CW01003730

The Ordeal of Elizabeth

By

Elizabeth von Arnim

The Echo Library 2012

Published by

The Echo Library

Echo Library
Unit 22
Horcott Industrial Estate
Horcott Road
Fairford
Glos. GL7 4BX

www.echo-library.com

Please report serious faults in the text to complaints@echo-library.com

ISBN 978-1-40680-025-8

Elizabeth.

The ORDEAL OF ELIZABETH

NEW YORK
GROSSET & DUNLAP
PUBLISHERS

Note on the Text::

Obvious typographical errors have been corrected. Inconsistent spelling and hyphenation in the original edition have been preserved, as has the frequent omission of punctuation before quotes.

There is no Chapter IV.

The ORDEAL OF ELIZABETH

Chapter I

THE Van Vorst Homestead stands close to the road-side; a dark, low-built, gloomy old place. The horse-shoe on the door, testifies to its age, and the devout superstition of the Van Vorst who built it. However effectual against witches, the horse-shoe cannot be said to have brought much luck otherwise. The Van Vorsts who lived there, a junior branch of the old colonial house, did not prosper in worldly matters, but sank more and more as time went on, in general respect and consideration.

There was a break in the deterioration, and apparently a revival of old glories, when Peter Van Vorst married his cousin, a brilliant beauty from town, who had refused, as tradition asserts, half the eligible men of her day, and accepted Peter for what seemed a sudden and mysterious caprice. The marriage was a nine days' wonder; but whatever the reasons that prompted her strange choice—whether love, indifference, or some feeling more complicated and subtle; Elizabeth Van Vorst made no effort to avert its consequences, but settled down in silence to a life of monotonous poverty. She did not even try, as less favored women have done under harder circumstances, to keep in touch with the world she had given up. She never wrote to her old friends, never recalled herself, by her presence in town, to her former admirers. As for the Homestead, it wore, under the inert indifference of her rule, the same neglected look which had prevailed for years. The foliage grew in rank profusion about the house till it shut out not only the sunlight, but all view of the river. Perhaps Madam Van Vorst, as people called her, disliked the idea of change; or perhaps she grudged the cost of a day's labor to cut the trees; or it might be that she liked the gloom and the feeling of confinement, and had no desire to feast her eyes on the river, after the fashion of the Neighborhood. It reminded her too much, perhaps, of the outside world.

She was a stately, handsome old lady, and made an imposing appearance when she came into church on Sunday, in the black silk gown which rustled with an old-time dignity, and her puffs of snow-white hair standing out against the rim of her widow's bonnet. Her daughters, following timidly behind her, seemed to belong to a different sphere; dull, faded women, in shabby gowns which the village girls would have disdained. If you spoke to them after church, when the whole Neighborhood exchanges greetings and discusses the news of the week, they would answer you shyly, in embarrassed monosyllables. Still, in some intangible way, you felt the innate breeding, which lurked behind all the uncouthness of voice and manner.

Their life, under their mother's training, had been one long lesson in self-effacement; they never even drove to the village without consulting her, or bought a spool of cotton without her permission. The stress of poverty, as time went on, grew less stringent at the Homestead; but with Madam Van Vorst the penury which had been first the result of necessity, had grown to be second nature. She let the money accumulate and made no change in their manner of life. Her daughters had no books, no teachers; no occupation but house-work; no interest beyond the petty gossip of the country-side.

With Peter, the son, the downward process was more evident and had taken deeper root. His voice was more uncouth than that of his sisters and his manner less refined; it was hard to distinguish him if you saw him in church, from any farmer, ill at ease in his Sunday clothes. He spent his days at work on the farm, and his evenings, more often than his mother dreamed of, at the bar in the village. Like his sisters, he bowed beneath her iron rod and lived in mortal fear of her displeasure. Yet he had his plans, well defined, and frequently boasted (at least at the village bar) of what he should do when he became his own master.

With the sisters a certain inborn delicacy of feeling prevented them from formulating, even to themselves, those hopes and aspirations which, nevertheless, lay dormant, needing only a sudden shock to call them into life. When that shock came, and it was known all over the Neighborhood that Madam Van Vorst was dead, the news brought a mild sense of loss, the feeling of a landmark removed; and people hastened at once to the Homestead with sincere condolences and offers of assistance to the daughters. Cornelia and Joanna were stunned, but not entirely with sorrow; rather with the sort of feeling that a prisoner might experience, who finds himself by a sudden blow, released from a chain which habit has rendered bearable, and almost second nature, yet none the less a chain.

It was not till the evening after the funeral that this stifled feeling found expression. The day had been fraught with a ghastly excitement that seemed to give for the moment to these poor crushed beings a fictitious importance. All the Neighborhood had come to the funeral; some grand relations even had journeyed up from town to do honor to the woman whom they had ignored in her lifetime; these last lingered for a solemn meal at the Homestead. The whole affair seemed to bring the Van Vorst women more in contact with the outside world than any event since their father's death, many years before. Sitting that evening, talking it all over, it might have been some festivity that they were discussing, were it not for their crape-laden gowns, and the tears they were still shedding half mechanically, though with no conscious insincerity.

"It was kind of the Schuyler Van Vorsts to come up," said Cornelia, wistfully. "I thought they had quite forgotten us—they are such fine people, you know—but they were really very kind, quite as if they took an interest."

"I'm glad the cake was so good," said the practical Joanna. "I took special pains with it, for I thought some of them might stay."

"It went off very nicely," said Cornelia, tearfully, "very nicely indeed. Mrs. Schuyler Van Vorst spoke of the cream being so good."

"She ate a good deal of it, I noticed."

"One thing I was sorry for," said Cornelia, reluctantly. "I saw her looking at the furniture. You know poor Mamma never would have anything done to it."

The sisters looked mechanically about the familiar room whose deficiencies had never been so glaringly apparent. The Homestead drawing-room had been re-furnished, with strict regard to economy many years ago, after a fashion too antiquated to be beautiful, and too modern to be interesting. The chairs and sofa were covered with horse-hair, and decorated, at intervals, with crochet anti-macassars. In the centre of the room stood a marble-topped table, upon which were ranged, at stiff angles, the Pilgrim's Progress, Paradise Lost, and several books of sermons. There were no other books and no pretty knick-knacks; but some perennially blooming wax flowers, religiously preserved beneath a glass case, contrasted with the chill marble of the mantel-piece. Above them hung one of the few relics of the past—a hideous sampler worked by a colonial ancestress. The room was much the worse for wear, the wall-paper was dingy, the carpet faded to an indefinite hue, some of the chairs were notoriously unsafe, and the sofa had lacked one foot for years.

"I think," said Cornelia, with sudden energy, as if roused at last to the truth of a self-evident proposition, "I think it is about time that the room was done over."

Joanna attempted no denial; but after a moment she remarked tentatively, as if balancing the claims of beauty against those of economy; "Some pretty sateen, I suppose, for a covering would not cost much."

Cornelia shook her head with melancholy decision. "It would be quite useless to do anything with the furniture," she declared, "if we didn't first change the carpet and the wall-paper."

Joanna was silent in apparent acquiescence; and Cornelia, after a moment's hesitation, brought out a still bolder proposition. "I've been thinking," she said "that we ought to have a piano. Of course I can't—we can't either of us play," she went on in hurried deprecation of Joanna's astonished looks, "poor Mamma would never let us take lessons; but people have them whether they play or not, and—it would give such a nice, musical look to the room."

Joanna sat lost for a moment in awe over this radical suggestion. "It would be very expensive," she said, practically "and—there are a great many things we need more."

But the more imaginative Cornelia refused to be daunted. "What if it is expensive!" she said boldly "and if we don't actually need it, that's all the more reason why it would be nice to have it. We've never spent money on a single thing in all our lives except for just what was necessary. Couldn't we for once have something that isn't necessary, that would be only—pleasant?"

Thus Cornelia struck the key-note of resistance to that doctrine of utility which had enslaved their lives, and Joanna, after the first shock of surprise, followed willingly in her lead. It was decided that the piano should be bought at once, and in discussing this and other changes, time passed rapidly, and they went to bed in a state of duly suppressed, but undoubted cheerfulness. It was altogether quite the pleasantest evening that they had spent for many years, though they would not have admitted this for the world, and sincerely believed themselves in great affliction. There was another being in the house who rejoiced in his freedom and meant to make the most of it.

The next morning at breakfast the sisters might have perceived had they been less engrossed in their own thoughts, that Peter was meditating some communication, which he found it hard to express. His words, when he spoke at last, chimed in oddly with his sisters' wishes. "I never," he said, speaking very deliberately and looking about him in great disgust, "I never saw a place that needed doing over so badly as this does."

There was a moment's pause of astonishment; and then Cornelia looked up in glad surprise. "Why, Peter," she said, "I had no idea that you would care"—

"Care!" said Peter, importantly. "Of course I care. I've always meant to have the place fixed up when—well, she couldn't live for ever, you know" he broke off half apologetically, as he caught the look of mute protest on his sisters' faces. "It did all very well for her and for you," he went on, coolly, "but it's not the sort of place I can bring my wife to." The last words came out with an air of indifference, that might have befitted the most commonplace announcement.

Upon Peter's hearers, however, they fell like a thunderbolt. It was several minutes before Cornelia repeated, in a very low voice:

"Your—your *wife*, Peter?"

"Yes, my wife." Peter rose and faced his sisters squarely, his hands in his pockets. He thrust out his under lip, and his florid Dutch face wore an expression of mingled defiance, exultation and embarrassment. "Why, I've been married some time," he said. "You didn't suppose I was going to stay single all my life, did you?"

"But who—who"—Cornelia's mind, moving with unusual rapidity, had already passed in review and rejected as improbable all the eligible young women of the Neighborhood, with none of whom she had ever seen Peter exchange two words. "Who can it be, Peter?" she concluded, lamely.

"Is it—any one we know?" chimed in Joanna, hopefully.

Peter looked them full in the face; he had always held his sisters in some contempt. "You know her well enough," he said, deliberately "or if you don't— you ought to. She's a young lady who lives near here, and her name is Malvina Jones."

There was a dead silence. The old Dutch clock on the mantel-piece, which had kept its place undisturbed through the trials and changes of several generations, seemed to beat in the stillness loudly and fiercely, almost as if it shared the consternation of Peter's sisters, who stared at him aghast. Cornelia was the first to speak. "Malvina Jones!" she repeated, slowly. "You don't mean the—the girl whose father keeps the bar?"

Peter flushed angrily. "There's only one Malvina Jones that I know of" he declared, "and she's my wife and will be the mistress of this house. And so, if you don't like it, you can leave—that's all I have to say."

With this conclusive remark Peter betook himself to his usual avocations, and his sisters were left to resign themselves to the situation as best they might.

"Malvina Jones!" Joanna repeated, still lost in astonishment.

"One of the village girls!" said Cornelia, bitterly, "a—a bar-keeper's daughter."

Joanna seemed to hesitate. "That isn't the worst of it," she said at last. "There are some very nice girls in the village, you know, but Malvina Jones is not— I'm afraid she really is *not* a very nice girl."

Cornelia was silent. She knew enough of the petty gossip of the village to be aware that Joanna was stating the case mildly. Before her mental vision there rose a picture of Malvina as she had often seen her on Sunday, with her glaring red hair, her smart attire and her look of bold assurance, undisturbed by the disapproving eyes of the congregation. Then she thought of her mother, the stately old dame whom they had been so proud of, even while they feared her. She looked at the breakfast-table, at the quaint, old-fashioned shapes of the glistening silver and the Dutch willow-ware which had been in the family since time immemorial; she thought with affection even of the old horsehair furniture, which must surely be preferable to such improvements as Malvina might suggest, and she pictured the bar-keeper's daughter entertaining her friends in the room where Madam Van Vorst had received with old-world stateliness the visits of the Neighborhood. To poor Cornelia the family dignity—what little there was left of it—seemed to be crumbling to ashes.

"I don't think we need to bother now about—about the piano," she said, and the words died away in a sob.

Chapter II

IT was a June morning twenty years later, and Elizabeth's hands were full of June roses.

"Look," she said, holding them out "how beautiful!" She placed them in a flat china dish and proceeded to arrange them, humming, as she did so, a gay little tune from some favorite opera of the day. The Misses Van Vorst, her aunts, who had been talking rather seriously before the girl entered, broke off in their conversation and brightened as they watched her.

There had been times in Elizabeth's childhood when the heart of each sister had been contracted by a secret fear, which they concealed even from one another, when they had offered up in seclusion fervent prayers that certain hereditary characteristics might not be revived in this treasure which fortune had unexpectedly bestowed upon them. These prayers had been to all appearance more than answered. Elizabeth did not look like her mother. It was true that the beautiful, wavy hair, which grew in soft ripples on her forehead, showed in the full glare of the sunshine or the firelight a trace, a suspicion of the deep red which in her mother's locks had been unpleasantly vivid; but with Elizabeth, it was a warm Titian shade which would delight an artist. In other respects, it was her grandmother whom she resembled, as very old people in the Neighborhood would sometimes inform you, wondering to see the beauty and distinction which had perversely skipped one generation, reproduced in this bar-maid's daughter. Certainly it was from Madam Van Vorst that the girl inherited the haughty turn of the head and the instinctive pride of carriage. The older woman's beauty may have been more perfect. Elizabeth's features were admittedly far from classical. Her nose tilted slightly, the chin was too square, the red, pouting lips were perhaps a trifle too full. But her skin was dazzlingly fair and fresh, and there was a glow of color and wealth of outline about her which disarmed criticism. The eyes, under their long lashes, were large and lustrous. Like her hair, they varied in different lights, or perhaps it was in different moods. They seemed a clear gray when she was thoughtful, blue when she smiled, and they grew, in moments of grief or acute emotion, singularly deep and dark. But such moments had, at this period of her life, been rare.

To her aunts, as they watched her that morning, she was the visible embodiment of all those stifled aspirations, to which Peter's marriage had apparently given a fatal blow. They could think now without bitterness of that great humiliation, and if they spoke of their brother's wife, it was with due propriety as "poor Malvina." They owed her after all, a debt of gratitude, since she was Elizabeth's mother, who had died most opportunely when Elizabeth was a baby.

The girl had been their sole charge from the first, for Peter concerned himself little about his motherless child. His death, when she was still very young, could hardly be considered an unmitigated affliction. As for Elizabeth, it was chiefly remarkable in being the occasion of her first black frock, on the strength of which she gave herself airs towards her less afflicted playmates.

Thus the Misses Van Vorst were free to carry out certain cherished plans in regard to their niece's future, which they had formed when, hanging over her cradle, they had fondly traced a resemblance to the grandmother after whom she had been named, through some odd, remorseful freak of Peter's. Impelled, as she grew older, by a wistful consciousness of all that they had missed, they heroically resigned themselves to part with her for a while that she might enjoy the advantages of a very select and extremely expensive school in town. And after five years she returned to them, not over-burdened by much abstruse knowledge, but with a graceful carriage, a charming intonation, a considerable stock of accomplishments, and the prettiest gowns of any girl in the Neighborhood.

Her return was the signal for the changes at the Homestead, which now made the old house a cheerful place to live in. The sunlight, no longer excluded by the overgrown foliage, flooded the drawing-room, and from the long French windows, opening out on the well-kept lawn, you caught a charming glimpse of the river. The fire-place was decorated in white and gold, the polished floor was strewn with rugs. Amid the profusion of modern chairs and tables and bric-à-brac were old heirlooms which had mouldered in the attic for generations, un-thought of and despised, till Elizabeth routed them out and placed them, rather to her aunts' surprise, in a conspicuous position. The walls were hung with fine engravings, books and magazines were scattered here and there. Across one corner stood the much-coveted piano.

The improvement was not confined to the furniture. The Misses Van Vorst, too, seemed to have progressed and assumed a more modern air, in harmony with their present surroundings. They were old women now, and people of the present generation placed carefully the prefix "Miss" before their Christian names; but in many ways, they were younger and certainly far happier than they were twenty years before. It was Elizabeth who had made the change, it was she who had filled their narrow lives with a wonderful new interest. And yet, it was on her account that they felt just then the one anxiety which disturbed their satisfaction in the warmth of her youth and beauty, nay, was rather intensified because of it.

"We were saying, dear," Miss Cornelia could not help observing after a moment "just as you came in, that it is a pity the Neighborhood is so dull. There is so little amusement for a young girl."

"We used to think it quite gay when we were young," said Miss Joanna, her knitting-needles clicking cheerfully as she talked. "There was always a lawn-party at the Van Antwerps', and Mrs. Courtenay was at home every Saturday, and then the fair for the church."

"But Mrs. Courtenay doesn't stay at home any longer," said Miss Cornelia, dejectedly, "and the Van Antwerps haven't given a thing for ever so long, and as for the fair—the church has everything it needs now—steeple, font, everything, so there is no object in having a fair."

"And so few people to buy if there were," sighed Miss Joanna, becoming despondent in her turn. "I quite miss it—I used to enjoy making things for it. Really now, if it were not for knitting socks for Mrs. Anderton's new babies, I should be quite at a loss for something to do."

Elizabeth, who had turned and stared from one to the other, as if in surprise at the introduction of a new subject, here broke in with a soft little laugh. "Well, auntie, Mrs. Anderton certainly keeps you busy," she said, consolingly "and as for the fair—why, I don't know that it would be such wild dissipation." Insensibly at the last words, her mouth drooped at the corners, the eyes, which an instant before had sparkled with amusement, grew thoughtful. A slight cloud of discontent seemed to drift over the buoyant freshness of her mood.

Miss Cornelia observed it and continued to lament. "Well, at least, a fair would be *something*," she insisted "and then in old times there used to be dances. If you went out to tea—oftener, my dear—even that would be a diversion."

The cloud on Elizabeth's face deepened. She bent down with elaborate care to place the last rose in position. "Oh, I don't know that it matters much," she said, and there was a sudden hardness in her tone. "There are no men for a dance, and as for the tea-parties—they don't amuse me very much. There are always the Andertons, or Johnstons, or both; and they talk about Mrs. Anderton's babies, of Mrs. Johnston's rheumatism, or the way the village girls dress; and the Rector asks me to take a class in Sunday-school, and looks shocked when I refuse; and—and it is all stupid and tiresome. I—I s-sometimes—I hate this place, and all the people in it," Elizabeth broke off, with a sound not unlike a sob.

Her aunts were paralyzed. This outburst of revolt was to them an entirely new phase in the girl's development. They did not attempt any response, or rebuke, and Elizabeth, after a moment, went over and kissed them each remorsefully. "There, don't mind me," she said. "I'm a horrid, discontented wretch." Then, as if to put an end to the subject, she added quickly: "I'm going to drive to Bassett Mills. Is there anything I can do for you?"

Her aunts gladly accepted the change of mood.

"It's a lovely morning for a drive, dear," said Miss Joanna, "and will do you good. But I wish, if you go, you would stop at the Rectory—the baby is ill, so the butcher tells me, and I have some beef-tea I'd like you to take."

Elizabeth's smile again lit up her face into its former brilliance. "What would you do without the butcher, Aunt Joanna?" she asked. "He's a perfect mine of information. Did he have any other news this morning?"

"Only that he had just come from the Van Antwerps'—they are up at last for the summer."

"Are they," said Elizabeth, carelessly. "Ah, well, they don't make much difference, one way or the other." She seemed to reflect a moment, while again her face clouded. "If I go to the Rectory," she said abruptly, "I suppose I must stop to see Aunt Rebecca. She will see me pass, and she is always complaining that I neglect her."

The Misses Van Vorst again looked distressed. The aunt of whom Elizabeth spoke, Malvina's sister-in-law, kept a small dry-goods shop, much patronized by the Neighborhood, and had risen considerably above the original position of the family. Yet the older ladies of the Homestead could never be reminded of her existence without a sharp recollection of a painful chapter in the family history. Had they consulted only their wishes, Elizabeth would never have been informed of the connection. They were just women, however, and admitted the claims of Elizabeth's only relation on her mother's side, and one who had a daughter, too, of about the girl's own age.

"Of course, my dear," Miss Cornelia said at last, reluctantly, "we wouldn't have you neglect your aunt."

"No, poor thing," said Joanna "we wouldn't have you hurt her feelings for the world. So perhaps you would better stop there, my dear; and if you do, will you get me some sewing-silk from the store?"

This proved by no means the only commission with which Elizabeth was burdened when she started, half an hour later; for Miss Joanna had had time to remember several other things she wanted from the store, to say nothing of the beef-tea for the Rector's wife, and numerous messages of advice and sympathy, which the girl was earnestly charged not to forget. Miss Cornelia had no commissions, and merely asked Elizabeth to remember, when she came home, every one whom she had seen, to inquire of the Johnstons, if she met them, how their grandmother was, and to notice, if she saw the Van Antwerps, if they had their new carriage, and what Mrs. Bobby had on. At last Elizabeth drove off, in the old-fashioned pony-chaise, behind the fat white pony whose age was wrapped in obscurity, and who trod, with the leisurely indifference of a well-bred carriage-horse, the road which he knew by heart.

It was a pleasant, shady road, that ran between stone fences, across which you caught the scent of honey-suckle. Beyond were fine places, once the pride of the Neighborhood, now for the most part neglected, or turned into pasturage for cows. The trees interlacing, formed an arch over-head, through which the sunlight flickered in long, slanting rays; the air was very still, except for the soft hum of bees, and a gentle wind that occasionally rustled the foliage and caressed the petals of the wild-roses, which grew in careless profusion along the road-side. Here and there, in sheltered nooks, wild violets still lingered, and the fresh green grass in the fields was thickly strewn with buttercups and daisies. But for all this beauty of the early summer Elizabeth seemed to have no eyes. Her brows were knit and her face clouded, and now and then she gave a vicious pull to the white pony's reins more as a relief to her own feelings than from any hope of hastening the movements of that dignified animal.

Her thoughts matched the day as little as her looks. Her mind still reverted with remorse to the outburst of an hour before. Why had she displayed that childish petulance, and given audible expression to the discontent which had smouldered unsuspected for many months? To speak of it was useless and only distressed her aunts; it was not their fault if the place was dull. And then she could, as a rule, amuse herself well enough. There were always drives and walks, the garden and the flowers, her books and her music, a hundred resources in which she found unceasing pleasure. There was even to her warm vitality a delight just then in the mere physical fact of living. And yet the times were growing more frequent day by day, when all this would fail her, when she would long passionately for novelty, for excitement, for something—she hardly knew what. There were desperate moments when it seemed to her that she would welcome any change whatsoever, when she thought that even storm and stress might be preferable to dull monotony.

After all, it was not the dullness of the place which lay at the root of her discontent. There was another trouble which went far deeper of which she never spoke; yet it affected her whole attitude towards the world, and more especially the Neighborhood. She did not feel at home in the small, charmed circle of those who knew each other so well, not even with the girls with whom she had played as a child. There had always been a tacit assumption of superiority on their part, which Elizabeth instinctively felt and resented. The most disagreeable episode in her life was a quarrel with one of her playmates, in which the latter had won the last word by an angry taunt against Elizabeth's mother, who was "a horrid, common woman, whom no one in the Neighborhood, would speak to—*her* mother had said so." Elizabeth, paralyzed, could think of no retort, but walked home in silence, shedding bitter tears of rage and mortification. She did not repeat the remark to her aunts—it was too painful and she somehow suspected too true; but that night she cried herself to sleep and had consoling dreams of a time when she should be a great personage, and able to turn the tables on her tormentors. This was a long time ago; but the old wound still rankled, and she held herself proudly aloof from her former playmates. They, on their part pronounced her hard to get on with, and their mothers made no effort to encourage the intimacy. In the conservative society of the Neighborhood, Peter's marriage was still vividly remembered, and could not easily be forgiven. Elizabeth was pretty and to all appearance, well-bred, but still people thought of her antecedents and maintained towards her an attitude of doubt. It was the perception of this fact, the consciousness of having begun life at a disadvantage, which embittered Elizabeth's thoughts as she drove through the country lanes that June morning.

The sun was high in the heavens when she reached Bassett Mills, a nondescript place, neither town nor village, and much over-shadowed by the glories of Cranston, not ten miles away. "The Mills" is not very prosperous, but it has its factory, and the mill-stream, dashing precipitously through its midst, lends some picturesqueness to the squalid houses on its banks. There was a certain life and movement this morning about the steep High Street, down which the white pony took his leisurely way. A stream of factory people passed by to their noon-day dinner; the street was full of wagons and carriages from the Neighborhood. Elizabeth saw the Van Antwerp dog-cart standing in front of the hardware shop, and caught a smile and bow from Mrs. Bobby, which surprised her by their graciousness. Later on she met the Courtenays, whom she knew better, but who greeted her more coldly. Elizabeth's own bow was stiff, and the cloud which Mrs. Bobby's cordiality had dispelled, again darkened her face.

She went on to the Rectory, but here she found that the baby's illness had developed into measles, and she could deposit her beef-tea at the door and take her leave with a clear conscience. Outside she stood in the hot sun debating if she should or should not stop to see her aunt and cousin. It was a long time since she had been there, and her aunt would be sure to assail her with reproaches. Amanda, too, would feel injured, and look the spiteful things which she never actually said. But then Elizabeth could usually rise superior to any spitefulness that Amanda might display. She felt on the whole very kindly towards her cousin, she liked to show her pretty gowns, and her good-nature had even stood the test of several bungling attempts on Amanda's part to imitate them. There were moments when, in the dearth of society, Elizabeth would turn with a certain affection to this uncongenial cousin, who at other times jarred upon her greatly.

It was the remembrance of Miss Joanna's commissions that on this occasion turned the scale in favor of the intended visit. Elizabeth left the white pony, who would stand an indefinite time, and entered the small dry-goods shop, where her aunt or Amanda generally presided. It was empty. Elizabeth hesitated a moment, then she crossed the hall that led to the living-rooms of the family. Here she paused in astonishment. From behind the closed door of the parlor came the sound of a man's voice; a rich, barytone voice singing from Tannhäuser the song of the Evening Star. Elizabeth waited till it was over; then she opened the door and went in.

Chapter III

THE young man who had just sung was still at the piano, softly playing variations on the same air. She gave him one hurried glance. He was tall and fair, with blue eyes and a silky blonde moustache, and he wore a velveteen coat, much the worse for wear, and a turn-down collar that showed to advantage the fine outlines of his throat and the graceful poise of his head. These details Elizabeth grasped at once before her gaze wandered to her aunt and Amanda, who were sitting idle as she had never before seen them in the morning, with eyes intent on the young man at the piano. Elizabeth noticed that Amanda had on her Sunday frock and her hair very much frizzed.

The girl had entered so softly that the three people already in the room did not at first notice her presence. When they at last did so, it seemed to cause something of a shock. Her aunt and Amanda stared at her in silence, and Amanda turned a trifle pale. The young man rose from the piano and looked at her intently for a moment with his bright blue eyes; then he re-seated himself and went on playing, but much more softly, and as if hardly conscious of what he did.

Elizabeth's aunt was the first to recover herself, and upon second thought it occurred to her that her niece had arrived at an opportune moment—when she and Amanda had on their best clothes, and were entertaining company. This reflection tempered the usual austerity of her greeting. "Why, Elizabeth, is that you? You're quite a stranger. It isn't often you honor us with your company."

"You know," said Elizabeth, quite used to the formula of reproach and excuse, with which these visits invariably opened "the white pony has been lame, and I have driven out very little."

"And you couldn't come on your wheel, I suppose? Nothing short of a carriage would do for you. I wonder you don't insist on a groom in top-boots. But well, never mind," Aunt Rebecca went on, feeling that she had sufficiently maintained her dignity "you're very welcome now, I'm sure, and you're just in time to hear some music. This is Paul Halleck, who has been kind enough to sing for us. Mr. Halleck, this is Amanda's cousin Elizabeth, whom you've heard us speak of." There was an odd note of grudging satisfaction in her voice as she made the introduction. Mrs. Jones's feeling towards her niece was a complex one, characterized on the one hand, by an involuntary sense of resentment at the elevation of Malvina's girl, on the other, by an equally involuntary pride in the connection. The latter sensation predominated when she introduced Elizabeth to a stranger whom she wished to impress.

Elizabeth's chief feeling was one of annoyance, and it brought an angry flush to her cheek. Then she caught the look in the young man's eyes, as he rose and bowed with much deference; and her own eyes fell and again she blushed, but not with anger.

"I have had the pleasure of seeing Miss Van Vorst before," said Paul Halleck, "though she has not, of course, noticed me."

"Why, yes, of course," said Elizabeth's aunt, still in high good humor, "you've seen her when you were out sketching. You see, Elizabeth, he's a painter as well as a singer; he's quite a genius, altogether. We find him a great acquisition to our parties here at The Mills. And to think that he was born here, and lived here part of his life! You remember the Hallecks that went West when you were a child? They settled in Chicago, you know. He only came to New York awhile ago, and thought he'd look up his folks in this place. But there, Elizabeth, sit down, and perhaps Mr. Halleck will give us another tune."

Elizabeth silently took the chair the young man placed for her, while her aunt still talked on volubly. The girl was bewildered by what she heard. She could not imagine this handsome young singer, with his air of picturesque Bohemia, as an acquisition to the parties of Bassett Mills; nor did he seem at home in her aunt's parlor. She glanced about the commonplace, gaudy little room, every detail of which impressed itself upon her with a new sense of its crudeness; the plush-covered furniture, staring wall-paper, the lace anti-macassars, the photographs of the family, the men in high hats, the women simpering in their Sunday clothes. It did not seem the fit atmosphere for an artist. And then, with a sudden, sharp misgiving, Elizabeth looked at Amanda, and asked herself for a moment if she could be the attraction. The doubt vanished instantly. Poor Amanda was not pretty at the best of times, and there was a sullen look on her face just then that made her appear at her worst. She had a dull, pasty skin and very light eyes. All the color seemed to be concentrated in her hair, which was a deep, dark red, all the more striking for the contrast to her pale face. The gown she wore, of a bright yellow, was peculiarly successful in bringing out the faded tints of her complexion and the jarring vividness of her hair.

Amanda at that moment felt to the full the unkindness of fate. She had not shared for an instant her mother's gratification at Elizabeth's entrance. It was hard, she thought, that, having arrayed herself in her best, and struggled long to look beautiful, she should be completely over-shadowed by Elizabeth in the cool white gown and shady hat, which had a provoking air of not being her best, but merely her natural and everyday attire. Amanda had seen, as well as Elizabeth, the look in Paul's eyes. Was it fair, she asked herself, that she should share her good things with Elizabeth, who had so many of her own? And so Amanda sat silent and sullen, while her mother talked on, and Halleck ran his fingers over the keys, as if he would fain be playing.

"What shall I sing?" he asked abruptly, in the first pause, and looking at Elizabeth as if her wishes alone were of any consequence.

"Oh, the Evening Star again," she responded eagerly. "I only heard the end of it, and it brought up so many delightful memories."

So Halleck sang the song again. A voice, artistically modulated, filled the little room, which vanished for Elizabeth. She saw pilgrims filing past in slow procession, Tannhäuser struggling against the power of the Venusberg, Elizabeth kneeling in her penitent's dress before the cross. The whole Wagnerian drama unrolled itself before her eyes while the song lasted. And then, as the last note died away, she came back to the present with a start, and realized that the young man who had just afforded her this pleasure was handsomer far than any Wolfram she had ever seen before.

"Ah, thank you," she said, drawing a long breath. "That is so beautiful. It is so long since I have heard any music."

"You are fond of it?" said Halleck, eagerly.

"Yes," she responded, earnestly.

"Ah, I saw it—I was sure of it," he declared. "You have the artistic temperament. I saw it in your face at once."

Elizabeth blushed for the third time that morning, and now with a distinct sense of pleasure. Amanda, too, flushed a dull red. She was not quite certain what the artistic temperament might be, but it was clearly one of those good things of which Elizabeth had an unfair monopoly.

"You play or sing yourself, of course?" Halleck went on.

"Oh, I play a little," Elizabeth pouted out her full under-lip, in charming deprecation of her own powers. "I am ashamed, before a real musician, to say that I play at all."

"I am not a real musician, alas!" said Halleck, "only a dabbler in music, as I am in art." A thoughtful look came into his blue eyes, and he went on absently playing fragments from Tannhäuser. "I am glad you like that," he said, abruptly. "You remember the heroine was called Elizabeth."

"Yes," said Elizabeth, "I remember." It gave her an odd little thrill of pleasure to hear him pronounce her name, and yet she wondered if his remark were not too personal to be in good taste. "But I don't think I am at all like that Elizabeth," she added, after a moment, following out his suggestion in spite of this doubt.

"No, perhaps not," said Halleck, regarding her with a calm scrutiny, in which he seemed to appraise her no longer as a woman, but purely from an artistic point of view. "You are not exactly that type; you have more life and color, less spirituality, perhaps; but you are fair, and your hair would do admirably. You would make a beautiful picture with your hair unbound, kneeling before the cross."

"I have never had my picture painted," Elizabeth murmured, trying to imagine herself in a penitent's garb.

"Will you let me try it?"

Elizabeth smiled and assented, deciding that no long acquaintance was necessary, when it was a question of having her picture painted, in a costume which she was quite determined should be becoming. She sat mentally reviewing the resources of her wardrobe, while Halleck struck sonorous chords on the piano, and asked if she recognized this or that Wagnerian theme, upon which he proceeded to extemporize. Amanda and her mother were distinctly left out, and the latter began to repent of her first satisfaction in her niece's visit. She broke in at last, brusquely, upon the very midst of the love-music from "Tristan and Isolde." "Well, I don't think much of this Wagner," she said. "His music all sounds the same—a lot of queer noises, with no tune to them. What I like now is 'Home, Sweet Home,' or 'Nancy Lee'—something real nice and catchy."

"I can play those, too," said Halleck, good-humoredly, and immediately played the first mentioned air, with variations of his own improvisation. At the end of it he rose from the piano. "Won't you play for me now," he said to Elizabeth.

"Oh, no, not after you." Elizabeth shook her head and rose to her feet, with a sudden recollection of the white pony and her aunt's dinner-hour. "Some other day," she said, "I'll be very glad to play for you, but really now I have not the time—or the courage." She spoke with a pretty, smiling deference, and she held out her hand, which he took in a long, lingering grasp. There was a soft glow of color in her cheeks, her eyes were cast down till he could see only her long lashes. "Thank you so much," she said "for the music." Then she drew her hand away from his and kissed her aunt and Amanda, with an unwonted display of affection. She felt an odd sense of excitement, a wish to be friendly with all the world.

Neither her aunt nor Amanda seemed to share it. They did not try to detain her, and Halleck, though he looked disappointed, said nothing. They all three escorted her to the door of the shop, where the white pony stood patiently enduring the heat and the flies. Elizabeth lingered over her farewells. She wished to ask her new acquaintance to come to see her, but disliked doing so before her aunt and cousin. It was he who finally said, leaning over her as he placed the reins in her hand: "And—a—how about that picture? May I come to see you about it?"

Elizabeth's eyes were still hidden as she answered demurely: "I am sure I— we shall be very glad to see you at the Homestead."

And then she drove off, and the others stood for a moment and looked after her in silence.

"She—she's pretty—isn't she," said Amanda, suddenly speaking for the first time since Elizabeth had appeared. Her voice, even to herself, sounded harsh and grating. Her lips were very dry.

Halleck started and looked at her as if reminded of her existence. Then a smile stole over his face and sparkled in his handsome blue eyes.

"Yes, she's rather pretty," he answered, carelessly "but—a little disappointing on a close view. However, she'll do very well as a model—she's picturesque, at least."

Amanda drew a long breath of sudden and intense relief.

Chapter V

"*And* so you say this young man lives at The Mills, my dear?" Miss Cornelia paused, the heavy, elaborately chased tea-pot suspended in her hand. Her gentle, near-sighted eyes looked anxiously across the table at Elizabeth.

It was the first time that the girl had spoken of her new acquaintance, though it was now some time since her return from Bassett Mills, and she had told at once of the measles at the Rectory. This piece of news, however, had lasted them well through dinner, and in the country it is improvident to use up all one's information at once. Perhaps Elizabeth thought of this; or it might be that the other item did not strike her as of any special importance. She only mentioned it very casually at tea-time; but her aunts' anxiety was easily aroused at any suggestion of new acquaintances at Bassett Mills.

"I don't think he lives at The Mills," Elizabeth made answer now reluctantly to Miss Cornelia's question. "I think he—he is just staying there—I believe Aunt Rebecca said something about his coming from Chicago. But his family used to live at The Mills."

"You don't mean those Hallecks who went West a long time ago?" exclaimed Miss Joanna. "Do you remember, sister?—the man was in jail the most of the time. The children used to play on the road behind the church—poor little neglected things, I was quite worried about them. It was a relief, I remember, when they all went away."

Elizabeth found this piece of ancient history peculiarly inopportune.

"Well, that was a long time ago, Aunt Joanna," she said. "It doesn't matter, I suppose, so much what people's parents were like. Mr. Halleck is very nice himself. He is an artist, and he wants to paint my picture." She brought out this last information, which she had been longing to tell for some time, with a certain triumph; but it fell unexpectedly flat.

"An artist!" Miss Joanna repeated. "Dear me! One of those little Hallecks who used to play in the road."

"To paint your picture, my dear?" repeated Miss Cornelia still more doubtfully. "When he has only met you once! I am afraid he is rather a pushing young man. But of course, dear, you won't encourage him."

Elizabeth's eyes were fixed on her plate; her cheeks were painfully flushed and she bit her lips to keep back the scalding tears that rose to her eyes. "I don't think he is pushing," she murmured, but she said no more. How could she explain to her aunts the vast difference that existed between this young man and any other friend of Amanda's? They were dear, good women, but so hopelessly narrow and antiquated, with their little old-fashioned ideas of propriety, their distinctions founded on the conventional laws of the Neighborhood. Elizabeth, too, was not without an involuntary respect for these distinctions. She had her full share of the pride of birth which was instinctive in every Van Vorst, even in the most ignorant country lout that had ever borne the family name and lowered the family credit. With Elizabeth it was only intensified, perhaps, by a doubt of her own position. But then she belonged to the new generation; and there was a side of her nature that recognized the futility of these old traditions. Elizabeth did not analyze her feelings; she was only conscious of a vague sense of revolt, a desire to beat her wings as it were, against the cages of conventional distinctions, and test her powers of flight.

But she did not put all this into words. Her aunts would not have understood. She did not understand herself. She rose from the tea-table presently, with a murmured excuse, leaving the food on her plate untasted, to Miss Joanna's great distress, and wandered into the drawing-room and sat down at the piano. The keys seemed to respond with unusual readiness to her touch, the music expressed in some vague way what she could not put into words. She played on restlessly, feverishly, for more than an hour, passing from one thing to another; Chopin nocturnes, waltzes, Hungarian dances, fragments from Wagner; anything she could remember.

The drawing-room remained dim for the sake of coolness; it was unlighted except for a lamp at a corner-table, beside which Miss Joanna sat with her knitting. As Elizabeth played she nodded comfortably and presently fell asleep. This was always the effect of Elizabeth's playing; she said she found it very soothing. Miss Cornelia sat upright in an old-fashioned, high-backed chair close to the piano. She moved her head in time to the music, and the thin little silvery curls that framed in her worn, delicate face seemed to sway in unison with the melody. She wore a black gown, a trifle antiquated in fashion but falling about her in graceful folds, and some rich old lace softened the outlines of her throat. There was a gentle, tremulous dignity about her nowadays. Miss Cornelia was very happy in moments like these. It was touching to see the pride she took in Elizabeth's music. But after awhile this evening the girl let her hands drop on the keys, and said impatiently: "Oh, it's no use, I can't say what I want to say. The music's in me, but it won't come out. If you could have heard that man to-day at Aunt Rebecca's."

"Do you mean that young Halleck, my dear?" said Miss Cornelia in surprise, and pronouncing his name with evident distaste. "I didn't know that he played."

"He can do anything," Elizabeth declared. "He paints, he can improvise by the hour, he sings as well as any opera-singer, and—he is very handsome. He would make a superb Lohengrin or Tristan," she added, thoughtfully "only, unfortunately, his voice is barytone. I wonder why Wagner showed such partiality to tenors."

"But he is not—going on the stage, is he, my dear?" asked Miss Cornelia, tentatively. She felt more anxiety than pleasure at hearing of this paragon.

"I don't know," said Elizabeth, "and it doesn't much matter. I am not to know him, you see, because his people used to live in the village years ago, and Aunt Joanna saw him playing on the road." She spoke bitterly.

"But, my dear, I—we never meant anything of the kind," protested Miss Cornelia. But Elizabeth went on without heeding her.

"Of course I know the rules of the Neighborhood. They would no more think of knowing a young man from Bassett Mills than they would a convict. But I don't really belong to the Neighborhood; I'm only on the outskirts, as it were—

tolerated for your sake and for Grandmamma's. I'm tired of being a sort of nondescript—neither flesh, fowl, nor good red herring." The girl's face was hard, but she spoke quietly, in a matter-of-fact tone, as if stating inevitable truths.

Miss Cornelia sat mute, bewildered, her whole soul wrung by a powerless resentment against fate. If by any sacrifice on her part she could have provided for Elizabeth congenial society—the charming young girls and attractive young men of whom she and her sister had often dreamed—she would have made it thankfully; but with all her love, there was nothing—or there seemed to her nothing that she could do. They had given Elizabeth every advantage, she was beautiful and charming; and the result of it all was that she felt herself to be "a sort of nondescript, neither flesh, fowl, nor good red herring." It was a very bitter thought for Miss Cornelia.

Elizabeth, seeing this, felt remorseful for the second time that day. "Don't look so unhappy, auntie," she said, quickly. "It's not your fault—no, nor mine either; and, I suppose, it's not the fault of the Neighborhood. People can't help being narrow and conservative; they were born so. But then, Aunt Cornelia, when—when I don't have so many friends, you can't expect me to draw the line so awfully closely." Something like a sob crept into the girl's voice, but she went on with hardly a pause: "You mustn't think that I would want to know—any one. This man isn't like the rest of Amanda's friends. Only wait till you hear him sing—you would lose your heart, I'm sure, on the spot. And now, confess, auntie, you would like me to have my picture painted. The girls at school used to say that I would make a glorious picture. Do *you* think I would make a pretty picture, auntie?" She went over to Miss Cornelia and put her arms around her, looking up into her face with laughing, brilliant eyes, from which all bitterness had disappeared.

"My darling." Miss Cornelia, bewildered by the quick change of mood, could not find words. She thought that Elizabeth would make the prettiest picture in the world; but to have told her so would have been to run counter to all her ideas of propriety. So she finally said, with due regard for accepted formulas: "You shouldn't think so much about looks, Elizabeth. If you are good, that's the main thing."

"Of course, it's the main thing," Elizabeth assented, "but I'm afraid if it came to a choice, I'd rather be pretty, auntie, and so would most people." She ended with a light little laugh, and Miss Cornelia, in spite of her principles, attempted no rebuke.

The look of gaiety soon faded from Elizabeth's face. With a quick, impatient little sigh, she walked over to the window, and looked out into the night. It was still and sultry; heavy storm clouds were gathering and obscured the sky. The old elm trees, growing close about the house, cast sombre shadows; they seemed to keep out what little air there was. Elizabeth, as she leaned her hot cheek against the cool glass of the window-pane, felt again a sense of stifling, of being in a cage. It was useless to beat her wings; life was outside, but she could not reach it. "Oh, I would give anything in the world," she thought "just to breathe, to be free, to know what life is."

Suddenly she turned around with a start. There was a voice in the hall; some one spoke her name. A moment later a young man was advancing towards her across the dimly-lighted room. Mechanically she went to meet him. She did not think of her aunts, she did not think of anything but his presence.

"Have I—come too soon?" Paul Halleck asked, as he took her hand.

Chapter VI

ELIZABETH drove again, a few weeks later, through shady, fragrant lanes, on her way to Bassett Mills. It was early in the morning, but the sun was already hot. The wild-roses along the road-side had mostly departed, the grass in the fields had a parched look. It was a long time since any rain had fallen, and the roads were thick with dust. All the freshness of the early summer had faded. But for these signs of premature blight and the scorching effect of the sun, Elizabeth seemed to have no eyes.

She drove along in a happy dream. There was a brilliant color in her cheeks, a radiant light in her eyes. She bloomed like a rose that has unfolded every petal to the summer sunshine. The fields through which she passed were not the familiar pasture-lands and "places" that skirted the road to Bassett Mills; they were the flowery meadows of poetic Arcadia, on the road that led to Paradise.

It was something of a bore, under the circumstances, that she must first of all go to Bassett Mills, but Miss Joanna had intrusted her with numerous commissions, that she could not very well refuse to discharge. That was the reason why she had started so early. There was a brook in a meadow near by; a brook shaded by weeping willow trees, under which nowadays a young artist sat sketching for many hours at a time. Elizabeth's drives, or walks had for the last few weeks led no further. But to-day she had decided to go first to Bassett Mills, and be back in time for the usual engagement, of which her aunts knew nothing.

The affair was not really so clandestine. There was no reason why she should have kept it secret beyond a vague embarrassment, an unwillingness to speak about the one subject that occupied her thoughts. Miss Cornelia and Miss Joanna had, after the one protest, yielded to the inevitable; they had not even discouraged young Halleck's visits to their niece. They had gone so far as to admit, when he had come to tea at the Homestead, and sung and played for them afterwards for hours, that he was an extremely talented young man. It had been a most successful evening, Miss Joanna had not even gone to sleep. And yet, with it all, in both sisters there was some innate distrust, some lingering prejudice perhaps, that prevented them from succumbing entirely to the charm of his handsome face and beautiful voice. They were civil to him—painfully civil; but they did not welcome him as they would have welcomed young Frank Courtenay, who used to stare at Elizabeth in church every Sunday, but had never apparently mustered up courage to come and see her. He was much under the influence of his mother, who considered Elizabeth's hair "conspicuous" and had remarked that it was bad taste for a young girl to be *too* well dressed—a fault that could not in justice be alleged against her own daughters.

Elizabeth, too, might have welcomed the visits of young Courtenay. There had been times when she had doubted, sadly, if she were really so pretty as the girls at school had seemed to think. But these times were past, and she had not a thought to spare for Frank Courtenay's heavy, commonplace good looks. Paul Halleck had assured her many times that she was beautiful, and had sketched her in every variety of pose, in that impressionistic style which Elizabeth had secretly thought rather ugly, before she learned to regard it as the last word in Art.

Elizabeth had learned many other things in the last few weeks. Halleck undertook her education in all artistic and literary matters, showing her how little she had hitherto known of this or that great light. He quoted Swinburne and Rossetti; he read her extracts from Maeterlinck and Ibsen; he opened for her the treasures of that school which Nordau calls degenerate. He had all the intellectual and artistic jargon of the day at his tongue's end. She sat at his feet and devoutly learned it all.

She knew his history, now. It was very romantic, and it lost nothing in the telling. He had a keen eye for artistic effect, and spared not one sordid detail of his early surroundings which served to throw into more brilliant relief his subsequent career. He told how the possession of a lovely childish soprano had raised him literally from the gutter, and procured him a position as boy soloist in a Chicago church, and how, later on, a patron was found, who sent him abroad to study. He had wandered from one European centre to another; learned to play in Dresden and to paint in Paris, and developed a fine barytone voice, of which great things were prophesied. In fact, he was a universal genius, and could do anything, except apparently earn a living, which indeed has been always hard for genius. And so at last he drifted back to Chicago, where he sang for a while in the same church where he had begun his career; but finally left for some reason or another, and tried his fortune in New York. He was debating now whether to go abroad again to study in earnest for the stage, and meanwhile he was on a walking tour, sketching about the country. He had come to Bassett Mills for the sake of old associations, and had stayed—well, he left it to Elizabeth to imagine *why* he stayed.

All this was very interesting and romantic; far more so, Elizabeth thought, than any ordinary affair could have been, with some commonplace youth of the neighborhood. She had only one regret; she could not help wishing in her heart that Paul's early surroundings had been, if not more exalted, less familiar. She would have preferred him to have no associations with, no friends at, Bassett Mills. The place seemed to her, as she drove through it that morning, so hopelessly common, so unusually prosaic. The ugly, sordid houses, the people with their faces of dull stolidity, jarred upon the ecstatic tone of her mood. She could not imagine that genius could be born in such surroundings.

The discordant note was still more striking when, having discharged the greater part of her commissions, she entered the dry-goods shop, and found Aunt Rebecca in her most trying humor.

"So that's you, Elizabeth," she said, looking her niece severely up and down, while her thin lips moved at the corners. "It seems to me you're very much dressed up, driving round these dusty roads. The way you wear white is a caution! But I suppose for a millionaire like you it don't matter about the washing."

Elizabeth bit her lip. "I'm not a millionaire, you know Aunt Rebecca," she said, "but I like to wear white, and it's as cheap as anything in the end. Is Amanda in?" she added quickly, anxious to stave off further criticism. "I'll go back and see her if she is."

"She's in the parlor," said Amanda's mother, shortly. "She's got a headache. I guess she don't feel like seeing company," she added hastily, but the words came too late. Elizabeth had already left the shop, and was crossing the narrow, dark little hall that led to the parlor. Her heart beat rapidly as she did so. She felt an odd, utterly irrational desire to feast her eyes on the spot where she had first experienced such new and delightful sensations.

There was no music in the room now, no air of festivity. The atmosphere was close and musty, the sun poured in at the window beside which Amanda sat sewing. She bent closely over her work, her skin was more pasty than ever and her eyes were red and swollen. Elizabeth remembered her aunt's words about the headache; otherwise she might have thought that her cousin had been crying. She went over and kissed her with a friendliness born of her own superabundant joy. The lips she touched were dry and hot. Amanda did not respond to the caress. She stared stupidly at Elizabeth, as if half dazed by her sudden entrance.

"How are you, Amanda?" Elizabeth said. "I'm sorry you have a headache. Perhaps it's the heat. It's a terribly hot day, and the roads are so dusty. Aunt Rebecca implied that my dress showed that very plainly. It was clean this morning—does it really look so badly?" She walked over to the mirror and inspected herself critically, setting her hat straight and adjusting the white ribbon about her throat. It was a long narrow glass, framed in black walnut, and there was a shelf underneath it, which supported a large sea-shell. The whole thing reminded her of a similar arrangement at her dressmaker's in town, and seemed in some way the crowning feature of the prosaic, painfully respectable character of the room. She hated to look at herself there—the glass brought out all one's defects. But to-day, in spite of the trying glare of the sunshine, her own image flashed back at her, so brilliantly fresh, in her white dimity gown, so redolent of health and beauty, that she could not help smiling back at it, as at some delightful apparition. Ah, yes, it was good to be young and pretty, and to have a lover waiting for one near by. Her eyes brightened unconsciously, and she gave a little caressing touch to the shining masses of wavy hair which stood out, like red molten gold, against the broad brim of her shady white hat.

The other girl sat and watched her.

"You like to look at yourself, don't you?" The words rang out harshly, suddenly. Elizabeth started and turned around. It seemed to her for a moment as if some third person had spoken—some one with a strange, mocking voice that she had never heard before. But there was no one else in the room.

"Yes, you like to look at yourself." Amanda went on after a pause, more quietly, "you think yourself a beauty, and a good many people, perhaps, might agree with you. *He* tells you so, I suppose. I daresay he tells you your hair's picturesque—he used to tell me that about mine. He was going to paint my picture, but it went out of his head when he saw you. Most things did, I guess. He—he hasn't been here since." The girl's voice broke in a quick, convulsive sob, and she stopped for a moment, but went on almost immediately: "If you hadn't come in that day, it would have been all right. We were keeping company; every one in The Mills knew we were. All the girls were jealous of me—as if he'd have looked at them! Some of them work in the factory, there's many of them don't even have a piano and sit in their kitchens. I know what's genteel, even if I can't talk all that rubbish about music and Wagner that you learned at school. And what good will all that do you when you're married? What do you know about mending and sewing and cooking? What sort of a wife would you make him? You'd ruin him in a month with your fine clothes. But men are such fools!" She gave a short mirthless laugh, her eyes glittered strangely. Elizabeth stared at her paralyzed, glued to the spot in helpless fascination. She had never heard Amanda talk so much before. Her words came quickly, fiercely, one upon another, like some overwhelming torrent that had been suddenly let loose.

"Why should you have so much more than me? Why should you have fine clothes, and a carriage, and go to school in New York, and have the swells in the neighborhood call on you? Was your mother any better than mine, or a hundredth part as good? She wasn't even respectable; no decent people at The Mills would speak to her before your father married her—I know that for a fact. And then to give yourself airs!" Amanda stopped short, panting, exhausted by her own vehemence. Elizabeth still stood before her powerless. When Amanda spoke of her mother the color rushed into her white face, and she made an effort to speak; but the words seemed to die away on her lips. Amanda, after a moment's pause, went on.

"It isn't that I care so much about that; you might have had everything else, if you hadn't taken—him. Why did you come in that day looking like a dressed-up doll? You hadn't been here for weeks, and I was glad. I didn't want him to know you—I wasn't afraid of the other girls. But you who've got so much—couldn't you have had the decency to leave him alone? Couldn't you see that he was mine?"

"Amanda," Elizabeth gasped out. "I—I didn't know. I—I never thought"—Her brain reeled, she stammered painfully, trying in vain for words to vindicate herself from this shameful charge. Amanda brushed her aside contemptuously.

"You didn't think?—no, you never do, of anything but yourself, your pretty face and pretty clothes! You're selfish and spoiled—every one knows it; you've had every wish granted till you want everything, and you won't be satisfied with less. But what's the good of saying all this to you?" she broke off suddenly, with a sharp change of tone. "I must be crazy; I've felt so, I'm sure, these last weeks. It won't make any difference—nothing I say can bring him back. And yet he'd have married me—if you hadn't come." She went to Elizabeth and gripped her by the wrist. "He kissed me once," she said. "Has he kissed you yet?"

"No," said Elizabeth, mechanically, "no." She shrank away a little and set her teeth. Amanda's grasp was painful, but she would not have cried out for worlds.

"Well, when he does," Amanda said, "remember this—he kissed me first. You can't take that away from me—I have the first claim." She let go of Elizabeth's hands and fell back a step. There were two deep red marks from her grasp. "Now go," she said, "go to him. I knew you were going to him—I saw you thinking of it, and it made me hate you. Go to him and tell him that I hope his love for you will last as long as it did for me." She laughed again harshly and then suddenly burst into violent weeping. "Oh, it's ignominious," she said, "it's contemptible. No one can despise me more than I do myself. I haven't any pride. I hate him—I hate him; yet I'd take him back now, if he'd come to me." She sank down on the sofa and hid her face in the red plush cushions, while her whole frame shook with convulsive sobs.

Elizabeth stood still in the middle of the floor. Mechanically she glanced at her reflection in the mirror; white, distraught, with startled eyes—a ghastly parody of the brilliant vision which had smiled back at her only a few minutes before. The hot sunlight, flooding the commonplace little room, seemed to bring out, with glaring vividness, all the tragic, sordid elements of the scene. A quarrel between two women about a lover! Could anything be more hopelessly vulgar and grotesque?

It was the sting of this thought that finally roused Elizabeth to speech. She raised her head with sudden haughtiness, and her words came clearly and fluently. "I don't know what you mean, Amanda," she said "by this scene. If there is any one whom you—you think I have taken from you, you can have him back to-morrow so far as I am concerned. I don't want any other woman's lover. It—it would be base. Whatever else you think me, I'm not—that. If it is Paul Halleck whom you mean, you can marry him, if you wish, to-morrow. At least you may be sure of one thing, that I never will." Her low, vehement voice died away, and she waited for an answer; but none came. Amanda only sobbed on hysterically, her face buried in the sofa-cushions.

Elizabeth stood looking at her for a moment, with a feeling in which pity, anger and repulsion were strangely mingled; then she hastily left the room by the door that led directly to the street. She had presence of mind enough to avoid the shop and her aunt's unfriendly eyes. She reached the carriage, and—un-heard-of thing—touched the white pony with the whip.

Chapter VII

THEY had left the last house behind; they were out in the open country. Elizabeth dropped the reins and let her tears flow unchecked—hot, blinding tears, the bitterest she had ever shed. At each familiar tree and landmark she sobbed with redoubled violence. Only an hour before she had driven along this same road in the ecstatic glow of her first romance. Now all the bloom had been rubbed from that romance, all the glory faded from the hero of her dreams; she herself was a woman who had been insulted, humiliated, dragged in the dust.

By degrees a few coherent phrases detached themselves from the confused mass of painful recollections, and stung more sharply than the rest. "My mother better than yours—she wasn't even respectable; no decent people would speak to her" ... Oh, it was too bad—too bad; she had not thought it was so bad as that. Amanda must have exaggerated—she would ask her aunts; but no, no she would never speak of that interview to a soul. It was humiliating enough as it was.... "He kissed me once. Has he kissed you yet?" No, thank Heaven! that indignity had been spared her. They had hovered as yet on the borderland of love; she had put off the inevitable declaration with instinctive coquetry, a vague unwillingness to be won too easily. She was glad now—glad and thankful; he did not know that she cared,—he should never know. She had no love for the man who had kissed Amanda.... "Selfish and spoiled—thinking only of herself?" Yes, she might be all that; but at least she would not take another woman's lover. The words "it would be base," rang in her ears. Had she spoken them, or Amanda? At all events, they were true. It would be base to marry Halleck now. In fact, she did not wish to marry him. It was he who had involved her in this horrible, sordid misery. Her aunts were right; there must be distinctions of classes. Had her father remembered this, people would not have it in their power to insult his daughter now.

Through all her complex feelings ran a sharp sense of anger against Amanda, mingled strangely with an involuntary pity, almost with an understanding of her point of view. It was not based on justice, but on fellow feeling. Amanda had resented her superiority; she, Elizabeth, knew what that was. She had felt the same herself, when smarting impotently under the patronizing friendliness of the other girls in the Neighborhood, and then had turned, with unconscious snobbery, to play the same part towards Amanda. The incongruous, grotesque humor of the situation struck her suddenly, and she laughed out loud in bitter irony. She had envied the other girls of the Neighborhood, Amanda had envied her, the girls at Bassett Mills had envied Amanda. Strange net-work of classes in a democratic country, of distinctions the more galling for their intangibility. Of one thing Elizabeth was convinced, that she could never herself "put on airs" as Amanda had said, again; there was not a girl in the whole countryside, blessed with a good mother, who could not look down on her, if she pleased.

Her tears were falling now so fast and blinding that she could not see the road; she was not even conscious that they had reached the spot where the white pony stopped now of his own accord. And even as he did so, a young man stepped forward and grasped the reins which had fallen from Elizabeth's nerveless hand; a tall, fair young man who had been standing for the last half hour, scanning anxiously, with his bright blue eyes, the glaring dusty road.

"Elizabeth," said Halleck (he had called her that for five happy days) "Elizabeth, why are you so late? And, for Heaven's sake, what's the matter?"

Elizabeth looked up and with great effort, stopped crying; but otherwise she made no sign of pleasure in his presence or even of recognition. She put up one hand, indeed, and straightened her hat, but this was a purely mechanical concession to the force of habit. She knew that her face was flushed and tear-stained, her eyes red and swollen; she was sure that she looked an absolute fright, and she did not care. She was past caring, at least for the moment.

"Elizabeth," Halleck repeated, more and more bewildered, "what is the matter? I've been waiting for you an hour. You've been crying," he added, stating unnecessarily an obvious fact. "Won't you tell me what it is?"

"Nothing—nothing," Elizabeth answered at last, in a voice that was still thick and choked with sobs. "I haven't been crying or," struck by the futility of denial, she added hastily "if I have it—it's no matter. Will you please let me pass?" She tried to take the reins from his hands, but he grasped them firmly, and laid the other hand on the bar of the wagon.

"Won't you let me pass?" she repeated stubbornly.

"Not till you tell me what's the matter."

He eyed her coolly, determinedly, all the habit of power depicted on the lines of his handsome face. She stared back at him defiantly, with her tear-swollen eyes. Her whole attitude breathed the spirit of rebellion; a spirit new in their intercourse. Halleck saw it, at the same time that he noted the disfiguring marks of tears on her face. Oddly enough, he had never admired her so much.

Nevertheless, he was determined to remain master of the situation. He glanced up and down the road; there were never many people passing, but it was not safe to rely on this fact.

"We can't talk here," he said. "Come into the field."

"I don't wish to," she said, stubbornly. "I'm going home."

He fixed his eyes upon her. "You shall not go home," he said quietly, "till you have told me all about it." She sat immovable, her pouting under lip thrust out in a way that she had sometimes, in moments of obstinacy and displeasure. She did not meet his eyes. "Don't be childish," Paul said, pleasantly, after a moment. "You know you must tell me what it is."

She looked up reluctantly, and met his steady gaze, under which she turned first white, then red, and slowly, as if fascinated, rose from her seat. Yet still her words were unyielding. "We may as well have it out at once," she said, coldly.

Halleck could not repress a thrill of triumph. It was sweet to test his power over this beautiful, high-spirited girl, to feel her will, her intellect, like wax in his hands. But he tried not to show this consciousness in his face. She was in a strange mood; he did not understand her. Gravely and respectfully he helped her to scale the stone wall, which separated the meadow from the road. Her hand barely rested on his, and her eyes were averted carefully, but he paid no heed. He fastened the white pony to a tree, then slowly and thoughtfully followed Elizabeth across the field.

The noon-day sun beat down upon them in all its scorching brilliancy; it was pleasant to gain the shade of their usual trysting-place. Here the little brook, which had rippled and sparkled over stones and moss all the way from the mill-stream, formed itself into a quiet pool, over which weeping willows spread out long branches, and seemed to admire their own reflection in the cool green mirror beneath. Elizabeth took her usual seat on a fallen moss-covered log, drawing, as she did so, her white skirts about her, with what seemed an involuntary gesture of repulsion, and Halleck, who was about to place himself beside her, flushed and bit his lip. After a moment's hesitation, he threw himself down sullenly on the grass a little way off.

"Tell me," he said, in a tone that was the more determined for this little episode "tell me now what the matter is."

Elizabeth's eyes were fixed upon the cool, green water at her feet. "I don't know why you think," she said, slowly "that it has anything to do with you."

"Not when you are a full hour late for our appointment? Not when you treat me like an outcast? Oh, Elizabeth,"—the young man's voice softened suddenly, skillfully—"how can you trifle with me so, when I love you?"

He caught, or thought he did, a quiver in her face, although her eyes were still resolutely bent upon the pool. "Yes, I love you," he repeated. "I've loved you, I believe, ever since the day you came into that horrid, stuffy little room, looking like an angel—with that hair and that skin—so different from Amanda."—

He stopped as an indignant wave of color flamed in Elizabeth's cheeks. "How can you speak of Amanda—like that?" she broke out passionately, "when you loved her too, or told her so at least, when you said the same things no doubt to her that you are saying now to me?"

A light broke in upon Paul. In his relief he laughed out loud. "Amanda," he said. "Amanda! So she has been talking to you? And you believed all the nonsense she told you? And that is why you acted so strangely. I thought it was something serious!" And he laughed again in sheer light-heartedness. So all this had been only jealous pique, after all.

The gloom on Elizabeth's face did not lighten. "You seem to find the idea amusing," she said, coldly. "I do not."

"Because you don't understand how absurd it is. I never made love to Amanda—if she made love to me"—Paul stopped, warned by a curious stiffening in Elizabeth's attitude that he was on dangerous ground. She was not like other girls whom he had known—he had noticed this before; she required special treatment. "My dear child," he said, in a calm, argumentative tone "really you are a little hard on me. A man can't measure every word he says to a girl. I may have paid Amanda a few compliments, flirted with her a little, if you insist upon it, but—that's not a crime, is it? And I never gave her a thought, I hardly remembered her existence, after I had once—seen you." There was unmistakable sincerity in his voice. "Look at me, Elizabeth," he went on anxiously, "look at me, and tell me that you believe me."

Elizabeth raised her troubled eyes to his. "I—I don't know," she said, slowly. She did believe him—to some extent, at least. But what he told her did not alter the fact that it was she who had taken him away from Amanda, that, but for her, he might have been her cousin's admirer still. And that, after all, had been the substance of Amanda's accusation.

"Tell me the truth," she said, suddenly "if I had not come in that day—if you had never seen me, would you—would you have married Amanda?" She fixed her eager eyes upon his face, and waited breathless for his answer. He gave it with a light laugh.

"Marry Amanda!" he declared, "well, hardly! Such an idea never entered my head."

"Then," said Elizabeth, slowly "you deceived her."

He shrugged his shoulders. "She deceived herself, I think," he said. "It's not my fault if she—imagined things. Why should I marry a girl like that? She's not pretty, she's stupid, ignorant. Bah, don't talk to me of Amanda." He disposed of the matter with a wave of the hand and another light laugh. Elizabeth felt a sudden conviction of the absurdity of her own behavior. The painful, scorching flush in her cheeks was beginning to cool; the burning, angry shame in her heart was dying away. The remembrance of Amanda's words grew fainter; Paul's handsome face, his air of triumphant health and life, were again in the ascendent.

He saw the yielding in her eyes and brought out his most effective argument. He took boldly the seat beside her on the log and though she shrank away, it was not, he thought, entirely with aversion. "My darling," he said, "don't let trifles come between us. I love you, you love me; isn't that enough? Elizabeth, you are the most beautiful woman in the world. Elizabeth, dearest" ... He put out his arm and drew her towards him. She still shrank away, fascinated yet trembling, frightened at this new delight, this thrill of pleasure in his touch.

"Don't," she gasped out, "Amanda"—He stopped her protest with a kiss.

And it was not till later, when she reached home, that she thought again of Amanda's words: "Remember, he kissed me *first*."

Chapter VIII

MISS Cornelia and Miss Joanna sat at the breakfast-table and looked aghast at Elizabeth, who had just informed them of her engagement. The old Dutch clock on the mantel-piece ticked loudly, the sunlight fell in shining bars upon the snowy table-cloth, the old Dutch china, the glistening silver. Miss Cornelia was reminded forcibly, painfully, of a morning in that same room many years ago, when Peter had announced his marriage. Now the shock was not so great, was not unexpected, perhaps; but it brought with it, if less horror, an even greater disappointment.

"Well," Elizabeth said, after a moment, when her important announcement had produced no response, and she looked proudly, yet half wistfully, from one to the other. "Well," she repeated, "have you nothing to say? Can't you—congratulate me?" Her voice faltered over the last words.

"My dear," Miss Cornelia tried bravely to respond to the appeal in the girl's tone. "Of course, we—we wish you every happiness," she stammered out. She stopped, for tears choked her voice. She looked despairingly at her sister. Was this the moment that they had so often talked of together, planning with delicious thrills of pleasure all they would say and do? "This china must be Elizabeth's when—when she marries, you know." "We must lay by a little for—for Elizabeth's trousseau." This in demure whispers to each other, for they would not for the world have suggested such a possibility to the girl herself. Nice girls, of course, must not think of getting married till the time came, but—with Elizabeth's beauty, that time could not be long delayed, not even in the Neighborhood. The fairy prince would appear some day; though he had never come to them, they believed devoutly that he would come to Elizabeth. And now—and now—the fairy prince had come, or Elizabeth thought so; but they were only conscious of an overwhelming sense of doubt.

"You know so little about him, my dear," Miss Cornelia could not help at last protesting.

Elizabeth opened her eyes wide in genuine surprise. "So little of him," she repeated. "Why, I—I know everything, Aunt Cornelia." And she smiled to herself in silent amusement. Had she not seen him, every day and twice a day, for a matter of four weeks. How long did they think, these older women, that it took to know a man? "I know that he loves me," she said, after a moment, descending to further particulars "and I love him, and that's enough."

"But you can't live on love," urged Miss Joanna, practically. "You must have some money, you know, and I shouldn't think he, poor young man, had anything—at least, judging by his clothes. Those artists never have, they say. And meat, and everything indeed, never was so dear as it is now."

"I didn't know you were so worldly, Aunt Joanna," said Elizabeth, loftily. "Do you want me to marry for money?" Miss Joanna was crushed. But as she reflected in her own justification, one had to have something to eat, let lovers say what they would.

"My dear," said Miss Cornelia, coming to the rescue with the little air of dignity that she could sometimes assume "we certainly wouldn't want you—not for the world—to marry for money. But one has to be—to be prudent. We have brought you up in a way—perhaps it was unwise—poor Mother would have thought so. But at any rate you know nothing about economy, and—and you have only a little money, my dear, and he, I suppose, has nothing."

"He—he expects to make a great deal of money soon," faltered Elizabeth, coming down a little from her heights of romance. All this prudence was like a dash of cold water in the face. She felt disconcerted, indignant, and yet conscious, through it all of some reason in her aunts' objections. Yes, it was true—she had not been brought up to economy, she was fond of luxury and pretty things. In all her wishes for change, she had never thought that it would be amusing to miss any of these.

Miss Cornelia saw that she had produced some effect. "I think," she went on, still speaking with unusual decision, "that the most important thing is to find out something about him. You can't marry a man whom we know nothing about, except that—that he was born at The Mills. We must investigate his character." Miss Cornelia felt, as she brought out this last sentence, that it sounded eminently practical, and it received from Miss Joanna, indeed, its full meed of respectful admiration. Elizabeth only smiled superior.

"You can investigate as much as you like, Aunt Cornelia," she said. "I know all about him." And so the matter rested.

But how could two elderly and innocent spinsters, who had never in their lives stirred two hundred miles from home, investigate the character of a young man who had lived in Chicago and Paris and Vienna and all the four quarters of the world apparently? They had no idea how to set about it. In this perplexity Miss Cornelia again rose to the occasion, and suggested that the Rector might be a fit substitute for that invaluable possession "a man in the family," who is always supposed to accomplish so much. And the Rector, when consulted, proved unexpectedly resourceful. He had made Paul's acquaintance, and learned the name of the church in Chicago where he had sung for so many years. He had discovered, too, that the Rector of this church was an old college friend of his, and he wrote to him at once, requesting full and confidential information as to the young man's character, antecedents, and prospects.

The answer seemed to the poor ladies a long time in coming; as a matter of fact, it arrived very promptly. The Rector of St. Anne's at Chicago regretted to inform his old friend and colleague the Rector of St. Mary's, at Bassett Mills, that he had no good account to give of Paul Halleck, who had not long ago been dismissed from the choir of his church, and had left behind him in Chicago many debts and a bad reputation. The young man was believed to have, as the Rector added, genuine musical talent; but like many artists and musicians, he was morally irresponsible, dissipated and reckless.

The Rector of St. Mary's repeated the verdict, as gently as he could, to the older ladies at the Homestead. They bore it better than he expected. There were compensations indeed in the very extent of its severity. Had Halleck been less evidently and irredeemably a black sheep, there might have been some doubts as to their own duty; but, as it was, they felt that they must break off the dreadful match at once, and at any cost.

Yet the heart of each sister misgave her as they sat in a solemn conclave, and summoned Elizabeth before it. She came, rosy, bright-eyed, fresh from talks with her lover and happy dreams of a brilliant future, which they were to share together. She stood listening in apparent indifference, while Miss Cornelia faltered out the painful result of their inquiries. And when the worst was told, she had turned perhaps a trifle pale, but otherwise she seemed unmoved.

"I don't know why you tell me all this, auntie," she said, slowly. "I—I am sorry to hear it, but it can make no difference."

"No difference!" Miss Cornelia repeated, stupefied. "No difference, Elizabeth?"

"No, it can't change my love for him," she said, defiantly. "He told me that he has enemies at Chicago, and that you would probably unearth a lot of old scandals; and I promised that it should make no difference. Perhaps some of them are true; I don't care. Auntie, I can't—I can't give him up," she went on with a sudden change of tone and clasping her hands appealingly. "I tried to once before, and—I couldn't. If he were to go away now and leave me, I—I should die. I couldn't bear to go on living without him." The girl's face was flushed, her voice tremulous with feeling; it was evident that she fully meant—or thought that she meant—what she said. Her aunts looked at her in helpless perplexity.

"My darling," Miss Cornelia faltered at last, "think how much better it is to give him up now than to—to marry him and be unhappy. You don't know—men are very bad;—one reads such things in the newspapers. If he were to ill-treat you, desert you."

"Ah, but he won't," said Elizabeth, smiling incredulously. "You needn't worry, Aunt Cornelia; we shall be very happy. But even if we were not," she concluded, with a sudden burst of defiance. "If I thought that he would beat me, treat me like a dog—I don't care; I should marry him to-morrow."

And she thrust out her full under lip, and stood facing them, with a look of obstinacy on her fair, girlish face, that for the moment bore a strong resemblance to her father.

To Miss Cornelia's mind there rose again, with startling vividness, the events of twenty years before. The recollection seemed to endow her with an unwonted and unnatural strength. She went over to where Elizabeth stood and took both the girl's hot hands in hers.

"Elizabeth," she said, desperately, "you don't know what you're saying. You will be miserable if you marry that man. You don't know what it is to live with a person who is beneath you, who—who drags you down. We know, my darling, we have seen it. Be warned by us, and give him up."

Miss Cornelia had never in all her gentle life spoken with so much vehemence. Elizabeth, in her astonishment, stood for a moment absolutely passive.

She stole a glance at Miss Joanna; she was weeping quietly. Elizabeth's own face worked, her lip quivered. "I know whom you mean," she broke out, suddenly, in a quick hard voice. "You're thinking of my mother." And then, in the dismayed pause that followed, she dragged her hands away from Miss Cornelia's grasp and fled from the room.

The two older women looked at one another in silence.

"I didn't know," Miss Joanna said at last in a low, awe-struck tone "that the child knew anything about—about poor Malvina."

Chapter IX

"*A*ND so you let all this nonsense influence you?" Halleck asked this bitterly, staring up with moody eyes into Elizabeth's face. They were sitting under a wide-spreading tree, in a field not far from the Homestead. It was late afternoon and the shadows were long and peaceful. A ray from the sinking sun shot through the foliage overhead lighting up the red tints of Elizabeth's hair. Halleck's artistic eye rested upon them fascinated. He had never, as he told himself, been so much in love before.

"You give me up because of a little opposition?" he went on bitterly, roused to increased irritation by the thought of losing her.

"Why, what can I do?" The girl's voice was weary, and she threw out her hands with a helpless gesture. "They will give in to me, I suppose, if I insist; but it makes them too unhappy. I believe it would kill them. If they were unkind, I shouldn't care; but they only cry, and are so wretched, and I can't stand it. It makes me feel so ungrateful."

"And yet," said Halleck, anxiously, "you think they will give in in the end?"

"Oh, yes, they'll give in," said Elizabeth, wearily. "They'll give in, if I insist; and that's the very reason why I—what makes it so hard, you see."

"No, I don't see," said Paul, bluntly. "If you think they will give in, why are you so unhappy? But I understand how it is" he went on, harshly, "you don't love me. I'm too far beneath you—a Bohemian and an outcast. You are glad of an excuse to throw me over."

"Paul!" The indignant color flushed into Elizabeth's face. "How can you say such things," she asked reproachfully. "You know they are not true. I told my aunts that I would never give you up; I told them that—that I would marry you to-morrow, if I could."

"You told them that?" Paul exclaimed exultantly. He put his arm around her and drew her towards him. "Then keep your word, darling," he said. "Marry me to-morrow."

Elizabeth shrank away, startled. "Marry you," she repeated. "To-morrow, how could I?"

"Why not," said Paul, quietly. "Come up to Cranston and we will be married. Then let them say what they please."

Elizabeth was very pale. "I couldn't do that," she said in a low voice. "I don't want to be married so soon; and besides—it would kill my aunts."

He laughed. "Nonsense! People soon resign themselves to what they can't help. And then they needn't know—yet awhile. Listen, darling, this is my plan. You know that I want to go abroad—well, I have had a letter offering me a position in an opera company in Munich. If I accept it I start this week."

He stopped as Elizabeth gave a little cry and stared up at him with reproachful eyes. "This week," she said. "You go away this week?"

"Why, I can't stay here forever, you know," Paul said. "I've idled away my time unconsciousably already—but that is your fault, Elizabeth. Now it is time I went to work. And that is why I say—marry me before I go. Then, while I am away, nothing can separate us."

Elizabeth, pale and thoughtful, seemed to ponder the suggestion. "Marry you," she repeated, slowly. "Marry you—now at once?"

"Yes, to-morrow," said Paul, boldly.

"And—and keep it *secret?*" she went on, with a troubled look.

"Yes, for a little while," said Paul, "for a few months, till I come back. I shall have made my name and my fortune, darling, I hope, by that time, and your aunts will be quite reconciled to me."

"Then wouldn't it be better," said Elizabeth, with much reason, "to wait till then?"

"Are you willing to wait—in uncertainty all this time?" he asked, reproachfully. "Ah, Elizabeth, it is evident that you don't love me as I love you. Such an absence would be unbearable to me, if I felt that some lover was likely to come along at any time and take you from me."

Elizabeth could not help reflecting that the danger of such a catastrophe did not seem imminent, in the present condition of the Neighborhood; but she did not put the thought into words. She only said, with some dignity: "I don't think that I am the sort of girl to change so easily."

"Ah, you can't tell," said Paul. "Women are fickle beings. I don't trust you, Elizabeth. I have a feeling that, if you don't marry me now, you never will. And why should you hesitate?" he went on eagerly. "It isn't so much that I ask. I don't even say—come abroad with me now; only give me the certainty that when I come back, I shall be able to claim you."

"You would have that certainty now," she still insisted. "I promise that I will marry you when you come back."

"Then why not marry me now," he asked, triumphantly.

Elizabeth could give no good reason to the contrary. The idea was vaguely alarming, yet it held for her a certain fascination. She sat listening in troubled uncertainty, while Paul discoursed with enthusiasm over the many advantages of his plan. He was exceedingly anxious, as he had said, to make sure of this beautiful girl, who was, he vaguely felt, a little above him—of a grade superior to that of the other girls whom he had known and made love to, for the space of a fortnight perhaps. He had been true to Elizabeth, now, for more than double that time. He really believed that he should be true to her always. There were other things that attracted him besides her beauty. The thought that Elizabeth was Miss Van Vorst of the Homestead was not unpleasant to him; the old house, the family silver, the family traditions, appealed to his artistic sense of fitness. And then though he was no fortune-hunter, and certainly would have made love to no girl whom he did not for the moment at least sincerely admire, he admitted to himself, frankly, that it was by no means inconvenient that Elizabeth should have a little money of her own and the prospect of more in the future. The Van Vorst property, while it was insignificant enough when measured by the standard of the Van Antwerps and other rich people in the Neighborhood, seemed by no means contemptible to Paul, who measured it by the standard of poverty-stricken Bohemia.

Elizabeth's feelings were more complex, less frankly selfish, much more anxious and uncertain. The money question did not enter into them to any great extent, though she had an instinctive dread of poverty, and she was convinced that, if once married to Paul, she would not be able to have the pretty gowns, and other luxurious trifles, which had hitherto seemed a necessity of life. But she was young and romantic, and this thought did not weigh with her very much. What most distressed her, and made her feel in some way vaguely in the wrong, was the trouble this, her first love affair, seemed to bring to others; to her aunts, to Amanda. She loved her aunts, and hated to run counter to their wishes; she did not love Amanda, and yet the thought of having injured her, though unconsciously, brought with it an uncomfortable sense of guilt.

She had not seen her since that terrible interview, which she still could not recall without a feeling of humiliation; but she had seen her aunt, who told her that Amanda was ill with some low fever—typhoid malaria, probably; there was always a good deal of that at The Mills. It was not considered wise that Elizabeth should see her; and besides, Amanda was delirious, and did not recognize any one. Elizabeth was more relieved than sorry to hear it. No doubt, she told herself, Amanda was already out of her head when she uttered that extraordinary outburst, and it was foolish to attach any importance to what she said in her feverish excitement. Still, Elizabeth did not like to think of it, much less of the promise she herself had given, voluntarily, in such forcible words. She had been so absolutely sincere in making it; she had broken it so completely within the hour. The whole affair was unpleasant, and weighed upon her more than those more serious charges against Paul, which had fallen vaguely upon her ear, not seeming to make any deep impression. His conduct to Amanda was at its worst a mere trifle in comparison.

Still she could not give him up. That broken promise to Amanda only proved this the more strongly. She could not face the prospect of life without him. And yet she could not face without terrible misgivings the prospect of further tears and remonstrances from her aunts. The two claims struggled for the mastery; on the one hand, the claims of the women who had brought her up, whose every thought for twenty years had centred in her; on the other, the claims of the man who had loved her in his light way some five weeks. Under these circumstances, it was inevitable that the claims of the man should predominate. And yet Elizabeth longed to satisfy them both.

Paul's plan seemed to suggest a compromise. And Elizabeth had not yet learned that compromise is never satisfactory to either side.

"Listen," she said, looking at him intently, with eyes that seemed to hold, even in the moment of yielding, a certain defiance of his power, "If I do as you wish, if I—I marry you to-morrow, I am free to—to come home at once, to go on with my life as if nothing were changed—not to tell my aunts, not to tell any one, till you come back? Do you promise this, on your word of honor?"

For a moment Paul hesitated. He had hardly expected her to yield so easily; perhaps if he pressed the matter she might be persuaded even to go abroad with him at once. But there were financial reasons which made that inexpedient just then. On the whole, Paul decided not to test his power too far.

"Upon my word of honor," he said, looking her steadily in the face "I promise that you shall be free as air, to go on with your life as you please, till I come back to claim you."

And so the thing was settled. Paul was to go to Cranston early the next morning to make all necessary arrangements; Elizabeth was to follow him a little later. They were to be married at once. Then Paul was to take an afternoon train for New York, Elizabeth was to return home, the whole affair should remain a secret.

Then Paul, radiantly triumphant, clasped Elizabeth in his arms, and pressed his lips to hers.

"To-morrow," he whispered, "to-morrow, my darling, at this time—though the world won't know it—still you will be my wife."

A strange feeling thrilled Elizabeth. She could not have told if it were pleasure, or some involuntary presentiment. But aloud she repeated mechanically: "Yes, I shall be your wife."

"You won't fail me, dearest," he said, scanning her face eagerly. "You won't break your word? You have promised—you won't fail me?"

"No," Elizabeth answered, "I have promised—I won't fail you."

And yet the thought crossed her mind irrelevantly, that she had broken a promise once already.

She left him and went home through the stillness and the fast gathering shadows of the evening. The days were already growing shorter. She noted the fact mechanically; noted too that the deep glowing crimson of the sunset foretold a hot day for the morrow. She entered the house and looked in at the dining-room; the table was set out for tea with all the wonted care. Her aunts sat each at one end; they were neither of them eating and both had red eyes. In the centre of the table stood Elizabeth's favorite cake—the kind with the raisins in it, which she used to beg for as a child, and which was reserved either as a reward for virtue, or for consolation in some childish trouble. Now in this trouble that was so far from childish, poor Miss Joanna had bethought herself of the old attention, and brought out the favorite cake as the only means of comfort within her power. Elizabeth could not see it without a lump in her throat.

She smoothed her ruffled hair before the glass and came in quietly to her usual place at the table. They looked up nervously at her entrance, but neither spoke; they did not reproach her with being late or ask where she had been. Miss Joanna pressed upon her the various dainties, reminding her that she had eaten no dinner; otherwise the meal was a silent one. It was not till near the end of it that Elizabeth spoke in a strained harsh voice unlike her own.

"Paul is going away." That was what she said. "He—has an engagement to go abroad. He goes to New York to-morrow. I—I hope you are satisfied."

And then she stopped, for the look of tremulous relief on both their faces was almost more than she could bear. The raisins in her favorite cake seemed suddenly to choke her. She began to doubt, after all, whether she would go to Cranston the next day.

Chapter X

THIS was Elizabeth's last thought that night; it was her first in the morning. She dressed herself carefully, putting on white, according to the custom which had aroused Aunt Rebecca's criticism; and all the while she asked of the reflection that stared back at her with perplexed eyes out of the mirror: "Shall I go, or shall I not?" She put the question to a rose when she got down-stairs, repeating as she ruthlessly destroyed each petal. "Yes, no, yes, no?" But the flower answered with a "no," and she threw away the last petal in disgust.

"I think I shall drive over to The Mills this morning," she announced quietly at the breakfast-table. "There is some ribbon I want to match." Her aunts looked up startled. They wondered simultaneously at what hour Halleck was to leave for New York. Yet what if after all the child wished for one last meeting?

"You don't think it's—it's too hot to go over there to-day, my dear?" Miss Cornelia ventured at last uncertainly.

"No, I don't mind the heat," Elizabeth answered indifferently, as she sat playing with her knife and fork. She was very pale and had no appetite. This seemed to them only natural. They hoped that when the young man were once out of the way, their darling would be herself again.

"We must take her to the sea-shore for a little while," Miss Cornelia observed when Elizabeth had left the room. "She needs change of air." Miss Joanna cheerfully assented. The idea and the sacrifice which it involved (since to go away from home, even for a few weeks, seemed a terrible undertaking) consoled them both greatly.

And meanwhile Elizabeth went her own way. It was not till she was seated in the carriage about to start on her drive, that she observed as if by an afterthought: "Oh, by the way, if I can't match the ribbon at The Mills, I may go to Cranston for it by the trolley, so don't be worried if I don't come back till late, and don't wait dinner." Her aunts looked at one another questioningly; but she drove off at once, before they could offer any objections.

And so Elizabeth drove towards Bassett Mills. The day was dry and hot, as were most days that summer. The sun beat down out of a brazen sky, the roads were white with dust, the grass in the fields was sere and brown. The locusts all along the way kept up a loud, exultant song, the burden of which was heat.

To Elizabeth, as she drove on, there began to be something ominous in it all; in the heat and the dust and the dazzling sunshine and the locusts with their eternal noise. They seemed all part, and she with them of some horrible nightmare; she was under some spell which benumbed her, deprived her of the capacity for thought, of all but the power to keep doggedly on the way to Bassett Mills. What she should do when she got there she did not know; her brain was torpid, there was a strange ringing in her ears. It was the sun, no doubt, that was affecting her head; it would be wise to turn back, or she might be ill. But still she kept on.

It was not far from noon when she reached Bassett Mills. There was little life about the place this hot morning; the mill-stream even seemed to dash less tumultuously, and showed signs of running dry. A group of men stood outside the drug-store, which was a great meeting-place, and discussed the drought. It was decided that if it continued the crops would be ruined; but hopes were founded on the fact that prayers for rain were to be offered in all the churches on Sunday.

"But there's not much use praying for rain," said one skeptic, "when the wind's due west."

Elizabeth heard the words as she drove up, and, alighting tied the white pony to a post and bribed a small boy to "keep an eye" on him. Then she joined the group in front of the shop, who were some waiting for the trolley, others merely passing the time of day. She did not go into the dry-goods shop to try to match her ribbon; she knew that such ribbon as she wanted was not to be had at Bassett Mills. She stood idly listening to the men's conversation, and wondering if it were indeed true, as the skeptic had declared, that it was useless to pray for an event already determined by natural causes. She had been brought up to believe implicitly in the efficacy of prayer, and had added to her usual formula that morning a petition of unwonted fervor that she might be enabled in this perplexing situation to decide for the best. But perhaps there was no use in praying; perhaps one was not a free agent. Fate, she thought, had evidently determined that she should go to Cranston that morning to be married, since it was a thing that might so easily have been prevented—by an objection from her aunts, an offer of company on the expedition, even by the white pony going lame; she would have yielded, or so she thought, to the merest trifle, glad to have the decision taken out of her hands. But everything had been made easy; it evidently was to be. And an implicit believer in heredity might have observed that the matter had been decided for her, by events and influences which had moulded her character even before she was born. It was in just such clandestine fashion as this that her parents had once gone up to Cranston to be married; and it might be that some mysterious hereditary instinct, some force over which she had no control, was now constraining their daughter, under the same circumstances, to act in the same way.

Elizabeth, fortunately or otherwise, did not think of this. She only knew that she was standing outside the drug-store with the other loiterers, straining her eyes along the dusty white road for a sight of the trolley; and that, even while she doubted the wisdom of waiting, some fascination held her rooted to the spot. When the trolley came she took her seat at once. After all a trip to Cranston meant nothing; she might simply buy her ribbon and come back.

The trolley started off fast and jerkily, creating a teasing wind, that seemed to blow from some fiery furnace. Elizabeth clutched her hat with one hand, while with the other she tried to shield her eyes from the flying dust and glare. Soon they were past the cemetery and the straggling outskirts of Bassett Mills, out into the open country, with rolling meadow and upland on either side, all withered, scorching under the sun's fierce rays. An occasional wagon met them, wrapped in a cloud of dust; the trolley was hailed now and then from some solitary farm-house, and came to a sudden stop. The ride seemed endless, but that they were approaching Cranston was at last made evident by unmistakable signs; by the advertisements staring at them from trunks of trees and the expanse of stone walls; by the asphalt pavement that succeeded the rough country road, the increasing quantity of bicycles, carriages and dust; and finally by the neat rows of Queen Anne villas, with their gabled fronts and terraced gardens sloping to the road. Then the car, with a last triumphant jerk, turned a corner and landed its passengers squarely in the High Street of Cranston.

Elizabeth alighted rather limply, and stood looking about her in a dazed sort of way. A country woman laden with parcels addressed her timidly. "Excuse me miss," she said, "but would you tell me the best place to go for stockings?"

Elizabeth started and stared at her, as if the simple question had been put in Hebrew. Then in a moment she recovered herself and directed the woman very civilly. She watched her bustle off upon her round of errands, then turned and slowly walked into the confectioner's shop. It was there that she had promised to meet Paul.

There was no one, as it happened, in the front part of the shop, where candy and cake were sold; no one in the little restaurant at the back. Elizabeth sat down at one of the small marble-topped tables; her head was aching, her eyes blood-shot, she was conscious of nothing but a feeling of pleasure in the coolness and darkness, of relief from the outside glare. Mechanically, she glanced at the small mirror, that hung at an unbecoming angle opposite on the wall, and felt a slight shock at the sight of herself—pale, worn, with blood-shot eyes, her white gown dusty and bedraggled. No, she did not look well—she had never looked worse in her life. Her lips curled in an unmirthful smile, as she thought irrelevantly of Aunt Rebecca, and of how she might have held forth on the folly of wearing white for such a dusty ride. And thereupon with a sudden pang, came the thought of Amanda—Amanda, tossing no doubt just then in the delirium of fever. The unpleasant idea struck Elizabeth of a resemblance between her own white face in the mirror, and her cousin's face as she had last seen it, with those staring, red-rimmed eyes. Certainly, there was a latent family likeness; but it took unbecoming conditions such as these to bring it out. She wondered languidly if any one else had ever noticed it.

Poor Amanda! Was she still, in her delirium, fretting over Paul? Or was she, perhaps, secure in Elizabeth's promise, and the pleasure of having separated them? What would she think if she knew that Elizabeth was even now waiting for him here in Cranston—waiting to be married to him? But with this thought the spell of indifference which had rested upon Elizabeth seemed suddenly to fall away, and there swept over her a sudden sense of revolt, of shame and repulsion. She started impulsively to her feet. No, she could not be married—not in that way; it was clandestine, disgraceful. There was still time to escape. If only she could reach home, without seeing Paul! She made one quick, blinded rush for the door, and then, a tall figure stood in her way, and her hands were seized in a man's eager grasp. His handsome, exultant face looked into hers.

"My brave girl," he said. "So you have not failed me."

Chapter XI

ELIZABETH with a great effort wrenched her hands away from Paul's grasp, and fell against one of the marble-topped tables. Her face was white, her dull eyes looked up at him with a sort of terror.

"I—I have failed you," she said, speaking slowly and thickly, with parched lips. "I have come, but I—cannot stay. I was going when you came in."

"Elizabeth!" The look of exultant joy faded slowly and reluctantly from Paul's face. "Elizabeth, what do you mean? Why did you come if you don't mean to stay?"

"Because I—was crazy." She was trembling now, and she clung to the table for support; but still she was firm. "I—I didn't think what I did. Now I—I know. It would be wrong to marry like this—so secretly. I must go home. Let me pass." She spoke the last words quickly, imperiously, and made a motion as if to brush past him; but he stood motionless in the door and blocked her way.

He was very angry; she had never seen him so before. The emotion lent a curious brute strength to his fair, sensuous beauty. His face was as white as hers, his full red lips were set in a curve of unwonted determination.

"Listen to me, Elizabeth." He had never spoken to her in such a tone before. "I won't be trifled with like this. I have made all the arrangements. I won't have you—jilt me now. You must come with me, or I—I'll know the reason why."

She met his gaze defiantly. "You can't compel me to come you know," she said. And again she would have passed him, and again he stopped her. She did not try a third time, but sank into a chair and put up her hands to her face. A sudden faintness came over her; it might have been the heat, or the sharp, conflicting play of emotion. He followed her and gently took her hands from her face and looked into her eyes.

"Don't be foolish, darling," he said, persuasively. "You know that you love me, that you are only playing with me. You wouldn't really throw me over now."

She looked up reluctantly, fascinated as she had often been before, by the mere physical attraction of his beauty. "I—I don't know," she began slowly, and then stopped frightened at the sound of voices in the shop. A dread flashed over her all at once of a scene in a place like this. The trifling, frivolous consideration turned the scale in Paul's favor. She rose, shook off his grasp, and gave a hasty glance in the glass.

"No, I won't throw you over," she said. "It's all wrong but—as you say, it's too late now. Take care—some one is coming." She gave a warning look at the door, as Paul pressed her hand.

So the threatened scene was averted and Elizabeth's fate was sealed. The people who, after buying candy in the shop, came into the little back room for some ice cream, saw a young woman arranging her hair before the glass, and a young man waiting for her—a not unusual sight.

What followed seemed in after life a dream to Elizabeth. There were times when she tried to think that it had never happened; that the whole thing was a mere figment of the imagination. But on that day she was quite conscious that it was she herself, in very flesh and blood, Elizabeth Van Vorst, who walked by Paul Halleck's side through the glaring, sunny streets of Cranston, went with him into a dimly-lighted church, let him place a ring upon her finger, spoke her share in the marriage service, and wrote her maiden name for what should have been the last time, in the parish register. The clergyman was very old and mumbled over the service; the witnesses, two servants of his, were old and feeble, also, and took but small interest. The church was damp like a tomb after the heat without; Elizabeth found herself shivering as from a chill. It was a relief to come out again into the heat which had been so oppressive before. But on the church steps Elizabeth gave a little cry. A funeral was slowly filing past, its black trappings standing out in incongruous gloom against the noon-day brilliance.

Elizabeth looked at Paul. He had turned very white, and he too was shivering. "It is a bad omen," he said, in a low voice, as if to himself. He said no more, but led the way carefully in the opposite direction from that which the funeral had taken.

They found themselves in a part of Cranston unknown to Elizabeth. The road was bordered on either side by flowering hedges and led apparently into the open country. There were no houses in sight; for the moment, even no people. Halleck suddenly turned and clasped Elizabeth almost roughly in his arms, while he pressed passionate kisses upon her brow, her lips, her hair.

"My darling," he cried "I can't—I can't give you up. I was mad to promise it. Let everything go and come with me to New York."

"No, no, I can't," she murmured faintly. "I can't." His vehemence stunned, bewildered her; but instinctively she struggled against it. "You promised," she cried out indignantly, "you promised that I should be free—till you came back. I've kept my word, you must keep yours."

He let her go and for a moment they eyed each other steadily. This time the victory remained with her. "Did I really make that promise?" he said at last with a sigh. "Well, if I did, I must keep it, I suppose. But, Elizabeth, you must be made of ice—you can't love me, or you wouldn't hold me to it."

Elizabeth was chiefly conscious of an overpowering sense of relief.

"I do love you," she said, soothingly, "but indeed it is better—much better to let things be as we arranged them. I can't go to New York in this dress"—she gave a little tremulous laugh, as she glanced at her fluffy muslin skirts. "Only a man could suggest such a thing. And then my aunts!—they would be distracted. No, no, I must go home at once. You will be back in six months," she went on, trying to console him. "They will pass very quickly."

"Six months," he sighed. "It is an endless time." He was the picture of gloom as they turned and walked steadily back to the busy part of Cranston. And she, too, had her regrets. The compromise was satisfactory to neither.

At the corner of the High Street they parted. There was no opportunity for more than a hand-clasp, a few hurried words of farewell. Then he went his way to the railroad station, and she hurried to the trolley. The country woman with the many parcels was there before her, and told where she got the stockings, and how much she paid for them.

Back again went the trolley, along the asphalted road past the Queen Anne villas with their terraced gardens, past bicycles, carriages, wagons, and always clouds of dust; out into the open country, with rolling meadow and upland on either side, simmering in the heat of the summer afternoon, to which the morning heat was as nothing; Elizabeth sitting upright, shading her eyes from the glare, with aching head and burning eyes, and throbbing brain that refused to take in the reality of what she had done. This was her wedding journey.

An hour later the white pony brought her home.

"Did you—did you match your ribbon, dear?" Miss Joanna inquired anxiously. Elizabeth stared blankly for a moment.

"I—I never thought of the ribbon," she cried at last, and burst into hysterical laughter.

Chapter XII

IT was that time of year when the Neighborhood, and the whole riverside, are in their glory. Day after day dawned clear and frosty, to warm at noon-day into a mellow brilliance. On every side stretched wooded meadow and upland all aglow, resplendent in varied tints of crimson and russet, magenta and scarlet, blending in a glorious scheme of color, till they melted at last into the soft gray haze, which rested, like a touch of regretful melancholy, on the tops of the distant hills. Over the fields the golden-rod was still scattered profusely, amidst the sober browns and purples of the bay, and the pale lavender of the Michaelmas daisies. Red berries glistened on the bushes, the ground was covered, every day deeper, with a carpeting of fallen leaves and chestnut burrs.

On one of these autumn days, when the light was fading into dusk, Mrs. "Bobby" Van Antwerp came to call at the Homestead, and found no one at home but Elizabeth, who was kneeling on the hearth-rug, staring into the fire.

Elizabeth's thoughts were not pleasant ones. She had refused to go to Cranston with her aunts that afternoon, for she had never been near the place since that hot July day, nearly three months before, when she had forgotten to match her ribbon. What construction her aunts placed upon the episode she never knew. They did not allude to it in words, but treated her with added care and solicitude, as if she were recovering from some illness. In pursuance of this theory, they took her to a highly recommended and very dull seaside place, where she was extremely bored. She returned in better health, though hardly better spirits. She had now a new trouble, which increased as the autumn advanced. Paul's letters, at first many and ardent, grew fewer and colder, till they ceased altogether. Elizabeth's last letter remained unanswered, and she was too proud to write again. No doubt, she told herself, his thoughts were occupied by some new attraction. With a sudden flash of intuition, she realized that for Paul there would always be an attraction of some kind, and generally a new one.

This unpleasant perception had one good result, at least; it lightened her sense of remorse towards Amanda. She had long ago got over the ordeal of seeing her cousin again, and the strange scene between them had been relegated to a curious phase of unreality, covered up and almost obliterated, as such scenes not infrequently are among relations and intimate friends, by the thousand commonplace incidents of every-day life. And yet some sort of apology had been proffered by Amanda, as she sat up in her white wrapper, very pale and hollow-eyed, with her red hair cut short, and just beginning to come in in soft waves like Elizabeth's—a thing she had always desired.

"You know," she said, in her weak voice "I was real sick that last time you saw me. I was just coming down with the fever."

"I know you were," Elizabeth said gently, conquering the thrill of anger which swept over her at the recollection.

"I guess I said some queer things," Amanda ventured next, and gave an odd, furtive look from her light eyes.

"You certainly did," said Elizabeth, coldly. Not all the pity she felt for Amanda's weakness could avail to make her speak in any other way.

"Well, I guess," Amanda said, after a moment and closing her eyes as if wearied out, "people aren't accountable for what they say when they're sick."

"No," said Elizabeth, "I suppose not." And with this tacit apology and its acceptance, this episode between the cousins might be considered closed. Certainly, on Elizabeth's side, it was not only closed, but forgotten, in the pressure of far more serious troubles.

As she knelt that afternoon looking into the fire, a vision of her future life—colorless, empty, without joy or love—seemed to stare back at her from its glowing depths. The years stretched out before her, a dreary waste—without Paul. She was sure that he would never come back; the bond between them seemed the merest shadow. He had forgotten her in three short months, while she was more in love than ever, since she had never fully realized, at the time, the void that he would leave behind him. For a short time her life had bloomed like the summer; and now nothing was left to her but the fast-approaching gray monotony of the November days, and the bleak cold of the winter.

Upon these cheerful reflections entered Mrs. Bobby Van Antwerp, in a short skirt somewhat the worse for wear, with dark eyes that shone brilliantly beneath her battered hat, and her small piquante face glowing with health and exercise.

"Don't get up," she said. "What a beautiful blaze!" She sat down to it at once and held out her small, gloveless hands to its pleasant warmth. "I walked all the way," she announced, triumphantly, "and I thought I would just drop in, and perhaps you'd give me a cup of tea."

One must have lived in the Neighborhood to appreciate the informality of all this. People paid calls in their carriages, with their card-cases and their best Sunday gowns—it was not good form to come on foot, even had the distances permitted. But the young woman always spoken of as "Mrs. Bobby" though her claims to a more formal designation had long since been established, was a law unto herself and cared little what the Neighborhood's laws might be. Elizabeth had already noticed that this great lady, the greatest lady in the Neighborhood, treated her with more friendliness than other people of less assured position with whom she was, theoretically, on more intimate terms. This curious fact, and the cause of it, occupied her thoughts while she rang the bell and ordered tea, a little flustered inwardly, but outwardly calm, and comfortably conscious of the becoming neatness of her serge skirt and velveteen blouse. Whatever her troubles might be, she had not yet reached so great a pitch of desperation as to neglect her appearance.

"Aren't these autumn days beautiful!" said Mrs. Bobby, making herself at home by unfastening her coat and tossing aside her hat, whereby she disclosed to view a somewhat tousled halo of curly dark hair. "I tell Bobby that just these few days in the autumn make up to us for the bother of keeping the place, though in summer it is fearfully hot, and unspeakably dull all the year round. It must be very dull for you," said Mrs. Bobby, coming to a sudden pause.

"Oh, yes, it's dull," Elizabeth admitted, with a little sigh.

Mrs. Bobby laughed.

"Why don't you say 'oh, but I am so fond of the place,' or 'but I'm not at all dependent on society,' as the other girls in the Neighborhood do?"

"I don't know," said Elizabeth, reflectively. "I don't think, for one thing, that I am so awfully fond of the place; and as for society—I have never had any, so naturally I get on without it."

"But you would enjoy it, if you had it?"

A curious brightness shone for an instant in Elizabeth's eyes. "Ah, yes, I should enjoy it," she said, quickly. "I'm sure I should."

"I'm sure you would, too," said Mrs. Bobby. She seemed to reflect a moment. "Don't you go away in August?" she asked at last.

"Yes, this year we did," said Elizabeth. "We went to Borehaven. It—it wasn't very amusing." She stopped short blushing as if the last words had been wrung from her unawares; but Mrs. Bobby's smile seemed to invite confidence.

"Tell me all about it," she said. "Was it very terrible?"

"Yes, very," said Elizabeth, frankly. "There were a good many girls who used to promenade up and down, and a number of old ladies who sat in rows on the piazza and criticized the people and grumbled about the table; and they one and all treated us as if we had committed some crime. We were quite distressed till we found out that it was nothing personal—only the way they always treat new arrivals."

"Ah, I know the type of place," said Mrs. Bobby "and the people. Were there any men?"

"A few who were called men—about sixteen, I should think—most of them—but they didn't interest me particularly." And Elizabeth blushed, as she remembered the reason which had made her indifferent, at least to such men as Borehaven could boast of. Mrs. Bobby noticed the blush.

"What!" she said to herself "another attraction in this wilderness? Not that stupid Frank Courtenay—I hope not. Yet there isn't and never has been another man in the place that I ever heard of." While she pondered this problem the tea-things were brought in, and Elizabeth seated herself at the small table, behind the old silver urn, in the full glow of the firelight, which played on her hair and brought out the warm creamy tones of her skin. Mrs. Bobby watched her silently with her bright dark eyes, her small, pointed chin supported on her hand.

"You ought to go to town for the winter," she announced at last abruptly. This seemed to be the upshot of her reflections. Elizabeth looked up with a little start, and a momentary brightening of the eyes, which faded, however, instantly.

"Oh, my aunts could never bear to leave here," she said. "They have so taken root in this place. Besides," she went on, constrained to greater frankness by the consciousness of that quality in Mrs. Bobby herself "what would be the use if we did go? We know so few people. It would be horrid to be in New York and not know any one or go anywhere."

"Yes, that wouldn't be pleasant," admitted Mrs. Bobby, to whom indeed such a state of things was inconceivable. "But you would know people," she went on, after a moment "every one does somehow. There are your cousins, the Schuyler Van Vorsts, for instance."

"Who would probably never notice us," said Elizabeth "or if they did, would ask us to a family dinner."

"Well, that certainly would be worse than nothing," Mrs. Bobby admitted. "But—how about your old school friends? You must have known some nice girls at Madame Veuillet's. You would see, no doubt, a great deal of them."

Elizabeth shook her head. "I doubt it," she said. "They spoke—some of them—of asking me to stop with them, but they have none of them done so. They don't even write to me any more. It doesn't take long for people to forget one, Mrs. Van Antwerp," said poor Elizabeth, putting into words the melancholy philosophy which experience had lately taught her.

"My dear child," cried Mrs. Van Antwerp, "you're too young to realize that—yet." She put out her hand in her warm, impulsive way, and touched Elizabeth's. "I can promise you one thing," she said. "If you come to New York, I'll do what I can to make it pleasant for you."

Elizabeth looked up with glistening eyes. "You're—you're awfully kind," she began, stammering. In another moment she would have burst into tears, and perhaps, in the sudden expansion, confided everything to this new friend—in which case her life's history would have been different. But just then she heard the sound of wheels, and immediately she stiffened and the habit of reserve, which had been growing upon her during the last three months, reasserted itself. When her aunts entered, in a little glow of excitement after their day at Cranston, Elizabeth was sitting quite cool and placid behind the tea-things, absorbed in the problems of milk and sugar.

The rest of Mrs. Bobby's visit seemed to her rather dull. They sat around the fire, and Mrs. Bobby drank her tea and ate a great many of the little round cakes which accompanied it, and which she praised warmly, to the gratification of Miss Joanna, who had made them. She told them all about her domestic affairs, and Bobby's affairs, and the family affairs generally, and was altogether very charming and as the Misses Van Vorst expressed it, "neighborly;" but still she said not a word further of their going to town, or of that pleasant if rather vague promise she had made in a moment of impulse, which perhaps she already regretted. It was not till she held Elizabeth's hand at parting that she invited her, as if by a sudden thought, to dinner on the following Friday.

"It will be dull, I'm afraid," she said. "Only the Rector and his wife, and the Hartingtons, and Julian Gerard, who is coming up over Sunday. You will be the only young girl, and I want you to amuse Julian. We dine at eight. Do come early, so we can have a talk beforehand."

Elizabeth, entirely taken by surprise, had only time to murmur an acceptance, when Mrs. Bobby hurried off, being hastened by the arrival of her husband, who had called for her and was waiting outside in the dog-cart. "Friday, remember," she called out from the yawning darkness beyond the door, "and come early." Then Bobby Van Antwerp's restless horse bore her off.

The Misses Van Vorst returned to the drawing-room, in a state of considerable excitement.

"Think of my dining at the Van Antwerps!" Elizabeth exclaimed, still rosy from the unexpected honor. "I was so taken aback that I could hardly answer properly. But how on earth am I to amuse Julian—whoever he may be, and what have I got to wear?"

"It's a—a very nice attention," said Miss Cornelia, complacently. "She's never asked the Courtenay girls, I know, from what their mother told me. She said they thought it a pity she was so unsociable. I think, sister, when we see them we might mention that we don't find her unsociable—just casually, you know. As for what you can wear, my dear—either your white crepe or white organdie is quite pretty enough, and much nicer than anything the Courtenay girls would have."

"To think of dinner at eight o'clock!" said Miss Joanna, who was only just recovering her powers of speech. "So very fashionable! I wish, dear, if you can, you would notice what they have. Mrs. Bobby says her cook is very good at croquettes. I wish you could tell me, dear, if they are better than ours."

"I'm afraid I shan't be able to think of croquettes," said Elizabeth, "what with the burden of being on my best behavior and entertaining Mr. Gerard. I think by the way, that he must be that dark man I have seen sometimes in their pew on Sundays. Which would he like me best in, do you suppose—the white crepe or the organdie? I must get them both out, and decide which to wear."

Elizabeth's spirits were as easily exhilarated as they were depressed. She ran up-stairs, humming a gay little tune which had not come into her head for many a day. This dinner at the Van Antwerps', with the prospect of meeting a few of her neighbors and apparently, one unmarried man, might have seemed to many people a commonplace affair enough; but to Elizabeth it was a great occasion, and for the rest of the evening, bright visions of future pleasure danced before her eyes. That night, for the first time in many weeks, she did not cry herself to sleep, thinking of Paul.

Chapter XIII

"*A*ND you really think I look nicely?" Elizabeth asked this question in tremulous excitement, as she stood before the long pier-glass in her room on the night of her first dinner-party. The maid was on her knees behind her arranging the folds of her train, Miss Joanna stood ready with her cloak, and Miss Cornelia hovered a little way off, admiring the scene. Elizabeth held her head high, there was a brilliant color in her cheeks, her eyes shone like stars. You would hardly have known her for the same girl who had struggled with sad thoughts and disappointed hopes in the twilight only a few days before. This seemed some young princess, to whom the good things of life came naturally, unsought, by the royal prerogative of beauty.

"You—you look lovely," faltered Miss Cornelia, forgetting her principles in the excitement of the occasion "and your dress is sweet."

"It is fortunate I had it cut low, isn't it," said Elizabeth, as she clasped a string of pearls, which had once belonged to her grandmother, about her round white throat. "There, do I look all right? You're *sure* my skirt hangs well? I wanted a white rose, but we have no pretty ones left." A slight cloud of discontent crossed her face, but vanished instantly; since really, as she said to herself, she looked very nice even without flowers.

"Don't be late," entreated Miss Joanna. "Just think if the dinner should be spoiled!"

"Yes, it would be very bad manners," added Miss Cornelia "not to be punctual."

"I don't know," said Elizabeth, doubtfully. "It's rather countrified to be too early." But still she drew on her gloves and put on her cloak, and started a good half-hour before the appointed time, in deference to Miss Joanna's fears for the dinner and Miss Cornelia's sense of the value of punctuality.

The clock was striking eight as she entered the wide hall of the Van Antwerps's house, and read, or fancied that she did, in the solemn butler's immobile countenance, an assurance that she was unfashionably prompt. The demure little maid who followed him and took Elizabeth's cloak, regretted to inform her that Mrs. Van Antwerp was not quite ready, but would be down directly, and hoped that Miss Van Vorst would excuse her unpunctuality. Elizabeth's heart sank, but the maid was ushering her into the drawing-room, and there was no retreat. Yet she shrank back involuntarily, as the long room yawned before her, empty, except for one person whom she did not know; and thus she stood for a moment hesitating, her warm Titian coloring framed against the dark plush of the portiere, and her white gown falling about her in graceful folds, of a statuesque simplicity almost severe, but from which her youth and rounded curves emerged all the more triumphant. Her heart beat fast and there was a deep burning color in her cheeks, but she held herself erect, with the proud little turn of the head that seemed to come to her by nature.

The tall dark man who was turning over the leaves of a magazine at the end of the room, looked up as she entered and gazed at her for a moment in silence. Their eyes met; for an instant he seemed to hesitate. Then he rose and walked slowly towards her.

"You must let me introduce myself, Miss Van Vorst," he said, and his voice was like his movements, very deliberate, yet it was clear-cut and pleasant in tone. "My name is Gerard. Mrs. Van Antwerp told me I should have the pleasure of taking you in to dinner."

He spoke so quietly and naturally, and seemed to accept the situation with such absolute indifference, that whatever awkwardness it might have contained for a young girl nervous over her first dinner, was instantly removed. Elizabeth felt grateful, and yet perversely a little piqued that this grave, dark man should place her at a disadvantage, that he should be perfectly at home and know exactly what to do, when she was nervous and flustered. But that kind Providence which had endowed Elizabeth with so many good gifts had given her among others a power to cover inward perturbation with a brave show of self-possession.

"I'm terribly early," she was able to say now, quite lightly and easily, though still with that uncomfortable beating of the heart. "My aunts are very old-fashioned, and insist on punctuality as one of the cardinal virtues."

"In which they are quite right, I think," said Mr. Gerard, smiling. "But when you know Mrs. Van Antwerp well, you will have learned that it is the one virtue in which she is utterly lacking."

"I—I don't know her very well," Elizabeth admitted, regretting somewhat that she could not assert the contrary. "I have never even been here before," she added, glancing about the room, whose stateliness was a little overpowering.

"Really! Then wouldn't you—a—like to come into the conservatory and look at the flowers?" suggested Mr. Gerard, who seemed to have charged himself with the duties of host. "Oh, you needn't wait for Mrs. Van Antwerp," he added, smiling, as Elizabeth hesitated. "I know the time when she went to dress, and can assert with confidence that she won't be down for another half-hour."

So Elizabeth found herself led, somewhat against her will, into the famous conservatory, of whose beauties she had often heard; but with which, it must be confessed, she was less occupied than with the man by her side, at whom she cast furtive glances from beneath her long lashes. He was tall—decidedly taller than herself, though she was a tall woman, and rather broadly built than otherwise. His dark, smooth-shaven face, which had lighted up pleasantly when he smiled, was in repose rather heavy and impassive, with an ugly, square chin, that seemed to indicate an indomitable will, of a kind to pursue tenaciously whatever he might desire. In contradiction to this, his eyes, except when a passing gleam of interest or amusement brightened their sombre depths, had a weary indifferent look, as if there were nothing in the world, on the whole, worth desiring.

"And this is the man," thought Elizabeth, "whom I am expected to amuse. He doesn't look as if it would be an easy task. But no doubt Mrs. Bobby has given him the same charge about me, and he is trying, conscientiously, to obey. That's why he's taken me in here to show me the sights, the way they do to the country visitors." Her heart leaped rebelliously at the thought, even while she was saying aloud mechanically: "'What a fine azalea!' I wonder if I look like a countrified production. My gown isn't, at least; but then—he wouldn't appreciate that fact. It probably would be the same to him, if it came out of the Ark; he isn't the sort of man to notice, one way or the other. I don't believe he cares for women—no, nor they for him. He's not at all good-looking, and he must be—thirty-five"—she ventured another glance. "Oh, that, at least. His hair is quite gray on the temples. 'Yes, those orchids are beautiful. I never saw anything like them.' I must do my duty and admire properly; he thinks me very unsophisticated, no doubt. I don't think I like him. Did Mrs. Bobby think it would amuse me to—amuse him? But perhaps he is thinking the same thing about me." And she stole another glance at his face, but could not read, in his half-closed eyes and unmoved expression, any indication of his real feelings.

They had made the round of the conservatory, when suddenly he stopped. "Don't you—want a flower for your gown," he asked. He looked about him reflectively. "Let me see," he said. "You would like it to be white." Elizabeth wondered how he knew that. After a moment's hesitation, he chose a white rose and gave it to her. She fastened it carefully in her gown, where its green leaves formed the only touch of color.

"How does it look?" she asked innocently, and raised her eyes to his, where unexpectedly they encountered an odd gleam, of something that seemed neither wholly interest nor yet amusement, and that made her look down again quickly, while the warm color mantled in her cheeks. It was a moment before he answered her.

"It looks well," he said then, quietly, "and suits your gown." And they sauntered back slowly to the drawing-room.

Mrs. Bobby came hurrying in by the opposite door, fastening as she went the diamond star in her black lace.

"My dear child," she said, kissing Elizabeth, "what must you think of me! It is all Bobby's fault for taking us such a long drive, and I see he is not down yet either, the wretch! But Julian has been entertaining you, so it is all right. I'm afraid though that he has been taking away my character unmercifully, telling you that I am always late, and other pleasing things of the kind."

Gerard's smile again softened his face. "Do me justice, Eleanor," he said. "You know I don't say worse things of my friends behind their backs than I do to their faces."

She laughed. "I should be sorry for them if you did," she returned. "But here," she went on, as voices were heard in the hall, "here, in good time, are the Rector and his wife. What a blessing they didn't arrive sooner!"

The words had hardly left her lips before the Rector and his wife were ushered in, the latter uttering voluble apologies for being late, and laying all the blame on the erratic behavior of the village hackman, who feeling an utter contempt for people who did not keep their own carriages, reserved the privilege of calling for them at what hour he pleased. The theme of his unpunctuality was so engrossing that the Rector's wife would have enlarged on it for some time, had she not caught sight of Elizabeth, and in her surprise subsided into a chair and momentary silence. And then strolled in Bobby Van Antwerp, fair, well-groomed, amiable, and mildly bored at the prospect of entertaining his neighbors; and immediately afterwards followed the Hartingtons, still more bored at the prospect of being entertained; after which they all went in to dinner, and Elizabeth found herself seated between the Rector and Gerard.

"You live here all the year round, don't you?" the latter said to her, somewhere about the third course, when he had given utterance to several other conventional remarks, and she had grown accustomed to the multiplicity of forks at her plate, and had decided that the light of wax candles, beaming softly under rose-colored shades, was eminently becoming to every one. She looked at him now with an odd little challenge in her eyes, called forth, in spite of herself, by the wearied civility of his conversational efforts.

"Yes, I live here all the year round," she said, in her clear, flute-like voice. "I—I'm a country girl, you see."

He smiled. "You are to be congratulated, I think."

"Do you think so?" asked Elizabeth, in genuine surprise.

"Why, yes, I love the country; don't you," he said tranquilly.

She was silent for a moment, her eyes resting absently on the graceful erection of ferns in the centre of the table, which rose, like a fairy island, from a lake of glass. "It's not a conventional thing to say," she answered at last, slowly "but if you want the truth"—

"I always want the truth," said Gerard.

"Well, then, I don't think I do care for the country," she said. "I've had too much of it. I—there are times when I detest it." She spoke with sudden vehemence, and she met his wondering gaze with eyes that were curiously hard.

Gerard's face clouded. "You don't care for the country," he said, slowly, "and yet you live here all the year round?"

"Ah, that's the very reason," she said, lightly. "People always tell you that you don't appreciate your blessings; but how can you reasonably be expected to, when you don't have any voice in choosing them?"

"If you did, you probably wouldn't like them any better," he retorted. "And it would be more annoying to think that you had had a voice in the matter and had chosen wrong."

"Perhaps," said Elizabeth, "but I should like to make the experiment." And she stared again thoughtfully at the feathery forms of the ferns.

"Well, if you had your choice," said Gerard, lazily, "what would you choose as an improvement on the present state of things?"

She turned towards him with a slight start. "What should I choose," she said, slowly "as an improvement on my life just now?"

"Yes, if you had a fairy Godmother," suggested Gerard.

"With unlimited power?" questioned Elizabeth.

He laughed. "Well, not quite that, perhaps," he said, "but—a fairy Godmother who could give you a good deal. A very charming one, too," he added, in a low voice.

Elizabeth knit her brows and pouted out her full lips, in apparently deep reflection. "If I had a fairy Godmother," she said, musingly, "and she were to give me three wishes—three, you know, is the magic number in the fairy tales—why, I should choose first of all, I think, a season in town"—

"Which you might tire of in a month," suggested Gerard.

"Not at all," said Elizabeth, decidedly, "because my second wish would be for the capacity to be always amused."

"And do you really think," said Gerard, "that you would like that—to go through life as if it were a sort of opera bouffe?"

"Why not?" said Elizabeth. "I'm a frivolous person. I confess I like opera bouffe."

"For an evening, perhaps," said Gerard, "but after a time you'd get tired of it—oh, yes, I'm sure you would—and you'd begin to think"—

"Ah, no, I shouldn't," she interrupted him, eagerly "for that's what my third wish should be. I should ask for the power never to think. Thought—thought is horrible." She spoke the last words very low, more to herself than him, and broke off suddenly, as an odd, frightened look crept into her eyes. Gerard watched her in some perplexity.

"This girl," he said to himself "who must be, I suppose, somewhere about twenty, and has seen, according to Eleanor, nothing of the world, talks sometimes like a thoughtless child, and sometimes like a woman of thirty, and an unhappy one at that. I can't quite make her out." Aloud he said, in an odd, dry voice that he had not hitherto used towards her, "Now that you have pretty well in theory at least, reduced yourself to the level of a brainless doll, why not ask, now that you are about it, for the power not to feel? Then you would really be a complete automaton, and nothing on earth could have power to hurt you."

Elizabeth had grown very pale, and her hands were tightly locked together under the table. "Ah," she said, wearily "I've exhausted my three wishes. And, besides, it's too much to ask. No fairy Godmother, I'm afraid, could give one the power not to feel."

"Be thankful for that," he said, quickly. "A woman who has no capacity for suffering is—is—would be unspeakably repellant."

"Would she?" said Elizabeth, dreamily. "I should think, for my part, that she would be rather enviable." She sat staring absently before her, and Gerard did not try to break the silence. In a moment Mrs. Hartington on his other side claimed his attention, and Elizabeth was not sorry. She felt vaguely resentful towards him for having made her think of unpleasant things, which she had resolved not to do that evening. The dinner went on, and she helped herself mechanically to dish after dish which was pressed upon her. The Rector turned to her and made a few labored remarks, adapted as he thought to her youthful intelligence, and she answered them absently. Bobby Van Antwerp told, in a languid way, a funny story for the benefit of the table, and the conversation grew general for awhile. Dinner was nearly over when Gerard said, turning to her with a pleasant smile:

"I'm not a prophet, and yet I am going to venture on a prediction. In a little while, I think, you'll find your fairy Godmother, and have your season in town, though I don't know if the other things will be thrown in; and then some time in the course of it, I'll ask you if you are satisfied, and you'll tell me perhaps, that you are sick of it all, and are pining for the country, the green fields, and—a—the view of the river"—

He stopped as Elizabeth interrupted him flippantly. "Oh, no, never," she cried. "I'd prefer city streets to green fields any day, and as for the river—I've looked at it all my life, and I'm afraid I've exhausted its possibilities." She was quite herself again, her cheeks were pink; she looked up at him with laughing eyes. "Confess that you think me terribly frivolous," she said; "confess that you disapprove of me entirely."

"On the contrary," said Gerard, with rather a cold smile "I think there is a good deal to be said for your point of view—and as for disapproval, that's a priggish sensation that I hope I don't allow myself to feel towards any one. Wait till I see you in town," he went on, more genially "and then perhaps we'll agree better."

"Ah, but you never will see me in town," she said, sadly.

"Never?" he returned, slightly raising his eye-brows. "That's rather a rash prediction. I think I may have the pleasure of meeting you there before very long. You see I believe in fairy Godmothers," he added, lightly, as Mrs. Bobby gave the signal, and, rising, he pushed back Elizabeth's chair.

She paused for a moment, as she gathered up in one hand the soft white folds of her gown. "I wish your faith could perform miracles," she said. And then she followed dreamily in the wake of the well-worn black satin gown, which had been seen, on many another festive occasion, on the broad back of the Rector's wife.

"He does disapprove of me," the girl thought to herself. "He would have liked me better if I were a little bread-and-butter miss, in white muslin and blue ribbons, who babbled of green fields and taught a class in Sunday school. That's the kind of woman he admires. He thinks me hard and flippant, but—I don't care. At least he dropped that weary, society manner. It is something to have inspired him with an emotion of some sort, even if it happens to be disapproval."

Chapter XIV

THE Rector's wife, after the first surprise, was very glad to see Elizabeth. It made her feel more at home, and she drew her down now eagerly, beside her on the sofa by the fire, whose warmth on that autumn evening modified the somewhat chill atmosphere of the state drawing-room.

"My dear Elizabeth, I never expected to see you here." Increased respect mingled with the surprise in her tone. Elizabeth had certainly gone up several degrees in her estimation. "It's quite an honor to be asked—the Courtenays never are, I know, though don't repeat that I said so. Of course we are asked every year, as is only due, you know, to the Rector's position, my dear; but almost always the children are ill, or something goes wrong, and it's three years now since we've been able to come. It was unfortunate our being late this time. Do you think Mrs. Bobby was much annoyed?" The Rector's wife lowered her voice anxiously, as she for the first time waited for a response.

"Oh, no," Elizabeth was able truthfully to assure her. "I'm sure she wasn't annoyed."

"Well, to be sure, the Hartingtons were later"—in a tone of relief—"but these great swells can do as they please. You look very nice, Elizabeth, very nice indeed. I never saw that dress before. It must be pleasant to have something new occasionally"—and the Rector's wife gave a gentle sigh. "You see I have had the color changed on this dress—red, I think, makes it look quite different, and it is warm and pretty for the autumn. Don't repeat this, Elizabeth, but I wore the same dress here the last time I came to dinner four years ago—only then it was trimmed with pale blue. It was summer, you see, so it looked cool. Do you suppose Mrs. Bobby would remember?"

"Oh, I don't suppose Mrs. Bobby cares"—Elizabeth began absently "much about dress," she added, hastily. She was looking vaguely about her, wondering as the familiar voice meandered on, if she were really at dinner at the Van Antwerps', or prosaically seated as she had so often been before, in the Rectory parlor.

Mrs. Hartington, a large fair woman, very splendidly dressed, had seized upon Mrs. Bobby and was talking to her on a sofa at the other end of the room.

"So you have taken up the Van Vorst girl," she was saying, as she surveyed Elizabeth through her lorgnette. "She is really quite pretty, and—a—not bad form. That gown of hers is effective—it's so simple. I wonder how she learned to dress herself, here in the country."

"Oh, she's learned more than that, Sybil, I imagine," said Mrs. Bobby, in level tones. "I think her very good form, and extremely pretty. Her coloring is very picturesque, and quite natural." This very innocently, without a glance at the conspicuously blonde hair which her friends said had not been bestowed on Sybil Hartington by nature.

"She inherits it from her mother, I suppose—a red-haired bar-maid, wasn't she?" said Mrs. Hartington, again subjecting Elizabeth to a prolonged scrutiny.

"After all, she lacks distinction," she announced, dropping her lorgnette and turning to more important subjects.

Mrs. Bobby did not enjoy that half-hour after dinner; neither, perhaps, did Elizabeth, who had heard several times already the account of the attack of measles from which the Rectory children had lately recovered, and was glad when the men appeared in the midst of it. But if she had expected Mr. Gerard to come up to her to resume their conversation, as perhaps she had, in spite of her consciousness of his disapproval, she was destined to be disappointed. Gerard did give her one long look, as she sat in the full glow of the firelight; but he turned almost immediately and spoke to Mrs. Hartington, who had, indeed, the air of confidently expecting him to do so. It was Bobby Van Antwerp who sauntered up to Elizabeth, hospitably intent on making her feel at home.

"It was awfully good of you to come to-night, Miss Van Vorst. These dinner-parties in the country are stupid things, but, after all, it's a way of seeing something of one's neighbors. I think you're too unsociable here, as a rule. It's a bore of course to take one's horses out at night, but if one always thought of that, one would never go anywhere."

"I'm sure," Elizabeth said sincerely, "I was very glad to come. A dinner-party is a great event to me."

"Ah, well, it is dull here for a young girl," said Bobby, kindly. "My wife finds it very dull; but she knows I'm fond of the old place, and she comes to please me. You and she must try to amuse each other. You know, between ourselves"— lowering his voice—"Eleanor doesn't always take to people; it has made some of our neighbors around here feel rather sore—I'm afraid. But she does take to you, and so I hope we shall see a great deal of you."

Elizabeth smiled and murmured her thanks, wondering greatly to find herself thus singled out from the rest of the Neighborhood; and just then Mrs. Bobby came up and took her hand.

"Come," she said, "I want you to play for me. I'm so fond of music, and I've heard that you play beautifully."

"Ah, but I don't," Elizabeth protested; but still she allowed herself to be led to the piano, without undue reluctance. And then that grand piano, with the name of the maker had been tempting her to try it ever since dinner-time.

After all, it is doubtful if Mrs. Bobby cared so very much for music; but it is possible she knew of some one else who did. Elizabeth had a gift which had come to her, Heaven knows how!—a gift in which far greater pianists are sometimes lacking—the power to throw herself into what she played and to infuse into it something of her own personality. Her playing seemed no mere, mechanical repetition of what she had been taught, but the unstudied, spontaneous expression of her own thoughts and feelings. As she passed at Mrs. Bobby's request from one thing to another, mingling more set compositions with fragments from operas and songs of the day, the conversation between Mrs. Hartington and Gerard slackened, and he glanced more and more frequently towards the piano.

"Music is rather a bore—isn't it—after dinner this way," drawled Mrs. Hartington, noticing this fact.

"I don't think I agree with you. I'm fond of music," said Gerard, and after awhile he found an opportunity to saunter over to the piano, where Elizabeth sat playing, a little absently now, bits from Wagner. She started and looked up, blushing slightly, as Gerard asked her if she could play the Fire-music.

"I—it is a long time since I have tried it," she began, impelled by some vague instinct to refuse, and then she stopped, and almost unconsciously her fingers touched the keys, as she caught a look that seemed to compel obedience. He smiled.

"Please play it," he said, and though the tone was caressing, there lurked in it a half perceptible note of command. She felt it, as she began to play, and he stood listening, his grave eyes fixed upon her face. "A severe judge," she thought to herself with a proud little thrill of rebellion. And then, as she played on, she forgot this thought, and the fear of his criticism; forgot the strange room, and the strange people, and the fact that she was dining at the Van Antwerps'; forgot everything but the eyes fixed upon her, and played as she had never played before.

Elizabeth had always put the best of herself into her music, her finest qualities of brain and soul. But now she put into it something of which she before was hardly conscious, a force and depth and fire, which stirred inarticulately within her, and found expression in the throbbing Wagnerian chords. All the magic of the fairy spell thrilled beneath her touch, as it rose and fell and wove itself in and out amidst the clash of conflicting motives, while Brünnhilde sank ever deeper into slumber, and the flames leaped and danced and played about her sleeping form, and there lurked no premonition in her maiden dreams of that fatal, all-engrossing love, which was yet to awaken her from the serenity of oblivion. Then, as the rippling cadence died away, Elizabeth hesitated for a moment, striking furtive harmonies, till she passed at length into the poignant sweetness, the passionate self-surrender of the second act of Tristan, and so on to the Liebestod, with its swan-song of triumphant anguish, of love supreme even in death. With the last sobbing chord, Elizabeth's hands fell from the keys, and she sat staring straight before her, with eyes that were unusually large and dark.

"Upon my word she *can* play," said Bobby Van Antwerp, and looked, for him, slightly stirred. "She has temperament," Mrs. Hartington coldly responded and again honored Elizabeth with a prolonged stare. "My dear child," exclaimed Elizabeth's hostess, "I had no idea you could play like that." The only person who said nothing was the man for whom she had played. He stood motionless by the piano, and his face was white and set. When the applause of the others had ceased, and Elizabeth, blushing now and smiling, looked up at him in involuntary surprise at his silence as if from a dream, he started and then, recovering himself, he spoke mechanically a few conventional words of thanks, and without comment on her performance, turned abruptly away.

Elizabeth still sat, a trifle dazed, at the piano, her hands tightly clasped in her lap. Her cheeks were burning painfully and she bit her lip to keep back the tears that sprang unbidden to her eyes. She seemed to have fallen suddenly from the clouds back to earth. After a moment she rose and went over to her hostess to say farewell.

"Don't go," Mrs. Bobby entreated, holding her hand, "I really haven't seen anything of you."

"I must go, thank you," Elizabeth said, quietly. "William,"—this was the gardener, who on state occasions officiated as coachman—"will be furious if he is kept waiting."

She felt a sudden eagerness to be gone, and Mrs. Bobby admitted the force of her excuse and parted with her reluctantly. Both Bobby and Gerard escorted her into the hall, but it was Gerard who placed her in the carriage, and yet, as he did so, said not a word further of seeing her again.

"He probably doesn't wish to," thought Elizabeth, "now that he has done his duty to the last." The reflection was the only unpleasant one that she brought away from an otherwise successful evening.

Gerard sauntered back into the drawing-room, and stood leaning against the mantel-piece, gazing with thoughtful eyes into the fire, while, as it leaped and flickered, and sent out glowing tongues of flame, a woman's face looked up at him framed in her shimmering hair, and the magic of the fire-music still rang in his ear, mingled with the more passionate strains of Tristan, the deeper tragedy of Liebestod.

He had been standing thus a long time when Mrs. Bobby came and stood beside him. The other guests had left and Bobby had gone off to his den.

"Well," she said tentatively, glancing up smiling into his face, "well, Julian, what did you think of her?"

He started and looked at her blankly for a moment. "Think of—whom, Eleanor?" he asked.

"You know whom I mean—Elizabeth Van Vorst."

Gerard's eyes wandered back to the fire, where they rested for a moment absently. "I think," he said at last slowly, and as if weighing his words with more than his wonted deliberation, "I think there's too much red in her hair."

"Too much red in her hair," Mrs. Bobby repeated blankly; then recovering herself: "But there isn't any, Julian, or very little. I call her hair golden, not red."

"Look at it in the fire-light," Gerard insisted imperturbably, "and you will see that it's a deep red."

"Well, and if it is," said Mrs. Bobby—"not that I admit for a moment that you are right—but if it is, red hair is all the fashion nowadays."

"No doubt," said Gerard. "It's a matter of taste. But for myself I never see a red-haired woman"—He stopped, but went on presently with an effort. "I never see a red-haired woman, that I don't instinctively avoid her. Yes, it's a—a superstition, if you will. I feel that she will be dangerous, somehow or another, perhaps to herself, and certainly to others." A note of unwonted feeling thrilled his voice. He broke off suddenly and stared again into the fire.

Mrs. Bobby sat and watched him in silence. "And so," she said to herself, "*that* woman's hair was red."

"You see," said Gerard, presently, looking at her with a smile, "I've shown the confidence I repose in you by confessing my pet superstition. Miss Van Vorst's hair is not *very* red, I admit, except in some lights, but still it's—it's red enough to be dangerous; and that fact, and certain other little things I've noticed about her, incline me to—to avoid her. She puzzles me; I can't quite make her out. Still, she is certainly a girl whom a great many men would—would admire. I'm no criterion, I believe."

"I hope not, I'm sure," said Mrs. Bobby, ruefully "for the sake of most of the women I know. My dear Julian, I despair of ever getting you married."

"My dear Eleanor, if you would only stop trying. Your efforts are, if you will excuse my saying so, a little too transparent. Do you suppose that I imagined this evening that your unpunctuality was entirely accidental?"

"Imagine what you will, you marvel of astuteness," said Eleanor, composedly. "I certainly did not intend to hurry down while I knew Elizabeth to be in such good hands, as I admit yours to be, in spite of certain faults which I hope marriage will improve. And that's why I don't relax my efforts, as you call them, while there is such a superfluity of nice girls in the world, and such an insufficiency of nice men to deserve them. But I'm disappointed about—about Elizabeth Van Vorst," she went on, musingly. "I thought—I don't know why, Julian—but I thought that you would like her."

Gerard started. "I never said that I—didn't like her," he observed.

"No, but your remarks seemed to point in that direction. Now I like her very much. Indeed, to return your confidence with another, Julian"—she looked up with a smile—"I was thinking, if Bobby approves, of asking her to spend the winter with me.

"I knew that," he returned, calmly, "and I approve of the plan highly. It will be a pleasant change for her, as she doesn't seem exactly satisfied with her surroundings; and for you it will be a—a"—he paused, apparently in search of an appropriate word—"an interesting study," he concluded.

She looked up in surprise. "A—a study," she repeated.

"Yes, a study—to see what a girl like that, with the somewhat odd antecedents that you told me about once, and some contradictory characteristics that I think she has—to see how she develops in the storm and stress of a New York season. I—I think you will find it quite interesting, Eleanor."

"I'm glad you think so," she returned, softly. "But—how about yourself, Julian? Couldn't you—just on general psychological principles—condescend to take an interest in it, too?"

A shadow fell on Gerard's face. "Oh, for myself," he said, carelessly, "I'm not easily interested in things nowadays, and above all not—thank Heaven! not in women." He paused. "All the same," he added, "you have the best wishes—for the success of your protégée." And with this he bade her good-night, and left her.

She sat for a long time without moving, and watched the fire flicker and die away.

"On the whole, I'm rather glad her hair is red—in certain lights at least," she observed at last, apparently to the smouldering embers. "It—it makes the study still more interesting."

Chapter XV

*W*HEN Eleanor Van Antwerp had uttered the words "If Bobby approves," she had given voice to a purely conventional formula; for when, in the eight years of their married life, had Bobby not approved of anything that she might chance to desire? She did not suppose for a moment that he would object to her asking Elizabeth Van Vorst, or any one under the sun, to spend the winter, and when, the next morning, she paid him a visit in his den, where he was supposed to be transacting important business, and proved to be enjoying a novel and a cigar, she was still, as she asked his permission to carry out her new plan, merely paying a graceful concession to the perfunctory and outworn theory of his supremacy. Bobby listened placidly, puffing at his cigar, his clear-cut, clean-shaven profile, outlined against the window-pane seeming absolutely impassive in the gray light of the autumn day. But when she concluded, and was waiting, all aglow with her own enthusiasm, for his answer, he turned his blue eyes towards her with an unusually thoughtful look.

"Well," she said, impatiently, as he still declined to commit himself, "what do you think?"

"What do I think," he repeated, slowly, "of your asking Elizabeth Van Vorst to spend the winter?"

"Why, yes, I don't want to do it, dear, of course, unless you approve."

"Well, then," said Bobby, calmly, "if you ask my candid opinion, I think it would be a mistake. I—I'd rather you didn't Eleanor, really I would."

"Bobby," Eleanor Van Antwerp stared at her husband in incredulous amazement. "Bobby, you don't mean to say that you don't want me to ask her?"

"That's about it." Bobby paused and reflectively knocked the ashes from his cigar. "You see," he went on, argumentatively "this is the way I look at it. The girl is good-looking, and all that, and it's very nice for you to see something of her up here, and I'm only too glad, for it's awfully sweet of you, darling, to come here on my account, and I've always been sorry that there wasn't some woman whom you could be friends with. But to ask a girl to spend the winter, and introduce her to people, is—is a responsibility; and if you want to ask any one—why, I'd rather it were some girl whom I know all about—that's all."

It was not often that Bobby made such a long speech. His wife could hardly hear him to the end of it. "But, my dear Bobby" she exclaimed, breaking in upon his last words, "you know all about Elizabeth Van Vorst!"

"Do I," said Bobby, quietly. "I know that her father was a fool, and that her mother was—worse. Perhaps it would be better if I didn't know quite so much, Eleanor."

"For Heaven's sake, don't harp on what happened centuries ago," cried Mrs. Bobby, who had not been born in the neighborhood. "I've always thought it a shame the way people here snub that poor girl. People can't help what their fathers and mothers were like. If mine were fairly respectable, I'm sure it's no credit to me."

"None at all," Bobby assented, "but still you'd feel rather badly if they were not. It's a natural feeling, Eleanor. I'm not a crank about family, but on general principles, I think a girl whose mother was a lady is more apt to behave herself than one whose mother was—well, quite the reverse."

"And on general principles," said Eleanor, quickly "I agree with you, but I think Elizabeth Van Vorst the exception that proves the rule."

"Then I would rather," said Bobby, tranquilly, "that it were proved under some one else's auspices than yours."

"But that doesn't seem likely, under the circumstances," exclaimed his wife, impatiently. "Really, Bobby, you disappoint me. I never supposed you had such narrow-minded ideas. The girl has been very well brought up by those dear old aunts, and she is perfectly well-bred. And I'm sure there is plenty of good blood in the family as well as bad. The Schuyler Van Vorsts are their cousins, and lots of old Dutch families. I dare say, if we went far enough back, we'd find ourselves related to them, too."

"I dare say," said Bobby, resignedly, "if we went far enough back, we'd find ourselves related to a lot of queer people. But we don't, thank Heaven! have to ask them to visit us."

"Ah, well, I see you are hopelessly opposed to my plan," said Mrs. Bobby, changing her tactics, "and of course, dear, as I told you before, I wouldn't think of asking any one unless you approve."

"Oh, I don't really care," said Bobby, somewhat taken aback by this sudden surrender. "Ask any one you please. You know I never interfere with your plans. Only don't blame me if they turn out badly—that's all."

"Ah, but they never do," cried Mrs. Bobby, "at least this one won't, I'm sure. I really have set my heart on it, Bobby," she went on, pleadingly. "The truth is, though I don't often speak of it, going out has been a weariness, and that big house in town seems horribly empty since—since the baby died." Her lip trembled and she paused for a moment, while Bobby turned and stared fixedly out of the window at the brilliantly-tinted leaves that a chill east wind was whirling inexorably to the ground. "I thought," she went on presently, in a voice that was not quite steady, "that if I had some one with me to make the house seem a little brighter—some young girl whom I could take with me on the same old round that I'm so sick of— why, I could look at life through her eyes, and it would seem more worth while. But of course Bobby," she concluded, earnestly, "I wouldn't for the world do anything to which you really object."

"My dear Eleanor," said Bobby, turning round at this and speaking for him quite solemnly. "You know I don't object to anything in the world that could make you happy."

And so Mrs. Bobby had her own way.

It was on Saturday that this conversation took place; and on Sunday afternoon they all walked over to the Homestead—Mrs. Bobby, her husband and Gerard. Elizabeth had been prepared for their coming, by a whisper from Mrs. Bobby after church; and tea was all ready for them with Miss Joanna's cakes, and a fire that was welcome after the cold out-doors, where the bleak east wind was still robbing the trees of their glory and ushering in prematurely the dull grayness of November. Mrs. Bobby was not satisfied till she could draw Elizabeth to a distant sofa, and deliver the invitation which she felt, in her impetuous fashion, she could not withhold for another day.

But though the first of Elizabeth's wishes was thus fulfilled with a promptness most unusual outside of fairy tales, she did not accept with the enthusiasm that might have been expected. For a moment, indeed, her eyes sparkled, her cheeks glowed with delight. And then of a sudden the color faded, her eyes fell, she shrank back as if frightened at the idea.

"I—I—it's awfully sweet of you, Mrs. Van Antwerp," she said, low and hurriedly, "but I—I can't go—I wish I could, but I can't. Don't—don't ask me." It was almost as if she had said, "Don't tempt me." Poor Mrs. Bobby, whose intentions were so good, was exceedingly puzzled and not a little piqued.

"Oh, well, if you don't care to come," she said, coldly, in the great-lady manner which she seldom assumed, "of course I shall not urge you. I shouldn't have mentioned the subject, if I had not thought from what you said the other day, that you were really anxious to come to town."

"So I was, so I am—for some reasons; but for others—Dear Mrs. Van Antwerp," the girl pleaded, "don't think me ungrateful. I should love to come beyond anything, but—but I can't. It doesn't seem right," she added, more firmly.

"Doesn't seem right," repeated Mrs. Bobby, wondering, "You mean on your aunts' account. You think it wouldn't be right to leave them?"

"Yes," Elizabeth assented, as if relieved at being furnished with an excuse of some sort, however feeble, "I don't think it would be right to leave them."

"But that is nonsense," cried Mrs. Bobby. "They will miss you terribly, of course, but it will be no worse than when you were at school, and they would be the first to wish you to go, I'm sure."

Elizabeth was quite sure of it, too. Mrs. Bobby, reading this conviction in her eyes, and all the more anxious for the success of her plan, now that it met with so many unexpected obstacles, went on to expatiate on the delights of a season in town, and all the possibilities that life can offer, to one who has youth, talent and beauty. Elizabeth listened eagerly with dilating eyes, which she only once withdrew from Mrs. Bobby's face, to glance across to the other end of the room, where Mr. Gerard was leaning forward in an attitude of respectful interest, as he talked to Miss Cornelia. For a moment Elizabeth's eyes rested, half absently perhaps, on the strong lines of his face, while the irrelevant thought passed through her mind: "I wonder what he would think." Then, quick as lightning, the answer followed. "I don't care," she said, under her breath, and drew herself up with a little flash of defiance.

She turned towards Mrs. Bobby. "Do you really want me?" she asked, caressingly.

"Should I have asked you, if I didn't," laughed Mrs. Bobby, triumphant, as she saw that victory was hers.

Elizabeth told the news to her aunts as soon as the visitors had left. Their delight was what she had expected. They were eager in approving her decision, and in assuring her that she should have all the pretty gowns that the occasion required, sustained by the conviction, which occurred simultaneously to the minds of both, that their old black silks, which they had foolishly thought of as shabby, would do admirably another winter. It would be the height of extravagance, as Miss Cornelia afterwards observed to replace them.

"It's just what we have always wished for you," she cried, her little curls all a'flutter with joyful excitement, "and so unexpected—quite like a fairy-tale."

"Yes," Elizabeth assented, "quite like a fairy-tale. There's only one difference," she added to herself, as she left the room, "from every well-regulated fairy-tale that I ever heard of. The fairy Godmother, coach and four, are just a little—too late."

Chapter XVI

"MY dear Elizabeth," said Mrs. Bobby, "I regret to say it, but you really are growing terribly spoiled."

The winter was far advanced when Mrs. Bobby made this remark. With Lent growing every day nearer, the whirl of gaiety grew ever faster and more furious. It was not often that Mrs. Bobby and her guest had an opportunity for private conversation. But to-night, as it happened, they had merely been out to dinner, and having returned at an unusually early hour, Elizabeth came into Mrs. Bobby's boudoir in her long white dressing-gown, and sat brushing out her masses of wavy hair, while she and her hostess discussed the evening's entertainment, and other recent events of interest.

Mrs. Bobby's eyes rested upon Elizabeth with all the satisfaction with which a connoisseur regards some beautiful object of which he has been the discoverer. Elizabeth's beauty, Elizabeth's conquests, formed to Mrs. Bobby just then a theme of which she never tired. Nor did she fail to make them the text for various sermons that she delivered to Bobby about this time, on the subject of her own wisdom, and his utter failure as a prophet.

"Confess, Bobby, that my plans turn out well," she would say, "and that I'm not such a fool as you thought me."

"Why, I never," Bobby would protest, "thought you anything of the kind." But she would go on unheeding:

"It would have been a shame for that girl to be buried in the country, and I do take some credit to myself for having rescued her from such a fate. But after that, all the credit is due to Elizabeth. I did what I could, of course, to launch her successfully, but when all is said and done, a girl has to sink or swim on her own merits. Elizabeth takes to society as a duck does to water; it's her natural element. And talk of heredity! There are not many girls with the most aristocratic mothers who can come into a room with the air that she has, as if she didn't care two straws whether any one spoke to her or not, and then of course every one does. Now explain to me, Bobby, if you can, where the girl gets that air."

"I suppose," said Bobby, "if I believed implicitly in heredity (which I am not at all sure that I do) I'd account for it by your own remark that she has plenty of good blood as well as bad."

"Oh, yes," said Mrs. Bobby, incredulously, "you can always make a theory fit in somehow."

But though Mrs. Bobby exulted in that air of indifference with which Elizabeth accepted, as if it were a mere matter of course, all the devotion offered up at her feet, she was beginning to realize that the most admirable qualities can be carried too far. And thus it was that she upbraided her this evening with being unreasonably spoiled, and not sufficiently appreciating the good things which had fallen to her lot.

"I don't know what you want me to do," Elizabeth said, quietly, when she had listened for some moments to this rather vague accusation. "I'm sure I go everywhere that I'm asked, and that, you must admit, is saying a good deal; I talk to all the men who talk to me, and that again you must admit, means a great deal of conversational effort; and—and I make no distinctions between them whatever, and do my duty on all occasions. I really don't know what more you can expect."

"But that," exclaimed her hostess, "is exactly what I complain of. You go everywhere you are asked—yes, and you never express a preference for any particular place; you talk to the men who talk to you, and you make no distinctions—no, for apparently it's all the same to you, whether it's this man or the other."

"Not quite," said Elizabeth, placidly, "for one man amuses me and another doesn't. But beyond that, I don't—thank Heaven! I don't care." She broke off suddenly, and she drew her comb with unwonted vehemence through her hair.

"I don't know why you should thank Heaven," said Mrs. Bobby, watching her narrowly, "for a fact that is quite abnormal in a girl of your age, who has some of the nicest men in town in love with her. There are times when I think you are quite heartless, and yet—with that hair, and those eyes, and the way you throw yourself into your music, you seem to have abundance of temperament. On the whole, Elizabeth, you are a puzzling combination. What was it Mr. D'Hauteville said of you—that you reminded him of a lake of ice in a circle of fire?"

"Mr. D'Hauteville," said Elizabeth, yawning, "is fond of glittering similes. This one sounds well, but doesn't bear close consideration. The fire, I should think, under the circumstances, would dissolve the ice."

"Perhaps it will," said Mrs. Bobby, "when the right time comes."

"Which will be never," said Elizabeth, with decision. Her hostess smiled as one who has heard such things said before.

"After all," she resumed, after a pause, returning to the grievance which had first started the conversation, "I could forgive you everything else, but this indifference about your picture. One would think that when a great artist asks as a special favor to paint your portrait, you might at least have the decency to go to look at it, when it is on exhibition, and all New York is talking about it."

"That's the very reason," said Elizabeth, "why it strikes me as rather bad taste for me to stand in rapt contemplation before it, while a lot of people are jostling me, and making remarks about my eyes, and hair, and mouth, as if it were I on exhibition, and not Mr. ——'s picture."

"Well, it *is* you whom they want to see," said Mrs. Bobby. "The New York public doesn't care much for art, but it does take an interest in the people whom it reads about in the papers—a weakness that we needn't quarrel with, since it has made the Portrait Show a success, and given us so many thousands for our hospital."

"Well, at least," said Elizabeth, "I have done my duty in contributing my portrait to the good cause; so don't ask me to be present in actual flesh and blood, and above all not to face such a crowd as there was the other day, when we tried to look at it and my gown was nearly torn off my back in the process."

"You could go early," suggested Mrs. Bobby, "as I did the other day. You have no idea how much better it looks in that light than it did at the studio."

"I am very tired of it, in any light," said Elizabeth. "People have talked to me so much about it. But, if you insist upon it I will go—I will go early. There are some of the other portraits too that I should like to look at, if I can do so in peace." And with this concession, the conversation was allowed to drop for a moment.

It was Elizabeth who resumed it, speaking slowly and tentatively, with many lapses, and eyes carefully turned away from her friend. "You talk," she said, "a great deal of my successes, and I suppose, in a way, I ought to be—satisfied. And of course I am," she added, hastily. "People have been very nice to me. I—I couldn't ask for anything more. And yet—there is one person—I don't know if you have noticed it—one person with whom I am a distinct failure, who I think almost dislikes me, and that is—your friend Mr. Gerard."

"What, Julian," said Mrs. Bobby, in a tone that was absolutely devoid of expression. "You think he—doesn't like you?"

"I am quite sure of it," said Elizabeth.

"But why," questioned Mrs. Bobby, in apparent bewilderment. "What reason have you for thinking so?"

"A great many, but any one of them would be enough. To begin with, he never speaks to me if he can possibly help himself. His avoidance of me is quite pointed—you surely must have noticed it?" She fixed her eyes anxiously upon Mrs. Bobby.

"I"—Mrs. Bobby checked the impulsive words that rose to her lips. "Julian is—is very peculiar," she said in a non-committal tone. "I don't think he cares for women."

"Perhaps not; but still I have seen him talk to them—in a bored sort of way, it is true. But to me he never talks, in any way whatsoever."

"He never has a chance. You are always surrounded."

"He would have the same chance as the others. No, it isn't that. He disapproves of me; I can feel it, as he looks at me through those dark, half-shut eyes of his, and it gives me an uncomfortable sense of wickedness. He thinks me flippant, and vain, and frivolous, and I am when he is there, or I seem so. When he is listening, I say all the horrid, cynical, heartless things I can think of. I have to say them, somehow. It is fate. It began the first night that I met him—it was in the country, do you remember?" She paused and again looked questioningly at Mrs. Bobby.

"Yes," the latter answered softly, "I remember."

"I was rather excited that night—it was the first time I had ever been out to dinner. I talked in a flippant sort of way about hating the country, and longing to go out, and wanting to be always amused. It was very *young*, I suppose." Elizabeth spoke with all the superiority of a girl half-way through her first season towards her more unsophisticated self of a few months before. "He didn't like it. The sort of woman whom he admires knows her catechism, and is satisfied with that situation in life where it has pleased Providence to place her. I shocked him; he has never got over it. He showed me, that very evening, how he disliked me—it was so pointed that it was almost rude. You asked me—do you remember? to play." She stopped.

"I remember," said Mrs. Bobby again softly. "I never heard you play so well."

"I never have—since. I seemed to have, just for the moment, some strange power over the keys—such feelings come to one, you know, sometimes. And then, when I stopped—he had asked me for the Fire-music—I felt, somehow, that he was fond of music—he *is* fond of it, passionately fond—but when I stopped, he looked at me blankly for a moment, till he suddenly remembered what was expected of him, and thanked me in a cold sort of way and walked off. And—I shouldn't think so much of that; but since then he has never—never once asked me to play, though he has often heard other people ask me."

"I have noticed," said Mrs. Bobby, quietly, "that you will never play when he is in the room."

"I couldn't," said Elizabeth, "it would have such a dampening effect to feel that there was one person in the room who disliked it, who, no matter how well I played, would always preserve his critical attitude.

"You see that I am reduced to the unflattering alternative that it is myself that he objects to or my playing. But it is the same with everything. There is my picture, for instance. He is the only person I know who has said nothing to me about it, has probably not even seen it."

"That must be rather a relief," said Mrs. Bobby, placidly, "since you are so tired of the subject."

"If I am," said Elizabeth, "that is no reason why he shouldn't go through the conventional formula of telling me that he has seen the picture, and adding something civil about it, as the most ordinary acquaintances never fail to do."

"No, of course," Mrs. Bobby agreed softly, "the most ordinary acquaintances never would. But perhaps he doesn't consider himself exactly that."

"Whatever he considers himself," said Elizabeth, with some heat, "he is not exempt from the common rules of civility. But I suppose he doesn't really admire the picture, and is too painfully truthful to pretend to the contrary." And then she stopped and laughed a little at her own vehemence, but without much spirit. "It really is very illogical," she admitted, "I don't care for Mr. Gerard's admiration, it would probably bore me extremely to have it; and yet—it's not pleasant to be so absolutely—ignored."

Mrs. Bobby was watching her with an odd little gleam in the dark eyes that were almost hidden by her long, curling lashes. "I will tell you," she said, "what it is that he doesn't like. It isn't you, or your playing, or your conversation; it's your hair."

"My hair!" Elizabeth took up mechanically one of her long shining locks and passed it through her fingers. "I may have been inordinately vain," she remarked after a pause, "but I never supposed before that there was much the matter with my hair."

"Nor would most people, I imagine. But he has some odd ideas, and among them, it seems, is a prejudice—a superstition, as he calls it—against red hair."

"But mine isn't red," said Elizabeth, quickly.

"Of course not," said Mrs. Bobby. "He is color blind, as I told him. But there's no use in arguing the point with him. He insists that your hair is red enough to—to be dangerous—those are his words, and he avoids you in consequence. He has had some unfortunate experience in the past, I should imagine, which has given him this prejudice. There, my dear, I shouldn't have told you," Mrs. Bobby went on, leaning back in her chair, and still watching Elizabeth narrowly through half-closed lids, "if I didn't know, of course, that it can make no real difference to you what Julian thinks."

"Of course not," Elizabeth made answer mechanically with dry lips, as she still drew her comb absently through the offending hair.

"You have so many admirers," Mrs. Bobby continued serenely, "it can't matter very much that one person should hold aloof. And then I shouldn't care about Julian's opinion, for he never admires any woman. Ever since that unfortunate experience, which happened, I think, when he was very young, he has been a confirmed cynic, avoiding all young girls, and horribly afraid of being married for his money. I really despair now of his ever falling in love; I have talked up almost every girl in town to him, and all in vain. No, even you, Elizabeth, spoiled as you are, couldn't expect to make a conquest of Julian."

"I don't know what I should expect," said Elizabeth, rather coldly, "but I certainly don't wish to. It would hardly be worth while." She rose, with one long look in the glass, and moved wearily towards the door. "I am so very tired, dear," she said. "I think I will say good-night."

"Good-night," said Mrs. Bobby, cheerfully. "Sleep well—you need to—and don't waste another thought on that tiresome creature, Julian."

"Oh, I'm not likely to," Elizabeth responded, with rather a pale smile. "I'm much too tired."

And yet she did think of him more than once, as she stood before her mirror, arranging her hair into two heavy braids, which reached below her waist, and repeating to herself that, as Mrs. Bobby had said, it could matter little about the one dissenting voice in the general chorus of admiration which had attended her triumphant career. In spite of which assurance, her last thoughts as she fell asleep might have been somewhat surprising to those who, having watched that career entirely from the outside, regarded her as the most fortunate being in the world.

Elizabeth's aunts were on the whole, more to be envied than the girl herself that winter. There was no alloy in their happiness, no under-current of dissatisfaction, even though they wore their old black silks, and Miss Joanna's friend, the butcher, was heard to complain somewhat bitterly of her sudden parsimony in regard to joints of meat. What did it matter? They would have dressed cheerfully in sackcloth and lived on bread and water, for the sake of such glowing accounts of Elizabeth's triumphs as Mrs. Bobby constantly transmitted, or of the girl's own brilliant letters which seemed to breathe the radiant satisfaction of a mind without a care.

Elizabeth's aunt at Bassett Mills also watched her career, which was chronicled at that time in the papers. Poor Aunt Rebecca, after a hard day's work, reading her niece's name, and possibly a description of her costume in the list of guests at some smart festivity, would look up, awe-struck, at Amanda. "Only to think," she would say, with the old contradictory note, half pride, half jealousy "to think that it should be Malvina's girl!"

But Amanda, still pale and wasted from the fever with her hair quite long and very soft and wavy, would give an odd, furtive look from her light eyes and say nothing.

Chapter XVII

IT was early at the Portrait Show. It was so early that what few people were already there had the place practically to themselves. There were only three or four in the large room at the head of the stairs, which at a later hour of the afternoon was invariably crowded, and where was hung that picture which had attracted so much attention, partly from the great fame of the artist, still more, perhaps, from the beauty of the subject.

A young girl in a long, white gown of some soft, clinging stuff, stood against the background of a dark green velvet curtain. There was no relief to the dead whiteness of the gown, and the roses that she held were white; all that brilliancy of color, for which this great artist is famous, he had expended upon the deep red-gold tints of the hair, the vivid scarlet of the lips, the warm creamy tones of the skin, as they were thrown into full relief by the dark background. The painter had lingered, with all the skill at his command, on the rounded, dimpled curves of the neck and arms, nor had he forgotten the haughty little turn of the head, which gave a characteristic touch to the picture. Seen at a glance, it was aglow with life and color, very human, very mundane, the embodiment of health and bloom. A study in flesh-tints, one critic had carelessly pronounced it, and nothing more. It was only when you looked at the eyes that you caught a discordant note, which, if you dwelt upon it, contradicted the joyous effect of the rest; a look, a latent shadow which the great artist had either surprised or imagined, and transferred perhaps unconsciously to his canvas, where, if you saw it at all, it held you with a haunting sense of mystery, the fascination of an unsolved problem. "What does it mean," a man said to himself that afternoon, "and did —— really put it in, or do I, with my usual superstition, imagine it? Am I the only person who sees it, or do others?"

Two young girls, who jostled up against him just then evidently did not.

"Portrait of Miss Van Vorst," said one, reading from her catalogue, "by — —." She passed the artist's name without recognition, as she delightedly pressed her companion's arm. "Say, Mamie, that's Elizabeth Van Vorst, you know, the beauty. I've seen lots about her in the papers."

"You don't say so?" returned the other, who was apparently less up-to-date. "I thought she must be one of the swells, but I didn't know the name. She's pretty isn't she?—but doesn't her nose turn up too much?—and I don't think much of her dress, it's so kind of simple."

The man who had been standing when they came up in front of the picture, turned frowning aside, and found himself face to face with the original. For an instant each stared at the other in silence, and it might have been noticed by a careful observer that the man was at once the more disconcerted and the less surprised of the two.

"So I see you have achieved fame," he said, recovering himself almost immediately and smiling, as he glanced at the two girls who were still criticizing Elizabeth's features, all unconscious that the subject of their remarks was within hearing.

"Yes, fame," she returned, lightly "of a kind that you despise." She, too, was quite herself again—that flippant, frivolous self, at least, which he had always the power to awaken.

"I suppose I'm a crank," he admitted. "I really don't like to hear my friends talked about, by their first name by people who have read about them in the papers."

"Oh, that," she said, carelessly "is a necessary penalty of fame."

"Which you share with a variety actress," he returned. "I realize more and more that I'm hopelessly behind the age. Look at those two girls," he went on, glancing at them with some animosity.

"They have spent, I should imagine, their little all on the admission fee and the catalogue; they don't care two straws for the portraits as portraits, and they have never spoken to the originals, but they are wildly interested in them because they represent to them the magic word 'society,' and they will go away and talk about them as if they knew them intimately."

Elizabeth laughed softly. "Ah," she said "let them be. They're getting their money's worth; don't grudge it to them. So far as I'm concerned, they may pull my face to pieces as much as they please. I know how it is—I've stood on the outside, too, of a thing, and tried to imagine that I was in it."

"Do you think they'd be happier," asked Gerard, "if they were?"

"Ah, that depends," she returned, oracularly, stroking down the long fur of her muff.

"Tell me how you find it yourself," said Gerard. He looked about the room. "The place is comfortably empty," he said. "Have you been around yet, or would you—a—like to sit down awhile?"

She hesitated. "I have been in several of the rooms," she said. "I came early on purpose. Eleanor is lunching somewhere, but she is to meet me here at three."

"Then suppose you—a—rest till she comes?" he suggested, as he led the way to a sofa which had been placed for the accommodation of weary sight-seers in the centre of the room. "It's a long while since I've had a talk with you. ('And whose fault is that,' thought Elizabeth.) This isn't a bad place to talk in, and if you've been around once, you've had enough of it for the time being."

"I am glad to rest for a few minutes," Elizabeth admitted.

She threw open the revers of her coat, and sank back in her seat as if physically tired. Gerard looked at her. She was exquisitely dressed. Her dark green velvet and furs set off the fairness of her skin, her large feathered hat suited her picturesque style. The subtle atmosphere of fashion, of distinction, lurked in every fold of her gown, in every movement and gesture. Three months had sufficed to endow her with it. They had also sufficed—or was this again the result of his imagination?—to take away the first freshness of her beauty. She looked brilliant, but a trifle worn; her color had faded, there were lines of weariness about the mouth, and deep black rings under the eyes.

"You don't look well," he said, abruptly. She smiled. ("I might have known that he would say that," she said to herself.)

"I know it," she returned, quietly. "The maid woke me up, as she generally does, with strong coffee. I refused at first to be waked. I haven't been to bed at a reasonable hour for weeks, and I'm so countrified that I show the ill effects of it."

"You shouldn't go out so much," said Gerard. "What is Eleanor thinking of that she allows it? You—you will be ill if this keeps up." He spoke almost angrily.

"Yet what difference would it make to him?" thought Elizabeth. "He is very unaccountable. Why should he look at my picture, thinking no doubt all the time how ugly my hair is? I don't want his advice—I won't have it. Oh, it's all in a good cause," she said lightly, aloud. "I complain sometimes, but I wouldn't stay at home, really, for the world. It's all too delightful. I may be tired, but at least I'm not bored."

"It has all come up to your expectations, then?" said Gerard. "You like it better than—a—the river view?"

"Ah, if you had looked at that view as many years as I have, you wouldn't need to ask the question."

"And you are always amused?" he went on. "That was the next wish, wasn't it? You see I'm putting you through the category, as I threatened to do once, and I expect only the truth for an answer. Are you always, every day and all day long, thoroughly amused?"

She met his gaze unflinchingly. "Don't I—seem to be?" she asked.

"I don't know," he said. "I've wondered—sometimes. You certainly ought to be," he declared.

"Then," she said "you may take it for granted that I am."

"And the third wish," he said, musingly, "follows naturally on the other. You never, in this whirl of gaiety—never, I suppose, get a chance to think?"

"Not a moment," she returned, triumphantly. "All my time is occupied, I'm glad to say, in being amused. That's hard work, too, sometimes, but then—the game is worth the candle."

"Well," he said "you are, I admit, a very fortunate young woman, and you have my congratulations. There are not many people whose wishes are fulfilled, as quickly and absolutely as yours have been."

"No," she said, with sudden thoughtfulness "that is very true." She sat for a moment staring straight before her, with the look in her eyes which had puzzled and haunted him in the pictured eyes at which he had looked awhile before. "Do you know," she said at last, speaking very low and hesitatingly, "it's very absurd, but it—sometimes it frightens me a little. Do you remember in Greek history—or was it mythology?—there was a king who had every wish fulfilled, till he grew at last to feel that it—was dangerous; he offered up sacrifices to the gods, he tried to escape but it was all of no use. Everything went well with him, till at last—his fate overtook him. And so I think, sometimes—mine will."

"Your fate?" Gerard repeated, utterly taken aback and puzzled.

"Yes, the penalty," she said, quickly "of having too much. I have an odd idea sometimes that there is—there must be some misfortune in store for me; that I shall pay for all this yet in some terrible way which no one expects. Oh, it's perfectly absurd, I know, but still I—I can't help it." She had turned of a sudden very white, and she stared up at Gerard with a frightened, mute appeal in her eyes, like that of some dumb animal or a child.

To him she seemed all at once very young and helpless, a being to be soothed and protected; very different from the gay, self-possessed young woman of a few minutes before. "My dear child," he said, very gently, yet with a note of authority, and laying his hand ever so lightly on the delicately gloved hand that rested on her muff "you're nervous and over-wrought. You couldn't otherwise have such a morbid idea. This eternal going-out has got on your nerves. I wish you would promise me to stay at home for a day or two. You will, won't you?" he asked, persuasively.

"Yes, I—I will," she said, mechanically, and still looking very white. "I'm over-tired, as you say."

"And now don't talk," he went on, peremptorily. "I'll get you a glass of water, and then I want you to sit quietly here, and not say a word, till you are better."

She shook her head. "I'm quite well, and I don't want anything," she protested, but he brought the glass of water and made her drink it, and then watched her anxiously, while the color slowly came back to her face, and her eyes lost their strained, appealing look. They sat in silence; he would not let her speak, and as time passed, a great calm insensibly stole over her, a feeling of peace, of security, such as she had not known in all those weeks of fevered gaiety. She was conscious vaguely of a wish that she might sit thus always, saying nothing, alone with him—all the more alone as it seemed for the crowd that was beginning to surge into the room, with a murmur that broke faintly upon her ear, like the sound of the sea a long way off.

The wish was, perhaps, the result of fatigue. She was no sooner fully conscious of it than she rose to her feet.

"Shall we walk through the rooms now?" she said. "It's more than time for Eleanor to be here. Oh, I'm all right now, thank you"—she met his question smilingly. "I don't know what was the matter—it was very silly. You see I boasted unwisely about never thinking, since I have such foolish thoughts; but I won't again. Look, there is a picture of Gertrude Trevor. A good likeness, isn't it? But you've seen it before, perhaps?"

"No," said Gerard, absently. "I haven't seen any of them before." They walked on slowly through the rooms, and she did the honors, pointing out the pictures, as it was apparently his first visit. They did not seem to interest him greatly.

"Have you really never been here before?" she asked at length. She could not have explained what induced her to put the question.

He answered it absently. "Why, yes, every day"—and then suddenly stopped and turned his eyes full upon her, while that strange light gleamed in their sombre depths which she had surprised once or twice before and had interpreted many different ways, which now set her heart beating wildly, and made her wish her question unspoken. "Every day," he repeated, quietly, "about this time, or earlier, since—since the thing began."

"Then why—why"—The words died away on her lips. They had reached the head of the great staircase, and the crowd came streaming up, a confused mass, to which she paid no heed. She had again the feeling of being alone, quite alone, in the midst of it all, while involuntarily their eyes met, and his were all aglow with a fire which she had never before seen in them, or imagined; a fire that dazzled and bewildered, and filled her with a strange, unreasoning joy, as it burned away the barriers of doubt and indifference, till for one short, breathless moment, which she could have counted with her heart-beats she read his inmost soul.

"I only looked at one picture," he said.

And then with the words the spell which held her seemed broken, and the crowd closed in about her, with a sound like the roar of the sea very near at hand, and she looked down the great staircase, and saw Mrs. Bobby coming towards them.

Chapter XVIII

"MY dear," said Mrs. Bobby, "I'm so sorry to be late. Luncheon was interminable. Why, Julian, who would have expected to see you here?" She gave him her hand demurely, with softly shining eyes. Neither her surprise nor her contrition seemed to ring quite true.

Gerard's dark eyes were again half closed beneath their heavy lids. He looked, if a trifle pale, more impassive than usual.

"I don't know why my presence here should cause so much surprise," he said. "Most people come here, don't they, some time or another. It's a—a meeting-place, isn't it?"

"It seems to have been on this occasion," Mrs. Bobby murmured under her breath. A young man had just stopped and spoken to Elizabeth, and the words might have referred to him. Gerard smiled.

"Won't you come and look at some of these pictures?" he asked. "I want to talk to you."

"You awaken my curiosity."

They walked slowly along the gallery which skirted the hall, too deep in conversation to pay much heed to the pictures which hung along their way. Elizabeth's eyes followed them, the while she was repeating mechanically "Yes, the portraits are extremely fine."

"But not one," the young man declared, with blunt gallantry "to compare with yours. It's by all odds the most beautiful picture here."

"Do you really think so?" said Elizabeth, gently. "I'm very glad." She had heard the sentiment, rather differently put, perhaps a hundred times. Yet it seemed now to have all the charm of novelty.

The young man, a very slight acquaintance, charmed to have called up that glow of pleasure to her face, redoubled his efforts to entertain her. He was sorry when Mrs. Bobby returned with Gerard, and bore her off. "She was delighted when I said that about her picture," he thought, "there's nothing like flattering a girl, if you know how to do it delicately."

"We really must be going, Elizabeth," said Mrs. Bobby, consulting her engagement-book. "We have at least a dozen visits, and we promised, you know, to go to Mr. D'Hauteville's musicale."

"That reminds me that I did too," said Gerard. "I'm glad you spoke of it."

"We shall see you there, then," said Mrs. Bobby, as he placed them in the carriage, and they drove off. "I am feeling utterly crushed," she continued, turning to Elizabeth, and looking under the circumstances, very cheerful. "Julian has been giving me a terrible lecture. He thinks me, I see very clearly, quite unfit to have the care of you. He says that you are not as strong as you seem, that I have been dragging you around—entirely for my own pleasure, apparently—from one thing to another till you are quite worn out, and that you will be ill if I don't take care. He has quite frightened me. But there, Elizabeth, you don't look so very tired, after all."

She certainly did not. There was color in her cheeks, a light in her eyes that was at once brilliant and soft. All the lines drawn by sleepless nights had, for the moment at least, disappeared.

"You don't look badly," Mrs. Bobby repeated. "You look, in fact, infinitely better than when I saw you this morning."

"I feel better," Elizabeth admitted. "Just for a moment, at the Portrait Show, I did feel tired and depressed, and he—Mr. Gerard got alarmed about me, but it was nothing. I am quite well now. And the portraits are really very interesting. I am glad you persuaded me to look at them again, Eleanor."

"I thought you might be repaid," said Mrs. Bobby, serenely. "What did you think of your own picture? Doesn't it look better in that light?"

Elizabeth's face was turned away, so that Mrs. Bobby could only see the rounded outline of her cheek and one small, shell-like ear. "Yes, I—I thought it looked better," she said, in a low voice. "Perhaps you were right. It must have been the—the light of the studio that made me feel—disappointed in it, somehow."

"Oh, there is everything in the light in which you look at things," assented Mrs. Bobby, cheerfully. And with this profound remark, the two women sank into silence, while the carriage rolled swiftly up the Avenue, stopping occasionally, as the footman left cards. To Elizabeth, as she sat gazing out of the window, the prosaic brown stone houses, and the more pretentious ones of marble which broke the monotony here and there, and the brilliant shops, which had intruded themselves like parvenus among their quieter and more aristocratic neighbors—all these familiar objects stood out in a softened perspective, which endowed them with lines almost of romance. The wide, commonplace streets had an unwonted charm, the people who walked on them wore an air of curious happiness, merely, no doubt, at finding themselves alive in this beautiful world. Yes, as Mrs. Bobby had so wisely observed, "there is everything in the light in which you look at things."

"I wonder if Mr. D'Hauteville's musicale will be pleasant," Elizabeth observed dreamily, as they neared Carnegie Hall. The remark was purely perfunctory. Pleasant? Of course it would be pleasant—she hadn't a doubt of it.

"There will be a lot of queer people there—musical, literary, and that sort of thing," said Mrs. Bobby, vaguely. "Some men with long hair will play, and the women, no doubt, will wear wonderful æsthetic gowns. If Julian were not to be there, I should not dream of going. My prophetic instinct tells me that we shall not know a soul."

"But won't that be rather amusing," suggested Elizabeth.

"Well, theoretically, yes," said Mrs. Bobby, in rather a doubtful tone, "but, practically, I'm afraid I prefer people whom I know, and who have the conventional amount of hair and lack of brains. Let me confess the truth to you, Elizabeth. I'm not really Bohemian—I only pretend to be so at odd moments, when I want to tease Bobby, or shock the Neighborhood. There isn't at heart, I believe, a more conventional little society wretch than I. However, as you say, that sort of thing is amusing—for one afternoon; and Julian will be there, and protect us from the celebrities and tell us who they all are."

Julian was fortunately on hand when they arrived, but the room was filled for the most part with people who looked very much like any one else, and only a few were sufficiently long-haired and eccentric to justify Mrs. Bobby's prediction of their being celebrities of some sort. The host, who came forward to meet them, was a well-known musician, a man with an intellectual face and dreamy eyes, which lighted up as he welcomed them with eager cordiality; but he could do no more for the present than seat them and give them programmes, for the music was about to begin.

It was a charming studio, well up near the top of Carnegie Hall, and like most studios, it was artistically furnished. The polished floor was strewn with rich rugs, the walls were covered in every nook and cranny, with plaques, and pictures, and rare tapestries, and strange Eastern weapons. A grand piano took up the whole of one corner, and in another a toy staircase seemed to have been placed entirely for ornament, till it was utilized as a seat by some picturesque-looking girls in large hats. From the broad casemented window near which Elizabeth sat, she could see an expanse of roofs and chimneys, far down from the dizzy height, and beyond them the river, and further still the winter sunset, fading in cold blues and greens and violets, on a still colder sky. Her eyes rested there with dreamy satisfaction. She had no wish to look back into the room, to where Gerard was standing close to them, on the other side of Mrs. Bobby. She was still living on the memory of that moment—was it an hour or was it years ago?—that long look of which the reflected light was still glowing on her face, and in her dreamy eyes. She had no wish to renew it; the recollection was sufficient, for awhile at least. Yet she was glad to know that he was there.

Mrs. Bobby meanwhile, having embarked on her trip to Bohemia, was disappointed to find it comparatively tame.

"I don't see any one I know," she said to Gerard, as the piano solo came to an end. "They look, most of them, depressingly commonplace. But they must be extraordinary in some way, or they wouldn't be here. Tell us who they are, Julian, and introduce them to us if you think we would like them."

"Why, there are some musical lights," he answered, rather absently "who, I hope, are going to perform for our benefit, and there are a few ordinary music-lovers like myself, and some literary people—whom I don't know that you would care about."

"You think us too frivolous, I see," said Mrs. Bobby. "But you don't realize how clever I can be if I try, and as for Elizabeth, she knows a lot more than she seems to know."

"Does she?" asked Gerard with a smile, and he glanced across at Elizabeth, who still would not meet his eyes. "She looks very innocent," he said, musingly, after a pause. "I should be sorry to think of her as—concealing anything."

A little pang, a thought sharp like a stone, struck Elizabeth for an instant. It was the first rift in the lute. She put it resolutely away from her.

"You think me too stupid, I see," she said "to have any knowledge to conceal."

He had no time to answer before some woman began to sing. She had a beautiful voice, and Elizabeth listened, yet chiefly conscious, all the while, of the fact that Gerard had managed to shift his position, and was standing directly behind her.

"I never thought you stupid," he said, under cover of the applause, in a low voice that no one but she could hear, "no, nor ignorant; but I have sometimes thought you frivolous, and flippant, and—and a little hard. You seem, I sometimes think, to take pleasure in showing these qualities to me. Why is it, I wonder?"

"I—I don't know," she murmured, in the same low voice, and gazing straight before her. "You—somehow you seem to compel it. You ought to be grateful, I think. At least you know the worst of me."

She spoke these words with an absolute unconsciousness of their falseness; and even as they died away on her lips, she glanced across the room and saw Paul Halleck standing in the door-way.

That old mythological king whom some vague reminiscence of her school-days had conjured up in Elizabeth's mind, he who had every wish fulfilled, till he grew at last to dread his own prosperity—was it, I wonder, in some such moment of foreboding that the final crash came, or was it when his fears were lulled and his senses stilled, by some delicious, over-powering sense of happiness that shut out for the moment all unpleasant thoughts? This, at all events, was the way in which fate overtook Elizabeth.

Paul Halleck stood in the door-way, having apparently just arrived. His blue eyes were wandering about the room. They did not fall, as yet, upon Elizabeth.

She did not faint, or cry out, or make herself in any way conspicuous. She turned deathly white, and her heart, which had been beating faster for Gerard's presence, seemed suddenly to stop entirely, as though a piece of ice had been laid on it. And then, in a moment, her heart began to beat again, though faintly. She drew a long breath. Gerard, who was standing directly behind her, could not see her face beneath the shadow of her large hat, yet he felt instinctively that something was wrong.

"Do you feel faint again?" he asked, anxiously, thinking to himself that she was really far from well. "Can I get you anything?"

"No, thank you," said Elizabeth. "I felt faint for a moment, but it is over." It took all the strength that she possessed to speak these words so clearly and distinctly. In making the effort she was not conscious of any plan of deception. She was merely bearing up, instinctively, to the end.

She never doubted that it *was* the end. It had fallen at last—that sword of Damocles, which she had learned to dread as the winter wore on, of which she had always been vaguely conscious even in her gayest moments, and had only forgotten, quite forgotten, in that short, delicious hour when she had allowed herself to float off in a dream of happiness never to be realized, from which she was awakened so soon and so rudely. And yet, though it was over, she was not sorry that she had dreamed it. It had been very sweet, worth even, she thought, the bitterness of the awakening.

Meanwhile the musicale progressed. A man with long, floating hair and fingers of steel thundered out a piano solo. Elizabeth shut her eyes and leaned back in her chair. How fortunate that there was so much music to prevent conversation! But at the first pause she opened her eyes and looked up at Gerard.

"I was wrong when I told you that you know the worst of me," she said, faintly. "You'll know it, soon."

"What a terrible prospect!" said Gerard, bending over her and the jesting words had a soft intonation, which thrilled her like a caress. "I really don't think I can stand it—quite."

Had she intended to tell him the truth? The moment was not propitious. The music had stopped, and there was a murmur of conversation all over the room. People began to move about, and in the general shifting of position, Paul Halleck, for the first time, caught sight of Elizabeth.

She had had some vague, childish idea of what would happen when he saw her. She had pictured him in her unreasoning terror, as stepping forward before them all and claiming her as his wife, like a scene in a play. Nothing of the kind took place. She saw at once how absurd her expectations had been. Paul merely started and looked at her, recognition and it seemed, pleasure sparkling in his eyes; but with a sudden, uncontrollable impulse, she turned her own eyes away, as if she did not know him.

"Do you see that man in the door-way?" said Gerard, who, standing as he was behind her could not note the changes in her face,—"that handsome fellow with the light curls? He has a very fine voice, and has just been engaged as soloist at St. Chrysostom's."

"Indeed. Is he to sing this afternoon?" She brought out the question with difficulty.

"I hope so," said Gerard. "I'd like you to hear him. But perhaps you know him," he went on. "He is looking at you as if he expected you to bow."

"No," said Elizabeth. "I don't know him." She told him this, her second lie that afternoon, without deliberate intention, in sheer lack of presence of mind. It was a piteous, involuntary staving-off of the inevitable. The next moment that fascination which leads us to our own undoing made her look in Paul's direction, and this time she could not avoid his eager gaze and bent her head mechanically.

"After all, I believe I must have met him somewhere," she said hastily. Mrs. Bobby, who for the last quarter of an hour, had been determinedly ignoring them both, apparently giving her whole attention to the music and the people, now turned towards them.

"Who is that handsome man who bowed to you, Elizabeth?" she asked. "I never saw him before."

"His name is Halleck. I—I knew him in the country," said Elizabeth, who had no natural talent for deception and entangled herself at once in contradictory statements. Gerard's face darkened, and he glanced across at Halleck, whose eyes were fixed on Elizabeth with a look that seemed, to the jealous, fastidious man by her side, an intolerable presumption; a look that was not only one of admiration, but, or Gerard imagined so, held in it a curious touch of proprietorship. "Confound the fellow," chafed Gerard—he who would fain have kept the woman he loved, as he certainly would have kept her picture, shut out from all profane eyes, even admiring ones. "He looks at her as if he had discovered her and she belonged to him. Where can she have met him, and why did she say she hadn't."

Mrs. Bobby, too, looked across at Paul.

"He is certainly very good-looking," she said. "And do you mean to tell me, my dear, that such an Adonis flourished in our Neighborhood, and I never saw him. Pray, where did you keep him hidden?"

Before Elizabeth could reply, and to her great relief, D'Hauteville came up with the long-haired musician, whom he introduced to them, and who proved to be, at last, one of the celebrities upon whom Mrs. Bobby had counted. In the diversion that ensued Halleck seemed forgotten. But a few minutes later, he sat at the piano and sang songs by Schubert and Franz, which she had heard him sing before, at the time when she had thought his voice the most beautiful voice in the world. Now, as she listened it left her cold. She had changed so much, and he—no, he had not changed. His voice was not so wonderful as she had thought it, but still it was a fine barytone voice. His art no longer seemed to her remarkable, but it had, if anything, improved, and he was as handsome as ever, in his fair, effeminate style. It was not the voice nor the art that was lacking. It was the answering thrill in herself. It was not his beauty which had failed him, it was she who no longer cared for it.

His success with the audience was instantaneous. Even Mrs. Bobby was impressed. "Your friend sings well," she whispered to Elizabeth, "and yet his hair is short. You may introduce him to me if you get a chance."

And this chance immediately presented itself, as Paul, amid the applause that followed his song, walked over to Elizabeth and quietly shook hands with her. It was the moment that she had dreaded all the time that he was singing, yet now that it had come, she met it in apparent unconcern, and smiling, though with white lips.

"I thought at first," Paul said, "that you had quite forgotten me."

"Oh, no," she said, "my memory is not so short." Then she turned and introduced him to Mrs. Bobby, and went on herself quietly talking to Mr. D'Hauteville. Nothing could have been more simple. Not even Julian Gerard, who from a distance watched their meeting, could have imagined any secret understanding between them.

The handsome young singer made a very favorable impression upon Mrs. Bobby, who went so far as to ask him to call, in that impulsive way of hers, which sometimes led to consequences that she regretted. In this case she realized, almost as soon as the words had left her lips, that she had done a rash thing, or what Bobby would consider rash. Still, the invitation was given and eagerly accepted, even though Elizabeth, standing cold and indifferent, said not a word to second it. By this time the music was over. They were about to leave, when some one claimed

Mrs. Bobby's attention, and she turned aside for a moment. Paul seized the opportunity, for which he had been anxiously waiting, to whisper in Elizabeth's ear.

"Darling, don't go. I must see you for a moment."

"You can't speak to me here," she said, impatiently, trying to escape from him.

"But I must see you. Can't you see that I must?"

"You have done without it," said Elizabeth, without turning her head, "some time."

"Because I couldn't help myself."

"There is such a thing as writing," she said, in the same low, bitter tone. Yet even as she spoke her conscience misgave her. It was not his neglect that she resented so bitterly, it was his return. But Paul, not understanding this was rather flattered than otherwise by the reproach.

"Darling, I will explain when I see you," he said, hurriedly. "There's no time now. Meet me to-morrow morning—at the Fifty-ninth street entrance to the Park, at eleven o'clock."

"To-morrow! Impossible! I have a hundred things to do."

"Ah, but you must," he pleaded. "I must see you. Darling you look so beautiful—fifty times more beautiful than before."

"Hush," said Elizabeth. "How dare you? Some one will hear you."

"Give me a chance of seeing you, then," he said. "It is necessary. You will meet me—will you not?—to-morrow morning?"

"If you insist upon it—yes."

"At the west entrance of the Park—you understand?"

"Oh, yes," said Elizabeth impatiently, and hastened to rejoin Mrs. Bobby, who was waiting at the door.

Julian Gerard came up gloomily. The whispered conference had not escaped his notice.

"We shall see you to-night at the Lansdownes' ball," said Mrs. Bobby. "It is the night for it, isn't it, Elizabeth? I never can keep track of these things."

Gerard looked reproachfully at Elizabeth. "You promised me," he said, "that you would stay at home for a night or two."

She smiled back at him with the old touch of wilfulness. "Did I really make such a rash promise," she said, lightly. "Ah, I'm afraid I can't keep it—not to-night. I must be amused. A quiet evening would be unendurable." Her cheeks were flushed, her eyes glittered with feverish gaiety, there was an odd, strained note in her voice. Mrs. Bobby looked at her in some perplexity, then she glanced up deprecatingly at Gerard.

"It is her first season, you see Julian," she said, as if in apology. "You can't expect her to give up things."

"No," he repeated, mechanically. "I can't expect her to—give up things." He fell back silently, in increased gloom. Elizabeth glanced towards him involuntarily as she left the room.

"Now," she said to herself, "I have disappointed him again and he won't come near me this evening. But it is better so—far, far better," she repeated to herself, with a little sob, as she followed her hostess to the carriage.

Chapter XIX

THE next day was unexpectedly mild. Winter, after reigning supreme, made sudden and treacherous overtures to approaching spring. The air in the Park was almost balmy, and the drives were gay, as though it were much later in the season, with carriages and riders and bicycles galore; yet the warm sunlight falling incongruously on sere, brown grass and bare branches, seemed but to emphasize their dreariness and the fact that winter had not really surrendered, and was only biding his time and the advent of the March winds, to make his power felt all the more strongly. Pedestrians, realizing this, refused to be inveigled out, even by the spring-like air, and there was no one to notice the young man and the young woman who sat on a bench in one of the secluded walks near Eighth avenue; the young woman, simply dressed in a dark tailor-made gown, with a small black hat pushed well over her face, which showed beneath it very pale and set, with hard lines about the mouth; the young man staring at her in bewilderment, a look of distress in his handsome blue eyes.

"And so," he said, "you don't love me any longer?" It had taken him some time to grasp this fact, which still seemed to him incomprehensible.

"No," she said, in a low, determined voice, "I don't love you any longer. I don't know if I—ever did. I was so young, I had never seen any men, I didn't know what I was doing. You flattered me; it was interesting, romantic. But if I had loved you, really loved you"—she stopped for an instant. "If I had really loved you," she repeated "do you think I could have hesitated—that day at Cranston? Do you think I could have let you go—without me? Why, I should have followed you—don't you see that I would?—to the end of the world." The color rushed into her face, there was a ring in her voice that he never heard before—no, not even in those early days, when she had sat at his feet, and worshipped him as a genius. Then, as he looked at her, he realized for the first time that he had lost her. The discovery was, for many reasons, unwelcome.

"Well, if you didn't love me," he said, hoarsely, "you certainly made me believe that you did. Elizabeth, you have treated me abominably. I didn't wish to leave you—do me the justice to admit that—it was your own doing entirely."

"I know it." She bent her head submissively. "I don't blame you for anything; not even for—forgetting me."

"I didn't forget you," he interrupted her, flushing hotly, and repeating assertions which she had heard already, and interpreted by that knowledge of his character, which she had acquired too late to be of value. She put them aside now with a gesture of weariness.

"What's the use," she said, "of going over that again, I have said already, I don't reproach you. We can't either of us—can we?—afford to throw stones. And yet, if you had not stopped writing"—She paused for a moment with knitted brows, as she seemed to weigh one possibility against another, in a sort of inward trial of her own conduct. An instinctive mental honesty, however, carried the day. "I don't know that that would have made any difference," she said. "I was very unhappy because you—had forgotten me, and that made me want to come to town, all the more; but—if I had been happy, and sure that you loved me, I should have come, I think, all the same. And no matter how I had felt, or what I had done, I should have known, sooner or later—oh, I couldn't but realize it—what a—what a terrible mistake we had made." She put out her hands in a sudden, despairing gesture, which hurt his vanity.

"Elizabeth, do you really mean that?"

"Yes," she said, in a low, monotonous voice, and staring straight before her with hard, hopeless eyes. "Yes, I mean it. I have been realizing it, little by little, all these months. And yet I put it away—I wouldn't think of it—till one day it forced itself upon me. I knew, all at once, that I—I dreaded your coming back, I hoped you never would—it was when I was enjoying myself, when I was thinking how delightful life was. And then, after that, the fear of your coming was always there—I could never get rid of it for any length of time, till just for a while—yesterday"—Her voice faltered, and for the first time the softening tears sprang to her eyes. "Oh, I can't help it," she cried out, "if I'm hard. When I think how happy I was—wildly, absurdly happy, just for a little while, and then to think how—how miserable I am now."

She stopped, half strangled with her sobs, and Paul sat staring at her in moody silence. He was clear-sighted enough now to grasp the truth. Such violent grief, he told himself, could have but one explanation. There was, there must be, some other man.

Yet the conviction made him only the more determined not to give her up. True, there had been a time, not long before, when he would have done so only too gladly; when he would have welcomed an opportunity to free himself from an irksome bond, which he regretted quite as much as she did. But now, since his return, when he heard her spoken of everywhere as one of the beauties of the season, when he saw her in D'Hauteville's studio in her velvet and furs, her whole appearance redolent of grace and charm, and that nameless distinction which Gerard had noticed, and which impressed the young musician even more deeply; when he saw her thus a hundred times more desirable, his fickle heart succumbed anew, with a sudden throb of joy, at the thought of the secret tie between them. She was his, this young princess, whom he had chosen when she was a mere Cinderella; he had but to hold out his hand and she would come to him. For he never doubted that she *would* come. Her first coldness he had looked upon as mere girlish pique at his neglect, a proof of her affection. Now, a sadder and a wiser being, he had learned that the privilege of forgetfulness is not confined to men alone.

Yet the situation, unflattering though it was, had its advantages, which dawned upon him gradually, while Elizabeth still sobbed. He rose and paced up and down in front of her, thinking the matter over. After all, a wife was the last thing that he wanted—just then, when his career was opening out before him in unexpectedly brilliant colors. He realized perfectly the value of his own good looks, and the loss of prestige that marriage would involve. Matrimony is a mistake for an artist—he had told himself this many times in the last few months. And yet, having once made the mistake, having won this beautiful girl for his wife, how could he give her up. There was the chance that she might change her mind again, and return to her first love. Then it was sweet to feel that she was in his power, that he could at any time bring her to terms by threatening to publish the fact that she had concealed all this time. True, the marriage might be dissolved—he had not much doubt himself that it could be; but either this plan did not occur to Elizabeth, or she dreaded the inevitable gossip and publicity. At all events, it was not his place, he thought, to suggest it to her. He held the mastery of the situation, and he was determined to improve it to the uttermost. And having arrived at this conclusion, he suddenly stopped before her and spoke in a tone of unwonted resolution.

"Listen to me, Elizabeth," he said. "I don't know why you are making this scene. In what has the situation changed since—let us say, last week? I don't ask you to acknowledge our marriage at once—indeed it is impossible for me to do so, as I am not—worse luck—in a position just now to support a wife."

Elizabeth, in her surprise, stopped crying and stared up at him blankly. "You don't want the marriage acknowledged?" she repeated, utterly taken aback.

"Not just now," said Paul, calmly. "It would be as inconvenient for me, as it seems to be for you. No, all I ask is for you to see me occasionally, to think of me more kindly, and in time—perhaps in time, dearest, you will care for me again as you used to."

He went on to dilate on this hope. Elizabeth's tears as she listened, ceased. A feeling of relief stole over her, the reaction which follows so often upon violent distress. "In time," Paul said. Ah, yes, her heart answered, there is no knowing what wonders time may accomplish. It might even—who could tell?—find a way for her out of this terrible perplexity.

Yet the thought was illogical. Of what use was it to put off the evil day? There was a side of her nature which was brave and straightforward, which detested false pretences and evasions, and all the net-work of deception in which her secret had already involved her; which called out upon her boldly to tell the truth, since every day that she kept it hidden only made the final disclosure more difficult. But there was another side which counselled compromise, which shrank from facing the inevitable, which lived only in the present and refused to take thought for the future. And finally there was a side which did not reason, which simply remembered the look in a man's eyes, when he had spoken to her the day before of her picture.

How would it be if he knew the truth? Would he make allowances for her, would he be magnanimous enough to forgive? Ah, no, he had judged her harshly for no apparent reason. Such a discovery would put an end entirely to all his faith in her.

For she felt instinctively how it would strike him—this impulsive action of a thoughtless girl, who had rushed into marriage as if it were a mere farce, and taken upon herself, lightly, the most solemn vows, only to repent of them quite as readily. He would pronounce her hopelessly light and fickle, he would never believe that she was capable of any deeper feeling. His presentiment, distrust—whatever it was that had kept him from her—would be justified, and—and there would be the end of it. And the best thing that could happen, that stern inner voice called out.

But she would not listen to it—not yet, at least. She must see him once or twice first, probe his feelings a little more surely, prepare him a little, perhaps, to judge her more gently.... Some time—very soon, perhaps,—she would tell him herself, but—not now, not now....

Her head ached, she was physically exhausted, and Paul was waiting, impatiently, for her decision. She had an engagement, too, for luncheon—she remembered that mechanically.... In this matter-of-fact world of ours, the every-day and the tragic incidents of life jostle one another so closely.

"I—I must go," she murmured, confusedly. "I've been here too long. We can talk about all this another time."

"But you consent," he said eagerly. "You wish to keep it secret, awhile longer? That is the agreement for the present?"

She hesitated for a moment. "Yes," she said at last, "that is the agreement, till—till I have time to think it over. And now I must go." She drew out the little jeweled watch that Mrs. Van Antwerp had given her, among other valuable things, at Christmas. "I am going out to luncheon, and I am supposed at present to be in my room, recovering from last night's ball."

"What a gay person you are!" Paul said, regarding her complacently. "Ah, Elizabeth, if you wanted to be nice, you could help me a great deal in my profession."

"Help you?" she repeated, staring at him blankly.

"Yes, in a social way," he explained. "It always helps an artist to be taken up by swell people. There's your friend Mrs. Van Antwerp—can't you—there's a good girl—persuade her to do something for me?"

"I heard her ask you to call," she returned, coldly.

"Yes, but she could do more than that," he said. "She could, for instance, have me sing and ask people to hear me. I need a start, I need patrons among society people; and that is exactly, my dear girl, what you can get me."

They were walking slowly by this time towards the entrance of the Park, and suddenly she turned and faced him with one of those flashes of defiance, which he rather admired. "Let me understand," she said, quickly, and a pale, cold gleam lighted up her white face, like the glint of steel upon marble. "You want me to—to get you invitations, to persuade people to ask you to sing? This is the—the price of your silence?"

He shrugged his shoulders, not much disturbed by the scorn in her voice. "If you choose to put it so plainly—yes," he said. "After all, it is not much to ask, and you ought, one would think, to be glad if you can help me."

She walked on beside him in gloomy silence. "It's not much to ask," she said, in a low, bitter voice, "but it involves—have you thought of that?—my seeing you constantly."

"And is that so terrible?" he asked, reddening.

"It's not pleasant," she said, shortly "but I suppose I must—submit. I'm in your power; you can ask what you please." They had reached the entrance of the Park, and she turned to him, as if to dismiss him. "I promise, then," she said. "I'll do what I can to help you—socially, and in return you must promise to treat me as you would any other acquaintance—not force me to meet you again, or let people suppose that there is anything between us. Do you agree to that?"

"I suppose I must," he said, disconsolately, "though it's a harder condition, by far, than mine."

Again that cold, scornful gleam flashed across her face.

"Oh, you'll resign yourself to it," she said. "It's much more to the point to get—the invitations. I'll see that my side of the bargain is fulfilled." She drew down her veil, glancing anxiously across the wide Square, where street-cars, bicycles and wagons all converge from different directions and in inextricable confusion. "Don't come any further with me," she said. "I don't wish people to see us together."

She left him abruptly as she spoke, and he stood for a moment and watched her cross the Square and take a car at the corner. He was not quite satisfied with the interview; she had been too independent, too scornful. It hurt his pride. But the situation was full of possibilities. He felt that his rash marriage had been a stroke of genius.

Elizabeth, meanwhile, was making her way home, with a feeling of tremulous relief, much as if she had escaped unexpectedly from shipwreck, with at least a plank to cling to, and bear her perhaps to ultimate safety. Yet how slight that plank was she might have realized, had she known that Julian Gerard, as he entered the Park on horseback, had seen her walk down one of the side paths, with the man who, only a day before, had aroused his jealous suspicions.

"And she said she didn't know him," he thought, with a fierce throb of pain, and rode on, frowning, into the Park.

Chapter XX

"*MY* dear Julian," wrote Mrs. Bobby Van Antwerp to Mr. Gerard a week later, "you are, I think, neglecting us shamefully. What has become of you? If you are inclined to perform a charitable action, do come in to tea to-morrow afternoon. You don't generally, I know, patronize such mild functions, but we are to have a little music"—

"A little music?" mused Gerard, knitting his brows and thrusting out his under lip, as the note dropped from his hand. "That means, of course, that young Halleck. It's something new for Eleanor to go in for music. But it's *her* doing, of course. I suppose she really cares for the fellow. And yet what a pity—what a pity that she should throw herself away like that!" He sat gazing absently before him, his pen in his hand, while the work upon which he had been engaged when Mrs. Bobby's note arrived—an article for a scientific magazine—remained without the finishing touches he had intended to bestow.

He had not seen Elizabeth since that morning in the Park.

He had carefully refrained from going where he might see her. He had denied himself, once for all, that unprofitable and mysterious pleasure of watching her across the ball-room, while he leaned inertly against the wall, or talked, in his weary way, to some woman to whom he felt himself indebted. No, thank Heaven, he had been warned in time; there was no danger of his being made a fool of a second time.

His mind wandered back across the gulf of years, to that other woman whom he had loved so desperately once, whose shadow still stood between him and the happiness which seemed, now and again, within his grasp. He thought of the mad infatuation, the bitter disillusion, the restless travelling to and fro, the final settling down into cynical indifference.... and then long afterwards, when the indifference had grown into a habit, and he dreaded nothing more than to have it disturbed, he had met this girl who had exercised upon him from the first a curious effect, half repellant, half attractive, and wholly baffling and alarming, whose hair he had objected to because it was "too red" and who played the piano with a force and fire and passion, which stirred his heart as he had resolved it should never be stirred again.

Gerard had always intended to marry, but he proposed, in spite of the efforts of Eleanor Van Antwerp and other anxious friends, to take his time about it. He had his ideal of the sort of wife he wanted—a being as different as possible from his first love, and almost as tiresome a compound of all the domestic virtues as that mythical personage whom Hannah More's hero had once gone in search of. But, unlike that estimable individual, he had fallen in love with a woman far removed from his ideal, of doubtful antecedents which he liked no better than Bobby Van Antwerp, of qualities the reverse of domestic, and the type of hair and coloring which he had long illogically, but none the less strongly, associated with a certain lack of moral sense.

Yet though Gerard could not help his feelings, he could certainly control his actions, and he was determined to keep away from Elizabeth Van Vorst—more especially now since there seemed to be some unaccountable understanding between her and that young Halleck.

Yet that very fact made him the more anxious to see her, and find out for himself how far his suspicions were justified. "Good Heavens," thought Gerard, getting up and pacing restlessly to and fro "how can she care for a fellow like that—so second-rate, so superficial, such a—such a cad? What is Eleanor thinking of to have him at the house? Some one really ought to give her a hint—not I; but—some one." ...

The end of it all was that he strolled into Mrs. Van Antwerp's drawing-room that afternoon, his usual air of well-bred impassiveness unmoved by the sight of Paul Halleck seated at the piano, and the cynosure of several pairs of admiring feminine eyes.

Elizabeth's eyes were not among them. She was in a back room pouring tea. But Gerard had no sooner assured himself of her being thus harmlessly employed, than his jealous heart suggested that there was something sinister in such apparent indifference.

He wandered into the other room as soon as he decently could. She was seated at the tea-table, for the moment, entirely alone. Seen thus off guard, for she did not at first perceive Gerard, there was something indefinably weary and listless in her attitude. She was paler even than she had been that day at the Portrait Show, and the lines beneath her eyes were not black, but purple. It would have gone ill with her reputation as a beauty had it been put to the vote that afternoon. But it was Gerard's peculiarity, his misfortune perhaps, that she appealed to him most at times when to the world at large she was looking her worst. He stood watching her for a moment. Presently she looked up. She caught sight of him. Instantly the warm, lovely color rushed into her cheeks, only to retreat, and leave her paler than before—but not till he had seen it.

His manner was very gentle as he approached her and asked for a cup of tea. She poured it out mechanically, with a hand that trembled.

"We have not seen you lately," she said, with eyes carefully riveted on the tea-things. "Eleanor was wondering—what had become of you."

"Indeed! It was very kind of her to give me a thought." Gerard stirred his tea absently. "I was busy," he said "with an article I had promised for a magazine."

"Ah! You write a great deal, don't you?" Elizabeth looked up with some interest. "I should like to see some of your articles, if I may."

He smiled. "You don't know what you're asking. You'd find them very dull."

"What, because I'm so dull myself?" she asked, with a flash of spirit.

"I told you once before," he said, in the tone that he had used to her at the studio "that I didn't think you—that."

"Ah, but you think me other things that are—worse."

"As what, for instance?" he asked, smiling.

"Oh frivolous, and vain, and heartless. A lot of horrid things."

"I only said you *seemed* so."

"Ah, then you think I'm better than I seem?" she asked, flippantly, yet with a swift inward pang.

He seemed to consider. "I think you are very—incomprehensible," he said at last.

She bent down over the tea-things, so that he could not see her face. "Oh, that's only," she said, in a low voice "because you haven't the key to the enigma. If you had it"—She paused. "You might not like the things you understood," she concluded.

Gerard put down his untasted cup. "I'm willing to take the risk," he said, deliberately.

He waited, as if for an answer, but none came. She appeared to busy herself with the tea-things. In the next room Paul Halleck began to sing the Evening Star song. It seemed to Gerard that Elizabeth turned a shade paler than she had been before.

"He has a fine voice," he said, when the song was finished. "Don't you think so?"

She started. "Yes, I—I think so," she said, mechanically.

"I was surprised a little at Eleanor's going in for music," Gerard went on. "It isn't her line, generally."

"No, it isn't her line," Elizabeth repeated, in the same mechanical tones. Suddenly she met his eyes defiantly. "I asked her to have him here," she said.

"Ah, you asked her?" Gerard drew his breath quickly. "I *thought* he was a—a friend of yours."

"You thought so?" she returned quickly, and then in a low voice, as if she dreaded the answer: "Why?"

"Why?" He repeated her question as if it surprised him. For a moment he seemed to hesitate; then, as if forming a sudden resolution: "I thought so," he said, steadily, and looking her straight in the face "for one thing, because I saw you walking in the Park with him one morning."

"Ah, you—you saw me?" She seemed to gasp for breath. Then, with a quick, impetuous movement, she pushed the tea-things away from her. "And so," she said, turning to him suddenly, her cheeks flushed, her eyes sparkling "you—you put the worst construction upon that, you think more ill of me than ever?"—

He had turned very pale, but still his voice was steady. "I don't know why I should think ill of you, for such a simple thing as that. But if there is any secret about it"—he fixed his eyes upon her coldly, haughtily—"if the meeting was not intended to be known, why I—I'm sorry I should have seen it. Of course I should not mention it—to any one else."

She flushed a little, then grew pale, before the scorn in his eyes. "There is—there is no secret," she said, in a low voice. "You can mention it—to whom you please."

"I confess I was a little surprised," he went on, without heeding her, and this time a note of keen anxiety pierced through the studied quietness of his voice, his gaze softened, as if imploring her to give him the explanation which he had no right to demand. "I was a little taken aback," he said, "because I understood you to say—the day before—that you hardly knew him."

"Yes, I—I remember." She leaned back in her chair, staring before her with hard, bright eyes. "When I told you that," she said, slowly "I—I lied."

It gave him a keen shock to hear her pronounce the word. He did not speak, and she looked up at him presently with a little, deprecating smile. "Now," she said, softly "I've shocked you, haven't I?"

He was silent for a moment. "No," he said, at last "not that; but—I'm sorry. I don't like to think of you as—misstating anything, even if the matter is of no importance."

She had taken up a teaspoon, and was playing with it absently. "I don't know," she said, slowly "why you should care."

"Don't you?" He turned his eyes away. "I wish to Heaven I didn't," he said, low and fiercely. The words were not intended for her, but she heard them and again the warm, beautiful color rushed into her cheeks. An answer trembled on her lips, but she struggled not to say it; struggled against the desire to bring that glow to his face, that light to his eyes, which she knew so well lay dormant, beneath the heavy lids. She knew, ah, she knew. While he stayed away she had her misgivings, but now that she saw him again, she read his heart, even as she had done at the Portrait Show. She had only to be herself, her best self, and she held him captive, he could not escape. Yet, paradoxically, her better instincts urged upon her to show him her worst side, to say the things which hurt and shocked him.

While she hesitated, people came crowding in from the next room. In the confusion that ensued, Gerard was forced away from the table. He fell back against the wall, and watched Elizabeth while, with instinctive self-command, she fulfilled the different demands made upon her. He saw Halleck go up to her gaily, flushed with his success, and bending over her, murmur a few jesting words, which she heard without a smile. Gerard could have killed him for the air of proprietorship which was even more pronounced than at the musicale. But she—how did she like it? He scanned her face eagerly. There was no softness there, no answering gleam of pleasure; rather a dull, dogged look of submission, which seemed to cover, or Gerard deceived himself, an instinctive shrinking, a powerless resentment.

"She doesn't care for him," he thought, with a quick, sharp sense of relief. "And yet—she has to be civil to him, she has to do things to help him. Why, for Heaven's sake, why?" He wandered into the other room, tormenting himself with this question, and found his hostess there.

"What do you think of my new protegé?" she asked, detaining him as he took his leave.

"What, Halleck? Oh, he sings very well," he returned, absently.

"I never before posed as a patron of rising musicians," she went on, "but Elizabeth knew him, it seems, in the country, and asked if I would mind helping him a little. She's so fond of music, you know." She spoke quite innocently. Gerard gave her a quick, searching glance. Apparently she suspected nothing. Yet she was a woman of quick perceptions. Perhaps, after all, it was he who was mistaken; his jealous, suspicious nature had led him into unnecessary torture. No wonder she had met his doubt with defiance, had not deigned to justify herself, or to dispel a distrust which he had no right to display. In the sudden, glad, unreasoning reaction, he was ready to heap all manner of insulting epithets upon himself.

"I think your efforts will be repaid," he said, inclined in his relief to be generous. "Halleck has a fine voice. I shouldn't wonder if he were quite a success."

"It was very nice of you to come in," she said. "You have been such a recluse lately. What have you been doing?"

"Oh, the whirl of excitement in which I've been living was too much for me," he declared "and so I've given up society for awhile, and am going in for hard study by way of rest."

"Good gracious! That sounds very impressive," she said. "I'm almost afraid to suggest, under the circumstances, that you should take a seat in our box at the opera to-night. And yet I wish you would, Julian, just by way of doing me a favor, for some people I've asked are not coming, and Bobby is away, and Elizabeth and I will be quite alone."

He smiled. "I don't think there's much chance of your being alone very long," he said. Yet he promised at last to take one of the vacant seats, though he had refused several other invitations for that evening. Mrs. Bobby's eyes sparkled as if she had achieved a victory.

"Julian is coming to-night," she announced to Elizabeth, when the musicale was over and the last guest had departed.

"Is he?" Elizabeth spoke without apparent interest, as she sank, with a weary look, into a chair in front of the fire.

"You are tired. Would you rather not go to-night?"

"Oh, no"—with a languid gesture. "Music doesn't tire me!"

"And yet," said Mrs. Bobby, who had taken the seat opposite her and was watching her thoughtfully, "you didn't seem to care enough about it to come in to listen to your friend this afternoon."

Elizabeth blushed. "I could hear him in the other room," she said.

"Where, besides, you seemed to be very well entertained," said Mrs. Bobby, serenely. "Still, I don't think it was nice of you. It is hard on the poor man, after flirting with him in the country, to treat him so indifferently in town."

"I didn't flirt with him," said Elizabeth, but her protest was faint, and seemed purely perfunctory. In fact, she was not sorry that Mrs. Bobby had adopted this theory, realizing that a half-truth may sometimes be the most effective barrier to a knowledge of the whole.

"Don't tell me anything so wildly improbable, my dear," said Mrs. Bobby. "My knowledge of human nature will not allow me to believe that a pretty girl and a handsome young singer, thrown together for weeks in the country, as I believe you were, did *not* indulge in a tremendous flirtation. But seriously, Elizabeth, I am glad that it went no further, and that you have recovered so easily. For I can imagine that you lost your heart to him a little. Confess, Elizabeth, didn't you?"

"Perhaps I did," said Elizabeth, staring immovably into the fire "but one gets over such things, you know."

"Indeed one does," said Mrs. Bobby. "I was desperately in love at seventeen, and cried my eyes out when they made me give the man up; and yet had I married him, I should have been the most wretched being in the world, instead of a much happier woman than I deserve to be, thanks to a husband far too good for me. (But that, dear, is between ourselves. I always try to make Bobby think it's the other way.) But imagine how dreadful it would have been, if I had had my own foolish way at seventeen. And so I am glad, Elizabeth, that you have got over your penchant for this young artist, who is good-looking, and sings well, and all that; but who is—even if I knew anything about him, which I don't—quite the last man I should like you to marry."

Elizabeth's face was turned away. "I don't know," she said in a low voice, "why you think of that."

"Oh, I was only speculating on what might have been," said Mrs. Bobby, lightly. "I know," she went on after a moment, stealing a furtive glance at the girl's averted face, "I know the sort of man I should like you to marry, Elizabeth. He must be older than you, considerably older; of a serious disposition, with a strong will, stronger than yours, for you might be perhaps a little hard to manage; fond of music and fond of books; rich, and with a good position of course; and—and I should like him to be every bit as nice as Bobby, if such a thing is possible."

Elizabeth turned her white face towards her friend. "And you think," she said, in a low, stifled voice, "that I should come up to the standard of a paragon like that?"

"My dear," said Mrs. Bobby, wisely, "paragons don't marry *other* paragons, or the world would be somewhat more dull than it is at present. A man who is very serious should marry a woman who is a trifle frivolous, and in that way they strike the happy medium."

"I don't know," said Elizabeth. "They would be more likely, I should think, to strike a—a discordancy. It would be fatiguing to try to please a man like that. One could never, do what one would, come up to his standard."

"You wouldn't have to," said Mrs. Bobby, softly, "he would think you perfect, if—he loved you."

"Do you think so?" said Elizabeth, with rather a dreary smile. "I think, for my part, that he would be harder to satisfy, he would exact all the more, because—he loved you." She sat pondering the idea for a moment, then with a careless little gesture, she seemed to dismiss the subject as a thing of small consequence. "It's much better not to try to satisfy people like that," she declared. "What a lot of time we are wasting! It must be time to dress." She got up and moved towards the door.

Mrs. Bobby followed her with her eyes. "I'll send Celeste to you," she said. "Wear your most becoming gown. Look your best, and do your hair the way I like it. I assure you, such trifles have their effect—even upon a paragon."

Chapter XXI

"LOOK my best!" Elizabeth repeated, standing before her muslin-skirted dressing-table, and staring at the haggard apparition that met her eyes. "Wear my most becoming gown, do my hair the most becoming way! It all sounds so easy. But what can bring back my color, what can take away these terrible dark rings, this horrible strained, anxious look? Any one can see, to look at me, that I've something on my mind....

"... I shall never tell him the truth—never, never. I may beat about the bush, but I shall always leave myself a loop-hole to crawl out of. And yet if I could only consult him—consult *some one*—find out what I really ought to do. But no, no, I don't dare risk it; it would be terrible to be advised—just the way I don't want. I must decide on some plan myself. But—Heaven knows what!" She stood for a while motionless, gazing helplessly into a mist of perplexities.

The little Sèvres clock on her mantel-piece roused her as it struck the hour, and she began hastily to dress. She drew the rippling waves of her hair into the fashion that Mrs. Bobby liked, she put on her favorite gown, a charming creation of white lace and chiffon, relieved by touches of pale green; she tried conscientiously to look her best, but still her cheeks were pale, there was the strained look in her eyes.

She was about ready when Mrs. Bobby's maid came to help her, bringing a box of flowers that had just that moment arrived. Celeste, a thrifty person, regarded them with some disgust. She could tell them, these gentlemen, that it was of little use to waste their money on Mademoiselle, who did not care about, sometimes hardly glanced at, the flowers which some other young lady would give her eyes to receive. Ah, well, that was the unequal way in which things in this world were arranged. Celeste disposed of the matter thus, with a philosophic French shrug of the shoulders.

But there was no counting on such a capricious person as Mademoiselle. To-night, as she glanced at the card in the box, she blushed beautifully, took out the flowers with care, and read with eager eyes the few lines that the giver had scrawled, apparently in great haste and in pencil:

"This afternoon I was unspeakably rude—even brutal. Forgive me—what right had I to take you to task for your actions? My only excuse is that I care—I can't help caring—so desperately. I send you white roses—they suit you best. You wore one that I gave you—do you remember?—but probably you don't—the first night I saw you. If you are very merciful, if you accept my repentance, wear one to-night—in token of forgiveness."

"In token of forgiveness?" Elizabeth pressed one of the exquisite, creamy-white roses against her glowing cheeks. "You wore one the first night I saw you—probably you don't remember?" Ah, yes, she remembered—but that was different. She could not wear one now. "Yet only in token of forgiveness?" With a quick, passionate gesture, she raised it to her lips, then fastened it carefully amidst the lace of her gown.

Celeste, whose presence she had forgotten, bent down discreetly, with a suppressed smile, to arrange the folds of her train. Ah, clearly, after all, there was one gentleman who did not waste his money on Mademoiselle.

"Madame wished Mademoiselle to look well to-night," she observed, after a moment. "I think Madame will be satisfied."

Mademoiselle glanced at herself again, and started as she looked. Could this brilliant young beauty, her small head proudly erect, her eyes brilliant, her cheeks aflame, be the same woman whose haggard reflection had stared back at her from the same mirror only half-an-hour before?

She did not feel like the same woman. The doubts, the fears, which had beset her then seemed mere chimeras, the fancies of a morbid brain. She felt gay, confident, strong enough to conquer even fate. Celeste was right—she looked her best. Mrs. Bobby's words rang in her ears. "Such trifles have their effect—even on a paragon." And then again—"He would think you perfect as you were if—he loved you." "No, he need not think me perfect," she murmured to her mirror, "but he must—he shall think me beautiful. And that is more to the point," she concluded, as she gathered up fan and gloves and left the room.

The opera that night was Carmen, which peculiarly suited her phase of mind. There is no other which so thoroughly embodies the spirit of recklessness, the triumph of the senses, the frank, impulsive, untrammeled enjoyment of life and of living. To be sure, there is the tragic ending—but before that, three acts of brilliant melody, glowing with color, with warm, sensuous pleasure.

Gerard was waiting in the box when they arrived. On the stage Carmen—that ideal Carmen of whom Mérimée dreamed and Bizet set to music—had just appeared upon the scene of Don Jose's misfortune, and was warbling, with bewitching abandon, the notes of the Habanera.

Gerard's face, which had an anxious look, brightened wonderfully, radiantly, as the two women entered the box. He murmured eagerly a few grateful words in Elizabeth's ear, and took the seat directly behind her, which he did not abandon, even though his predictions were justified, and Mrs. Van Antwerp's box was filled, after the first act, with men who looked anything but pleased at finding that particular place monopolized. Mrs. Bobby, however, seemed delighted to entertain them, was gracious, charming and piquante, and elicited from a stern dowager in the next box severe criticisms on the wiles of young married women, and their reprehensible manner of diverting to themselves the attention due to the young girls under their charge.

Elizabeth hardly noticed the men who entered the box. She sat with eyes fixed upon the stage, upon that intensely real music drama which she had seen many times already, but which never lost its fascination; yet acutely conscious all the while through every fibre of her being of Gerard's presence, of his watching her, of his bending over her, now and again, to murmur a word in her ear. And as for him, she had appealed to him most, perhaps, at least to a certain side of his nature, that afternoon in her pale languor; and yet he could not but feel his senses thrilled, his pulses throb, when she was so warmly, vividly, humanly beautiful as she was tonight. For the moment he was carried beyond himself, his doubts dispelled, or at least forgotten.

And yet, as the evening wore on, some subtle influence in the music or the play seemed to recall them. At the end of the second act she turned to him, the strains of the Toreador song still ringing in her ear, and felt, insensibly a sudden lack of sympathy, a cloud that seemed to have drifted between them. His brows were knit, his face moody.

"You don't like it!" she said, staring up at him with wondering, disappointed eyes.

"What, the opera?" He started as if his thoughts had been elsewhere. "No, I don't like it," he said, frankly. "It jars upon me somehow, brings up memories"—he paused. "Oh, it's some drop of Puritan blood, I suppose," he went on, impatiently, "that asserts itself in me. I can't view the thing from an artistic standpoint. I can't forget for a moment what a heartless creature the woman is. When I see her ruining men's lives, luring them on, turning from one to another—it's too realistic—there are too many women like that"—He was speaking low and bitterly, with a strange vehemence, but suddenly he broke off, with a short laugh. "Oh, it's absurd," he said, "to take a thing like that seriously."

Elizabeth did not smile. She leaned back in her chair as if she were suddenly weary. "Poor Carmen!" she said, in a low voice. "You're very hard on her." She held up her fan before her eyes, as if the light hurt them. A shadow seemed to fall upon her beauty, effacing its color and brilliance, bringing out again into strong relief the dark rings under the eyes, the lines about the mouth. She sat in silence for awhile, but suddenly she turned to him.

"I'm going to shock you, I'm afraid," she said, "but—do you know—somehow I can't help seeing the other side. What is a woman to do, if she changes against her will? Is she to abide always, inexorably, by the results of a mistake?" A note of passionate feeling thrilled her voice, she fixed her eyes anxiously, intently, upon Gerard. "There are so many questions that might arise," she went on, eagerly, as he did not answer at once. "One might, for instance, make a promise—a very solemn promise, and find out afterwards that it was—a mistake, that it would ruin one's whole life to keep it; and—and one might break it, and the other person might think himself very much injured; and yet—would you think the woman in that case so very much to blame?"

Gerard thought he understood. With the conviction came a sense of passionate relief, which yet he hesitated, with the fastidious scruples of a proud and honorable man, to grasp in its entirety.

"I—I don't think I'm competent to express an opinion," he said, in a low voice. "You should ask—some one else."

"There's no one else whom I can ask," she said quickly, and with her eyes always fixed imploringly upon him. "Tell me—what you think. What should a woman do in a case like that?"

"I—it's a difficult situation," he said, still holding under control his eager desire to advise her in the only way in which it seemed to him possible to advise her. But how could he trust his own judgment? "I"—he hesitated—"Personally," he said, "I can't imagine holding a woman to a promise that she has—repented of; but other men might—probably would feel differently."

"Yes," she said, sadly, "he—this man does."

"And you—the woman is quite sure she has made a mistake," he asked, eagerly.

"Yes, yes, quite sure," she said, quickly, "a terrible mistake."

"Then," said Gerard, and he drew a long sigh as of intense relief, "I don't think there could be two opinions on the subject. No one could advise you—this woman to ruin her life for a mistake, especially if the—the man were unworthy?" He looked at her questioningly.

"He seemed to her unworthy," she said, in a low voice.

"Then, for Heaven's sake," he asked, almost fiercely, "how can you hesitate?"

She did not speak, but turned her eyes towards the stage and again placed her fan so that it shielded them. All over the house there was the subdued rustle of people returning to their seats. The orchestra sounded the first notes of the third act, the curtain rose upon the gypsy camp. During Michaela's solo and the scene between the two men, Elizabeth still sat silent, her fan before her face. The act was well advanced before she turned to Gerard.

"Then," she said, "you would advise me to—to break my word?"

"Under the circumstances—yes," he said, steadily. "But don't," he went on quickly, and passionate vibration thrilled his voice, more unrepressed than ever before, "don't be guided by my opinion. In this particular case it is—impossible for me to judge impartially."

"Is it," she asked softly, and then added quickly, as if to avert an answer, "still, I'm glad to know your opinion. I feel sure you wouldn't say what you don't think. Thank you—thank you very much." Her tone was low and subdued, like that of a grateful child. She leaned back in her chair with a look of relief, that seemed both physical and mental. She did not speak again till near the end of the act, when Carmen reads her fortune in the cards. "I wonder," Elizabeth said then, softly, "what she sees in them."

"I had my fortune told once," she observed, turning to Gerard, as the curtain fell. "It was when I was at school, and I went with one of the girls to a famous palmist. He told me all sorts of strange, true things about the past, and about the future."—She paused.

"Well, about the future?" he asked, smiling. "One doesn't care about the past. But he predicted, no doubt, all sorts of delightful things about the future?"

"No." She stared thoughtfully before her with knit brows. "He said"—she spoke low and hesitatingly—"he said there was luck in my hand—plenty of it; I should have splendid opportunities. But—he said there was a line of misfortune, which crossed the other line and might make it utterly useless; that there was danger of some kind—he couldn't tell what, threatening me about my twenty-first year, and that, you know, is very near; he said there were strange lines—tragic, unusual,"—

She stopped. "It sounds very ridiculous," but though she tried to smile, her voice trembled, "and yet—I remember it frightened me at the time, and does still—a little—when I think of it."

"But you don't surely," cried Gerard, "my dear child, you don't suppose he knew a thing about it?"

"I don't know. I believe I'm superstitious—are not you?"

"I'm afraid I am," he said, "but not about things like that. I've seen too many predictions of the kind prove false, to give them a thought."

"It *is* foolish to worry about them," she admitted, but still she sat apparently deep in thought and played absently with her fan. At last she looked up with her most brilliant smile. "I don't know why it is," she said, "but we seem to be fated on unpleasant subjects. And yet the opera is so gay. Do let us try, for the rest of the evening, to think of pleasant things." She turned and held out her hand, smiling, to a man who entered the box. For the rest of the opera she was brilliant, animated, beautiful, as she had been at first.

"And now you are satisfied," she said, looking at Gerard with laughing eyes, as the curtain fell for the last time. "Carmen comes to a bad end. According to your principles! she deserved it."

"Ah, my principles!" he said, smiling. "I'm afraid I don't live up to them very much."

"Don't you?" She gave him a quick, searching glance, as he stood with her cloak in his hand. "I wish I could believe that," she murmured. "I should be a little less—afraid of you."

He placed the cloak about her shoulders. "It is I who am afraid of you," he whispered, bending over her, "and have been ever since I knew you."

Her eyes fell, and she fumbled nervously with the fastening of the cloak. "Ah, you were afraid of me?" she said, under her breath. "And now"—

"Oh, I've grown very brave," he murmured, as he followed her out of the box, "you can't frighten me away any longer." The jesting words lingered in her ear as they left the Opera House.

"Ah, if he knew!" she said to herself, as she sank into her corner of the carriage. "He doesn't know. And yet I told him the exact truth. It's not my fault, if he—misunderstood."

And Gerard meanwhile was telling himself that he understood it all.

"Poor child!" he murmured to himself, as he lit a cigar and sauntered slowly home. "So that was it. Of course, she thought she loved him—the first man she met, and when he turned up felt herself bound—I see it all! And she has suffered— had terrible pangs of conscience over this thing. And I who misjudged her all this time—imagined I don't know what—could I have advised her differently? Surely not. The fellow's not worthy of her. Neither am I. She won't look at me, probably. And yet—one can but try"—

Chapter XXII

IT was mentioned generally, at various sewing-classes and other mild functions during Lent, that Julian Gerard was very attentive, all of a sudden, to Elizabeth Van Vorst. Some people, less accurate or more imaginative than the rest, went so far as to announce the engagement as an actual fact.

"And, if so, it's all Eleanor Van Antwerp's doing," Mrs. Hartington observed in private to her intimate friends. "She was determined to make the match from the beginning. I saw the way she threw the girl at his head at a dinner in the country, but I never for a moment thought she would succeed—with Julian Gerard of all men, who is so desperately afraid of being taken in."

Julian Gerard, by that time, had well-nigh forgotten that such a fear had ever disturbed him, or if he did remember it, it was to regard it, so far as Elizabeth was concerned, as profanation. Since that evening at the opera, his remorseful fancy had placed her on a pinnacle, which she found at times, it must be confessed, a little difficult to maintain. It was his misfortune and hers, that he could never view her in the right perspective, never realize that she was neither a saint nor the reverse, but merely a woman, and painfully human at that.

But since he chose to consider her a saint, she did her best to live up to the character. She kept Lent strictly that year as she had never done before, went to church morning and evening, denied herself bonbons and other luxuries, and worked with unskilled fingers but great diligence at certain oddly-constructed garments which were doled out to her and other young women every week as a Lenten penance, and incidentally for the good of the poor. If in most cases the actual penance fell to the lot of their maids, why, the poor were none the wiser, and certainly much the better clothed. But Elizabeth insisted on putting in all the painful stitches in the hard, coarse stuff herself, and looked very pretty bending over it, as Mr. Gerard thought when he came in one day and found her thus employed.

It pleased him, of course. He did not attach much importance, himself, to these things—this constant church-going, these small penances; yet, manlike, it seemed to him right and fitting that she should regard them differently. And then it was pleasant, after service, to meet her in the vestibule. How many incipient love affairs have been helped along, brought to a climax perhaps, by the convenient afternoon service, and the sauntering walks home in the lingering twilight!

To Elizabeth there was an indefinable charm in those ever-lengthening Lenten days, rung in and out to the music of church bells, and marked, as the season advanced and Easter approached, by the growing green of the grass, and the budding shoots of the trees, and the intangible feeling of spring in the air. That sense of dread, of impending misfortune, which had been for a short time almost unbearable, was lulled to sleep as by an opiate. She did not think of the past or the future, she simply drifted from day to day, and each of these was pleasanter than the last.

For one thing, she had grown hardened, indifferent almost to the constant meeting with Paul Halleck. She had kept her word and obtained for him all the invitations in her power, until he no longer needed her help. He was a great success. Mrs. Van Antwerp's informal little musicale had been only the first of a series of more elaborate ones, at which Halleck was often the chief attraction. Young girls admired him extremely. Elizabeth could hear him talking to them, just as he had once talked to her, about Swinburne and Rossetti and the last word in Art, and she saw that, like herself, they thought him very brilliant. It was an admiration which had tangible results, since it led to an interest in music, and a desire to take singing-lessons from the talented young barytone. Before long, he took a studio in Carnegie, near D'Hauteville's, and furnished it luxuriously, on the strength of his new prosperity. He was very much the fashion and absorbed in his success, and seldom had the time, or perhaps the inclination, to encounter Elizabeth's unflattering indifference. So for the most part he left her alone, to her intense relief.

One incident, a chance word, in a retrospect of that time, afterwards stood out in Elizabeth's mind, though at the moment it seemed to make but a slight impression.

It was one Sunday afternoon when a number of people, Paul Halleck among them, had dropped in to afternoon tea, and the conversation happened to turn upon palmistry. Elizabeth did not proffer her own experience. She listened silently to what the others said on the subject.

"I can't say I have implicit faith in it," observed Mrs. Bobby. "I was told by a fortune-teller that I should marry a dark man, who would beat me and treat me horribly; and as you see, I've married a fair man—who treats me pretty well on the whole."

Bobby, who was leaning against the mantel-piece his tea-cup in his hand, smiled serenely.

"Don't boast too soon, Eleanor," he said, lazily, "there's no knowing what brutal tendencies I may develop yet."

Mrs. Hartington, who was seated near him on a low chair, looked up into his face with a sympathetic smile. "Are you one of those long-suffering husbands who turn at last, Mr. Van Antwerp?" she asked, sweetly. "It would be good discipline, I think, for Eleanor not to have her own way *always*."

Bobby looked down at her coolly for a moment with his calm blue eyes. "No doubt, it would be good discipline for all of us, Mrs. Hartington," he said, in his pleasant, clear-cut tones, "but as my wife's way and mine are generally the same, I'm afraid I'm not likely to inflict it."

Mrs. Hartington looked down with an injured air, adding another to her list of grievances against her dear friend and neighbor, Eleanor Van Antwerp.

"I should never go to a common fortune-teller, my dear," she observed in a louder tone, for the benefit of the assembled company. "Yours was probably just an ignorant person. But I did go to ——, who, you know, charges a small fortune, and he told me the most extraordinary things. I have perfect confidence in him; every one I know thinks him quite infallible."

"Do they?" said Paul Halleck, suddenly turning from the piano. He shrugged his shoulders. "I devoutly hope you are mistaken," he said. "—— read my hand in Paris, and told me some very unpleasant things; among others that I was probably destined to a violent death. This year of my life, by the way—the twenty-seventh—was to be my fatal year."

He spoke half laughingly, but the words produced an effect. There was a general exclamation of horror, and Elizabeth, who was pouring tea, dropped the cup that she held in her hand. Julian Gerard, who was standing behind her, bent down to recover the fragments.

"It's odd," he said, as he placed them absently on the table, "his year of danger and yours seem to correspond." The words rose involuntarily to his lips, and an instant later he wished them unspoken.

She flushed a little, then grew pale. "Oh, I'm sorry you remembered that nonsense," she said. "I don't really believe in these things." But her hand trembled as she poured out the tea, glancing furtively at Halleck as she did so.

He was enjoying the sensation that his announcement had created. "Yes," he was saying, "if I live to be a year older, I am safe; but till then—Heaven knows what danger threatens me!" He shrugged his shoulders with a light laugh. The prediction did not seem to trouble him greatly. Elizabeth wondered if he had not invented it, for the sake of the effect. And then, involuntarily, the thought crossed her mind—what if it were really true, and the prediction were fulfilled? Such things had been known to happen—there might be something in it.... Quick as lightning the thought flashed through her mind of all that his death might mean to her—the merciful release, the solution of all difficulties.... Just for a moment the idea lingered, while the others talked, and she shuddered.

"You are quite pale," said Gerard, fixing his eyes upon her. He was still sensitive to any sign of feeling which Halleck seemed to arouse in her. "I believe you are really superstitious. These things seem to frighten you."

"Am I superstitious?" She looked up at him dreamily. "Perhaps I am. It would be nice, I think, if there were something in it, if one could tell what is going to happen. One could act accordingly. I should like, for instance"—her voice sank—"I should like to look into the future one year, and see what fate has in store for me."

"If I had any control over fate"—Gerard crushed back the impetuous words that followed. Not yet—the moment was not propitious. Besides, he was not sure of her. There was still at times something in her manner that was baffling, uncertain.—And just then Paul Halleck sauntered up and bent over her in that intimate manner which still annoyed Gerard's fastidious taste, even though he had long since convinced himself that he had no cause to fear him as a rival.

"Did you hear ——'s terrible prediction, Miss Van Vorst?" Paul asked, smiling, "and aren't you sorry for my untimely fate?"

Chapter XXIII

"WHY will you never play for me?"

Gerard stood leaning on the piano, his eyes half smiling, yet with a look of mastery, fixed upon Elizabeth. She was sitting in a low chair by the fire, the book on her lap which she had been reading when he came in. It was a stormy March afternoon, and the dusk was closing in prematurely. The room was already in shadow, except where the firelight formed a little circle of radiance, illumining Elizabeth's face and hair. Seated thus in the full glow of light, with the shadows in the foreground, all the little details of her appearance—the broad sweep of rippling hair on her forehead, the soft laces at her throat, the pale, dull green of her gown, even to the buckle on her slipper, and the one white rose in her belt—each trifling part of the harmonious whole, impressed itself on his memory, haunting him afterwards with a keen sense of pain.

She looked up at him now from under her long lashes, with the old light in her eyes, half defiant, half tantalizing—that spirit of revolt which still glanced forth at times to baffle and disturb him.

"I don't want to play this afternoon. I don't—feel in the mood."

"You are never in the mood when I ask you." Silence. "Confess at once," said Gerard, with some heat—"for it would really be quite as civil—that you don't wish to play for me."

Another swift upward glance. "Perhaps I don't"—demurely.—"You're too severe a critic."

"You know," said Gerard, "that that is not the reason."

Silence again. "Will you tell me the reason?" he asked.

She answered him this time with a flash of defiance. "I don't know," she said, "what right you have to demand it. But if you insist upon it, I'll tell you. You—you don't like my playing, and—it's very absurd, of course, but I never can play for people who don't."

"I—don't like your playing?" He shielded his eyes for a moment, as if from the glare of the fire. When he spoke again his tone was peremptory. "You foolish child," he said, "come and play for me, and I'll tell you, afterwards, what I think of it."

She looked up at him—startled, rebellious, met his eyes for a moment, then rose, pouting, like the child that he called her, constrained against her will, put down her book, and moved slowly toward the piano. "You are so terribly determined," she complained.

"And you are so terribly perverse! But when I want a thing very much, I can be determined, as you say. Play me the Fire-music," he went on, "and—and 'Tristan and Isolde,' as you did—do you remember?—the first night I met you."

She paused, with her hands on the keys. "I—I thought,"—she began, and then broke off suddenly, and began to play as he bade her—at first faltering, uncertainly, with a strange hesitation; then more firmly, as the keys responded with the old readiness to her touch, and she lost herself in the music. Outside the storm increased, the rain beat against the windows, the room grew dark, and once Elizabeth paused—she could hardly see the keys. But Gerard murmured, "Ah, the love-music!" and she played on. All the terrible distress, the maddening perplexity, of the last few months seemed to express themselves, in spite of herself, in those surging, strenuous chords; all the hope, too, and the wild unreasoning happiness. She was startled, almost as if she were telling the whole story in language so eloquent that he must surely understand it without further words. But Gerard, as was natural, read into it only his own feelings. He stood leaning on the piano, his hand shielding his eyes, which were fixed intently upon her.—It was so dark now that he could hardly see her face, only the shimmer of her hair standing out against the dusk, the movement of her white hands on the keys.

She faltered at last, struck a false chord, and broke off in the very midst of the love-music. "I—I can't see," she murmured, and let her hands fall in her lap.

"Do you remember," Gerard said, "that first night you played? I had talked to you at dinner, you know, you—you repelled me a little. I thought—I am telling you the bare truth, you see—you were a little cynical, a little hard—it seemed a pity when you were so"—he paused for a moment and his voice softened as he lingered over the word—"so beautiful. I couldn't understand you. I thought—I wouldn't try. It wasn't worth while—most things were not. And then—you played"—He paused again for a moment. "You know what most girls' playing is like. Yours has a soul, a fire—I don't know where you get it. It moved me, set me thinking, as no other woman's playing has done for years."

He paused again. Elizabeth looked up quickly. "I thought," she murmured, "that you didn't like my playing, that you were bored"—

"Ah, you thought," he said, "that when a man feels very much, he can make pretty speeches? I can't, at least. Oh, I've no doubt"—he made a resigned gesture—"I've no doubt that I behaved like a brute. Women have told me that I generally do. I said to myself—that girl is dangerous, she could make a man fall in love with her—even against his will. I was in love once—but that's another story. I never wanted to repeat the experiment. And so, as you know, I avoided you; like a fool, I used to go and look at your picture, and then—keep away from you, evening after evening. I struggled—with all the strength I have—I struggled not to love you. And then, as you know"—he looked her straight in the eyes—"as you have known well these last few weeks,—I failed."

There was silence for a moment. She was very white, her hands were tightly clasped in her lap. "I"—she gave a little shuddering sigh—"it would have been better if you hadn't."

"Elizabeth!" She felt rather than saw how his face changed. "Elizabeth," he said, hoarsely, "do you mean that? Then"—as she sat silent—"you don't love me?"

Oh, for the strength to answer "No," and end this scene—this useless, perplexing scene, which she should have been prepared for, which yet seemed to have come upon her unawares! One firm, courageous "No," and a man like Gerard would not ask her twice. Instead, a compromise, useless, feeble, hovered on her lips. "I—shouldn't make you happy," she faltered out, despising her own weakness.

"Is that all?" He laughed out loud in sheer relief. "My darling,"—the triumphant tenderness in his voice was hard to bear—"don't you think that I can judge of that?"

She was silent, and he drew nearer to her and took her hands in his. "You needn't be afraid," he said. "I shall worship the ground you tread upon, if—if you will only consent. You will, Elizabeth, won't you?" She had not known before that his voice held tones so caressingly gentle.

For a moment she sat motionless, passive beneath his touch, and then suddenly: "I can't," she broke out, hoarsely, drew her hands away from him, and going over to the mantel-piece, she leaned her arms upon it and hid her face.

When he spoke again, after a long silence, his voice was entirely changed. "There is something here I don't understand," he said, coldly. "One moment you seemed to yield, and the next"——He made a step towards her. "Tell me the truth," he entreated, "don't spare my feelings. It's a false kindness. You love someone else—is that it?—then tell me so, and I won't reproach you—or—trouble you again."

She turned her face towards him. It was white, quivering with emotion; but she answered firmly: "No, you are entirely wrong. There is—no one else."

"Not Halleck?" he asked, watching her intently, his face dark with the old distrust.

She made a quick, involuntary gesture of repulsion. "Not he—not he, of all people," she said, bitterly.

He still eyed her doubtfully, unsatisfied. "You are sure?" he insisted. "You are telling me the whole truth? Don't deceive me—now, Elizabeth; I could forgive anything but that."

How many chances were given to Elizabeth, only to be thrown away! She answered him steadily; "I'm not deceiving you. I tell you frankly that when I first met Paul Halleck I thought I cared for him—he was the first man I had ever known; but now he is nothing to me, and I have told him so—I think I almost dislike him." There was no mistaking the accent of sincerity in her voice. It was fortunate for Elizabeth, since she was no adept in lying, that the truth and the falsehood were in this case so nearly identical.

Gerard was satisfied.

"Then what," he urged, eagerly—"if there is no one else—what stands between us?"

She hesitated. There were voices in the hall, some visitors requesting admission, the butler parleying a little—the discreet, intelligent butler, who had so considerately refrained, for the last quarter of an hour, from coming in to light the gas.

Gerard was too absorbed to notice anything outside of the cause he was pleading. "Tell me," he repeated, his eyes fixed intently upon her face, "what stands between us?"

She put out her hand with a deprecating gesture. That threatening interruption seemed to give her courage. She was quite herself again. "Can't a woman hesitate for no definite reason?" she asked. "You, yourself—didn't you hesitate—for reasons that I must confess seem to me rather vague and—not very complimentary."

The argument struck home. He changed color. "Don't cast that up against me, Elizabeth," he pleaded. "It's not worthy of you. I told you the plain truth, badly as it sounds, because it seemed due to you—I wanted you to know the worst. And you must remember that I had no reason to suppose that you cared, or would ever care, anything about me. It was only I who suffered when I kept away from you. But you—now that you know how—how madly I love you—don't trifle with me—be generous—give me a definite answer?"

"But I—I can't," she returned, in her old wilful way, "just on the spur of the moment, like this. I don't want to marry any one—not just now, at least. I—I like my freedom"——

The words died away on her lips. She broke off suddenly, turning very pale, as the importunate visitor, whom the butler had vainly endeavored to show into another room, drew aside the portière and entered brusquely. It was Paul Halleck. He had a strangely excited look, which increased as he surveyed the two people on the hearth-rug, whom he had evidently interrupted at a critical moment.

To one of them, at least, his entrance was most unwelcome. Not all of Gerard's carefully cultivated self-control could avail to hide his annoyance; he uttered under his breath an angry exclamation, and going over to the piano, stood moodily turning over sheets of music. Elizabeth, to whom Paul's appearance was for some reasons still more disconcerting, showed greater self-possession. She held out her hand coldly, but composedly, with a few mechanical words, to which he barely responded. There was an embarrassing pause, broken by the butler, who made his belated, majestic entry, lighted the chandeliers and drew the curtains. The effect of the illumination was startling, as it threw into strong relief the look of agitation on each of their faces.

"It—it's storming still, isn't it?" said Elizabeth, and then remembered that she had asked the same question already. Gerard started up and reflecting gloomily that it was of no use to try to "stay that fellow out," he took his leave. Paul and Elizabeth were left alone.

His presence seemed a matter of absolute indifference to Elizabeth, who sank again into the low chair by the fire, and picking up the book she had laid down, turned over its pages with an air of icy unconcern. He came and stood beside her, leaning against the mantel-piece, a look of brutality on his handsome face.

"So," he said. "I've driven Gerard away. A case of 'two is company,' evidently."

Her expression did not change. "Oh, he had been here some time," she said, coldly. "No doubt he meant to leave in any case."

"Oh, no doubt." He sneered angrily. "Do you know what I heard to-day?" he went on. "I heard that you were engaged to him."

She flushed a little. "Did you?" she said, and then, quietly: "But that means nothing, you know."

"But you are together all the time. I can't come to the house without meeting him. You encourage him, accept his flowers, lead him on.—Pray, how long is this sort of thing going to last?"

They eyed each other for a moment, he flushed with anger, she cold and hard. "You have no right," she said, icily, "to ask an account of my actions."

"No right!" he repeated, as if thunder-struck. "I should like to know who has a better."

"No right that I acknowledge, at least," she amended her first sentence.

He paced up and down the room, struggling for self-control. "Whether you acknowledge it or not, is immaterial," he said, stopping suddenly in front of her. "I claim it, and that is enough. You must give up this infernal flirtation with Gerard, or"——

"Or what?" she insisted haughtily, as he paused.

"I shall go to Gerard at once and tell him the truth," he concluded, defiantly.

Dead silence. The book she held fell from Elizabeth's nerveless hand. The steady ticking of the clock in the stillness seemed to beat an accompaniment to these words: "Don't deceive me—now, Elizabeth; I could forgive anything but that."

"Paul?" Her voice was no longer icy, but soft, with caressing tones. "Paul, you wouldn't be so unkind?"

"What difference does it make to you?" he said, eyeing her keenly, "whether I tell Gerard or not? You can't marry him, you know—it's impossible."

"I don't want to marry him," she said, gathering all her powers of resistance, "but—he's a friend of mine. I don't want him to be told things about me by—an outsider."

"Ah, you call me that!" he said, his anger roused again. "Well, outsider or not, I hold the cards. I shall go to Gerard at once and tell him that we were married—at Cranston, last July. If he doubts my assertion, the record is there, and it won't be very hard for him to verify it."

Silence again. Elizabeth sat musing, her brows knit, her under lip slightly thrust out, in a fashion that seemed to express all the obstinate resolve of her nature. "I will do as you wish, if you will keep silent."

"Will you write a note to Gerard," Paul demanded, "sending him away?"

"No," she said, sullenly. "I won't do that."

"Then there is nothing else you can do," he declared.

Elizabeth mused again. "I would give—money," she said. The last word was spoken very low.

He started and flushed. "Do you want to bribe me?" he asked, angrily.

She shrugged her shoulders. "I am quite aware that you will not do anything for nothing," she said.

Paul fell again to pacing up and down the room. His face showed traces of a mental struggle. Elizabeth watched him from the corners of her eyes; she saw that her offer tempted him more than she had dared to hope.

He stopped at last in front of her. "How much can you spare?" he asked, in a voice in which a certain bravado strove to gain the mastery over inward uneasiness and shame. "The truth is, I am most confoundedly hard up just now, what with furnishing the studio and everything, and if you could help me a little, it would be very convenient. I can pay you back later with interest a hundred times."

"I have told you," she said, coldly, "what payment I want."

He shrugged his shoulders, with an attempt at nonchalance. "Oh, as to that, I never really intended to tell Gerard." Elizabeth's lip curled.

"How much money do you want?" she asked, curtly. "A hundred? Two hundred?" Her ideas on such matters were vague. Paul's face fell.

"I should need five hundred at least, if—if it is to be of any use," he said, gloomily.

It was more than she expected, but she showed no signs of flinching. "Five hundred, then," she said, rising as if to conclude the interview. "Will it do, if I let you have it to-morrow?"

"Perfectly. Elizabeth, you are an angel. I can't thank you enough." He advanced towards her with outstretched arms, but with a gesture of repulsion she waved him aside.

"Don't thank me," she said, coldly. "This is a bargain for our mutual advantage. I will fulfil my share of it if you remember yours. And now, as we have nothing more to discuss, I think I will ask you to excuse me." She made him a stately inclination, picked up her book and sailed from the room in undiminished dignity and apparent unconcern.

But when she was alone and had locked herself into her room to think over her misery, then, indeed, the situation stared her in the face in its true colors. Her own words, "I like my freedom," rang mockingly in her ears. She was not free, but a slave; slave of a man who had her in his power, and would use it, as time went on, more and more unscrupulously. This time it was five hundred that he demanded; next time it would be a thousand. What could she do? Somehow or another, he must be satisfied. Anything was better, any sacrifice, any humiliation, than to allow him to go to Gerard with that bare statement of facts, "We were married at Cranston, last July!" The truth, devoid of any of the softening evasions by which she cloaked it to her own mind; the redeeming circumstances which excused, if they did not justify, her silence.

Her bitterest enemy must admit that the position was a hard one. A contract entered into hastily by a thoughtless girl, on the impulse of the moment; a quarter of an hour in an empty church one summer day; a few words spoken before a sleepy old clergyman and indifferent witnesses—could such things as these have power to ruin one's whole life? No, no—her heart cried out wildly to the contrary. The whole episode seemed, in the retrospect, so dream-like. It was easy to imagine that it had never happened. And yet, had she the courage to ignore it?... And, even if she had, there was always Paul to remind her of it, who would not give her up without a terrible struggle, that must, without fail, come to Gerard's ears.

There was only one hope that she could see, and that was wild and irrational; the hope Paul had himself suggested. If that prediction could be fulfilled! Elizabeth shuddered. It was terrible to think of such a thing; terrible to obtain one's own happiness at the cost of another person's life. She did not really wish Paul dead—that would be wicked. And yet—and yet—the thought pressed irresistibly upon her—if it had to be!—if it had to be! What a blessed relief—what an end to all this misery! "Oh, I do wish it, I do wish it!" she broke out, speaking aloud, unconsciously. "I would give anything in this world to hear of his death."

She stopped, startled at the sound of her own voice. The wish shocked her, even in the moment of expressing it. Her wishes were so often fulfilled—she had an almost superstitious faith in their efficacy. If this one were fulfilled, what then?— For a moment she, thinking it over, balanced possibilities; and then with a stifled cry, fell on her knees and hid her face in her hands.

"Oh, I'm growing so wicked," she sobbed out. "It's because I'm so miserable. Only let me have what I want, and I'll be different; I'll be the kind of woman that he admires; only—I must find a way, I must have what I want—*first.*"

Chapter XXIV

THE next day dawned clear and bright; a beautiful morning in early spring after a night of storm. Upon Elizabeth's spirits as she dressed the weather produced the illogical effect that it does upon most of us. Reviewed by daylight, the situation seemed to her many degrees less desperate. The night before, there had seemed to her only one way out, and that a tragical one; but now there were—there must be—a hundred ways, if only she could gain the time to think of them.

The first thing was to obtain the money; but this in itself was no easy matter. She had promised it to Paul as if it were a mere trifle; yet, as a matter of fact, she was as badly off herself at the time as was to be expected of a young woman who had gone out a great deal, and established and lived up to an expensive reputation for being always well and appropriately gowned.

She reviewed her resources. Mrs. Bobby would have lent her the money at once and asked no questions; but from this course Elizabeth's pride shrank uncontrollably. She preferred to take a sum she had just laid aside to satisfy to some extent the claims of a long-suffering and complaisant dressmaker; but even with this sacrifice determined on, she was still far short of the amount required. She took out, in desperation, her various jewels and trinkets, and looked them over, wondering how much they were worth. There were many pretty things her aunts had given her, none of them probably of any great intrinsic value, and there were the beautiful gifts that Mrs. Bobby had showered upon her; and, finally, there was the string of pearls which she always wore about her neck, one of the few heirlooms which old Madam Van Vorst had once kept under lock and key, and which her daughters had of course made over to Elizabeth. The girl stood now hesitating with the pearls in her hand. She had worn them to every ball that winter, she was wont to say, with her half-joking, half-real touch of superstition, that they brought her luck; as if, with their possession, something of the spirit of that proud beauty of a by-gone day had entered into her, enabling her to conquer the world in which the older woman had been naturally at home. Would the power leave her with the pearls? The fantastic thought lingered for a moment, and then impatiently she thrust it aside, and put the precious heirloom in with the rest of her possessions, which she had resolved to sacrifice. It was not a moment when she could afford to dally with sentiment.

Yet what a strange, disreputable proceeding it seemed! She was haunted with a vague sense of losing caste, as she took her trinkets to one of the smaller jewelry-shops, and faltered out her improbable tale of their being unbecoming and of no use to her. The jeweler, well used to the straits of fashionable young women, listened without a smile, and offered her on the whole a fair price, though it was much less than she expected. There was nothing that she was not obliged to part with—from the jeweled watch which Mrs. Bobby had given her at Christmas, to the pearls, which proved to be the most valuable of all. When she left the shop she had deprived herself of all her ornaments, but she held the necessary bribe in her hand, and as the simplest way of conveying it to Halleck, she got on a cable car and went up at once to his studio at Carnegie. There was nothing startling in the proceeding, for he had now a number of pupils, who came to him at his studio; and though the girls whom Elizabeth knew always brought their maids, or a chaperone of some sort, she was not in the mood to waste much thought on conventionalities. Her one idea was to fulfil her share of the bargain before he should, perchance, have repented of his, and she did not think of the chance of meeting any one. Her own affairs had reached a crisis which blinded her to the fact that to other people, the world was progressing peacefully, in the usual order of events.

This dream-like state of indifference to all but the one anxiety continued till she reached Carnegie and was borne up in the elevator to Paul's studio, which was directly opposite to Mr. D'Hauteville's. And here, for the first time, she paused, seized by a sudden panic. From behind the closed curtain at the end of the small vestibule, there came the sound of a woman's voice, strained, nasal, raised high in what seemed a tirade of denunciation. To Elizabeth's mind, as she heard it, there arose an involuntary recollection of Bassett Mills, and of the gaudy little parlor behind her aunt's shop, and some bitter words directed against herself, in what seemed a past period of her history. She stood hesitating, terrified; then the curtain was pushed aside, and a woman came out. It was her cousin Amanda. Her face was white and set, her eyes blazing. She stared at Elizabeth for a moment as if dazed, then brushed past her without a word.

Paul stood on the threshold, a picturesque object in his velveteen coat and turned-down collar, against the artistic background of the luxuriously-furnished studio. He looked flushed, annoyed; the scene which had just taken place had evidently been a trying one. But when he saw Elizabeth standing doubtful in the hall, his face cleared and he came forward to greet her with effusion.

"Darling, how good of you to come here!" He evidently hailed the visit as an overture towards reconciliation. She hastened to disabuse him.

"It was the easiest way to bring this," she said, handing him the package which she had clasped nervously all the way up. "Will you be kind enough, please, to count it and see if it is all right?" It was impossible to speak with more icy brevity, or to impart to any proceeding a more severely business-like air.

He flushed uncomfortably, but did not allow his vexation to interfere with the evident necessity of counting the money. "It is all right," he said, biting his lips, as he put down the last roll of bills. "Do you wish me to give you a receipt?" he asked, with fine sarcasm.

"No," said Elizabeth, gravely. "I rely on your word."

Paul bowed. "Thank you," he said. "And now—is there anything else I can do for you?"

"Nothing," said Elizabeth, briefly, "except what you know already. And now, I must go." She moved towards the door, but he placed himself in her way.

"Come, come, Elizabeth," he said. "I'm not going to let you go like that— the first time you make me a visit. Give me a kiss now, just to show that you don't bear malice."

Elizabeth's only reply was a look of ineffable haughtiness. "Will you let me pass, please?" she said, in a low tone of concentrated wrath, and with an uneasy laugh, he obeyed her.

"What a virago you are!" he said, "almost as bad as your cousin Amanda. It must be the hair," he added, with a sneer, but Elizabeth did not pause to reply. Anxious only to escape, she closed the studio door hastily behind her, and a moment later the elevator bore her swiftly down, and she regained the street, with the feeling of having staved off misfortune, for the moment at least.

She found, when she got home, a note from Gerard, informing her that he had been unexpectedly called out of town for a few days on business, but hoped to see her on his return. There were the flowers, too, which he sent her daily. He had no intention, evidently, of taking her answer of the day before as final. She realized this, with a thrill that held in it more of pleasure than alarm. Still, she was glad that he was out of town. His absence was a reprieve, giving her more of the time she wanted, though it is hard to say what she expected to gain by it. But very little often sufficed to restore Elizabeth's spirits. She was going out to dinner that evening, and she dressed for it with a mind that was comparatively at ease.

But poor Elizabeth's moments of tranquillity just then were short. She was nearly dressed when Celeste entered with the information that a young person had called to see Mademoiselle, who insisted upon seeing her at once. "I told her that Mademoiselle is dressing," said the maid, with expressive gestures; "that she has an engagement, it is most important, but—but she is a most determined young person, she insists that I bring up a message at once."

"It is Amanda, of course," thought Elizabeth, with a terrible sinking of the heart. She had forgotten, until that moment, the meeting in the studio. She glanced at the clock. "I have fifteen minutes, Celeste," she said. "Show her up. She may want to see me about something important." The maid departed, and Elizabeth bent down nervously to sort out gloves and handkerchief, wondering as she did now at each unexpected incident, what danger it might portend.

"I thought," said Amanda, "I might come up—seeing we're first cousins." She stood in the door-way, her eyes roaming about the room, taking in every detail—the soft prevailing harmonies of pale blue and rose, the firelight flickering on the tiled hearth, the shining silver ornaments on the dressing-table, the profusion of bric-à-brac, of cotillion favors, the roses in the china bowl, the general air of luxury—all a fit setting to the proud young beauty, standing before the mirror in her shimmering white satin and laces.

"My, but you look fine!" said Amanda, under her breath. A slightly awed expression crossed her face, modifying the assurance of her entrance. "You're going out?" she asked, looking almost ready to retreat.

"To dinner—yes; but not just yet. Won't you sit down, Amanda?" Elizabeth said, trying to speak easily. "I—I'm glad to see you. How is Aunt Rebecca, and—every one at Bassett Mills?"

Amanda sat down, her eyes still wandering eagerly around the room. Elizabeth, looking at her, saw the unfavorable change that a few months had made.

True, she was smartly dressed, with the cheap, tawdry smartness that can be bought ready-made at the shops, and her hat was tilted carefully at the fashionable angle; her hair, growing low about her forehead, had still the pretty, natural wave to it, which was a legacy from the fever, and the general effect at a first glance was striking. But the face, under the jaunty, be-feathered hat, was white and haggard, the eyes had a wild restless look, there were hard, vindictive lines about the mouth. Her hands moved incessantly, plucking at the fringe on her gown.

"Glad? Well, I guess you're not very glad to see me," she said, with a strange, mocking smile, ignoring the latter part of Elizabeth's speech. "There never was much love lost between us, and now—but still I thought I'd pay you a visit. I'm staying with Uncle Ben's folks, and they told me I ought to look up my swell cousin—since you were so sure to want to see me"—she gave a short, jarring laugh. "That stuck-up maid wouldn't believe me—thought I was crazy, when I said we were first cousins. I don't see why—I'm sure I don't look so—so different as all that." Her voice sank into rather a wistful key, and she stole a glance at the long pier-glass that stood opposite her. "I got my suit at a bargain sale," she said. "The girls said it was—real stylish."

"It's very pretty," said Elizabeth, gently. She glanced at Amanda with a sudden pity that overpowered her first annoyance and alarm at the inopportune visit. What had brought her to town? Some vague, irrational hope of winning back Paul's admiration, perhaps, with this gown that was "real stylish," and the new hat, and the general, tawdry attempt at smartness. It was that, probably, which had taken her to the studio, and no doubt Paul had been disgusted with this attempt to revive an old flirtation, and in his irritation, had convinced her somewhat rudely of his indifference. Poor Amanda! Really she had not seemed quite right in the head since the fever.

"Were you surprised to see me this morning?" said Amanda, watching her and seeming to read her thoughts. "I went to call on another old friend, and—I wasn't welcome"—she gave another jarring laugh, which ended this time in a sob. "He—he didn't seem glad to see me, considering how well he used to know me—once." Her voice broke piteously, she paused for a moment, and then: "I hate him, I hate him!" she broke out, fiercely. "I'd give anything in this world if I'd never known him."

"So would I," said Elizabeth, low and bitterly, and then stopped, frightened at what she had said. But Amanda showed no surprise.

"Ah, you think that now," she said, slowly, "but you didn't use to. You've got so many rich beaux now that you don't care about him any longer. But I wonder what they'd think—these rich beaux of yours—if they knew how wild you used to be about him, how you went wandering about the country with him, if they knew"—Amanda leaned forward and spoke in an impressive whisper—"if they knew that you have to do what he wants now, that you're afraid of him."

There was a silence. Elizabeth, faint and giddy, sank into the nearest chair, and put up involuntarily her hand to her heart. So here was another danger threatening, another person who knew something—everything, perhaps? Her brain reeled. Amanda leaned back in her chair, watching her triumphantly, a hard, bright glitter in her eyes.

"Amanda!" Elizabeth's white lips tried in vain to frame a coherent question. "Amanda,"—she made another attempt—"what do you mean?"

Amanda smiled contemptuously. "Oh, you know well enough what I mean," she said. "Why did you go there this morning when you don't care for him any more, and are sorry you ever knew him, unless you're afraid of him, and have to do what he wants?"

"Oh, is that all?" Elizabeth drew a long sigh of relief. "I went there this morning because—because I wanted to meet a friend"—she broke off in confusion before the look on Amanda's face. Then, with a sudden reaction of feeling, she raised her head haughtily. "It doesn't matter," she said, "*what* I went there for. It's a—a studio; all his pupils go there. I might have wanted to see him about singing-lessons, about anything.—If that is all you base your suspicions on, Amanda"——— She stopped.

"Ah, but if it isn't?" said Amanda, in her impressive whisper, which seemed fraught with a mysterious consciousness of power.

Another silence. The defiant look on Elizabeth's face faded; she leaned back in her chair and half closed her eyes. Ah, she was weary, deathly weary, of these constant nervous shocks. How much did Amanda know—how much? If she could only be sure!

"I think they'd be rather surprised," Amanda went on, in unnaturally quiet tones, "these swell friends of yours, if they knew all about you. They think you very sweet, they give you lots of things"—Amanda's hard, restless eyes roamed again about the room and rested on Elizabeth's beautiful gown. "It don't seem fair," she broke out, suddenly, with a fierce little sob; "it don't seem fair, that you should have so much—and then to be so pretty too, as well as all the rest!"

She was silent for a moment, struggling with the tears that threatened to break forth, and Elizabeth began to breathe more freely. All this bluster, after all, these vague threats, seemed to resolve themselves into the old, unreasoning, powerless jealousy—nothing more. And with the relief came again the sense of pity, of a certain justice in Amanda's point of view.

"It isn't fair," she said, softly. "I don't deserve it, but"———

"Well, fair or not, I guess it don't make much difference," Amanda interrupted her, drearily, rising to her feet. "You've always had the best of me, and probably, you always will. But, if ever you don't"———She broke off suddenly and moved towards the door. "I guess I'd better be going," she said. "You'll be late for your dinner. Only, before you go"—she paused with her hand on the knob of the door, that hard, mocking glitter in her eyes—"before you go, just put on some of your jewelry, won't you? Seems to me you look sort of bare without it."

"My—my jewelry?" Elizabeth's heart, which had been beating more quietly, suddenly stood still. "I—I don't wear jewelry, Amanda," she said, in a dull, toneless voice.

"What, not your pearls?" Amanda's hard, mocking eyes seemed to read her through and through. "Your pearls you were so proud of in the country, that you said you'd always wear. Seems to me you need them—with that fine dress!"

She stood hovering by the door, a weird figure in the exaggerated smartness of her attire, with her white face framed in the deep red hair, and that strange, uncanny smile gleaming across it, lighting it up into an elf-like suggestion of mysterious power. Elizabeth stared at her helplessly, fascinated; then, with a great effort, she roused herself and hurried towards her.

"Amanda!" she cried, desperately. "Amanda, for Heaven's sake, stop these insinuations! Tell me plainly what you mean?" She gripped her fiercely by the arm, her face was white and set. For a moment Amanda's eyes met hers. Then, as if in spite of herself, they fell, she freed herself sullenly from Elizabeth's grasp.

"Well, I guess I didn't mean much," she said, awkwardly, "or if I did, it don't matter. I wouldn't tell tales against—my first cousin"—She turned the knob of the door, but again she paused, that weird smile still flickering in her eyes. "Good-night," she said, "I hope you'll enjoy your dinner. Too bad you haven't got your pearls." She gave one last jarring laugh, opened the door and went out.

Elizabeth, white and trembling, sank into the nearest chair.

"How she frightened me!" she gasped out. "These constant shocks will kill me. Does she know anything definite? Probably not. But what can I do, how can I find out?—Ah, Celeste!"—as the maid appeared with an anxious expression in the door-way. "The carriage is waiting? Very well." She hurried to the dressing-table, caught up her gloves and gave one hasty glance at her white face. "How ugly I am growing," she thought, turning away with a shudder; "quite like Amanda! I see the resemblance. It is this awful life. I wish—oh, how I wish I were home!" The thought swept over her, thrilling her with an intense, passionate longing for her aunts' presence, for the country quiet, for rest and peace.

"Yes, I will go home," she thought, as Celeste adjusted the cloak about her shoulders and she hastened down to the carriage. "I will go home," she repeated to herself at intervals during the evening, while she talked and laughed with a restless light in her eyes and a feverish flush on her cheeks. "The country will be so peaceful. I shall be quite safe there, away from all this agitation, this trying to keep up appearances. It is the best way out. How fortunate that he is away! I won't see him again before I go."

It was, she felt, an heroic resolution. Yes, she would go at once. And she resolutely crushed back the thought: "He will follow."

Chapter XXV

"THE Van Antwerps have come up for the summer," said Miss Joanna, who had made the same announcement, if you remember, not quite a year before. "The butcher says they came last night. They never got here so early before."

Elizabeth, who was arranging flowers, looked up suddenly. "Yes, I know," she said, quietly, "Eleanor wrote me." She left her roses half arranged, and wandered restlessly over to the long French window. Before her stretched the well-kept lawn, with its flower-beds and rose-bushes and beyond, field and wooded upland, all clothed in their newest, most vivid dress of green; further still the river, with the white sails on its surface—that river from which, more than half a century before, another Elizabeth Van Vorst had resolutely turned away her eyes, refusing to be reminded of the life that she had given up. But that woman of an older generation was made of sterner stuff, perhaps, than her grand-daughter. And then there was not much travel in those days, no daily mails, no guests coming up to neighboring house-parties over Sunday.... "It will be nice for you, Elizabeth, to have Mrs. Bobby," said Aunt Joanna, in her comfortable monotone, her knitting-needles clicking peacefully. "You have found it a little dull, you know, dear, since you came back."

A little dull! Elizabeth could have laughed out loud at the words. A little dull—with such exciting subjects to discuss as the new Easter anthem, and the latest illness of the Rectory children; with such diversions as a drive to Bassett Mills, a tea-party at the Courtenays! ...

"If I am dull," she said, turning round presently with the ghost of a smile "It certainly isn't the fault of the Neighborhood. I didn't tell you that Mrs. Courtenay has asked me to tea—a third time. She says 'Frank will see me home—no need to send the carriage.'" She laughed a little, not without a shade of bitterness. "Fancy Mrs. Courtenay suggesting that—last summer!"

"Well, dear, she means well, I suppose," said Miss Joanna, puzzled but kindly. Miss Cornelia raised her head with a little, involuntary touch of pride.

"The Courtenays are—are really quite pushing, I think," she said, a most unwonted tone of asperity in her voice. "I told Mrs. Courtenay, Elizabeth, that you had been so *very gay*"—with emphasis—"you really needed a complete rest."

Elizabeth laughed. "And of course," she said "that only made her—dear good woman!—all the more anxious to provide me with a little more amusement. I never realized before how fond the girls have always been of me. But then that's the case, apparently with the whole Neighborhood. They always concealed their affection for me very successfully—until this spring!"

She paused, her aunts made no reply. She went over to the piano and began absently turning over sheets of music.

"Do you remember, auntie," she said, abruptly—Miss Joanna had left the room in response to a summons from the maid, and Elizabeth and Miss Cornelia were alone—"do you remember that I told you once that I felt myself a sort of nondescript—neither flesh, fowl, nor good red herring? But now I seem to be considered a very fine fowl indeed—the ugly duckling, probably, that turned into a swan."

"You never were an *ugly* duckling, my dear," Miss Cornelia could not help protesting, in spite of her principles. "It certainly wasn't that."

"Perhaps not," said Elizabeth, "at all events, I'm no better-looking than I was—let us say, last year. I heard a woman at The Mills say the other day that I had "gone off terrible," in my looks. But that doesn't prevent Frank Courtenay from coming here day after day, boring me to death, since he has discovered as his mother tells me, that I am "just the style that he admires"—it doesn't prevent the Johnston girls from going into raptures over my beautiful hair, and asking if I mind their copying my lovely gowns. They *have* copied my new spring hat, if you notice. Oh, it would be amusing, if it wasn't—so very petty!" She put out her hand with a weary, contemptuous gesture. "And then the funny part of it all is that I am not really so nice, if they only knew it, as I was last year, when they all treated me as if I had committed some sort of crime, merely in existing."

"My dear," remonstrated Miss Cornelia, "how can you talk like that? I'm sure you're not a bit spoiled—every one says so."

"Ah, they think so," said Elizabeth, quickly, "they think me nice, because I've acquired a society manner, and say the correct thing, but if they knew—everything"—she stopped suddenly and stood for a moment staring steadily before her, with knit brows. "Do you know, Aunt Cornelia," she said abruptly "what I think I am?—a sort of moral nondescript, neither good nor bad. I see the right way—oh, I see it so very plainly, and I want to take it; and then I choose the wrong—always and inevitably I choose the wrong, and shall all my life, until the end. It's not my fault, really—I can't do right, no matter how hard I try."

"My dear!" Miss Cornelia looked at her, puzzled and shocked. "There's no one," she said, putting into trite words her own simple conviction "there's no one, Elizabeth, who can't do right, if they try hard enough."

"Do you think so, auntie?" said Elizabeth, very gently. "Then probably I don't try—hard enough." She went over to Miss Cornelia and kissed her on the cheek. "If I were like you," she said, "I should." Then without further words, she sat down at the piano and began to play, as she did every day for hours at a time. Such restless, passionate, brilliant playing! A vague uneasiness mingled in Miss Cornelia's mind with her pride in the girl's talent, as she listened to it. Something was troubling Elizabeth, evidently; something which had brought her home so unexpectedly, which had changed her in looks and manner beyond what could be accounted for by excitement and late hours. Yet innate delicacy and timidity prevented Miss Cornelia from forcing in any way the confidence which seemed to tremble, now and again, upon the girl's lips. She had a vague idea that the difficulty, whatever it was, would soon be decided one way or another, that the Van Antwerps' arrival, which Elizabeth seemed at once to dread and look forward to, would bring matters to a crisis, and the whole thing would be explained.

Elizabeth was still playing when Mrs. Bobby interrupted her. That she had not allowed a day to elapse before hastening to the Homestead was a fact noted with jealous care by the Misses Courtenay, who met her at the gate.

"He is desperate." Mrs. Bobby's visit had not lasted many minutes before she murmured this, holding Elizabeth's hand, and scanning eagerly her averted face. At Mrs. Bobby's words it quivered, the color flushed into her cheek; but otherwise she made no sign.

"When you first went away," Mrs. Bobby continued, as no answer came, "he was all for coming up here at once. He thought it a caprice, a morbid, unaccountable whim; he was sure that if he could see you, remonstrate with you— And then there was your letter, forbidding him to come. He was beside himself! It was all I could do to keep him from taking the first train up here. I said—Wait—it doesn't do, always, to force a woman's will; give her a little time. At least she has paid you the compliment, which she has paid to no one else of—running away from your attentions."

She paused, her eyes still eagerly fixed upon Elizabeth's face. The color in the girl's cheek was now brilliant, her lips were parted; but still she did not speak.

"Day after day," said Mrs. Bobby, "we have talked it over—he walking up and down, restless, wild; I trying to soothe him, urging him to be patient— Sometimes he thinks that you are revenging yourself in this way for his former neglect, that it is a little scheme to pay him back—the idea drives him frantic, makes him furious with himself, yet he is always encouraged when he thinks of it. And then again—he thinks that you don't care for him, that you never will, that there is some one else.... Ah, my dear, if you really do care, you are cruel, unpardonably cruel, to torment him like this."

Again she paused. Elizabeth, with a quick, impatient movement, dragged her hand away from her grasp, and began to pace up and down, gasping as if for breath. "Cruel," she cried out, "cruel! And you think it gives me pleasure—to torment him!"

"If it doesn't," said Mrs. Bobby, following her with her eyes and speaking with some coldness, "I confess I am at a loss to account for your behavior."

Elizabeth stopped suddenly and bending down, almost buried her face in the roses, whose fragrance she inhaled.

"There never was a man," said Mrs. Bobby, "who loved a woman more than he loves you, Elizabeth. And there isn't a man, who, I believe, deserves a woman better."

"Deserves her!" murmured Elizabeth, "deserves *me*! Oh, good Heavens!" The exclamation was barely audible, and apparently addressed only to the roses.

"I said to him yesterday," said Mrs. Bobby, "'You'll come up Saturday, of course?' But—he's proud now and hurt, Elizabeth—he said: 'I won't come, I won't force myself upon her without—her knowledge and consent. If she knows, if she's willing, why, then, I'll come—not otherwise.'"

There was a pause. Elizabeth turned presently a face which seemed to reflect the glowing color of the roses over which she had bent. "What do you— want me to do, Eleanor?" she asked, softly.

"Tell me what I shall say," said Mrs. Bobby "in the letter which I must write when I get home." She went over to Elizabeth and put her hand on her arm. "Shall he come, or shall he not? It rests with you."

Elizabeth's eyes were again averted. "It isn't for me, Eleanor," she murmured, "to drive your guests away, if—if they really want to come."

And so Mrs. Bobby, when she got home, wrote her letter. It consisted of only one word.

The Saturday following was extremely warm. The Rector and his wife came to take tea at the Homestead, and they all sat afterwards in the dimly-lighted drawing-room. Elizabeth wandered to the long French window, and stood looking out upon the moon-lit lawn. "It's so warm that I think I shall go for a walk," she said, half aloud, but no one heard her. The Rector was telling Miss Cornelia about the death of an old clergyman in Cranston, who had lived alone with two old servants. Elizabeth stood and listened for a moment to the deep, impressive tones which mingled strangely with the comfortable monotone which the Rector's wife was addressing to Miss Joanna.

"And so," she was saying "you see I have had blue put on it again, being more summery"—

"I feel particularly sorry," the Rector's voice broke in, "for the old servants. They were quite prostrated, I fear, poor things! They too have not long to live."

"Black satin at four dollars a yard," said his wife, "is sure to last forever."

"He was an excellent man," said the Rector. "His death is a great loss." But here Elizabeth, weary of listening, softly turned the knob of the window and stepped out on the lawn.

What a beautiful night it was outside! The long twilight was fading into dusk, but the moon silvered the shadows that the trees cast across the road. Elizabeth walked to the gate and stood leaning against it. In the distance she heard distinctly the sound of a horse's hoofs. It grew nearer and nearer, and in a few moments a man on horseback was beside her, and drew his rein abruptly before this figure in white, which stood like an apparition in his path.

"Elizabeth," he said. "Elizabeth, is it you?"

"Did you think it was my ghost?" she asked, with a soft laugh. Her white gown shimmered in the moonlight, her hair framed in her face with a vivid halo, her eyes shone like stars. Gerard sprang from his horse.

"Elizabeth," he said "were you waiting for me?"

"Yes," she answered, "I was waiting for you."

And the next moment he had her in his arms, and she had forgotten all other thoughts, all other claims, beneath the fervor of his kisses.

Chapter XXVI

THE summer passed for an eventful one at Bassett Mills, being marked by at least two subjects of conversation; the one the engagement of Elizabeth Van Vorst of the Homestead "that girl of Malvina Jones," to a gentleman from town, who was reported to be "rolling in wealth;" the second, the illness of Amanda Jones, of that fashionable disease called nervous prostration, which no other girl at Bassett Mills but Amanda, who had always given herself airs, would have had the time or the money to indulge in. She had been taken ill while visiting her relations in New York, and her mother had gone up to nurse her, and announced on her return that Amanda was "that nervous" the doctor—"the best that could be had," as she observed with pride, had recommended complete rest, and sending her to a sanitarium for a few months.

"But there really ain't much the matter with her," Amanda's mother explained rather tartly to Elizabeth, who inquired for particulars as to her cousin's illness. "She has fits of crying, and then of sitting still and staring straight before her, like as if she was in a trance, and then she'll get up, and walk up and down the room for hours, and sometimes she'll notice you, and sometimes she won't—but dear me, it's all nonsense, I say. If she had some hard work to do, it would be better for her—but the doctor didn't seem to think so, and so I let her go to the sanitarium. No one shall say that I grudge the expense, as, thank Heaven! I don't have to, though there ain't another person at The Mills that wouldn't."

"I'm sure I hope it will do her good," Elizabeth said, kindly. She felt so glad to have Amanda, whatever the reason, away from Bassett Mills that she was conscious of a sudden pang of remorse, which increased when she received a letter from her cousin, congratulating her upon her engagement. It was a perfectly rational letter, with only slight references to her illness, and none at all to that unpleasant last interview in town; and Elizabeth answered the congratulations in the same amicable spirit in which they were offered, reflecting that, after all, much of Amanda's peculiarity must be excused on the ground of her persistent ill-health. And yet, as she sealed and directed her own letter, she breathed again a fervent thanksgiving that Amanda was safely out of the way.

There was another person for whose absence just then she felt devoutly thankful. When her engagement was announced, early in July—against her own wishes and in deference to Gerard's—she had received a terrible letter from Halleck, denouncing her perfidy, and threatening to come up at once. She had answered it as best she could, imploring his silence, and enclosing a sum of money which she borrowed from her aunts, on the plea of urgent bills—far from mythical, unfortunately, but which remained unpaid. Whether or no Paul granted her request, he pocketed the money, and she next heard of him as having gone abroad for the summer. The piece of news, casually mentioned one day in the course of conversation, thrilled her with a sense of overpowering relief, a suggestion, against which she struggled in vain, of possible accidents, of all the things that might reasonably happen to those who travel by sea or land. Elizabeth breathed a devout wish—it might almost be called a prayer—that this particular traveler might never return.

Meanwhile, the summer passed; a cool, delightful summer, rich with a succession of fragrant, sunshiny days and long, balmy evenings; and signalized by what for the Neighborhood was an unusual amount of gaiety. Several entertainments were given in honor of Elizabeth's engagement, among others a large dinner at the Van Antwerps'. And for this Elizabeth wore—it was Gerard's fancy—the same white gown in which he had first seen her, which he vowed that he cared for more than all her other gowns put together. And though she had pouted a little and declared that the others were far more smart, she yielded to his wishes in this, as she did in most things. Yet during the evening she noticed now and again his eyes fixed upon her with an odd, doubtful expression, as one who searches his memory for the details of a likeness, and finds inexplicably something lacking.

"I know what it is," he announced, abruptly, when they had wandered after dinner for a little while into the conservatory. "I was wondering what it was I missed, and now I know. You haven't got on your pearls. You wore them that night—in fact, I never saw you in full dress without them."

She flushed beneath his wondering gaze, reflecting how constantly he had observed her, wishing—almost—that he had not observed her quite so much.

"Did you forget them?" he asked smiling, as she made no response, but merely put up her hand to her white neck, as if just reminded of the fact that it was unadorned.

She plucked a rose from a plant near by, and began, nonchalantly, to pull it to pieces.

"Oh, I—I didn't feel in the mood to put them on," she said carelessly. "I—somehow I think I shall *not* be in the mood to wear them again for a long while."

He was watching her lazily, an amused smile gleaming in the depths of his dark eyes. "What an odd, capricious child you are!" he said. "You're all made up of moods. I never know what to expect next."

She was picking the rose to pieces very deliberately, petal by petal, her eyes cast down. "Yes, I'm all made up of moods," she echoed, softly. "You must never be surprised at anything I do or say."

"I'm not," he returned, smiling. "And yet," he went on, after a moment, "I confess I'm a little surprised—and disappointed at this last one. I was thinking, to tell the truth, as I had an idea you valued those pearls particularly, of asking you to let me have them, so that I could get you another string to match them exactly."

The last petal of the rose fell from Elizabeth's hand, she stared up at Gerard with an odd, frightened expression. "Don't," she broke out, harshly. "I—I hate pearls." Then with a sudden change, as she saw the absolute bewilderment in his face, she laid her hand gently on his arm. "Dear," she said, very sweetly, "you must have patience with my moods. I've got an idea, just now, that pearls are unlucky. It's very silly, I know, but—don't argue with me. Bear with me, Julian, let me have my own way—a little."

They were alone in the conservatory. He put his arm around her and pressed his lips to hers. "A little," he murmured. "Have your own way—a little! Didn't I tell you, my darling, that you should have your own way in everything?"

She seemed to shrink away with an involuntary shiver at the words. "Ah, but I don't want it," she protested. "It's the last thing I want. If"—she freed herself from his hold and stood looking him, very sweetly and steadily, in the face—"if we are married, Julian"—

"*If?*" he echoed, reproachfully.

"It's always safer to say 'if'" she said.

"Ah, but that's a suggestion I won't tolerate," he declared, firmly. "I'll have my own way in that, if in nothing else. But, *when* we are married, Elizabeth"—he paused.

"When we are married, then,"—she ceded the point resignedly, blushing rosy red—"when we are married, Julian, it must be your way, not mine. Yours is far better, wiser—yes"—she stopped his protest with an imperious gesture—"I feel it, even though I try sometimes to dispute it. I shall never do that—later. I shall try, with all the strength I have, to be more worthy of your love. But now—just now, Julian"—she looked at him anxiously, and a note of appeal crept into her voice—"if I seem odd, wilful, don't blame me, don't—doubt me"—

"Doubt you?" He took her hand and raised it reverently to his lips. "I shall never doubt you—again, my darling, no matter what you do or say."

There was the ring of absolute confidence in his voice. Yet it might have been that which made her shiver and shrink away, almost as if he had struck her a blow.

"I—I think we had better go back to the others," she announced, abruptly, in a moment, and her intonation was quick and sharp, almost as if she were frightened and trying to escape from some threatened danger. "It"—she smiled uncertainly—"it's not quite good form, I think, for us to wander off like this."

"Hang good form!" said Gerard, but still he followed her back resignedly to the other room, and she gave, as they reached the lights and the people, a soft sigh of relief, which fortunately he did not hear. Yet he noticed that for the rest of the evening she was paler than she had been at first.

This pallor increased when Mrs. Bobby, too, voiced the question which had been perplexing her all the evening, as to why she did not wear the pearls. Elizabeth did not mention her moods—it is evident that women cannot be put off, in such important questions as that of jewelry, with the vague answers that might satisfy a man. She said that the string had broken, and she had sent them to town to be re-strung. Her aunts knew that they had been there for that purpose since early spring, and they could not understand why she did not send for them, since other things had been left at the same jeweler's—notably that little jeweled watch, which they had heard of, but never seen. It was odd that Elizabeth should have lost, to so large an extent, her taste for pretty things.

Gerard, too, noticed this, but he would not ask her any more questions. Later he gave her a string of emeralds set with diamonds, which she wore to entertainments in the Neighborhood that autumn, and no one asked any more questions about the pearls, since it was natural that she should prefer to wear his gift.

His trust in her was absolute, as he had said. It seemed as if he would make amends now by the plenitude of his confidence, for that former instinctive, reasonless distrust. And then she was so different from the frivolous girl he had first imagined her. Every day he reproached himself with his old estimate of her character, as he discovered in her new and unexpected depths of brain and soul. She read all the books that he recommended—some of them very deep, and she would once have thought very tiresome—and she surprised him by the intelligence of her criticisms, she took a sympathetic interest in those articles by which he was making a name for himself in the scientific world, and she entered with an apparently perfect comprehension into all his hopes, thoughts and aspirations. There was only one thing in which she baffled him, one point where her old wilfulness would come between them. This was her obstinate and unaccountable refusal to name their wedding day.

The Neighborhood was exercised on the subject. It had been decided by unanimous consent that the wedding should be in the autumn—"quite the best time for a wedding" as the Rector's wife observed, and lay awake one whole night planning the most charming (and inexpensive) decorations of autumn leaves and golden-rod. But all the reward she received for her pains was the information that Elizabeth did not care for autumn weddings, and as the Misses Van Vorst at Gerard's request, had taken a small apartment in town for the winter, the Rector's wife had many pangs at the thought that the Bassett Mills church and her husband would lose all the prestige that would attend this great event—to say nothing of the fee.

But when Gerard, as a matter of course, spoke of their being married in town, Elizabeth looked up deprecatingly into his face.

"Wait till I'm twenty-one," she pleaded. "This is my unlucky year, you know. Do please, Julian, wait till it's over."

But Gerard's face was set in rigid lines, like that of a man who is determined to stand no more trifling. Elizabeth's unlucky year would not be past till April.

Chapter XXVII

IT was a bleak December day and Central Park seemed the last place where one would wish to loiter. The sky hung lowering overhead, gray, cold, heavy with the weight of invisible snowflakes. The wind made a dull moaning sound, as it stirred the bare branches of the trees. The lake, where at another season you see children sailing in the swan-boats, was nearly covered with a thin coating of ice. But Elizabeth Van Vorst as she stood with eyes intently fixed upon the small space of water still visible, did not seem to notice either the cold or the dreariness of the scene. She was leaning against a tree, and looking at nothing but the lake, till at the sound of foot-steps on the path, she turned to face Paul Halleck.

"So you got my note," she said, speaking listlessly, without a sign of surprise or satisfaction. She did not give him her hand, which clasped the other tightly, in the warm shelter of her muff.

"Yes, I got it; but I could wish you had chosen a warmer meeting-place, my dear." The last months had changed him, and not for the better. His figure had grown stouter, his beauty coarser. She shrank away in invincible repugnance from the careless familiarity of his manner.

"It was the best place I could think of," she said, curtly. "At home, we are always interrupted; at your studio—it is impossible. I had to see you—somehow, somewhere." She sat down on a bench near by, and shivering drew her furs about her.

"You do me too much honor," Paul returned, lightly. He took the seat beside her, his eyes resting, in involuntary fascination, on the rounded outlines of her cheek, the soft waves of auburn hair beneath her small black hat. "It's a long time since you have wished to see me of your own accord, my dear," he said, in a tone in which resentment struggled with his old, instinctive admiration of her beauty.

She turned to him, suddenly, her eyes hard, her face very white and set. "You know the reason." "I had to see you, to—to talk things over. You assume a right to control me, you ask me for money, you try to frighten me with threats. There must be an end of it. I"—she paused for a moment, and drew her breath quickly, while she flushed a dull crimson. "I have promised—Mr. Gerard," she said "to—to marry him next month."

He interrupted her with a scornful laugh. "To marry him—next month," he repeated. "And how about that ceremony which we know of—you and I—in the church at Cranston?"

The crimson flush faded and left her white, but still she did not flinch. "I have thought of that," she said, steadily, "and I have decided that it should not—make any difference. I don't believe the marriage would be legal—but that's neither here nor there. I don't want a divorce, I don't want the thing known, I don't consider that we were ever married. I don't think such a marriage as ours, which we both entered into without the slightest thought, which we have repented of"—

"Speak for yourself," he interposed.

"Which I have repented of, then," she went on, "ought to be binding. The clergyman who married us is dead; the witnesses, so old that they are childish, probably remember nothing about it. There is no one now living who remembers, except you and I. And for me I have determined to think of it as a dream, and I want you to promise me to do the same."

"But—there is the notice in the parish register." He was staring at her blankly, admiring in spite of himself, the calm resolution of her manner, the business-like precision with which she was unfolding her arguments, as if she had rehearsed them many times to herself.

"I have thought of that, too," she said, in answer to his last objection, "and I don't think it in the least likely that any one will ever see it. Why should they, without any clue? At all events, this is—the only way out." She faltered as her mind wandered for a moment unwillingly to another way which she had now despaired of—too easy a solution to her difficulties ever to come true. What a fool she had been to think that he would die! People like that never die. As she saw him now, in the full pride of his health and good looks, it seemed impossible to believe that any misfortune could assail him—least of all death! ...

"There is—no other way," she repeated, with a little, involuntary sob. "The risks are not great—but, at any rate, I must take them. Now, there is only one other thing"—She paused for a moment and then drew out of her purse a plain gold ring, and showed it to him. It was the ring which she had once worn on her finger for a few minutes, which she had kept carefully hidden ever since. She glanced about her; there was no one in sight except the policeman, who in the distance near the carriage-drive, was pacing up and down at his cold post and beating his hands to keep them warm. Elizabeth rose and went to the edge of the lake. With well-directed aim, she threw the tiny circlet of gold so that it struck the fast-vanishing surface of water and quickly disappeared. She drew a long sigh of relief. "There," she said, "that is over."

Paul watched her curiously. He saw that she attached to this little action a mysterious significance. He sneered harshly. "Very pretty and theatrical," he said. "But do you really think that by a thing like that—throwing away a ring—you can dissolve a marriage?"

She turned to him, her white face still resolute and intensely solemn. "I don't know," she said, quietly, "but I wanted to throw it away before you, so that you would understand that everything is over between us, and that day at Cranston is as if it never had been. *Never had been*, you understand," she repeated, with eager emphasis. "I want you to promise to think of it like that."

He shrugged his shoulders. "How we either of us think of it, I suppose, doesn't make much difference so far as the legality of the thing goes," he said. "But,—have your own way. If you choose to commit a crime, it's not my affair."

"A crime!" She started and stared at him. "Do you call that a crime?"

He smiled. "It's a rough word to use for the actions of a charming young girl," he said "but I'm afraid that the law might look at it in that light."

Elizabeth returned to the bench and sat down. She seemed to be pondering this new view of the matter. "I can't help it," she said at last, in a low voice. "If that's a crime, why—I understand how people are led into them. And I can't ruin his happiness, crime or no crime."

"And my happiness?" he asked her bitterly. "You never think of that? You professed to love me once. You took me for better, for worse, and how have you kept your word? If my life is ruined, the responsibility is yours. If you had gone with me as I wanted you to, I should have been a different man." There was a curious accent of sincerity in his voice. He really believed for the moment what he said.

The reproach was not without effect. She looked at him more gently, with troubled eyes that seemed to express not only contrition, but a certain involuntary sympathy. "It's true," she said. "I have treated you badly, and broken the most solemn promise any one could make. I don't defend myself; but—I'm willing to make what amends I can. I can't give you myself, but at least I can give you what little money you would have had with me. When I am married to"—she paused and flushed, but concluded her sentence firmly—"to Mr. Gerard, I will give you—all the money I have."

Paul paced up and down, apparently in deep thought. It was evident that her offer tempted him, yet some impulse urged him to refuse it. He stopped suddenly in front of her. "Principal or interest, do you mean?" he asked, in a tone in which the thirst for gain distinctly predominated.

The doubtful sympathy in Elizabeth's eyes faded, and was replaced by a look of unmistakable disgust. "I suppose I could hardly give you the principal," she said, coldly. "But I will pay over the income every year." She named the sum. "Isn't it enough?"

"That depends," he said, looking at her coolly. "It is enough, of course, for Elizabeth Van Vorst, but for Mrs. Julian Gerard"—

He stopped as an electric shock of anger seemed to thrill Elizabeth from head to foot. "You don't suppose," she cried, "that I would give you *his* money?"

"Then," said Paul, curtly, "he doesn't know?"

"Certainly not," she said, haughtily.

He began again reflectively to pace up and down. "I don't see," he said, "how you are to pay me over this money without his knowing it."

"Don't trouble yourself about that," said Elizabeth, contemptuously. "Mr. Gerard will never ask what I do with my money."

"Well he has enough of his own, certainly," said Paul, philosophically. "And yet, poor fellow, I am sorry for him if he ever finds out how you have deceived him."

"He never *shall* find out," said Elizabeth. She rose and pulled down her veil. "It is so cold," she said shivering, and indeed she looked chilled to the core. "I cannot stay here any longer. This thing is settled, isn't it? You will promise?" There was a tone of piteous entreaty in her voice.

"How am I to know," he asked, still hesitating "that you will keep your word? Once married to Gerard, you might—forget."

"If I do," she returned quietly, "you will always have the power to break yours and ruin my happiness."

"So be it, then. I won't interfere with you. After all, we probably shouldn't have got on well. Come—let us part friends, at least."

He held out his hand, but hers was again securely hidden in her muff, and the smile that gleamed on her face was pale and cold as the winter day itself. "Good-bye," she said, and turned away. He fell back, with a muttered oath.

"Upon my word, my lady," he said, "you might be a little more gracious." At that moment Elizabeth came back. There was a softer look on her face.

"I loved you once," she said. "Good-bye." And she held out her hand. He took it in silence. Thus they parted for the last time.

It had been a successful interview. She had gained all that she dared hope for. Seated in the warm car going home, and shivering as from an ague, she told herself that she had silenced forever all opposition to her wishes. Yet it did not seem a victory. Words which Paul had said lingered in her mind, stinging her with their contempt, the fact that even he could set himself above her. "A crime!" She had never considered it in that light. Surely it was impossible on the face of it that she, Elizabeth Van Vorst, could commit a crime.... And then again—what was it he had said? "Poor fellow, I am sorry for him, if ever he finds out how you have deceived him."

"But he never shall," she said to herself, resolutely as before. "Crime or no crime, his love is worth it. He never shall find out."

Chapter XXVIII

ELIZABETH had little time in those days for thought. There was still less time, even, when she was alone with Gerard. The days passed in a whirl of gaiety, in which she had been swallowed up since her return to town. It was a state of things which bored Gerard extremely, but secure in the promise he had at last obtained from her that the wedding should be at the end of January he possessed his soul in such patience as he could muster. And when he requested as a special favor, that she would refuse all invitations for the thirty-first of December and see the Old Year out in peace, she consented at once, and the hope of a quiet evening buoyed him up through other weary ones, when he would lean in his old fashion against the wall, and watch her across a ball-room, the center of an admiring court. Yet, even as he did so, the proud consciousness of proprietorship swelled his heart. She was his—his! He had no longer any doubt of her, or jealousy of the men who talked to her.

Why then was the expected evening, when it came, fraught with an intangible sense of gloom, of oppression, which made the time pass heavily? The old Dutch clock, which the Misses Van Vorst had brought with them from the country seemed to-night to mark the hours with extraordinary slowness, as if the Old Year were in no hurry to be gone, even though the noises in the street, the blowing of horns and of whistles were enough, one might have thought, to hasten his departure.

Elizabeth was pacing restlessly up and down the room. Her hands were clasped carelessly before her, her long house-dress of white cashmere, belted in by a gold girdle, fell about her in graceful folds. There was a flush in her cheeks, a somewhat feverish light in her eyes; she started nervously now and then as some enterprising small boy blew an especially shrill blast on his horn.

"I don't know why it is," she said at last with a petulant little laugh, coming back to her seat by the fire opposite Gerard, and taking up a piece of work, in which she absently set a few stitches, "New Year's Eve always gets on my nerves, I think of all my sins—and that's very unpleasant!" She broke off, pouting childishly, as if in disgust at the intrusion of unwelcome ideas.

He was watching her lazily, with the amused, indulgent smile which certain of her moods had always the power to call forth; the smile of a strong man, who felt himself quite able to cope with them. "With such terrible sins as yours, Elizabeth," he said, "it must be indeed a dreadful thing to think of them."

She turned quickly towards him. "You don't think that they can be very bad?"

"I should be willing to take the risk of offering you absolution."

She bent down over her work so that her face was hidden. "Ah, you—you don't know"——she rather breathed than spoke. He only smiled incredulously, as one who knew her better than she did herself.

"Play for me, darling," he said, after awhile, and she went mechanically to the piano. But her playing was always a matter of mood, and to-night her fingers faltered, the keys did not respond as usual. She passed restlessly from one thing to another—snatches of Brahms, Chopin, Tschaikowski, with the same jarring note running through them all.

She broke off at last, with a wild clash of chords. "I can't play to-night," she said, and came back to the fire. "How calm you are!" she said, standing beside Gerard and looking down at him with eyes almost of reproach. "This horrible evening doesn't get on your nerves at all."

"How can it?"—Gerard possessed himself of her hand and raised it to his lips.—"How can I waste any regrets on the Old Year," he said, "when the New Year is to bring me—so much happiness?"

She started and caught her breath, as if the words held a sting. "Ah, yes," she repeated, very low "it is to bring you—so much happiness!" For a moment she left her hand in his and then withdrew it with a stifled sigh. She went back very still and pale, to her seat on the other side of the fire, and taking up her work, she fixed her eyes upon it intently.

"And so you think it is to bring you happiness?" she said, in a low voice, continuing the subject as it seemed in spite of herself. "You are quite sure of that, Julian, you have—no doubts?" She raised her eyes with a wistful questioning that puzzled him.

"Doubts, Elizabeth!" He stared back at her reproachfully, his brows drawn together frowning. "Why do you harp so much on that, my darling? Why should I have doubts?"

"Why, some men might, you know."—Her eyes were bent again upon her work.—"You yourself—you had them, you know, when you first knew me."

He flushed. "Don't remind me of that," he said, hastily.

"Well, it may have been a true presentiment."—She gave him an odd, furtive look. "I've wondered—sometimes—if I were as nice naturally as other girls I know. I hadn't, to begin with, the sort of mother that—most girls have"——She hesitated, a painful crimson flooded her face, her eyes filled with tears. Gerard stared at her in amazement. He had never heard her allude to her mother before, and had supposed her entirely ignorant of all painful facts in the family history.

"Darling," he broke out, indignantly, "who has told you—things like that?"

"Who? Oh! I don't know."—She put the question aside listlessly.—"One always hears unpleasant facts, somehow. I always knew that she wasn't the—the sort of person that the Neighborhood would call on"—a painful smile hovered about her lips. "It used to make me very unhappy—but lately—it hasn't seemed to matter. And yet—I think of it sometimes"——She broke off suddenly and looked at Gerard with a strange light in her eyes. "Doesn't it make a difference to you? Doesn't it occur to you sometimes that I may be—my mother's daughter; that it would be wiser to—distrust me?" Her voice died away at the last words into a hoarse whisper.

"Elizabeth!"—Gerard sprang to his feet. He went over to her and took both her hands in his strong grasp. "Elizabeth, never let me hear these morbid fancies again. Never suppose that anything your mother did or left undone, can make a difference in my faith in you!"

He stood looking down at her with eyes full of an imperious tenderness. She trembled and shrank away before them, as if frightened. "You trust me, then?" she repeated, and she drew a long sobbing breath. "You're quite *sure* you trust me?"

"Absolutely."—Gerard's smile lit up his face.—"How often, you exacting woman," he asked, "do you want me to promise that I will never doubt you again."

There was silence for a moment. The noises in the street sounding suddenly with redoubled violence in the stillness, seemed to punctuate Gerard's words with an outburst of derision. To Elizabeth's fancy the whole atmosphere of the room was tense, vibrant, filled with jarring echoes of the noise without. Even the old Dutch clock, whose ticking was one of her earliest memories, seemed to beat with a new, discordant note of mockery, as if it too were uttering its ironical comment on the wisdom of a man's faith.

Elizabeth shuddered and thrust Gerard's hands away. "I wish—I wish I deserved your trust, Julian," she broke out, wildly. Then she laid her face on the arm of the chair and sobbed. He fell back and stared at her aghast. The tender smile was arrested, frozen on his lips. For him, too, as for her, the room was suddenly filled with discordant vibrations, a sense of unreasoning dread.

In a moment Elizabeth looked up; with a great effort she conquered her tears. She went to Gerard and put her hand on his arm. The face she raised to his was white, trembling in a pathetic appeal. The tears still glistened on her long lashes, there was a tremulous sweetness in her great dark eyes, in the quivering lines about her pale lips. "Julian," she said, "if I'm not—not worthy of your trust—not worthy of your love, even"—she faltered—"if I had deceived you—*were* deceiving you still"——she paused and looked him in the face with an agonized questioning.

"Yes?"—Gerard's hoarse voice urged her on.—"If you were deceiving me? It isn't—it can't be true, but if you were?"——

"If I were," she went on, steadily, "if I had kept one thing from you—against my will—oh, God knows! sorely against my will"—her voice broke—"if it had been a weight on my mind day and night—if I had longed to tell you and had tried to do it and always—my courage failed me, and—and—if at last—at last, I told you—would you—think me so very much to blame, couldn't you—forgive?"— Her voice again faltered piteously, the last word was barely audible.

He broke away from her and took two or three turns up and down the room, breathing heavily, like a man who had been running. "Tell me what this secret is?" he broke out, fiercely, pausing suddenly in front of her. "How can I tell if——I could forgive, till I know what it is?"

Again the silence. Elizabeth's white lips tried, apparently in vain, to form an answer. The courage which a moment before had possessed her, seemed to shrivel up and die away, before that fierce light in his eyes.

"Tell me," he repeated, inexorably, "what it is."

She put out her hand suddenly with a pleading gesture. "Ah, let us first see the Old Year out together," she murmured, "as we planned. I should like to feel that you loved me till—the very end of it. You may not—afterwards. It won't be long. See—it's nearly time." She glanced up at the clock. It was ticking faster now, as it seemed, and steadily, the hour hand well towards midnight.

Elizabeth went to the window and flung it open. The current of cold air which flooded the room seemed to give her relief; she leaned out as far as she could, inhaling it in long, fevered gasps. Gerard followed and stood behind her, in an agony of impatience, distraught by a hundred incongruous, terrible suggestions. The prolonged suspense seemed, in his over-wrought state, a very refinement of cruelty, yet some instinct kept him silent, left to her the mastery of the situation.

In the street there was unwonted stir and bustle. A crowd assembled to greet the New Year. Small boys, whose horns made the night hideous, pranced about like uncouth imps of darkness; the street-lamps, as they flickered, cast a weird, uncertain light on the snow-covered ground. But the moon, riding overhead, shone peacefully, and myriads of stars studded the wintry sky. Down towards the Battery one could hear, above all coarser sounds, the chimes of Old Trinity ringing faint but true.

Elizabeth's eyes were riveted upon St. George's clock, which stood out, not many blocks away, above the roofs of intervening houses. Her lips moved, but no sound came; one hand grasped convulsively the curtain behind her. To Gerard as he watched her those fifteen minutes before the New Year were the longest of his life.

Suddenly all noises slackened; upon the listening crowd outside there fell a pause, a hush of expectation. St. George's clock boomed out the hour in twelve majestic strokes. The old Dutch clock within the room echoed it in quieter tones. And then, as the last stroke died away, the crowd stirred, there arose a hideous Babel of sound—cat-calling, shouting, blowing of horns and whistles; pandemonium set loose. It raged for several minutes, and stopped abruptly, exhausted by its own violence. There was again silence, and then a burst of laughter. Some one in the crowd cried loudly and heartily: "Happy New Year!"

Elizabeth shivered, as if with a sudden consciousness of the cold. She shut the window and faced Gerard. Against the vivid background of the crimson curtain, in her clinging white dress, her pale beauty, crowned by her red-gold hair, stood out with a strange, unearthly quality, like that of some pictured saint. There was a look on her face which was tragic in its despairing resolution, yet which had in it a certain exaltation, as if she had risen for the moment at least, above herself, to heights hitherto unknown.

"You shall know the worst of me, at last. You won't"—she gave an odd little laugh—"you won't grant me absolution, Julian, I'm afraid. But oh, I'm sick— God knows, I'm sick of lies!" She paused and caught her breath as if for one supreme effort. "This is the truth," she said. "I was married to Paul Halleck—before I knew you, more than a year ago."

He staggered back, as if she had struck him a blow. "You were—married— to Paul Halleck?"

"Yes," she repeated, in a dull monotone, "married to him—more than a year ago."

He was still staring at her as if stupefied. "Married!" he repeated, "married all this time!—when you professed to love me! When"—a pause—"you promised to marry me! Oh, it's impossible," he cried, with a sudden flash of incredulity, and he put out his hand and touched her involuntarily. "Say you're only playing with me," he begged her, "trying my faith—say it's not true." His voice shook, unconsciously his hand closed upon her wrist with a grasp that might have hurt her, had she been capable just then of feeling physical pain.

"It—it is true," she said, and stood motionless, white and rigid as a statue, her head bent.

He still stared incredulous for a moment, and then the reality of what she said seemed to sink into his soul. With a quick, involuntary gesture, which wounded more than words, he let her hand fall, and began to pace up and down the room.

"Good God!" she heard him mutter. "Married all these months!—and I, who loved you, trusted you!"——He broke off with a gesture of angry despair. Her lip quivered, her eyes followed him for a moment and then filled with tears. She went over to the mantel-piece, and resting her arms upon it, she hid her face.

It was a long time before he stopped beside her, but then his voice showed recovered self-control. "Will you tell me," he said, "exactly how and when this marriage took place?"

She turned with a little shuddering sigh and raised her white, exhausted face to his. "It was at Cranston," she said, quietly, "one day in July. I did it hastily. My aunts were opposed to it, and—I hated to make them unhappy. But I—I thought I loved him. It was a mistake. I went up to Cranston to meet him, and—we were married. It was in church—there were witnesses, we signed a register—it was all legal, or at least I suppose so. And then—when we came out"——she paused.

"Yes—when you came out?"—Gerard repeated the words hoarsely, his brows drawn together, his eyes fixed upon her in an agonized questioning.—"What then, Elizabeth?"

She hesitated, staring straight before her, as if she were trying to recall the whole thing exactly as it happened. "When we came out of the church, I felt—I don't know why—I felt frightened. I seemed to realize—indeed, I think I *had* realized all the time—what a mistake it was. He begged me to come away with him, and I—I refused. He had promised me that I should go home, and that he wouldn't claim me for six months, and—I held him to it. He gave in at last, and so—we parted"——

"Ah!"—Gerard drew a long breath.—"You—parted?"

"Yes. I left him and came home. I got there about four—my aunts suspected nothing. He went abroad. And—after a while he stopped writing, I thought he had forgotten me. It all began to seem like a dream. And then—Eleanor Van Antwerp asked me to come to town, and—the rest you know."

"No, not all." Gerard insisted. "When the fellow came home, why didn't he claim you? How have you kept him quiet, all this time?"

"Ah, that was easy."—She spoke listlessly.—"He didn't care anything about me; I used to give him money. I sold my pearls—all my jewelry, in fact. Yes"—as

Gerard uttered a horrified exclamation—"it was a terrible bondage, but what could I do? He had me in his power. I used to wonder if the marriage were legal, but there was no one whom I dared ask. And then I thought sometimes that he might die—I had all sorts of wild ideas; but nothing happened, and meanwhile he threatened—to tell you everything. I bought him off twice, and then—this last time"—she paused—"this last time I promised him all my income if he would give me up forever, and never trouble me again. Ah, you think it unpardonable, I see"—she put out her hand with a deprecating gesture—"but you don't know what it is to be tempted—desperate. I was determined I wouldn't ruin my life. And then—then"—her voice faltered—"this evening when you seemed so happy, so trustful—that was what hurt me, Julian—it was easier when you were jealous, suspicious, as you were at first—it came to me suddenly that I couldn't begin the New Year—I couldn't begin our life together with this—this terrible secret weighing on my soul. And so I—I told you"——

Elizabeth's voice faltered, she raised her eyes in a half conscious appeal. It seemed to her for the moment as if the agony of that confession must make amends to some extent even for such deceit as hers. But Gerard's face did not soften. Her whole conduct seemed to him monstrous, incredible. He could not accept as atonement this tardy repentance, the fact that she had told him the truth—at the eleventh hour.

The thought occurred to him, which she had herself suggested, earlier in the evening. He remembered chance gossip of the Neighborhood about her antecedents, listened to vaguely even before he knew her, and haunting him afterwards in the first days of their acquaintance, till love had made him cast it aside, as a thing of no importance. Now it recurred to his mind as the only explanation—he did not accept it as an excuse—of this weakness which seemed otherwise inexplicable. No doubt there must be, he told himself, in the child of such parents,—it would be strange if there were not—some hereditary taint, some lack of moral fibre, which curiously imperceptible in other ways, must needs assert itself in any great moral crisis. The thought, which might have softened him, seemed at the time only to steel him the more against her.

He fell again to pacing up and down, thinking it over; seeing past incidents afresh in the merciless light of his present knowledge; recalling this or that insignificant circumstance which at the time had aroused, unreasonably as it seemed, his distrust;—her occasional uneasiness and distress, that air she had of being on her guard, the look in the picture—ah, he understood it now! It was the shadow of falsehood, which for months had clouded her every thought and action. What a fool he had been, he reflected fiercely—how he had allowed himself to be deceived—made an easy prey by the extent of his infatuation—how she had juggled with the truth, telling him the worst of herself in such a way that he had believed, all the more determinedly, the reverse.

He stopped at last his restless pacing to and fro and paused beside her. The fierce tide of anger, the first bitterness of his disillusion, had subsided. He was cold, with the coldness of despair. His face was worn and haggard, as if from the suffering of years, but it was set in rigid lines, from which all feeling seemed to have vanished. His eyes were dry and hard.

"I think," he said, and there was a dull, toneless sound in his voice; he spoke slowly, like one who either weighed his words with great care, or was afraid to trust himself too far, "I think there had better be an end to this. I should only say, if I said all I thought, things I might afterwards—regret; and I wouldn't"—his voice broke ever so little—"God knows I don't want to be unjust! But I cannot"—he let his hand fall with a look of dull despair—"I *cannot* understand how you have kept this from me all these months!"

He paused, as if expecting an answer, an excuse, perhaps of some sort; but she said nothing, and he went on, after a moment, his voice growing more uncertain: "It isn't so much the marriage—that could be, perhaps"—He hesitated, his heavy brows drawn together frowning—"The man must be an absolute wretch," he said, suddenly, "there must be—for your sake I hope so—some way out"——

"Oh, for me"—she made a little gesture of utter carelessness—"for me it can make no difference—now."

"For myself," he went on, not heeding her words, perhaps not fully grasping their meaning, "I couldn't—whether the marriage held or not—I couldn't forgive—being so deceived."

He stopped and again seemed to expect some protest, but she only repeated, in a dull voice of complete acquiescence: "No, I didn't think you could forgive—being so deceived"——

"Even if I could forgive," he said, "I could never trust"——

"No," she repeated, "you could never trust." Her face was colorless, but impassive, as if it had been turned to stone, her voice was almost as firm as his. "You are quite right," she said. "I deserve all the harsh things you could say. It is kind of you to say—so few. Perhaps, later, you'll judge me more gently; but—I couldn't expect it now. And so"—she faltered and caught her breath, as if her strength failed her—"and so good-bye," she said at last. "I think it can only hurt us both to—discuss this any longer."

Her calmness stunned him. He had been prepared for tears—excuses—but she offered no defence and made no effort to arouse his pity. There was a dignity in her complete submission. He looked at her, his face working with varied emotions; and then he said "Good-bye" mechanically and took her hand for an instant. It was icy cold and lay impassively in his. He dropped it and moved towards the door, as if under some spell, deprived of all capacity for thought or feeling. Involuntarily, her eyes followed him. Was this the parting, after so many months? But at the door he paused, he looked back. The firelight played on her hair, on her white dress, the drooping lines of her slender form, the deathly pallor of her face, the despair in her eyes.... He softened, perhaps, or it might be that the mere physical spell of her beauty held him, even when all that made the glory of his love, had been rudely shattered. He came back, caught her in his arms, and pressed burning kisses on her lips. She trembled as if they had been blows, but she made no effort to free herself. And then, as if ashamed of his weakness, he let her go and went out hastily. A moment later she heard the front door close, with a dull sound that echoed through the quiet rooms.

She stood where he had left her, staring blankly about her at the familiar objects which seemed to have acquired, during the last hour, an air of change, of unreality. What had happened, what had she done? Awhile ago she had been borne up by a courage that seemed almost heroic, a sense of moral victory. Now that had failed her. She was simply a woman despised and heart-broken, who by her own suicidal act had destroyed her happiness.

"How—how can I bear it?" she broke out, at last, fiercely, and sinking down on the hearth-rug, she lay prostrate, her face hidden, while her whole frame shook with convulsive sobs. The old Dutch clock ticked softly, pitifully, in the silence; the fire flickered and died away. But outside in the street spasmodic whistles kept on blowing, and belated wayfarers still bade each other, with laughter and jollity, "Happy New Year."

Chapter XXIX

It was eight days later. Elizabeth's trouble and the New Year were both a week old. She had lived through the time somehow or another, had even faced those smaller trials which follow in the wake of any great catastrophe. She had told the whole truth to her aunts—it was only less hard than telling Gerard—she had written to her friends to announce the breaking of her engagement, and had countermanded the orders for her trousseau. These affairs disposed of, she was ready to face the world with such strength as she had left.

For Gerard the situation was simpler. He had taken at once his man's way out of it, and pacing the deck of an ocean steamer, he tried to distract his mind and forget his trouble in plans for extensive travel and scientific research. They had been his resource once before, when a woman had disappointed him.

He had not seen Elizabeth again. He dreaded, perhaps, to trust himself, or perhaps his anger was still too great. But he had written before he left to her aunts, urging them to consult a lawyer and take steps at once to free her from the results of her rash marriage. To himself, he justified this weakness—if it were weakness—by the thought of Halleck's baseness. "I could not bear to think of her as his wife," he said to himself, "a fellow who could give her up for money!"

Upon Elizabeth's aunts the affair had come like a thunderbolt. They were quite unprepared for it, though many suspicious circumstances—the mystery as to Elizabeth's jewels, her own occasional words—might have suggested the idea that something was amiss. But absorbed in their delight in the engagement, their affection for Gerard, they had not the heart to formulate any doubt they might have felt. Now, in the first shock of their awakening, they remembered unwillingly the same facts of family history which had occurred to Gerard. What could they have expected from Malvina's child but deceit, folly and disgrace? But they were gentle souls, and had no reproaches for Elizabeth, only a silent, sorrowful pity, which hurt the girl's proud spirit more than the sharpest words.

She was lingering that morning, pale and languid, over her untasted breakfast, and Miss Cornelia, from behind the coffee-urn, stole anxious glances towards her, all sense of injury lost in her distress over the girl's wretched looks, and fear that she was going to be ill. They two were alone, Miss Joanna having already started to do her marketing, when the maid entered with the belated newspaper. Miss Cornelia held out her delicate, tremulous hand for it, nervously apprehensive of that paragraph which no doubt in the society columns, announced that the engagement between Miss Van Vorst and Mr. Gerard had been broken "by mutual consent."

It was not this notice which met her eyes, but some exciting head-lines on the first page which had already attracted the attention of the cook and the housemaid.

"Elizabeth," said Miss Cornelia, in a stifled voice. "Elizabeth—what is this?"

Elizabeth raised her vacant eyes, and saw Miss Cornelia deathly white and staring in horror at the paper. "Is it?" she said. "It must be. What a dispensation! So young, too."

"Auntie," said Elizabeth, impatiently, "why don't you say what it is?"

"I am afraid he was very ill prepared," said Miss Cornelia, apparently talking to herself and oblivious of her niece's presence. But suddenly she seemed to realize it and placed her hand over the paper. "My dear, don't look at this yet," she faltered. "You—it will be a shock, Elizabeth. Prepare yourself."

Elizabeth did not wait to hear more, but went to her and seized the paper from her hand. The headline told, in large type, how Paul Halleck, the prominent young singer, had died the evening before of a mysterious draught of poison, which had been sent to him by mail.

There followed in smaller type the details of the affair, but Elizabeth did not read them. She sank into the nearest chair and sat staring before her with dilated eyes, that seemed to express less surprise or terror than a sort of awe, as at some unexpected manifestation of Providence.

"It was I who killed him," she said. She spoke in a dull, dream-like way, not in the least conscious, as it seemed, of anything extraordinary in the words. Poor Miss Cornelia could form no other conclusion than that she had suddenly lost her mind.

"Elizabeth, my darling," she remonstrated, "what do you mean?" But Elizabeth was still staring before her vacantly, absorbed in her own thoughts.

"And so it has happened!" she said, in a low voice, "at last!—when I had given up hope!"—She was quite oblivious of her aunt's horror or of the staring eyes of the maid, who stood listening, the coffee-pot in her hand, her mouth wide open. But at that moment Miss Cornelia suddenly remembered her presence and signed to her to leave the room—an order obeyed reluctantly.

"Now, Elizabeth," Miss Cornelia faltered out, as the door closed, "do, my darling, explain what you mean. It's quite absurd, you know, to say that you had anything to do with this."

"I wished it," said Elizabeth, gazing at her with dull, expressionless eyes. "I wished, I even prayed, that he might die. And my wishes always come true—only it is in such a way that it does no good."

"But you can't," urged Miss Cornelia, in desperation, "you can't kill people by *wishing*, Elizabeth. Of course, there are things that one can't—feel as sorry for as one would like"—Her voice faltered, as she thought of certain individuals connected with her own life, whose death it had been hard to regard in the light of an affliction. "We can't help our thoughts," she murmured, "we can only pray not to give way to them."

"Ah, but I didn't," said Elizabeth. "I encouraged them. And now I shall have remorse, I suppose, all my life." She sat pondering a moment, while the expression on her face grew softer. "I am sorry he is dead," she said, at last. "It does me no good now—and he seemed so full of life the last time I saw him. But it was his fate, no doubt—a fortune-teller told him he would die before the year was out.

It was his unlucky year, as well as mine. And the prediction has come true—in both cases."

"But how did it happen?" urged Miss Cornelia. "Do read, Elizabeth, how it was. Did he drink poison by mistake?"

Elizabeth took up the paper and read the story, which grew to be a famous one in the annals of New York crime. Halleck had received on New Year's Eve a package which contained a small hunting-flask of sherry. There was no name or card with the present—if present it *were*; nothing to identify the giver, except the hand-writing on the package, which he did not recognize.

He suspected nothing, however, imagining the card to have been forgotten, and accepted the flask as a belated Christmas present; but kept it unopened, in the hope of discovering from whom it came. He had brought it out and showed it the night before to some friends, and the flask and the box in which it arrived were passed from one to the other, but each disclaimed all knowledge of them.

"To me," said D'Hauteville, who happened to be present, "it looks like a woman's handwriting, disguised to seem like a man's. Perhaps"—he smiled—"it contains a love potion."

"Or a death potion," suggested another man, laughing.

"I'm not afraid," said the young singer, lightly, "of either catastrophe." With a smile he poured some of the wine into a glass and raised it to his lips. "To the health," he said, "of the mysterious giver." He emptied the glass and put it down, observing that it must be, after all, a woman's gift, since no man would have chosen such poor wine. "Try it," he said, but by some fortunate chance no one did. And in a few minutes Halleck was taken desperately ill, and died before the hastily-summoned physician could save him.

This is, briefly put, the account which Elizabeth read, at first with a strange sense of unreality, as if such tragedies, of which she had often read before in the papers, could not possibly occur within the circle of her own acquaintance. Then followed a growing horror, a feeling of passionate remorse for her own indifference.

"Read it, auntie," she said, thrusting the paper into Miss Cornelia's hand. "I—I must be alone to think it over." She went quickly and shut herself in her room. But when there she did not lie down and cry, as might have been best for her; she had not shed any tears since New Year's Eve. She paced up and down, going over the whole thing in her mind, imagining the details with a feverish vividness, struggling, above all, with this irrational, yet terrible sense of guilt.

It *was* irrational—this she realized even in her state of feverish excitement. The vindictive wish which had crossed her brain would never have gone beyond it and resolved itself into action. She would not even—she knew this now—have been a passive factor in Paul's death; she would have been the first to go to his aid, had she seen him suffering. No selfish remembrance of her own gain would have stopped her. And yet—and yet—with all her reasoning, her mind always returned to the same point. She had wished for his death, and her wishes had been fulfilled, too late for her own advantage, only as it seemed, to add to her punishment.

The idea occurred to her all at once that she must go and look at his dead body. It presented itself, in some irrational way, in the light of an atonement. The fever in her blood, the beginning of an illness, made the strained, hysterical thought seem natural and almost inevitable. She was not conscious of doing anything unusual. Hastily, she dressed herself, choosing instinctively a black gown and tying a black veil over her face, and went out into the street, where the cold air, which she had not faced for a week, blew refreshingly on her burning cheeks. She walked all the way, rapidly, choosing unfrequented avenues, and looking neither to the right nor the left, her mind intent on the one object, yet with a strange relief in motion and the intense cold. She reached Carnegie Hall in a surprisingly short time, but here she encountered unexpected difficulties.

"Take you up to Mr. Halleck's studio?" said the elevator-man, looking with surprise and suspicion at this veiled young woman, who made such an extraordinary request. "I can't take you up. The police has charge, and there ain't a soul allowed to go in but Mr. D'Hauteville."

Elizabeth was not in a mood to be gainsaid. She placed a coin in the man's hand. "I must see him," she said, in a hoarse whisper. "If you won't take me up, I'll walk. I am his wife," she went on, as he still stared at her, wondering. "I have a right to see him."

"Well, it's the police that settles that," he rejoined, gruffly, but still he took her up, reflecting that, after all, it was no business of his. He brought the elevator to a stand-still, with a shake of the head and an anxious look towards the fatal studio, but Elizabeth moved towards it as if she had no doubt whatever of entering. And at the same moment, Mr. D'Hauteville opened the door of his rooms on the same landing, and came face to face with her.

"Miss Van Vorst!" he exclaimed, staring at her; then, in a lower voice: "For Heaven's sake, don't come here. Halleck is dead. Haven't you heard?"

"Yes, I—I have heard." She looked pleadingly at him. "Mr. D'Hauteville," she said, "take me in to see him. I—I must see him. It was such a shock. I am his wife, you know," she added. The disclosure, which she had once so dreaded, fell from her lips indifferently, as if it were a thing of small importance, compared with the gaining of her purpose.

"His wife!" D'Hauteville fell back and stared at her incredulously. Then his mind quickly grasped the explanation of facts which had puzzled him. He looked at her and saw that she was suffering from terrible distress and excitement. "Do you really wish to see him?" he said. "It would be painful."

"Yes, I—I must see him." Elizabeth raised confidingly her troubled eyes, and D'Hauteville apparently could not resist their appeal. Slowly and reluctantly he unlocked the studio door and allowed Elizabeth to enter. The hall was empty, but from behind the portière at the end came the sound of voices. D'Hauteville cast an anxious glance towards them, but he opened quickly another door, and led the way into the bedroom, which was still and dark, and close with a strange, oppressive atmosphere. D'Hauteville, treading softly, drew up the shade. Then he fell back and turned his eyes away.

Elizabeth felt no fear, though her only recollection of death was connected with a horrible moment in her childhood, when they had led her in trembling to look at her father in his coffin. But now she felt indifferent to any trivial terrors. She stood by the bedside looking down at the dead man, and put out her hand and touched the curls which clustered about his forehead. He was not much changed; the greatest difference which death had made was in a certain look of dignity, which his face had never worn in life. It was impossible, standing there, to think of his faults, or of any harm that he had wrought in her life. She only remembered that he had been her first lover—nothing more.

A few moments passed, and then D'Hauteville pulled down the shades and drew her gently from the room. The tears were falling fast behind her veil, and the hand that rested against his was icy cold.

"I had better see you home," he said anxiously, but she shook her head.

"No, no, thank you. You have been very kind, but I—I would rather not. Mr. D'Hauteville," she said, raising piteous eyes to his "who—who could have done it?"

"God only knows!" said D'Hauteville, with a sigh. "No one else, I believe, ever will."

He had rung the bell, and they stood waiting for the elevator, when she turned to him. "It was not I," she said, "don't ever think that it was I." And at that moment the elevator stopped and she was borne away, before there was time for further words. But D'Hauteville stood paralyzed.

"For Heaven's sake," he asked himself, "why did she say that? Who accused her?"

Elizabeth, as she went her way, was quite unconscious of the impression her words had produced. Her head felt confused, and after she left Carnegie there followed a blank interval, during which she wandered aimlessly, but found herself at last, as if led by some involuntary instinct, in the Park beside the lake, into which a few weeks before she had thrown her wedding ring. Now, as before, it was nearly covered with a thin coating of ice, yet there was a strip of water visible, and upon this her eyes fastened with a thrill of terrified fascination. She pictured it involuntarily, closing over her, dragging her down, blotting out all thoughts, all feelings.... A moment of agony, perhaps, and then? Rest, oblivion, an end of all struggle, no more to-morrows to be faced, no more regrets.... The thought of death, the one way out, the only remedy, swift and sure, appealed to her with a force almost irresistible.

If only the water were not so cold!—In an instant there swept over her, quite as inevitably, the natural, healthy reaction; the revulsion against the icy pond, and all the weird, uncanny, frightful, unpleasant associations that it conjured up. Ah, she had not the courage!—not then, at least. She closed her eyes, shutting out the strange fascination of the water gleaming in the pale chill sunlight, and promising its sure and terrible relief—she closed her eyes and turned resolutely away. A horror seized upon her of herself and of loneliness, of the bleak desolation on every side.

She hastened, breathing heavily, towards the entrance of the Park, her hurried footsteps on the crisp, hard path sounding unnaturally loud in the wintry silence.

Chapter XXX

SEVERAL weeks later the Halleck poisoning case was still, so far as the general public was concerned, an impenetrable mystery. For a day or two various clues were investigated, with a great appearance of zeal; and then a lull fell upon the efforts of the police. Their final investigations, if they made any, were conducted behind closed doors. But no result appeared from their labors; the coroner's inquest was postponed from week to week for lack of sufficient evidence. The public grew impatient, and clamored that some one should be arrested;—it did not seem greatly to matter whom. And then there began to be strange rumors of influence exerted to conceal the truth, of suspicion which pointed in such high quarters, that the police were afraid to continue their search.

These rumors were still comparatively new when Eleanor Van Antwerp took up one day a scandalous society journal—(one of those papers which no one reads, but whose remarks, in some mysterious way, every one hears about)—and came across a paragraph, which seemed to her at once insulting and inexplicable.

"They say"—it began with this conventional formula—"that certain highly dramatic developments are to be expected soon in the famous poisoning case. The evidence that the District Attorney has collected is now said to be complete and to inculpate rather seriously a well-known beauty. The lady is related, though on the father's side only, to one of our old Dutch houses, and was introduced to society, where she was before entirely unknown, by the representative of another old Knickerbocker family. Under such circumstances her success was certain. Not content with taking the town by storm, she made special capture of a certain prominent society man and eligible parti, to whom her engagement was announced. This gentleman has, however, according to latest reports, left the forlorn beauty and fled to parts unknown."

What did it mean? The hot, indignant color rushed to Mrs. Bobby's cheek, and then, retreating, left her deadly pale. She took the paper to her husband, and pointing out the offending paragraph, she stood beside him as he read it, her dark eyes fixed intently upon his face, and seeing there, to her dismay, more indignation than surprise.

"Well," she said, as he looked up at the end. "Tell me—what does it mean?"

"It—the editor of that infernal thing ought to be horsewhipped," he said, fiercely.

She put the remark aside as irrelevant. "Why, that should have been done long ago. But what does it mean?" she persisted, holding to the main point.

He put the paper down with a sigh. "It means what it says, Eleanor, I'm afraid," he said.

She stared at him, a shade paler, while the dread in her eyes grew more pronounced. "Means what it says?" she repeated. "Then it isn't merely a wild concoction of the kind they're always inventing?"

"It's more than that, I'm afraid." Bobby rose and began to pace up and down. "They do say nasty things," he said, apparently addressing the walls, or anything rather than his wife.

Her eyes followed him with an intense anxiety, as her white lips barely framed the question: "At the clubs?"

He nodded. "Yes, there, and—at other places besides. At the District Attorney's, for instance"—

"You don't mean?"—she began incredulously.

"That they suspect her? Yes."

Mrs. Bobby sat down as if her strength suddenly had failed her. "But that's absurd—impossible!" she said, after a moment.

"Perhaps; but—it's the impossible that some times happens." Mrs. Bobby was silent in incredulous horror; and he went on, after a pause: "You see, she's in a confoundedly unpleasant position. There are all kinds of queer stories going the round. They say now that she was secretly married to Halleck; that he had some kind of power over her, at least; and then having every motive to get rid of him, being engaged to Gerard"—

"Bobby," said his wife, in a horrified tone "how can you repeat such disgusting gossip?"

"I'm only telling you what they say," said Bobby, apologetically.

"I don't wish to know it." Bobby held his peace. "Why should she have any motive?" said his wife, after a moment's reflection "when her engagement was broken?"

"They say—but I thought you didn't wish to know."

"I don't, but I suppose, I must know. What do they—these disgusting people—say?"

"They think that Gerard found out something which made him break the engagement. As for the poison, that was sent before, you know"—

"Bobby," said his wife, with a little cry, "you don't mean to suggest that she—that Elizabeth Van Vorst"—She paused as if at a loss for words, and Bobby concluded the sentence.

"Sent the poison?" he said, quietly. "No, I don't suggest it—not for a second; I don't *believe* it, even," he cried, with sudden emphasis, "but there are other people who—who do both."

"Then they must be fools." Bobby made no reply. "Where," she said, in a moment, "do they suppose she got it—the poison?"

"That they don't know—as yet; but they know—or they think they do—where she got the flask. There's a shop in Brooklyn where they sell others like it"—he stopped.

"Well," she said, "what of it? I daresay there are a good many shops where they sell them."

"The man who keeps this particular shop, said, I believe, that he sold one on the twenty-third of December to a young woman thickly veiled, rather tall and with wavy red hair."

"Her hair isn't red," said Mrs. Bobby, quickly.

"Some people call it so, you know," said Bobby. She was silent.

"Hundreds of women have that sort of hair," she said, presently. "Half the actresses in town"—

"He said it seemed to him natural."

"How should he know?" said Mrs. Bobby, contemptuously. "And why on earth should she choose a place like Brooklyn? I don't think she ever went there in her life."

"She seems," said Bobby, gently, "to have done a great many things that you—didn't think of, Eleanor." And again his wife fell silent.

"Have they any other evidence?" she asked, after thinking a moment, "or what they call evidence? I might as well know the worst."

"They have her letters, which were found among Halleck's papers—she told him to burn them, but he didn't. They were signed 'E. V. V.' One of them was about her engagement to Gerard—it seemed he had threatened her, and she offered him money to keep him quiet; the other was just a line, asking him to meet her in the Park. It's evident that she was afraid of him and had to keep him supplied with funds. She sold all her jewelry, they say, to do it."

"Ah—her jewelry!" Mrs. Bobby drew a long breath. "That is what she did with it, then," she remarked, involuntarily.

Bobby turned to her sharply. "You noticed, then," he said, "that she didn't have it?"

"Of course. There were her pearls, which she never wore last summer; the watch I gave her, too—I used to feel hurt that she never carried it, but I never suspected—Oh, what a fool I was—what a fool! And I who thought myself so clever in bringing about a match between her and Julian!" She stopped and suddenly burst into tears. "I made a nice failure of it all, didn't I?" she said. Then in a moment, her mood changed, and she turned upon Bobby indignantly. "Why didn't you tell me all this before?"

"I didn't want to tell you," said Bobby, slowly, "a moment sooner than was necessary. Personally, I don't see the use of having all this exploited—as a matter of fact, I'd pay a good deal to have it kept quiet; partly for your sake, and partly because—well, I like Elizabeth. She may not have behaved well, but I don't think she deserves to be made conspicuous in this way. I don't mind confessing that I've done what I could to arrest the zeal of the police, but I'm sorry to say, without success."

"You don't mean," she said incredulously, "that they refused money?"

"Well, the new District Attorney is very zealous," Bobby explained, "and, between ourselves, I think he wants the éclat of a sensational case. To put a young society woman in prison, against the efforts of all her friends, shows Roman stoicism,—or so he thinks."

"But you don't believe," said his wife, piteously, "you don't think it could come to that, Bobby?"

"To prison?" he said. "I don't know, Eleanor—upon my word I don't know." And he began again thoughtfully to pace up and down.

"What did Gerard say," he asked presently, "when he wrote to you before he sailed?"

"It was just a hurried note, hard to make out. He said the engagement was broken by her."

"Of course he'd *say* that. What did she tell you?"

"That it was his wish, but he was not to blame, and she would tell me more some other time. She looked so unutterably wretched that I couldn't ask any questions just then."

"Ah," said Bobby, softly. "I don't believe, poor child! that it was her doing, Eleanor."

"If it was Julian's," she said, "he must have had some good reason." And with that they both fell into thoughtful silence.

"I don't see," was her next objection, uttered musingly, "I don't see how they ever thought of Elizabeth in the first place. It seems such a wildly improbable idea."

"It certainly does," Bobby agreed. "Then Elizabeth, poor child, as it happens, rather put the idea into their heads herself. It seems that she went to the studio the day after the poisoning and insisted upon seeing him. She said she was his wife. D'Hauteville saw her, I believe, but he said nothing about it. It was the elevator man who told the story—he took her up and he heard D'Hauteville call her by her name. He says that D'Hauteville took her into the studio, and when she came out she was crying. And the man vows he heard her say 'I didn't do it, don't think I did it,' or something of the kind."

"Why, I never," broke in Mrs. Bobby, "heard anything so extraordinary. The man must have been drinking. It's impossible that Elizabeth could have done such a thing. Why, it was that day—that day"—she paused and thought—"that day after the murder," she continued, triumphantly, "I remember distinctly going to see her in the afternoon, and she was ill in bed with grippe, and her temperature very high."

"I can believe that," said Bobby, rather grimly, "after what she went through in the morning. For I'm afraid there's not much doubt, Eleanor, that it's true. One of the detectives, too, saw her pass through the hall, and I don't think that D'Hauteville denies it. They want him to testify at the inquest, but so far, they can't get him to say one thing or another."

"He would deny it, of course, if it were false," said Mrs. Bobby, in a low voice. Her husband bent his head. "Well," she said, rallying, "after all, I don't see anything in that. It would be pretty stupid, if she were really guilty, to defend herself before she was accused. No one but a fool would have done that, and the person who sent that poison couldn't have been a fool. And she wouldn't have gone near the studio; that's the last thing the real culprit would have done."

"That's what I say," said Bobby. "It doesn't seem on the face of it the act of a guilty woman. But they have some theory of hysterical remorse, and there is other evidence I haven't heard which fits into that. They say that when she heard that it had really happened she lost her head completely. There have been such cases, you know. Oh, and then another thing. They're comparing the handwriting on the package with the letters"—

"The letters?" broke in Mrs. Bobby, anxiously.

"Yes, that I told you of, you remember—written to him—they've got experts examining them now."

"Ah, well, if the experts have got hold of the case," said Mrs. Bobby, resignedly, "we might as well give up hope. They'd swear away any person's life to prove a theory."

"Well, at least," said Bobby, "it's the life of a young and beautiful girl. That really seemed to me, when I heard all this, the only hope. Even handwriting experts are human." But his wife only sighed despairingly.

"I think," she said, after awhile, "I must go to Elizabeth. I haven't seen her for several days, and she mustn't think that her friends are giving her up."

"You won't—tell her anything?" asked Bobby, anxiously.

"Do you think she doesn't know?"

"She would be the last person, in the natural order of events, to hear of it."

"Then I shall say nothing," said his wife, after a moment's reflection. "You wouldn't, would you?" she added, as she caught an odd look in her husband's eyes.

"I—I don't know." Bobby seemed to reflect. "If—if she were to go abroad just now," he said, doubtfully, "it might not be a bad plan."

"Bobby!" Mr. Van Antwerp's wife faced him indignantly. "You wouldn't have her—run away from all this? You wouldn't have her frightened by anything those people can threaten?" Eleanor Van Antwerp's dark eyes sparkled, she held her head proudly. Her husband looked at her half in doubt, half in admiration.

"You would face it?"

"Yes, if it cost me my life."

The look of admiration on Bobby's face brightened and then faded to despondency. "Ah, well, you are right—theoretically, of course, but—would Elizabeth, do you think, have the same courage? Or, if she had, could you, knowing what you do, take the responsibility of allowing her to face it?"

This was the doubt—the horrible doubt, which troubled Mrs. Bobby as she drove to Elizabeth's home, and at the thought of it her heart failed her. Her husband had judged her rightly—she could be braver for herself than for others. Would it not be better, after all, to suggest to the Misses Van Vorst the desirability of a trip abroad? She looked thoughtfully out of the carriage window. It was a bleak February day, and people in the street had their coat-collars turned up against the chill east wind. The climate of New York at this time is detestable; a change would do any one good. She would go herself to the Riviera and take Elizabeth with her.

Mrs. Bobby had hardly reached this conclusion before the carriage stopped in front of the quiet apartment house in Irving Place where the Van Vorsts were spending the winter. It was an old-fashioned house with an air of sober respectability, that seemed to make such wild thoughts as filled Mrs. Bobby's brain peculiarly strained and improbable, like the hallucinations of a fevered brain. It was a shock, keyed up as she was to the tragic point, to enter the peaceful little drawing-room with its bright coal fire and general air of comfort, and to find Elizabeth prosaically engaged in looking over visiting-cards and invitations. And yet Mrs. Bobby was shocked by the change in her appearance, which every day made more apparent. Her face was haggard, there was a deep purple flush in her cheeks; her lips were dry and feverish, there was an odd, strained look in her eyes. The hand she held out to her visitor burned like fire.

"I'm so glad you came in," she said, with a wan smile. "I've been looking over these stupid things and my head aches. You see, I've neglected my social duties shamefully—not sending cards, or even, I'm afraid, answering some of my invitations. People must think me horribly rude."

"Oh, they know you've been ill," Mrs. Bobby answered vaguely. She sat down, all the wind taken out of her sails, and stared wonderingly at Elizabeth. How could she—how could she look over visiting-cards and talk about invitations, with this terrible danger hanging over her head? Was it possible that she had no suspicions? And yet—did not her eyes betray her? But Mrs. Bobby could not think of any way of introducing the subject of which her mind and heart were full, and there was silence till Elizabeth spoke again.

"It's odd, isn't it," she said languidly, "that Mrs. Lansdowne hasn't asked me to her ball. Have you cards for it?"

"I—I believe so."

"Well, she has left me out," said Elizabeth. Mrs. Bobby started and looked at her with some interest. "I suppose she thinks," Elizabeth went on, "I—I'm not much of an addition just now. I certainly am not, to look at." She laughed a little, in a feeble way. "Of course I shouldn't go," she added, "but it isn't nice to be—left out."

"Perhaps it's a mistake," suggested Mrs. Bobby, not very impressively. She was quite convinced to the contrary.

"Perhaps," Elizabeth acquiesced, "but if so, several other people have done the same thing. The Van Aldens never asked me to their dance, and I haven't had an invitation to a dinner for weeks. People forget one quickly in New York, don't they?" And she made another painful attempt at a laugh.

"I suppose," said Mrs. Bobby, "they think you don't want to go."

"I don't," said Elizabeth, "but they might at least give me the opportunity of refusing." And then there was a pause, in the midst of which Miss Joanna entered.

"Oh, Mrs. Van Antwerp," she said, "how glad I am to see you! Do tell Elizabeth that she ought to be in bed. You can see for yourself she has fever. It is the grippe, of course—she has never really got over it."

"Yes," said Mrs. Bobby, looking doubtfully at Elizabeth, "it is the grippe, of course."

"The grippe is a convenient disease," said Elizabeth, in a low tone, "it means—so many things." She took up a sheet of paper and began to write hastily.

"It does me good," she said "to employ myself. And I can't stay in bed—it drives me wild." Miss Joanna, as if weary of expostulation, moved to the window.

"Yes, I declare," she announced, in the tone of one who makes a not unexpected discovery, "there are those men again. Every time I look out, one or other of them seems to be watching the house."

"Watching the house?" repeated Mrs. Bobby, startled.

"Yes, that's what it looks like, at least. And the other day, when I went out, one of them stared at me so—most impertinent. I declare, if it goes on, we shall have to make a complaint. And one of them followed Elizabeth—didn't he, my dear?"

"I thought he did," said Elizabeth, indifferently, "but I didn't notice much. I have thought several times lately that there were people following me. Perhaps it is because my head feels so queer."

"What do the men look like?" asked Mrs. Bobby.

"Oh, quite respectable," said Miss Joanna. "They don't look like beggars, certainly. Cornelia thought they looked rather like detectives—she said they made her feel nervous; but that, of course, is quite ridiculous."

"Quite ridiculous," echoed Mrs. Bobby. To herself she was saying, "Ah, that trip abroad!"

"Eleanor has an invitation for Mrs. Lansdowne's ball, auntie," said Elizabeth, suddenly changing the subject, which did not seem to interest her, by the introduction of one that evidently rankled in her mind. "She thinks it is odd I wasn't asked. I told you," she went on, with a bitter smile, "that people are giving me up since my engagement was broken off."

"But that is nonsense," remonstrated Miss Joanna, in distress. "Tell her," she said, turning pleadingly to Mrs. Bobby, "that that isn't so."

Mrs. Bobby started up and took Elizabeth's hand. "I don't know," she said, speaking with strange earnestness, "who gives you up, Elizabeth dear, and I don't care. I never will. Remember that, dear child. I will stand by you whatever happens." And then, as if conscious of having said too much, or fearful perhaps of saying more, Mrs. Bobby swept hastily from the room, leaving her hearers petrified.

Miss Joanna was the first to speak. "How very strange she was!" she said, in a low voice. "What—what do you think she meant?"

Elizabeth was staring vacantly at the door, but at her aunt's words she turned.

"I don't know," she said, "what she meant, but one thing I understand—that my social career is ended." With a little pale smile, she swept aside the cards of invitation, locked them into a drawer and left the room.

Chapter XXXI

MRS. Bobby regained her carriage, and consulting her engagement book, she ordered her coachman to drive her to the house of one of her friends, whose "day at home" it was. It was a sudden resolution. She had gone about very little that winter, since she had no longer the incentive of chaperoning Elizabeth, and had not paid a visit for weeks, on the plea of mourning for an uncle. But now she set her teeth and said to herself that she must mingle with the world to find out, if possible, what the world was saying.

Was it fancy, or did she distinguish, as she stood in the hall of Mrs. Van Alden's house leaving cards, amidst the hum of voices in the drawing-room, words that bore upon her own fevered anxiety? "Shocking affair," and "so she is really involved in it"—surely she heard those sentences. And then the conversation ceased abruptly as the butler drew aside the portière and she stood for a moment on the threshold. Her eyes were bright, her head erect; she glanced around taking mental stock as it were of the company. Five or six women were seated about a blazing wood fire, with an air unusual at functions of this kind of having come to stay and of forming—or this again might have been her fancy—a sort of council of justice. There was Mrs. Lansdowne, to whose ball Elizabeth had not been invited; and there was Sibyl Hartington, and one or two others who knew Mrs. Bobby and did not, as it happened, love her very much. "Enemies," she thought, drawing her breath sharply, "and discussing Elizabeth and me! It's the same thing—I'm sure I feel as if it were I under suspicion." Eleanor Van Antwerp had certainly never known such a feeling before, but her bearing had never been more instinct with the nonchalant confidence of a woman who seems absolutely unconscious of her position, for the reason that it has never been questioned.

"I seem to have interrupted the conversation," she observed, lightly, after she had been rather nervously greeted and kissed by her hostess, and had taken her place in the circle. "Some one was telling a very interesting story—I caught fragments of it as I came in." She glanced her eye round the group. "It was you, Kitty, I think," she said. "Won't you—please—begin the story over again and tell it for my benefit?"

"Kitty," thus appealed to, colored and bit her lip. "Oh, the story isn't really worth repeating," she said, hastily. She had no wish to offend Mrs. Van Antwerp, and was heartily wishing that she had not spoken so loud. Sibyl Hartington helped her out by observing, with her placid smile:

"It's a story about a friend of yours, my dear Eleanor, so Kitty is afraid to tell it."

"About a friend of mine?" said Mrs. Bobby, and she opened her eyes very wide. "Then there's all the more reason," she said, decidedly, "why I should hear it."

Her glance challenged the group, but no one spoke and at last the hostess interposed. "My dear Eleanor, I'm sorry you should have heard anything about it. We were only talking about poor Elizabeth Van Vorst, and regretting that there is all this unfortunate gossip about her. For my part, I don't believe there is a word of truth in what they say, but it is certainly—uncomfortable."

"It makes it hard to know what to do," said Mrs. Lansdowne, a woman with a deep bass voice and an air of being not so much indifferent to, as unconscious of other people's feelings. "I couldn't for instance ask Miss Van Vorst to my ball while there are these queer rumors about her. I was sorry to leave out any friend of yours, Mrs. Van Antwerp; but if a young woman gets herself talked about, no matter how or why, I can't encourage her—it's against my principles. Let the girl behave herself, I say, and keep out of the papers. I'm sure that's simple enough."

"It's not always so simple," said Mrs. Bobby, and though the indignant color had rushed into her cheeks, her tone was seraphic, "not so simple for every one as it is for your daughters, Mrs. Lansdowne." A subdued smile as she spoke went the round of the circle. Fortunately Mrs. Lansdowne was not quick in her perceptions.

"No, it's true," she admitted, "my daughters have had unusual advantages. I can't expect every one to come up to the same standard. But one has to draw the line somewhere, and when a girl has done such queer things as Miss Van Vorst, there seems nothing for it but to drop her."

"But what—what has poor Elizabeth done?" asked Mrs. Bobby, with eyes of innocent wonder, and again there followed an awkward silence.

"Well, you know, Eleanor, they tell very queer stories," the hostess said at last, deprecatingly. "I never pay any attention to gossip, but these things are sometimes forced upon one. Haven't you seen that thing in *Scandal*?"

"I don't," said Mrs. Bobby, unmoved, "read '*Scandal*,' Mary."

"And *Chit Chat*," chimed in some one else. "There was a long paragraph in *Chit Chat*. It seems that she was mixed up in some way in that dreadful poisoning case. They say that she was actually married to that young Halleck."

"At the same time that she was engaged to Julian Gerard," said Mrs. Hartington, with her calm smile. "It's no wonder that he, poor man, when he found it out, got out of the affair as best he could."

Mrs. Bobby looked steadily at the speaker. "As a friend of Mr. Gerard's, Sibyl," she said, "I can state on his authority that the engagement was broken by Miss Van Vorst."

Sibyl Hartington's calm, faintly amused smile again rippled across her face. "I never doubted, my dear Eleanor," she said, "that Mr. Gerard is a gentleman."

The entrance of another visitor at that moment was not altogether unwelcome to Mrs. Bobby, who felt that she was being worsted; but the new-comer immediately continued the same subject.

"I've just been hearing the most extraordinary news," she exclaimed, sitting on the edge of her chair, and too much excited to notice Mrs. Bobby's presence, "I heard it at luncheon. They say that Elizabeth Van Vorst"—But here the speaker suddenly caught sight of Mrs. Bobby, and stopped short.

"Well, what do they say?" said Mrs. Bobby, with rather a bitter smile. "Don't keep us in suspense, Miss Dare, and above all, don't mind my feelings. I would rather know the worst of this."

"Well, I don't believe there is any truth in it. They say that she is really seriously implicated in that dreadful poisoning case; that the police have letters she wrote to Halleck, and all sorts of unpleasant things. But of course it's impossible—a girl like that, whom we all know!"

"Do we?" said Mrs. Hartington, softly. "Do you think that we, any of us, know much about her? You didn't, Eleanor, did you?"—turning to Mrs. Bobby— "You just took her up in that charming, impulsive way of yours—didn't you?— because people in the Neighborhood didn't have much to do with her, and you felt sorry for her?"

Mrs. Bobby made a scornful little gesture. "You flatter me, Sibyl," she said. "I'm afraid I'm not so charitable as all that. I 'took up' Elizabeth Van Vorst, as you say, because I liked her, and for no other reason. It was for my own pleasure entirely that I asked her to stay with me, and I have never regretted it."

Mrs. Hartington gave a barely perceptible shrug of the shoulders. "I congratulate you," she said. "It was a rash action, some people thought at the time. A girl whom you knew so slightly, whose mother was such an impossible person— or at least, so they say. I don't of course," she went on, in her soft, drawling tones, "know much about it myself, but it does make all this gossip seem less extraordinary—doesn't it?"

"Why, yes, of course, that accounts for it," said Mrs. Lansdowne, looking relieved. "That sort of thing runs in families. A girl who has a queer mother is sure to be queer herself and get herself talked about."

"I never thought her very good style," some one who had not yet spoken now found courage to observe. "Her hair is so conspicuous. I never could understand why men seemed to admire her."

Mrs. Hartington raised her eye-brows. "Ah, the men!" she said, with serene scorn. "She is exactly the sort of girl who would appeal to men."

Mrs. Bobby felt that she had stayed as long as the limit of human endurance would permit. She rose to her feet, her cheeks were flushed, her eyes brilliant, her voice rang out with crystal clearness. "It's hardly necessary for me to tell you," she said, "that Elizabeth Van Vorst is my most intimate friend. I love her very dearly and always shall. What her mother may have been is no affair of mine. But as for the men liking her"—she turned suddenly to Mrs. Hartington—"they do like her, Sibyl, and I think they show good taste. But if you mean the inference you seem to draw from that"—she paused and drew her breath quickly—"why, it's not very flattering, I think, to either men or women."

Mrs. Hartington gave a short little laugh. "My dear, I'm not drawing inferences one way or another. I merely stated a fact—complimentary, one might think, to your protegée. But you take things so seriously!"—She drew herself up with an air of some annoyance.

Mrs. Bobby's hands were tightly locked together inside her muff, she faced the group appealingly, her dark eyes wandering from one to the other. "Certainly, I take this thing seriously," she said, and there was a thrill of earnestness in her voice which moved more than one of her hearers. "It's no light matter for me to hear my friend spoken of—like this. I had Elizabeth Van Vorst with me all last winter, I feel as if I knew her like my own sister. I believe in her implicitly, no matter what any one may say. And if—if some of you"—instinctively her eyes fastened upon one or two whom she felt she was carrying with her—"if you would try to think the best, give her the benefit of the doubt, show that women can stand by one another—sometimes"—Her voice faltered and she broke off suddenly; there were tears glistening in her eyes as she held out her hand to her hostess. "Forgive me, Mary," she said. "I don't want to make a scene. But I can't help feeling strongly, and in this case I want every one to know exactly how I feel." And with that she left the room quickly before any one could speak, yet conscious as she went of a subtle wave of sympathy, which seemed to have made itself felt since her entrance.

"But it's useless—useless," she said sadly to her husband when she got home. "You might as well try to stop the course of a torrent as fight against the world's disapproval, when it is once roused against any poor, defenceless girl. And it isn't as if she were a great personage, or even as if she were still engaged to Julian! They've nothing to gain by standing by her. Yet there were one or two, I think, even of those women this afternoon, who felt with me. And at least"—she consoled herself a little—"at least they shall see that she has friends!"

"She'll need them, poor girl. The—the inquest—I've just heard—is coming off next week." He took up a paper knife and played with it, while he stole a furtive glance at his wife. "I think you had better—prepare Elizabeth," he said.

"Prepare her?" she repeated anxiously, as he paused.

"For some confoundedly unpleasant questions! Yes. Have you the strength to tell her?" His eyes questioned her anxiously. She was white to the lips, but she met them without flinching.

"One can always find strength."

"It's confoundedly hard, I know." Bobby began to pace up and down helplessly. "You don't know how I hate to have you mixed up in all this, Eleanor," he said. "I'd give anything to have you out of it. Wouldn't it be better for you to go abroad for awhile?"

"And desert Elizabeth? My dear Bobby, you wouldn't have me do that?"

"Well, you can't help her, you know," he urged.

"I can show that I believe in her. And, thank Heaven! social position does count for something. It may help me to fight Elizabeth's battles."

"It doesn't count for much, unfortunately, before the law."

"Not theoretically, no," said his wife, sceptically. "But practically—it counts with every one and everywhere. By the way," she added, struck with a sudden idea, "what sort of man is the District Attorney? I might ask him to dinner." And she looked prepared to send the invitation on the spot.

"My dear Eleanor, I'm afraid it's too late for that now. The thing to do now, since matters have gone so far, is to prove Elizabeth's innocence, and for that, the first step is to prepare her, so that she won't be taken unawares. Her aunts too—they must be told, I suppose. Poor things, I believe it will kill them!"

"People don't die so easily. It would be more merciful, I sometimes think, if they did." She sat and thought for a moment. "I think I had better go there at once," she said, at last, nervously. "I couldn't sleep to-night with this hanging over my head."

And so, for the second time that day, she drove to the Van Vorsts' apartment, feeling that her unexpected appearance in itself must prepare them for some calamity. And indeed the telling proved easier than she feared. She saw Elizabeth alone, and sat holding the girl's hand, trying by many tender circumlocutions to break the force of the blow. But Elizabeth understood almost immediately.

"They think I sent the poison—is that it?" she said, going at once to the point which her friend was approaching so carefully. "Well, that isn't so strange. Sometimes I feel," she added, wearily, and putting her hand to her head, "as if I had done it myself. I think I—I might have done it."

"Elizabeth, Elizabeth, what do you mean?"

"Because I wished it, you know," Elizabeth went on to explain quite calmly. "I was married to him, and I wished that he might die, so that no one would ever know it, I didn't tell any one but Julian—I wouldn't have told him if I could have helped it. That was the reason he gave me up—because I told him that I had been secretly married all the time. He was angry because I hadn't told him before."

"But," interrupted Mrs. Bobby, with intense anxiety, "you did tell him, at last?"

"Yes, of course I told him," said Elizabeth, in surprise. "I told him New Year's Eve. Why else should he have given me up?"

"Then," cried Mrs. Bobby, rising to her feet in her excitement, "that seems to me an unanswerable argument. If you had—had expected Paul Halleck's death, you certainly wouldn't have told Julian Gerard of your marriage. That's clear as daylight. Oh, Elizabeth, how fortunate that you told him!"

"Fortunate?" said Elizabeth, listlessly. "I don't see that it is very fortunate, since he has given me up and will never forgive me."

"But it may save you." Elizabeth looked at her blankly. "Oh, my dear child," cried Mrs. Bobby, "don't you understand that they suspect you of—of the murder?"

"You don't mean that they would put me in prison?"

Mrs. Bobby only answered by her silence. Elizabeth sat staring at her for a moment, then the color rushed into her white face, her eyes flashed. "How would they dare do that," she cried, "when I am innocent?"

"Of course you are," said Mrs. Bobby. "No one but a fool would think otherwise. And we will prove it, never fear. But you mustn't talk any more of this morbid nonsense about being guilty of his death and all that. I know what you mean well enough, but the general public doesn't understand such psychological subtleties. And besides, it's not true. The guilty person had no thought of doing you a service—be sure of that. Paul Halleck would have died, my dear, if you had never known him. And now keep up a brave heart, Elizabeth. Your friends will stand by you, and when all this is over—happily over, you will look back upon it as a bad dream—nothing more."

Mrs. Bobby had almost talked herself into feeling the confidence she expressed; but Elizabeth listened languidly, with drooping head. All color had faded again from her face; it looked haggard, worn; her hands plucked nervously at some fringe on her gown. When she wiped her eyes at the last words, the smile she conjured up was piteous.

"It's a dream," she murmured, "that is lasting—a terribly long time."

Chapter XXXII

THERE is an old prison well in the heart of the city, which presents a grim, mediæval front to the busy world outside. Elizabeth knew that it existed, but had never seen it. She did not know even where it was, till she found herself condemned to spend eight months within its walls.

This was after the inquest, when the evidence had gone as she had seen herself, very much against her. It was a curious feeling—this bewildered perception of a net closing round her, whose meshes she had woven herself. The verdict of the jury was hardly a surprise. And then they broke to her gently the fact that bail was refused, and they brought her across the Bridge of Sighs, the name of which gave her an odd little thrill, into the prison.

The inmates of The Tombs are mostly of the lowest class. Such a prisoner as Miss Van Vorst was disconcerting to wardens and matrons alike. The situation was unprecedented, they hardly knew how to deal with it.

Elizabeth was placed in one of the ordinary cells; no other indeed was to be had. It was small and dark, and had for furniture a cot-bed, a faucet set in the wall, and one cane chair. Light and air—what there was of either—came in through the corridor, above and below the iron grating which barred the doorway. There was no window.

Elizabeth, to whom an abundance of light and air had been one of the necessities of life, who had a passion for space and luxury, for fresh, dainty surroundings, looked about her in blank dismay. Yet she said nothing. From the first she seemed to school herself to a silent stoicism, which her friends called courage and her enemies insensibility, and which may have been a combination of both. The last two months had been crowded with so many startling events, so intense, conflicting a tumult of thought and emotion, that her capacity for acute suffering was for the moment exhausted.

Yet the mere physical horror that the cell inspired her with was very great. The first time that the key was turned upon her, and she was left entirely alone, with the twilight coming on, with no power to free herself, nothing to do but wait for the matron's return, she felt as she had felt once when for some childish offence, she had been locked into a dark closet. Now as then she threw herself against the door, trying with fierce, unreasoning efforts to force the lock, uttering hoarse cries for help. Then the door had been quickly opened, her aunts had let her out with remorseful tears, and the experiment had never been repeated. Now no help came to her, and she was left to adapt herself to the situation as best she might. The struggle left deep marks on her young face, a look in her eyes which they never afterwards lost.

There were many ways in which the prison routine was softened in her favor. Social distinctions count, as Mrs. Bobby had said, with every one and everywhere. Money is powerful, even in The Tombs. The warden and the other officials reaped in those days a harvest of gold coins from Mrs. Bobby.

A more comfortable bed, a hand-mirror, all sorts of forbidden luxuries, found their way into Elizabeth's cell. Neither warden nor matron apparently recognized their existence. She was permitted to receive her visitors alone, to have a light in her cell after dark, to walk for an hour a day in the corridor or the court. At these times she would see those other women, her fellow-prisoners, huddled together in an abject group, and feel thankful that at least she was not obliged to mingle with them. Her meals were served to her in her cell, and she could order what she wanted. Her friends sent her constantly an abundance of fruit and flowers.

The people who came to see her, and there were many of them, used to go away wondering at her calmness. They went prepared for tragedy, and Elizabeth received them as she might in her own drawing-room. They noticed no change in her, except that her head had never been held so proudly, and she had never looked so pale. But there were no confidences, no tears, no consciousness apparently of the extraordinary state of things. Even to her aunts, even to Eleanor Van Antwerp, she maintained this attitude of proud reserve. They could only guess at the thoughts which lay beneath it. There were times, indeed, when she did not think, when her brain would seem dazed. In those days she would read eagerly all the books that people brought her; read them through from beginning to end, but she had never any idea of what they were about.

There was one form of reading which no one suggested, which she did not, apparently, think of herself. No one brought her a newspaper, and she never asked to see one. Perhaps she did not realize how much her case was discussed, perhaps she realized it only too well. Her aunts were thankful for her lack of curiosity. They could not themselves open a paper, or enter a street-car, without an agony of dread as to what they might see or hear.

For the yellow journals, of course, were exploiting the affair—it was Mrs. Bobby's opinion, indeed, that it had been started originally on their account, for the enlivenment of a dull season. This may or may not be true; but certainly they made the most of it. They published Elizabeth's picture, and long accounts of her conquests. There were pictures, too, of her grandmother, that stately beauty whose fame was traditional, and of old Van Vorsts who had held important offices, and served city and state with credit in colonial and revolutionary times. Then, by contrast, there were accounts of her mother's past and her mother's kindred through several generations of moral and social disrepute. The Neighborhood was overrun by disguised reporters who made copious notes of local items, and took photographs of the Van Vorst Homestead, of the village, of Bassett Mills and even of the church—thereby causing the Rector's wife nervous spasms in her anxiety lest any of Elizabeth's moral perversions should be laid to the account of the religious teaching that she had received. Bassett Mills was all a-flutter in its excitement over this gratuitous advertisement. But in the Neighborhood—the staid, aristocratic old Neighborhood—there was a feeling of humiliation, a presentiment that it could never recover from the disgrace of such notoriety.

And yet, in spite of all discredit, what a subject for conversation—in the Neighborhood as well as Bassett Mills! Nothing else was talked of at the various tea-parties, of which so many had never been given before. People who had guests took them over on Sunday afternoons to the Homestead, and wandered about the grounds relating the family history, while the strangers stared with interest at the old house, and the horse-shoe on the door. There was a dreary look about the place for the Misses Van Vorst were not coming back that summer, and the old gardener left in charge had not the heart under the circumstances to keep it in order. Grass grew in the gravel-walks, the flowers in the garden hung their heads, the foliage was sadly in need of clipping. A shadow seemed to brood over house and grounds, as in the day of old Madam Van Vorst.

In town, where there were more things to talk about, the great poisoning case still took precedence of all other subjects, and society was divided on account of it into warring camps. There were those—a very large number—who followed Mrs. Hartington's lead, and spoke of Elizabeth as a sort of adventuress, who had thrust herself into circles which she had no right to enter; a party which disowned her entirely and believed implicitly in her guilt. But there was another party, smaller perhaps but not less influential, which took uncompromisingly the opposite side. The people who composed it were friends, many of them, of Mrs. Van Antwerp, and there were others who had cared for Elizabeth for her own sake, and again others to whom the romantic facts of the case appealed irresistibly, inducing them to espouse her cause regardless of reason. These all spoke of her as a suffering martyr and regarded her imprisonment as an outrage. They did not discuss the evidence, but met all doubts with the one unanswerable argument of their own intuitions.

But the first side had in point of logic, so much the best of it! This conviction intruded itself reluctantly on Eleanor Van Antwerp's mind, as she looked up from an exhaustive summary of the case for the prosecution. The article presented, in clear, remorseless details, all the links in the terrible chain of evidence—her hasty marriage, and then her repentance; her efforts to buy off her husband; the trouble she had to supply him with money; her evident fear of his betraying her to Gerard; her refusal to name her wedding day, till she had in sheer desperation decided on the murder; then when the thing was at last accomplished, her sudden remorse, her strange actions; the rumor that she had in the first excitement confessed her guilt before witnesses; the description too, of the woman who had bought the flask, and which fitted Elizabeth exactly in height, coloring and general appearance; the resemblances which the experts were said to have discovered between her letters and the handwriting on the package—never was chain more strongly forged! And what, the article further demanded, had her friends to offer in rebuttal but her social position, her youth and her beauty?

"It's not much, certainly," Mrs. Bobby's anxiety admitted. "And yet a good deal, too," her aristocratic instincts involuntarily responded; "and will have their weight with the jury," her cynicism added. But then again despair overwhelmed her, and she put the unavailing question: "Bobby, is there—do you think there is any hope?"

Bobby stared back at her, his face hardly less white than hers.

"God only knows, Eleanor! If she were just a man, or even an ordinary woman, I should say 'no;' but for a young girl, there's always a chance. Let her"—he dropped his hand on the table beside him with a deep sigh—"let her look as pretty as she can. It seems to me about the only hope."

"She won't look pretty," his wife returned, with a little sob. "She is just the shadow of her old self; if she stays in that place much longer, I believe it will kill her. Bobby," she cried, with a sudden burst of indignation, staring up at him with tragic eyes, "if that child dies—there, it will be murder! And yet you say the law is just!"

Bobby had said so much in the last few weeks in perfunctory defence of the law that he was weary of the subject, and so he attempted no further protestations, but watched his wife sadly as she walked impatiently to and fro; a slight, childlike creature, her cheeks flushed, her eyes brilliant with impotent anger, dashing herself as it were against impenetrable barriers. Only once before in her life had Eleanor Van Antwerp been confronted with an obstacle that did not yield to her wishes. That was when the baby died, and she had resigned herself to what she believed to be Divine Providence. But this seemed mere human stupidity.

"If only men were not so logical!" she exclaimed, despairingly. "Women, if they intended to get her off, would do it, no matter what the evidence was; but men!—they are so bound hand and foot by their sense of justice, their respect for law, and Heaven knows what! that they are quite capable, even if they believe her innocent, of finding her guilty, just because the evidence was against her."

"Well that's what they're supposed to do," Bobby put in, deprecatingly, "they've got to abide by the evidence." It was the twentieth time that he had made this explanation, and for the twentieth time, she brushed it aside.

"What does it matter," she demanded, "about the evidence, when any one with common-sense must *know* the girl is innocent? But I see how it is, Bobby," she went on, her lip quivering. "You don't really believe in her the way that I do. You have doubts—at the bottom of your heart you have doubts. Tell me the truth, and I'll try to forgive you—*haven't* you?"

She stopped before him, her dark eyes, fastened upon his, seemed to read his soul, but he answered steadily: "Eleanor, upon my honor, I believe in that child's innocence as you do. I'd give anything in the world to get her off. (Yes, and I would," he added to himself "for your sake, if she had committed twenty murders.")

She drew a long sigh of relief. "Oh, Bobby, you *are* nice," she said, gratefully. "You've been very good to me all this time—never once saying 'I told you so,' when the whole thing has been all my fault for not taking your advice."

"Your fault, you poor child! How do you make that out?"

"If I had never asked Elizabeth to stop with me," she said tremulously, "all this wouldn't have happened. You warned me—don't you remember?—and you were right. I've come to the conclusion, Bobby, that you generally *are* right and I wrong."

Her tone of submission was as edifying as it was surprising, but Bobby with unwonted quickness cut it short. "Nonsense!" he said almost roughly. "You were right in that case, as you generally are, and I was wrong; and no harm would have come of it if Elizabeth—well, I don't want to hit people when they're down," he said, apologetically "but if she had only been frank with us from the first, all this wouldn't have happened. My dear"—this in response to a reproachful look from his wife—"I don't mean to be hard on her, but I can't hear you blame yourself for what has been poor Elizabeth's own fault, helped out by a most extraordinary train of circumstances."

"She was to blame, certainly," faltered his wife, reluctantly, "but I can understand—I believe I should have done the same in her place."

"No, Eleanor," said Bobby, briefly and with some sternness, "you would not."

"It's true," she admitted, "I don't think I could keep a secret if I tried. But then neither apparently could Elizabeth—to the bitter end. That is one thing I can't understand," she went on, "why you don't any of you attach more importance to the fact that she told Julian herself."

"Because," said Bobby, slowly, "we have only her own word that she did so."

"But her aunts"—began Mrs. Bobby.

"They can't know what passed between them. What people think is that he discovered the marriage and charged her with it. It seems improbable that after deceiving him so long she should suddenly repent. And of course he would shield her as far as possible, so his version goes for nothing."

"All the same, I should like to hear it," said Mrs. Bobby decidedly. "If I were Mr. Fenton, I should summon him at once as witness." (Mr. Fenton was the counsel for the defence.)

"Why, Fenton thought of it," said Bobby. "He spoke about it to Elizabeth, and she cried out 'Oh, not he—not he of all people' in such a way that he—well, he thought he'd better not send for him, for fear of discovering something that would go very much against us. It did look badly, you know, that she should dread Gerard's evidence so."

Mrs. Bobby's reply to this was unexpected. "Is Mr. Fenton considered a clever lawyer, dear?" she asked.

"The best that money can get," said Bobby, somewhat taken aback. "But why, Eleanor?"—

"Oh, well—I hope he knows more about law than he does about women, that's all. Now I say, send for Julian at once."

"Well, you know, Eleanor, I can't help thinking that if he knew of any evidence in her favor he'd have turned up of his own accord before this. It looks badly, I think—his staying away; as if he were afraid of being questioned if he came."

Mrs. Bobby sat for a moment reflecting deeply, her brows knit. "I don't believe," she said, suddenly, "that he knows a thing about it. Where is he, do you know?"

"Some one saw him ages ago in London," said Bobby. "Goodness knows where he is now. But in all events, he must have heard."

"I doubt it. It happened, you know, while he was on the ocean, and by the time he had landed, the first excitement was over, and there was nothing about it in the papers for a long time. So that, even if he bought an American paper, he might not see anything about it, and the foreign ones of course would have nothing—you know how little interest they take in us over there. Oh, it might easily happen—strange as it seems, that he has heard nothing."

"But why is it, do you think," said Bobby, "that Elizabeth doesn't want him here?"

"My dear Bobby, how dull men are! Of course, she doesn't want to call upon him in a time like this. She's too proud. But nothing will prevent him—if I know him rightly—from coming at once, if there is anything he can do to help her."

"Well, if you think it's any good, I'll send a detective after him," said Bobby, with the composure of one to whom money is no object.

Chapter XXXIII

THE services of a detective proved imperative in finding Gerard. His banks when applied to by cable, regretted to reply that they did not know his address. He had left no directions to have his mail forwarded. Apparently his one idea had been to efface himself and break with some home ties. It was a proceeding which did not altogether surprise Mrs. Bobby, who understood the phase of mind which it indicated; but to Mr. Fenton it was proof positive of his own suspicions, that Gerard dreaded to be summoned as witness on behalf of the woman whom he had once loved.

"She is glad to have him out of the way," thought the astute lawyer to himself. "No doubt he has evidence which she is afraid of. Yes, she lied no doubt when she said she had told him herself of her marriage, just as she lied when she said she couldn't remember what she had done on the twenty-third of December. She remembered—I could see that plainly—very well." The counsel for the defence was reluctantly convinced of his client's guilt, but he had good hopes of saving her nevertheless, though he did not think it was to be done by means that were strictly legal. He said little and accepted Gerard's disappearance with philosophy, even though he did not absolutely discourage Bobby Van Antwerp from sending a detective on his track. It could at least, the lawyer argued, do no harm, since he was quite certain that Gerard however urgently summoned would not come. Bobby lost heart and would have let the matter drop, but his wife's influence again carried the day. The detective started, with urgent directions from Mrs. Bobby to find the witness at any cost, and equally urgent directions from Mr. Fenton by no means to find him, unless his evidence were desirable.

Meanwhile the summer came and life in The Tombs assumed a different phase.

The atmosphere in Elizabeth's cell grew unbearable, and the warden allowed her to spend a large part of her time in the prison court. Here, too, since the intense heat, the other women assembled for an hour every day, and she was brought in actual contact with them for the first time. The court was large, and she could sit on the bench which the warden had placed for her in the shadow of the wall. And yet, though she tried to, she could not ignore them; she found herself, little by little, observing them, taking even some faint interest in them. She grew to know them by name, and would talk to some of them, asking timid questions, partly with an instinctive desire to get away from her own thoughts, partly with the feeling that they were human beings, in trouble like herself. There was a lurking sympathy in her heart for even the most depraved. She would share with them her fruit and flowers, or make little presents of one kind or another, even though the matron, discovering this assured her that they were in many cases quite unworthy of her kindness.

"They won't thank you for it, Miss," she said "they won't indeed. They're just as likely as not to say the worst things of you behind your back."

Elizabeth stared at her thoughtfully for a moment beneath knit brows.

"I don't know that I care about their thanking me," she said at last, "and even if they're not worthy, that doesn't make it any the less hard for them, does it?"

To the matron this sentiment had a taint of immorality and she drew herself up primly. "Why, on that principle, Miss," she said, "there's no use at all in good behavior." Her point of view was the correct one, of course—at least for a prison official. But it was natural that Elizabeth, in revolt against the hard judgment of the world, should take the opposite side. And certainly the women, even the roughest of them, seemed to be grateful in their own way for her kindness, and respected absolutely the intangible barrier between them. There were one or two, indeed, younger and more imaginative than the rest, who would follow her with wistful eyes as she passed, or flush in involuntary, awkward delight if she spoke to them; to whom her presence in their midst appealed irresistibly, touching some latent sense of romance, and lending a new interest to the prison routine. There was something wraith-like, spiritual about her, as she grew from day to day, more frail, her face more thin and wasted, her eyes more unnaturally large and strained, and the shadows beneath them deeper and darker. Her gowns, since the hot weather began, were always white, unrelieved by color even at throat or belt. Only her hair made a gleam of brightness, the more vivid for the pallor of her face and the grayness of the prison walls.

It was this soft, wavy hair at which visitors to The Tombs looked most curiously, recognizing one of the strong pieces of evidence against her. There was a number of visitors to The Tombs, even on those hot summer days; people who only stared at one prisoner and asked before they left one question of the prison officials, which met the one answer. The warden—a gruff old man, hardened by long contact with the lowest offenders—seemed when his turn came to hesitate.

"Guilty, she?" he repeated, staring up at the questioner with his shrewd old eyes. "Well, there ain't a guilty person in The Tombs—not to hear them talk; but—she"—he paused a moment. "She never says nothing; but—bless you"—carried beyond himself by an unwonted burst of sentiment—"I'd as soon suspect an angel from heaven."

"Ah, he has had a large fee," the more cynical would observe as they left, and it was true. But the canny old warden was quite capable of accepting all the money in the world, and reserving the right to his own opinion, which he had stated in this case with absolute honesty. And it was shared, moreover, by the entire prison,—jailers and criminals alike.

Elizabeth grew conscious of the general sentiment and it cheered her more than its intrinsic value seemed to warrant. For it was based on no tangible evidence, was the result of a hundred unconsidered, unimportant words and actions, the effect of which, to those who had not seen or heard them, it was hard to explain; and it could penetrate little to the outside world. But she felt strangely indifferent to the outside world. Her horizon was bounded by the prison walls.

One day, sitting dull and languid on her bench in the shadow of the wall, she chanced to overhear a fragment of a conversation between the warden and a visitor. They stood within the door of the office, and their voices came to her distinctly. "I tell you," the warden said, apparently bringing his argument to a conclusion, "they'll never put a woman—let alone a young and pretty one like her— in the electric chair."

"Ah, but if she's guilty,"—the visitor's voice demanded. And then, with an odd grunt from the warden, they passed on. She could not hear the rest.

But what she had heard thrilled her with a new, sharp pang of terror, the reason of which she could not have explained. There was nothing in the warden's assertion, nothing even in the visitor's protest. She knew of course that there were people who believed her guilty, and the man's words were rather than otherwise. Yet something in them called up before her vividly for the first time the very danger which he disclaimed. Yes, she was to be tried for her life! Incredible stupidity!— how was it she had never realized it before?

There was after all nothing extraordinary, unprecedented in the idea; it was one which had exercised over her in times past a curious fascination. She remembered well having read a graphic account of the last hours of a noted criminal, everything that he had said and done, the way in which he had met his fate, his last words ... it all came back to her with startling distinctness. She had tried at the time to put herself in his place, to think how she would have felt.... It was so futile, she had desisted from it at last with a smile at her own absurdity, the healthy instincts of her warm young life asserting themselves, as they generally did, against the occasional morbidness of her imagination. Now, looking back on it, the whole thing seemed one of those presentiments with which people doomed to misfortune are visited.

Yet the idea was absurd, even now. There was no danger, for she was innocent. That man was guilty—or so the papers said. She remembered that he had protested his innocence—to the end. And perhaps he had spoken the truth.

What did the papers say about her own case? The evidence against her was strong—she had always vaguely known that. But—what was it the man had said?— they'd never put a woman, guilty or innocent, in the electric chair. But what woman would accept her life on such terms as that? Elizabeth raised her head with that characteristic, proud little motion which not all the humiliations of prison life had availed to break her of entirely. "I would rather die," she said to herself, "I would rather die."

And then she remembered how she had shrunk from death—that morning months ago in the park. She felt again the intense physical repulsion, the instinctive clinging to life, the dread of the unknown....

That evening when the younger matron—the one she liked the best—came with her dinner, she put her through a series of questions, which embarrassed the kind woman not a little. Had she ever, Elizabeth demanded, seen people who were condemned to death and how had they behaved? Did they seem frightened, or were they calm and brave? Were they—did the matron really believe that they were guilty, beyond possibility of doubt?

"Are innocent people ever condemned," asked the girl, sitting huddled together on her bed and staring at the matron with haggard eyes. "Surely there couldn't be—you don't suppose there could be—such a terrible mistake?"

"I"—The matron's voice suddenly failed her, her eyes filled with tears. "Heaven knows I hope not, Miss," she said and went out hastily.

Elizabeth sat still, staring before her. "She believes me innocent—but she is afraid I will be found guilty." A little shudder passed through her, in spite of the intense heat. And then again the dull cloud of weary indifference descended upon her, and she said to herself that she did not care.

But as time went on, she knew that this was false.

A few days later Mrs. Bobby came back, after spending a week in the country much against her will. It seemed to her that Elizabeth looked much worse than when she saw her last. She sighed as she realized, more emphatically than ever, how much of the girl's beauty had left her with that wealth of color and outline which had been its most striking characteristic. Certainly any one who judged of her by the famous picture, taken in her first bloom, would be wofully disappointed now. There was only the soft sweep of the hair, and the strange shadow in the eyes—of which the first premonition as it were had somehow crept into the picture—but for these points of resemblance one would hardly know her for the same woman.

"No," Mrs. Bobby reflected, "they won't acquit her for her beauty." But aloud she talked cheerfully, giving the Neighborhood news—what there was of it, skimming the cream of her letters from friends at gayer places—profoundly uninteresting just then, and mocking the scene about them with its frivolous incongruity—but what matter. Anything to keep going the ball of conversation! But at last, in spite of herself, there came a pause.

It was intensely hot. The sun beat down upon the rough uneven stones which paved the prison court, it baked the wall against which the two women leaned. Before their eyes there rose up sharply the walls of the men's prison, and beyond a fragment of the Court-house, with which the Bridge of Sighs formed a connecting link, invisible from where they sat. A little way off, in a small circle of shade, a group of women prisoners gathered silent, inert. A great stillness brooded over the place, broken only by the buzzing of flies and the noises in the street, which sounded dreamily as if it were many miles away. A man was crying "Strawberries, fresh strawberries!" and his voice floated in to the prison, bringing with it a tantalizing suggestion of coolness and freedom and green fields.

Involuntarily Elizabeth made a gesture of weariness, and raised to her parched lips the great bunch of roses, fresh from the country, which Mrs. Bobby had brought. They already hung their heads.

"I suppose," the girl said dreamily, her eyes half shut, "our flowers must be all out at the Homestead. It always looks so pretty there now, before the heat has lasted too long. I can see it—the river with the sails on it, and the fields covered with daisies—they must be out now—ah, and the wild-roses!"—She drew a long breath. "Oh, I am sick sometimes for a sight of it all," she broke out with sudden vehemence. "I'd give anything to lie down in the grass with the trees over me, and the cool wind in my face, and so—sleep"—Her voice sank away, she made a weary gesture. "I'm so tired," she said, "I'd like to sleep forever."

"My dear child." Mrs. Bobby caught her breath, a mist of tears in her eyes. "Don't you ever sleep here?"—she asked tentatively after a moment, and Elizabeth answered in the same dreary way, unconscious, apparently, that she was departing from her usual reserve.

"No, I don't sleep often," she said, "especially since the nights have been so hot. But when I do"—she paused and stared reflectively before her, while the shadow in her eyes grew deeper. "There's a dream that haunts me now," she said at last, "whenever I fall asleep. I dream about my trial, and—it always goes against me. I stand there all alone, the judge pronounces sentence, and I—I try to speak, I try to tell them that I'm innocent, but—the words won't come—I wake up half strangled"—she broke off shuddering. "Ah, you can't imagine how horrible it is," she said, "worse even than—lying awake."

Mrs. Bobby was silent for a moment, but when she spoke her voice was steady. "It's a horrible dream," she said, "but it's impossible—quite impossible that it should come true. You won't be left alone, we shall all stand by you, you will be acquitted surely—surely"—in spite of herself, her voice suddenly faltered, in a way that belied her words.

"You think so?" Elizabeth said, quickly. "You *hope* so. But—if you should be mistaken?" She put out her hand and grasped Mrs. Bobby's wrist. "Tell me the worst," she said. "I'd rather know it. Is there much danger, do you—in your heart of hearts, do you think that I shall be acquitted?" Involuntarily her grasp tightened, her strained, dilated eyes searched her friend's face with a look that seemed to compel only the truth—to tolerate no evasions. And Eleanor Van Antwerp, with all her courage, could not meet it. She turned her face away with a little sob.

Elizabeth sat rigid for a moment, waiting for the answer that did not come; then her fingers relaxed their hold, she took her hand away and sank back against the wall.

There was a long silence. The noon-day sun crept towards them, dazzling the eyes, a few flies buzzed aimlessly about. Upon Eleanor Van Antwerp's mind the prison court, as she saw it then, baking in the noon-day heat—the group of women huddled together, the rags of some, the tawdry finery of others, the look of dogged misery on their coarse faces—the whole scene impressed itself, calling up always in after years a sense of powerless despair.

At last Elizabeth turned to her, and a faint smile hovered about her white lips.

"Do you know," she said, "did the warden show you? in that corner there they have—the old scaffold—what's left of it, at least. They keep it as an interesting relic. Oh, he wouldn't show it to me"—she smiled again painfully—" he's too considerate—I heard him telling one of the visitors. They don't have anything of the kind now, he said,—there is—Sing Sing and the electric chair. And that is—or so they say—more merciful. But is it—do you really think it can be?" She paused and stared up at Mrs. Bobby with eyes full of a dawning terror. "To have a hood put over one's face," she went on, her voice trembling, "that's how they do it, isn't it?— to wait—wait for the shock." ... She stopped, the look of terror in her eyes grew deeper. She lifted the roses from her lap and held them up before her face, as if to shut out, with their color and fragrance, some horrible vision. "Oh, I see it day and night," she said, "day and night! If I see it much longer, I shall go mad."

Mrs. Bobby's hand tightened convulsively upon hers.

"Elizabeth, my dear," she cried, "you mustn't think of such possibilities. It could never—come to that, they would never—carry their cruelty to that extent"— Her voice faltered.

Elizabeth put down her roses and looked up at her. Her face showed recovered self-control. "Why—because I'm a woman?" she asked, with a pale little smile. "That's what the warden said—that they wouldn't condemn a woman to death. But even if they—stopped short of that, would imprisonment—would this sort of thing, or worse"—she swept her hand with a comprehensive gesture round her—"wouldn't death, on the whole, be better?"

And Mrs. Bobby could not answer, for she thought in her heart it would be—infinitely better.

But in a moment she rallied her energies.

"Elizabeth," she said, "there's no necessity to consider—either alternative. I believe firmly that we shall get you off. But in order to do it you must help us—to defend you. You seem indifferent about it; Mr. Fenton complains that you keep things back. You can't afford to trifle—tell us everything. Isn't there"—she leaned forward eagerly and grasped Elizabeth's hand—"doesn't Julian Gerard know something that would help us?"

She felt Elizabeth start and shiver; then stiffen into sudden rigidity. The hand she held was withdrawn, and with the action the girl seemed to release herself, mentally and physically, from her grasp.

"I don't know," she said, and her voice was cold, almost as though she resented being questioned, "I don't know why you think that."

"I don't think—I feel it! There is something that he can say." Mrs. Bobby's eyes seemed to challenge a denial. Elizabeth met them with a look of defiance.

"There is nothing," she said. "He knows nothing; or if he did"—she lowered her voice with a sudden change of tone—"if he could save me, I'd rather die than have him sent for."

"Ah—you'd rather die?" Mrs. Bobby caught her breath. "And you think that is fair—to yourself, to your aunts, to us all?"

"I don't know." The girl's voice had the ring of weary obstinacy that suffering will sometimes assume. "I only know I don't want him—sent for."

Mrs. Bobby seemed to reflect. "We can't send for him," she said at last, "we don't know where he is."

Elizabeth started. "You don't," she repeated, in a low voice, "know where he is?"—

"No, he left no address. His mail is at his banker's—they don't know where to forward it."

Elizabeth turned her face away. "Ah, I see," she murmured, "he doesn't wish to be reminded of—anything at home." A pale cold smile flitted across her white face. "It is better so," she said, firmly, "far, far better. I am glad that he is away and that there is no use in sending for him."

"But if there were"—all Mrs. Bobby's self-control could not keep the tremor from her voice—"if there were, Elizabeth, isn't there something that he could testify in your favor? Do tell me, dear," she urged; the girl sat silent. "You see I have guessed it—it can do no harm for me to know what it is."

Elizabeth spoke at last, low and hesitatingly. "He knows that on the twenty-third of December, when—when that man said he saw me in Brooklyn, I was with him—with Julian. I went out that morning, meaning to do some shopping, but I met him accidentally. He persuaded me to go up to the Metropolitan Museum—there was a picture he wanted to show me. We were there some hours. And—and that is all."

"And that was," said Mrs. Bobby breathlessly, "on the twenty-third of December. You are *sure*?"

"Quite sure," said the girl listlessly, "but what difference does it make? I wouldn't tell Mr. Fenton—I said I couldn't remember what I did that day, and I wouldn't tell you now, if I thought that you could send for him. You can't send for him, can you?" She looked at Mrs. Bobby with sudden alarm. "You really don't know where he is?"

"Upon my word and honor," Mrs. Bobby assured her, "I don't." And then she said little more, but kissed Elizabeth presently, bade her keep up her courage, and left sooner than she generally did.

"No, I don't know where he is," she said to herself, as the hansom bore her swiftly up-town, and she stared out absently at the deserted streets. "We don't know, but please God, we shall soon. If only that man finds him, if he can only get him here in time."

Chapter XXXIV

THIS was in the early summer; and Elizabeth's trial was to be in November. The time approached, and nothing had been heard of Julian Gerard. Efforts were made to postpone the trial, that this important witness might have time to appear. But the influence of people like the Van Antwerps, which seems in some ways all-powerful, is in others curiously slight. The District Attorney was acting in the interests of the yellow journals and they, according to their own account, in the interests of the people, which required, as they set forth in high-sounding editorials, that no more favor should be shown to Miss Van Vorst than to the lowest criminal.

After all, the girl's health had suffered so severely from the long confinement that it seemed a cruelty to lengthen it, even with the hope of Gerard's return. Mr. Fenton himself was of opinion that the trial should not be postponed. He had done his best for his client, though hampered more, perhaps, than he realized by his secret doubt of everything she said. He did not believe in this alibi, which she had trumped up, as he decided, when the one person who could confirm or deny it was safely out of the way. Yet he tried to find some other witness who remembered, or imagined having seen her at the Museum on the morning when she was supposed to have been in Brooklyn. No such person could be found. The case for the defence was lamentably weak. Mr. Fenton admitted the fact to himself with a shrug of the shoulders, and fell back philosophically on his conviction that no jury would send a young woman of Elizabeth's position and attractions to the electric chair.

Perhaps the person most to be pitied in those days was Miss Cornelia, who had been summoned as witness for the prosecution to corroborate the testimony of Bridget O'Flaherty, her former waitress, as to her niece's words and manner on the morning after the murder. The poor lady was in a pitiful state of agitation. "What shall I say?" she asked, looking appealingly from one to the other of Elizabeth's friends and advisers.

"Say anything," said Mrs. Bobby, hastily, "any—any lie that you can invent."

She stopped. Miss Cornelia drew herself up with dignity. "I don't think our child's cause can be helped by—by lies, Mrs. Van Antwerp," she said.

Mrs. Bobby felt herself rebuked. "Well, I am not given to lies myself, as a rule," she explained, apologetically, "but in a case like this it seems to me that the end justifies the means. It's a doctrine brought into discredit, I know, by the Jesuits, but still it seems to have a certain foundation in common-sense."

"I don't know anything about the Jesuits," said Miss Cornelia, with some stiffness, "but I shall try to act as our Church would advise, even—even if Elizabeth"—here her voice broke.

"I think," said Bobby Van Antwerp, coming to the rescue, "that Miss Cornelia is right, Eleanor. It is much better to tell the exact truth, and Fenton will make the best of it.—Good Heavens," he said afterwards to his wife, "you don't suppose that the poor lady could invent a plausible story, or even keep back anything that wouldn't be brought out in cross-examination and make a worse effect than if she gave it of her own accord!"

But upon Miss Cornelia the opposite side of the question was beginning to make an impression. Her mind moved slowly. It was not easy for her to break from old tradition. Her conscience had hitherto recognized the broadly drawn line between right and wrong; no indefinite, subtle gradations. As she had said once to Elizabeth, fully meaning it, one could always do right if one tried. But if—if one could not tell what the right was?...

Miss Joanna, sitting opposite to her in the twilight, broke the silence hesitatingly. "I suppose, sister," she said, "I suppose you remember—exactly what the poor child said—that morning? You haven't"—Miss Joanna caught her breath—"you haven't forgotten?" There was a note of entreaty in her voice.

Miss Cornelia could see it so plainly; the breakfast table and the paper with those startling headlines, and the look on Elizabeth's face, when she had made that extraordinary assertion. A confession of guilt! That was the way in which it would be construed—there seemed no way out of it. Miss Cornelia did not think that the most merciful jury could acquit her after that. And yet the child was innocent— Miss Cornelia knew that as surely as she knew that the Bible was inspired. Was it reasonable, was it right that she should be required to give evidence against her? Over Miss Cornelia's mind there swept a sudden, sharp sense of injustice, a passionate rebellion against fate.

But a life-long habit of truth-telling is hard to overcome. She answered Miss Joanna after a moment. "I—I haven't forgotten, sister," she said, and the hot tears scorched her eyeballs.

Miss Joanna put away her knitting with a hopeless sigh. "Well, of course, sister, you must speak the truth," she said, drearily, "but—it does seem hard." Then she went out of the room, crying quietly.

Miss Cornelia sat motionless in the twilight, while that new tumult of rebellion still raged within her. Ah, yes, it seemed more than hard—it seemed cruel, unjust, that such a thing should be required of her. Those strange people, the Jesuits, whom she had always held in horror, had some reason on their side after all. There were cases to which the simple, old-fashioned rules of right and wrong did not apply, which were extraordinary, unprecedented.... Miss Cornelia could not help asking herself—with a thrill of self-condemnation, indeed, and yet another feeling which defended the question—whether in certain circumstances, the wrong were not more to be commended, wiser, better than the right.

She spent a sleepless night, thinking it over. The whole foundations of her life, of her faith seemed shaken. She looked the next morning so exhausted, when she went down as usual to The Tombs, that Elizabeth at once divined that some new misfortune had happened, and it was not long before she drew it out of her.

She sat for a long time very still, one hand clasping Miss Cornelia's, the fingers of the other tapping on the ledge of the wall beside her.

"Of course, auntie," she said at last, quietly, "you must tell exactly what happened. There's no good to be gained by lies; at least"—she made an attempt at a smile—"my own success in that line hasn't been very striking. I was a little out of my head that morning, and I don't remember exactly what I said! but whatever it was"—she raised her head proudly—"I don't want anything kept back. Let them know the whole truth; then, if they condemn me, well and good. At least I shan't have anything"—her voice faltered—"anything *more* to reproach myself with."

"Elizabeth!" The older woman gazed up at her admiringly. "You are so brave—you are a lesson to me! But you—you don't realize, my darling—" sobs choked her voice.

"Oh, yes—I realize." A pale smile flitted across the girl's face. "I have realized—quite clearly—all these months. But that's no reason, auntie, why you should save me by lies."

And then she turned the subject, and began to talk calmly enough, about one of the women prisoners, in whose case she took a keen interest. Nothing more was said about her own affairs. She had relapsed, since that conversation months before with Mrs. Bobby, into her old reserve, and spoke very little of herself. The cooler weather was helping her. She seemed stronger, and always quite calm. Miss Cornelia went away, feeling rebuked for her own cowardice. Elizabeth was right, she thought with a pang of self-reproach; nothing but the truth must be told in her defence. But meanwhile Miss Cornelia tried to reconcile two opposite instincts; offering up day and night two apparently irreconcilable petitions; that she might be enabled to speak the truth exactly, and yet do no harm to her niece's cause.

Chapter XXXV

IT was the first day of Elizabeth's trial. She could hardly realize that it had come—this event which they had anticipated so long, the thought of which had lately crowded out every other. There was nothing alarming about the present proceedings—the appearance of one jury-man after another, generally followed in each case by a peremptory challenge. One was objected to because he was thought to have formed a favorable opinion, another an unfavorable one, and still another because he was apparently incapable of forming any opinion at all. If she had not been on trial for her life, she might have thought it dull.

Her gaze wandered to that wide court-room window opposite, from which she could see an expanse of roofs, flag-staffs and chimneys, full of charm and excitement after the unbroken outline of blank walls, which for many months had bounded her view. Then, forgetting herself, she glanced about the room, quickly turned and shrank back, while the color rushed into her white face. There were some women whom she knew, thickly veiled, in the crowd behind her—women who were against her. Those who were her friends had the consideration to stay away. And there were others whom she did not know, who crowded as close to the bar as they could, eying her with eager curiosity, making remarks about her in a stage whisper. As the heroine of this sensational case, she was a disappointment both in dress and appearance.

"Well, her hair waves prettily"—the words came distinctly to Elizabeth's ears in a lull in the proceeding—"but that's about all. I don't see why she was ever called a beauty, do you?"

"Why, no, indeed. Her features aren't regular—not a bit. And isn't she thin and white!"

"Hush!" a kindlier voice broke in, suppressing the others. "It's no wonder, poor thing. Most people would lose their looks, if they'd been through what she has."

A pang shot through Elizabeth none the less distinct because the reason was, in view of what was going on, so trifling and absurd. She had dressed herself that morning with unusual care, resolved to present as far as possible an undisturbed front to the world; and she had not realized that the plain black gown, and the unrelieved sombreness of the black hat, which would once have thrown into more dazzling relief her fresh young beauty, now emphasized with startling plainness the change in her appearance. For a moment, the fact forced itself upon her and hurt even then. When a woman has always been regarded as a beauty, it is hard to become accustomed to a different point of view. After all, what difference did it make? She had not realized the effect which her looks were supposed to produce on the jury.

For a while the prospect of any jury at all seemed dubious. The hours passed, the day came to an end, and there were exactly two men in the box. It was not till the end of the third day that the number was complete—twelve most unhappy men, whose faces Eleanor Van Antwerp scanned eagerly. Some, she decided, were kind; others—too logical; all of them were more or less intelligent. There were one or two, she thought, to whom the pathos of Elizabeth's pale and faded looks might appeal with an eloquence that fresh coloring and rounded curves would have lacked entirely. Upon these men she based her hopes.

And so the trial, once fairly started, dragged on its weary length. Mrs. Bobby spent her days there, sitting beside Elizabeth; her whole life, just then, seemed bounded by the court-house walls. She had no interest in anything outside. And Elizabeth's aunts, too, came every day. It was pathetic to see these timid, elderly women, plunged for the first time in their sheltered lives into this fierce glare of publicity, under which they bore up unflinchingly, in the effort to show to all the world their firm faith in their niece's ultimate acquittal.

As for Elizabeth, she had little hope; but neither had she, except at times, any great fear. The worst had been that first day, and now she was used to being stared at; used even to the thought that she was being tried for her life. The scene and its accessories—the listening, eager crowd behind her, the judge before her with his impassive face, in which she thought she could perceive, now and again—or did her hopes deceive her?—a gleam of sympathy; the jury weary but resigned, the reporters taking notes, scanning her with eyes that noted every detail of her manner and bearing, placed upon them Heaven knows what construction! Bobby Van Antwerp moving restlessly about, holding long conferences with the lawyers; her counsel and the District Attorney wrangling, glaring at each other over the heads of unfortunate witnesses—the whole thing lost its terrors, grew to be an accepted part of her life's routine.

The evidence at first was technical. There was much she did not understand—she wondered if the jury did. There were the doctors, showing with many long words and tedious explanations, with what sort of poison the murder had been committed; and then there were the handwriting experts, with still longer words and more tedious explanations. Now—what was it that they had brought out? Those unfortunate letters which she remembered so well having written, in great haste and anxiety. The experts were pointing out numerous points of resemblance between them and another piece of paper, which she had never seen before. And now it was the secret marriage they were proving—though what was the use of that, when no one denied it? The question of motive was absolutely clear; the District Attorney had expatiated upon it at great length in his opening speech.

All this Elizabeth grasped more or less distinctly. She realized that the evidence was strong against her. But she could not, weak and dazed as she was, keep her mind on it. The voice of the witnesses would grow indistinct, a mist would pass over the anxious faces around her, a lull would come in the nervous tension of the atmosphere; the blue sky, which she saw from the window, would seem very near, and she would float off into phases of oblivion, from which she would be roused, perhaps, by a touch on her arm, or a voice in her ear. "Listen, darling, that was a point in your favor," her aunts or Eleanor Van Antwerp would say.

These points were few and far between. But there was one which Elizabeth understood—she hoped that the jury did.

Mr. Fenton was examining one of the medical experts for the prosecution, a man who had had large experience in poisoning cases. The counsel for the defence was putting him through series of questions, the drift of which was not altogether plain. What sort of a crime did he consider poisoning? An atrocious one, was it not?—generally committed by hardened criminals? Had the witness ever been in contact with a case of poisoning where the whole scheme had been concocted and carried out by a girl of twenty, far removed by education, friends and antecedents from any connection with crime? No, the witness could not, in his own experience, recall any such case, but he had no doubt that it had been known, though he agreed in response to Mr. Fenton's next question, that it would be slightly abnormal. And here the District Attorney interposed with one of those objections which each lawyer seemed to make mechanically, whenever a question proved inconvenient to his side; but the Judge decided in favor of Mr. Fenton, and he went on imperturbably, shifting his ground a little.

"Poisoning is a crime—don't you think so?—that calls for a great deal of thought and calculation?"

"Yes," the witness thought it would undoubtedly.

"The person who planned it would have plenty of time to consider the consequences?"

The witness responded: "I should think so."

"He or she—whoever it was that planned it—would be probably of a cold-blooded and calculating disposition?"

"Probably."

"And not likely, do you think so?—to suffer from hysterical remorse as soon as the act was accomplished?"

Here the opposing counsel again intervened, and was again silenced by the Judge. Mr. Fenton repeated his question.

"I ask you," he said, addressing the witness with a certain solemnity, "as a man who has had experience with criminals and human nature, whether you think it likely that a woman, strong-minded and cold-blooded enough to commit this diabolical crime, on hearing of its accomplishment—a thing she has been expecting for days—would be seized with a fit of hysterical remorse, would utter wild, incriminating words, in the presence of—no matter whom, any one who chanced to be present, and would rush up at once to look at the body of the man whom she had murdered?"

The witness hesitated. "It—it doesn't seem likely," he admitted at last.

"It would be much more, don't you think," said Mr. Fenton quietly, "like the conduct of an innocent woman, who was suffering from a nervous shock, and had no thought of controlling her actions because she had no idea of being suspected?"

The witness, after a long pause: "Yes, it—would certainly seem so."

"It certainly does," said Mr. Fenton. "Thank you, doctor. I have no more questions to ask." And he sat down with the air of one who has scored a point.

Thereupon the prosecution, as if to prove the strength of the evidence which he had anticipated, placed upon the stand Bridget O'Flaherty, formerly maid-servant to the Misses Van Vorst, who swore upon her solemn oath that the prisoner had in her hearing declared herself guilty of the murder of Paul Halleck. Yes, those were her very words, the maid declared—"that she had killed him," and she had added that "it had come at last—just as she despaired of it" or something of the kind, referring no doubt to the fact that Halleck had kept the poison some time before taking it. The woman's testimony was full and circumstantial, and she gave the impression of telling the truth.

Mr. Fenton, on cross-examination, proved that she had been dismissed without a character from the services of the Misses Van Vorst, also that she had been paid for her evidence by a yellow journal. Its effect was distinctly undermined when he permitted her to leave the stand. And with that the prosecution called upon Miss Cornelia to corroborate the maid's statement.

Miss Cornelia was deathly white; her head shook, her thin, silvery curls fluttered, as if they had caught the infection of her own nervousness. In one hand she grasped her smelling-salts desperately, with the other she revolved in an agitated way a small black fan. A murmur of sympathy ran through the court-room as she took her place. Even the District Attorney seemed sorry for her and put his opening questions with unwonted gentleness. His tone was still bland when he came to the important point—had she noticed anything peculiar in her niece's manner on the morning after the murder?

Miss Cornelia's answer was low, but it was quite audible. "She was— shocked, naturally."

"Naturally. But did she seem surprised?"

Miss Cornelia's answer was this time still lower, and given with more hesitation. "I—I think so."

"You mean you are not sure?"

"I—I was so upset myself"—began Miss Cornelia.

"That you did not notice?"

"No, I—I did not notice," said Miss Cornelia, relieved.

"You thought that her manner was unremarkable, and simply what you might have expected under the circumstances?"

"Yes, I—I thought so," said Miss Cornelia. She added to herself the mental reservation that she had no idea what sort of manner under the circumstances, she should have expected.

The District Attorney assumed a more impressive manner. "Miss Van Vorst," he said, "do you believe in the sacredness of an oath?"

"Yes, I—I certainly."

"You would not speak anything but the truth?"

"No," said Miss Cornelia, this time more firmly.

"Then I ask you," said the District Attorney, suddenly drawing himself up to his full height, and fixing his eyes upon her, "I ask you, on your sacred oath, did your niece, or did she not, on the morning after the murder of Paul Halleck, say to you that she had killed him, or words to that effect?"

There was a long silence. Miss Cornelia looked desperately about her; at the Judge, whose face showed more than ever a touch of human sympathy; at Mr. Fenton, white with anxiety, trying to telegraph a hundred things which she could not understand; at the jury, bending eagerly forward; then back at those most interested,—her sister in an agony of suspense, Mrs. Van Antwerp flushed and trembling in her vain desire to intervene. Lastly, Miss Cornelia's haggard eyes sought Elizabeth herself; the girl was sitting white and rigid, motionless as a statue, her hands clenched, her eyes resolutely bent upon the floor. If it was a terrible moment for her; how much worse was it for the aunt who had brought her up, who was now called upon by a refinement of cruelty to destroy what seemed to be her only chance. Oh, for the courage—it seemed to her almost noble!—to utter one good lie! But there were the lynx-like eyes of the District Attorney fixed upon her, there was the oath she had taken, weighing upon her conscientious soul.... Suddenly she felt, with a sense of despair, that her silence had already spoken louder than speech. And, even as the thought passed through her mind, her answer framed itself on her lips and seemed to be uttered without her own volition; one word, barely audible, but caught at once and registered by twenty reporters, while a suppressed sigh went the round of the court-room.

"Yes."

"Thank you," said the District Attorney. "That is all I wished to know."

Chapter XXXVI

THERE was still cross-examination.

Mr. Fenton, too, began with unimportant questions. He gave Miss Cornelia, who looked ready to faint, time to recover herself a little. The questions he asked were easy to answer. Had her niece, in the course of her education, given them much trouble, had she ever deceived them, kept anything from them before this fatal secret? Ah, no, no! Miss Cornelia gave her answers tremulously, yet with a fervent relief, an eager desire to make herself heard throughout the court-room.

"Then with your knowledge of your niece's character," Mr. Fenton asked, speaking almost carelessly, "you didn't think of her as the sort of person likely to commit a crime?"

Miss Cornelia drew herself up with sudden dignity and her voice was plainly audible, and without a tremor. "Most certainly not," she said.

"Then how," inquired Mr. Fenton calmly, "did you account for her extraordinary assertion that she had committed this murder?"

Miss Cornelia hardly hesitated. "I thought she was out of her mind," she said. "I couldn't account for it in any other way."

"It never occurred to you for a moment that it was true?"

"Not for a moment." The words came out indignantly.

"You naturally did not suppose that were she really guilty, she would proclaim it quite so readily as that?"

Miss Cornelia stared. "I never," she said, simply, "thought of such a thing as her being guilty."

"But you asked her, did you not, for some explanation of her words?"

"I asked her," faltered Miss Cornelia, "what she meant by saying such a dreadful thing. And she said—she said"——

"Yes," said Mr. Fenton, encouragingly. "Take your time and tell us the exact truth. What did she say?"

"She seemed to be rather dazed—She said that she had wished so much for it to happen that when it did, it seemed almost like an answer to her wishes—as if she were accountable for it."

"And you accepted her explanation?" said Mr. Fenton. "It seemed to you plausible?"

"I knew what she meant—yes. But I could see that she was over-wrought and excited, or she wouldn't have thought of it."

"Did she seem distressed over Halleck's death?"

Miss Cornelia hesitated. "N—not at first," she said. "She couldn't seem to realize it."

"And afterwards?"——

"Yes, she seemed distressed then. I thought," said Miss Cornelia firmly "that she felt very badly indeed when she realized it."

"And there was nothing in her manner that could induce you to believe that she expected it, or knew a thing about it beyond what she read in the papers?"

"Nothing."

With this word, firmly pronounced, Miss Cornelia's ordeal came to an end; she descended white and dazed. Elizabeth leaned over as she returned to her place and pressed her hand with a faint little smile. "It's all right, auntie, I'm glad you spoke the truth." And so the episode passed.

"She really has done no more harm than we expected," Bobby Van Antwerp observed to his wife. "It is one of those things which sound much worse than they really are. After all, what does it amount to? The hysterical assertion of an excited girl! A guilty woman is more careful what she says."

"I will tell Elizabeth," said his wife, in relief, "what you say." But though she found an opportunity after the day's session, to whisper this encouragement into the girl's ear, Elizabeth listened vacantly and did not seem fully to grasp it. The maid's evidence, her aunt's corroboration, had brought up vividly to her mind the danger that existed all the time behind these slow, technical deliberations. That night the horrible waking dream, from which for awhile she had been free, returned more startlingly real than ever, and the face of the Judge who sentenced her was the same face in which, during the long days in the court-room, she had thought she detected some involuntary gleams of sympathy. It had seemed a kind face in the day-time, but in her dream it was inexorably stern.

The next morning, at the trial, her mind did not wander; she kept it resolutely fixed on the evidence. Mr. D'Hauteville was on the stand, and she wondered what more fatal revelations were to be made of her words and actions on that unfortunate morning, when she hardly knew what she said or did. But no new developments were brought out. There was no trace in Mr. D'Hauteville's evidence or his easy, unembarrassed manner of the suspicions which he had been perhaps the first person in town to entertain.

Yes, he had seen Miss Van Vorst on the morning after the murder, and had himself taken her into the studio. Was there anything peculiar in her manner? Certainly; she seemed much distressed, as was natural, he thought, under the circumstances. Had she tried to possess herself of the fatal flask, or of any other incriminating objects, as for instance her own letters? No, most emphatically no. Was it true, as the elevator man had already stated, that she had defended herself against his accusations? He could not remember anything of the kind; certainly he had not accused her, as he had no reason to suspect her.

Mr. Fenton on cross-examination, drew from him a description of her tears, of the fearless way in which she had entered, her apparent indifference to being observed. Was it, Mr. Fenton demanded, the manner of a guilty woman? The witness fully agreed that it was not. And then he left the stand, saying to himself philosophically that all was fair in the cause of a beautiful and unfortunate girl, whom he had admired extremely, and with whom his friend Gerard had been, and might be still, desperately in love.

The next witness was the Brooklyn tradesman, whose evidence had been already so much exploited by the yellow journals that it lacked the force of novelty. He deposed to having sold the flask on the morning of the twenty-third of

December, to a woman in black, thickly veiled, slight and tall, and with reddish hair. The witness was quite sure about the date, and as to the time he was less explicit, but convinced that it was somewhere between the hours of ten and twelve. He was a middle-aged man with a plain, honest face, and evidently anxious to tell what he knew and no more. When the District Attorney, in a dramatic manner, desired him to look at the defendant, and declare if she were the woman to whom he sold the flask, he seemed to shrink in distress from the terrible responsibility thus placed upon him.

"I—it is so long ago," he protested, "and—you—must remember that she wore a veil."

"Which entirely obscured her face?"——

"No, not entirely," the witness reluctantly admitted.

"Look at the defendant," the District Attorney insisted, "and tell the court if her general appearance recalls that of the woman to whom you sold the flask."

He turned to Elizabeth and requested her to rise. She grew a shade paler and stared at him for a moment as if startled; then slowly, she obeyed him, and stood facing the witness, who brought reluctantly his anxious gaze to bear upon her. She was ashy-white, but she held her head erect, her eyes met his without flinching. Thus they stood for fully a minute, and the silence in the court-room was tense with nervous excitement. Then the witness spoke.

"I—there is a certain resemblance," he said.

"Then you identify her?" said the District Attorney.

The witness was silent. He looked again at Elizabeth. She was trembling now, and caught hold of a chair as if for support. The witness cleared his throat. He was thinking that he had a daughter of about Elizabeth's age.

"I—I really could not tell," he began.

"Take your time," said the District Attorney, impressively. "This is a very important point."

And then there was again a long silence. In the midst of it the sun, bursting through a gray mass of clouds, touched Elizabeth's hair with a wave of light. It stood out, a shining halo, against the rim of her black hat. The witness stared at it as if fascinated. Then he uttered a sound—it might almost have been a sob—of relief.

"That is not the same woman," he said. "The hair is quite different! That other woman's hair was a much deeper red—it didn't shine and glisten. And her whole air, the way she held herself was different. I am sure it is not the same."

And this opinion, once announced, he clung to tenaciously—nothing the District Attorney said could shake it. Mr. Fenton would not even cross-examine, and there was great rejoicing in the ranks of the defense.

But the next day the prosecution placed upon the stand a druggist's clerk, who remembered having sold a bottle of arsenic to a woman dressed in black on the morning of the twenty-third of December. The occurrence was impressed on his mind because he had demurred as to selling poison, and she had presented a physician's certificate. She was handsomely dressed and seemed like a lady; he had noticed particularly that her hair was reddish. And when asked to identify Elizabeth, he swore unhesitatingly that she was the same woman.

Upon Mr. Fenton's cross-examination, it became evident what important questions may hang on the color of a woman's hair.

Mr. Fenton: "You said, did you not, that the woman's hair was red?"

Witness, cautiously: "I said, reddish. That's not quite the same thing."

Mr. Fenton: "Explain the difference."

Witness, confused: "Well, I—I don't know. I meant to say it was sort of— sort of light"——

"You meant to say, in other words, that it was not black?"

Witness, recovering himself and speaking stubbornly: "No, I meant to say that it was reddish—sort of sandy"——

"Ah—like the District Attorney's moustache, for instance?"

There was laughter in the court-room. The District Attorney's moustache was a brilliant carrot color, which at the opposing counsel's words, was emulated by his face.

"I object to these personalities," he said.

Mr. Fenton was instructed by the Judge to be more serious, but held to his point.

"Your Honor, it is necessary to find out what the witness means by the vague word 'reddish.' If he thinks it applies to the District Attorney's moustache"——

"But I don't," objected the aggrieved witness, to the renewed amusement of the court-room. "I call that carroty."

"Then point out, among people present, what hair you consider reddish."

The witness's eyes wandered till they alighted upon the distinctly sandy locks of one of the experts for the prosecution. "I call that hair reddish," he announced, with some satisfaction at finding a way out of his dilemma.

"Ah—now oblige me, by looking at the defendant's hair and tell us if you think it is like that of this gentleman."

The witness glanced helplessly at Elizabeth. "It—isn't much like it," he admitted.

"And yet you describe both as 'reddish?'"

The witness was desperate. "Well, I—I don't exactly know"—he said.

"What you mean by 'reddish?'" said Mr. Fenton.

"Well—no," said the witness.

"I see that you don't. It's not necessary for you to tell us that. You are color blind evidently, and by 'reddish' you simply mean anything between black and tow-color. But you can't swear away a woman's life with such vague descriptions as this. You can go now. I have no more questions to ask."

The crestfallen witness gladly retreated. But in spite of his discomfiture, his evidence had been a serious blow to the defense, and when, a few days later, the prosecution closed its case, it was admitted on every side to be a strong one.

The defense opened quietly enough. Mr. Fenton, too, brought out his handwriting experts, who were prepared with an equally startling array of technical details, to swear to the exact opposite of what had been solemnly declared by the experts for the prosecution. The court settled down into a dreamy mood, and the spectators for the most part went to sleep.

There was a break in the monotony, and one which created much excitement, when Elizabeth took the stand on her own behalf. She had been very anxious to do this, and Mr. Fenton had reluctantly consented, with many misgivings and elaborate instructions, to which he saw, to his alarm, that she listened almost vacantly. But when she began to testify his doubts disappeared. She gave her evidence very simply and directly, and there was something in the soft, low tones of her voice, an indefinable ring of girlishness, of youth and inexperience, which carried with it an illogical thrill of conviction.

She had never, she said, bought the flask which contained the poison, nor had she ever seen one exactly like it. She had not gone to Brooklyn on the twenty-third of December—she had never gone there in her life. She had spent the morning of the twenty-third of December at the Metropolitan Museum. She had not bought the bottle of arsenic, and knew nothing of it. She had no reason to expect Paul Halleck's death. She had read of it in the papers. No, she had not meant the assertion literally when she said that she had killed him; she had been startled because his death had seemed to come in direct answer to her wishes, and she had somehow felt accountable for it. Yes, it was a morbid idea—she realized it now, but she had not been at all well at the time. That was the reason she had gone up to the studio; she had been in a state of nervous excitement and hardly knew what she did. No, she had not thought of the police suspecting her in consequence; such an idea had never entered her mind.

On the whole, Mr. Fenton was satisfied with the effect that she was producing. He had made the agreeable discovery that he was beginning to believe in her himself; and if this conviction was impressing itself more and more upon his own suspicious mind, it must, he thought, be all-powerful with the jury, whom he had already mentally appraised as kindly men, anxious to escape from an unpleasant duty, and willing to give the prisoner the full benefit of every doubt.

But when Mr. Fenton at last sat down and the District Attorney took his place, then, indeed, began a very bad quarter of an hour for Elizabeth. Question by question, the lawyer drew out of her her reasons for keeping her marriage secret and for wishing Halleck dead, her engagement to Gerard and the manner in which she had deceived him. Her color changed from white to red and back again to ghastly pallor, her voice faltered and broke piteously, but still the terrible inquiry proceeded. Behind her, her aunts were biting their lips in agony and Mrs. Bobby was beside herself with indignation. "I'd give anything in the world," she said to her husband, "to get even with that man." Elizabeth's counsel was keeping up a running fire of objections, but in vain. The District Attorney got in his questions somehow or another, and Elizabeth answered them as best she could.

"Why," she was asked among other things, "was your engagement to Mr. Gerard broken off?"

"Because," she faltered, "I—I told him of my marriage."

"Why did you suddenly tell him, when you had kept it concealed so long?"

Elizabeth looked up with a piteous appeal in her eyes, which was answered by an objection on the part of her counsel, and she was told by the Judge that she need answer no question unless she wished. But by this time she had recovered herself.

"I am quite willing to answer," she said. "I told him because I was sorry I had deceived him. I had no other reason."

"You are quite sure that you *did* tell him, and that he did not—find out for himself?"

There was an insulting tone to the question, but she answered it steadily, without anger. "I am quite sure," she said.

"Who was with you on the day that you say you went to the Metropolitan Museum?" This was the next question, put with disconcerting suddenness.

She turned still whiter, if that were possible, than before, and her answer was barely audible. "Mr. Gerard."

"Was any one else with you?"

"No one."

"Is he the only person who can corroborate your statement?"

"Yes."

"Then it is a pity he is not here."

She was silent.

"Mr. Gerard," observed Mr. Fenton, "when he went abroad left no address. We made efforts to communicate with him, but so far, we have not succeeded. It is most unfortunate."

"Most unfortunate, certainly," echoed the District Attorney, "for the defendant. But perhaps he was not anxious to be summoned. We have heard of witnesses who went to the ends of the earth to avoid it."

He turned to Elizabeth. "Do you know of any reason," he asked, "why he should not wish to come?"

Elizabeth's hands were clasped together nervously. "I—I cannot tell."

"Did you send for him, as soon as you knew that his testimony was needed?"

"I did not."

"*Why* did you not?" said the District Attorney, in his sneering voice.

The color flushed into her face. "Because I—because I"—Her voice faltered and broke. "I did not *wish* him sent for," she said, with a sudden flash of defiance. Then she turned deathly white, and put up her handkerchief to her lips. "I—will not answer any more questions," she added, faintly.

After all, it had been very bad—worse, far worse, than she had expected. She felt as she left the stand that she had done her cause only harm. It seemed to her moreover, that whether she were acquitted or found guilty, she could never, after the abasement of that cross-examination, hold up her head again.

The outlook was gloomy, and the case for the defence was almost closed. But when Mrs. Bobby arrived in court the next morning, she was greeted by Mr. Fenton with a broad smile.

"We must put the handwriting experts on again," he said, cheerfully. "It will be dull, but anything to gain time. I have had a cable from Mr. Gerard. He will be here in a few days."

Chapter XXXVII

JULIAN Gerard paced impatiently the deck of the steamer on which, for eight miserable days, he had existed without sight of a newspaper. It was early dawn; the outlines of the Goddess of Liberty loomed uncertainly through a thick fog. He remembered how, when he had last seen his native shores, he had been distraught with bitter anger against the woman to whom his heart now turned with an eager longing, a passionate remorse.

For the hundredth time his mind analyzed and condemned that strange whim, the expression of a passing but very real phase of his disappointment and disillusion, which had led him to cut himself off from the world he had left behind. He had no wish to hear from home, to be reminded of home ties, or of the woman whom he had resolved to forget. Beneath his self-repressed exterior there was a strain of adventure in his blood, which made him turn, in a crisis like this, to the primitive resources of uncivilized life.

He had left home with no definite plans; but in London he met a friend, who was about to start for his farm in South Africa. Gerard at once decided to accompany him. South Africa was as good a place as any other, when all one desired was solitude and hardship, and to get away from one's self, and the unsatisfactory tone of the world.

The farm was deep in the interior of the country, many miles distant from railroad or telegraph station. For months the two men saw no one but the natives; they had no connection with the outside world. Gerard rode and hunted and studied, and took notes on the condition of the country. It was not a bad life on the whole, with a certain charm for a man satiated with all that wealth can give. He might even have enjoyed it, if he could have forgotten what had driven him to it, or erased from his memory the one face which haunted him.

The worst of it was, that she always seemed to be unhappy; he always saw her as he had left her, white and sad, with pathetic eyes. The thought of her which he had carried away that night seemed to have entirely effaced his earlier impressions of her, as she had first flashed upon him in the vivid radiance of her fresh beauty, as he had seen her often in a ball-room, a being meant only for smiles. He had never pictured her then as suffering; but now, he could not think of her in any other way.

One evening, as he and his friend sat together smoking, he found himself impelled, as it were, in spite of himself, to tell his story. The doubts, the misgivings which tortured him had grown too strong; it was a relief to put them into words. He spoke low and bitterly, in hurried phrases that were evidently the expression of his constant thoughts; not excusing the conduct of the woman who had deceived him, dwelling upon it rather with some harshness, for the very wish perhaps which he was conscious of to do the reverse. The other man, as he spoke, scanned his face keenly. At the end he made only one comment. "And yet she loved you?"

Gerard stared at him for a moment, the color flushing into his dark cheek. And then his face softened. Yes, it was not his money and position—he could at least do her that justice. "I believe she did," he said at last in a low voice.

"Then, for Heaven's sake," the other man flashed out, "what more do you want? Why, good Lord, if a woman *loved* me!"—and here he broke off and sat in silence, staring fixedly into the fire.

Gerard paced the floor that night, and his friend in the next room smiled grimly to hear him. The same smile flickered across his impassive features when Gerard, the next morning, announced his departure. His reasons were plausible; he wished to go about the country and study for himself the political situation of which he had hitherto seen little or nothing. His host, after that first involuntary smile, heard him through unmoved and expressed his approval. He escorted him to the nearest town, wrung his hand at parting, and went back, with a grimmer look than ever, to his own solitude.

Gerard had no plans; he was conscious of only one wish—to be where he could have news of home. At Cape Town he met the detective, who had followed him, led astray by various false clues, till he had at last found the right track. An hour later the two men started for New York. And now at last the wretched journey was over, and Gerard paced the deck of the ship and wondered miserably what new developments might have occurred.

There was a sensation in the court-room when he appeared. There had been rumors for days that the trial was being delayed for the arrival of an important witness, but it had hardly been expected that this would prove to be Elizabeth's missing lover, who had disappeared from view, as the prosecution had asserted, to avoid testifying against her. At least that reason for his absence could not be true, since it was Mr. Fenton who was bringing him in, with an evident air of triumph. Gerard himself had a worn and haggard look, which showed even through the sun-burn which had darkened his face. He had grown very thin, and there were white threads in his hair which were not visible a year before; his features were set in lines of absolute, impassive rigidity. He glanced neither to the right nor left, but sat down at once in the ranks of witnesses.

There was a short pause of breathless expectancy, and then the prisoner was brought in. Her aunts and Mrs. Van Antwerp were with her as usual, and behind followed the police officer—a little in the background, and with the air he considerately wore of effacing himself as much as possible. Those who were near Gerard saw him wince and flush painfully. He had been prepared for this, but the reality shocked him, almost beyond his powers of self-control. How changed she was! Paler even than he remembered her, and thin and worn till, but for her eyes and hair, he might scarcely have known her. It gave him a shock, too, somehow to see her all in black; he had always pictured her, illogically, in white as she had been that last evening.... For a moment she hardly seemed the same woman he had thought of, dreamed of, all these months. A rush of remorseful tenderness swept over him, all the greater because she was so changed. He would have liked to go to her before them all, and proclaim to the whole world his love and faith. But what he actually did was to turn his eyes away, to spare her.

She knew that he was there. She had read the news in the trembling joy depicted on her aunts' faces, before Eleanor Van Antwerp had whispered: "Darling, prepare yourself! He has come—he has come to save you." It hardly seemed a surprise, now that it had happened; she had always known in her heart that he would come. But she was not glad, she did not wish to be saved—by him. She still felt as she had felt from the first, that she would rather die than sit in her place of humiliation and see the pity in his eyes.... Ah, thank Heaven, he had turned them away; for him, no doubt, as for her it was a painful moment. He felt sorry for her, of course—a woman whom he had loved once, who was being punished more than she deserved. But there was an invincible pride in her nature which rebelled against his pity, which would have preferred condemnation, contempt. Yet, after all, pity was all that she deserved; she had never been worthy of his love. Let her take what poor remnant of it was left and be thankful. Yet deep down in her heart, there was, in spite of herself, a feeling of joy that the world would know that he had not forsaken her.

There was little time for these conflicting thoughts to oppose each other in Elizabeth's weary brain. Gerard was called to the stand, and then she could do nothing but listen—and listen gratefully—while in quiet, even tones, speaking very simply and to the point, he corroborated all that she herself had testified. Yes, he remembered perfectly the morning of the twenty-third of December. He had spent it with Miss Van Vorst at the Metropolitan Museum. They had been at the Museum for several hours, and he had left her at her home at half-past one. Had he known then of her marriage to Halleck? No, not then, but soon afterwards. She had told him on New Year's Eve. No, he had not suspected it, or drawn out the avowal in any way. It had been entirely voluntary. Naturally their engagement had been at an end, and he had gone abroad immediately. That was his evidence. It materially strengthened the defence on two points; first, that the prisoner had not bought either the flask or the poison; second, that she had not expected Paul Halleck's death.

The District Attorney, realizing this, tried to undermine its credibility. It was not an easy thing with a man of Gerard's character and high standing; but after all, a man in love is hardly an accountable being. The District Attorney dwelt sarcastically on the improbability of his having remained in ignorance all this time of the impending trial, and insinuated that he must have had serious objections to returning, which had been finally overcome by the efforts of the defense. He asked his questions in a blustering way, which fell just short of insolence. Gerard answered them quietly, apparently unmoved. Yes, he admitted, it seemed improbable that he should not have heard of the trial, but it was nevertheless absolutely true. He had spent the greater part of his absence on a farm in South Africa; he had led a rough, solitary life, read no newspapers, received no letters. He had first heard that his evidence was needed at Cape town, five weeks before. No, he had not received a letter from the defendant, urging him to come to her rescue, nor did he believe that any such letter had been sent. It would have been quite unnecessary.

"Your disinterested chivalry, in other words," sneered the District Attorney, "was sufficient, without such an appeal?"

"It is not a question of chivalry," said Gerard, coolly, "it is a question of telling the truth."

"Which of course you are anxious to do."

"Of course."

His imperturbability seemed proof, against all the offensiveness of the other's manner. The District Attorney, shifting his ground, questioned him as to the broken engagement; and here he was rejoiced to find his man more vulnerable. A tremor would cross Gerard's face, he changed color more than once. But still his answers were given quietly, in low, measured tones. Yes, it was true that Miss Van Vorst had kept him in ignorance of her marriage; but he did not think that her reasons for her silence need be discussed, since they were quite irrelevant.

"And you mean to assure us," said the District Attorney, incredulously, "that she told you at last of her own accord, without the slightest necessity?"

"Most certainly."

"And what she told you then was the only information you received of her marriage?"

"Yes."

"It was the only reason for breaking the engagement?"

"Yes."

"And now that that reason no longer exists," said the District Attorney, "the engagement, I suppose, is likely to be renewed?"

The question was so unexpected that Mr. Fenton was not ready with an objection, and Gerard spoke before he could interpose.

"I don't think that I am bound to answer questions as to what may or may not occur in the future."

Mr. Fenton hastily agreed with him, and he was sustained by the judge. But the District Attorney defended his line of inquiry.

"Your Honor, it is important for me to show how far this witness is biassed in favor of the defendant. He has wished to marry her once, it is possible, apparently, that he may be in the same position again. You won't deny," he went on, turning to Gerard, "—that there *is* such a possibility?"

Gerard hesitated for perhaps a second. Then he looked the lawyer squarely, defiantly in the face. He was very pale, but there was an angry light in his eyes; his voice rang out clearly. "I deny nothing," he said, "except that my feelings toward Miss Van Vorst have influenced the truth of anything I said."

Mr. Fenton again formally entered his objection, and after some wrangling, question and answer were stricken from the record. Still, the jury had heard them and could form their own conclusions. Mr. Fenton was not dissatisfied; there was a romantic element in the situation which must, he thought, appeal irresistibly to the popular imagination. And indeed, as Gerard left the stand, the general sympathy was on his side, even among those who secretly thought that he had stretched a point here and there, on behalf of the woman he loved. It was possible that his evidence was false; but the people who thought thus, if they were men, did not blame him; if they were women, they admired him rather the more.

The eyes of the court-room were fixed upon him as he crossed over to where Elizabeth sat and shook hands with her quietly, as if they had parted yesterday. And then he seated himself near her, in the little circle of her supporters. Eleanor Van Antwerp put out her hand to him, her dark eyes shining through a mist of tears.

"Julian, you don't know how happy I am to have you back."

He shuddered, "Don't speak of it, Eleanor. I can never forgive myself for having gone."

Elizabeth heard the words, but her eyes were resolutely bent on the ground, and she refused to take any of the comfort that his presence might have imparted. It was natural that he should feel remorseful, eager to show to the world as much as possible that he had not forsaken her, that he thoroughly believed in her innocence. But for anything more, such a possibility as the District Attorney had suggested, which he did not deny, could not, of course, very well deny under the circumstances?... Ah, no, there could be no question any more of love between them. Her own pride would not permit it, even if what she called his pity could influence his judgment to that extent. And then, with a start, she remembered that she was still on trial for her life, and that all thoughts of love and marriage were incongruous, almost grotesque. The case for the defense was closed, the District Attorney was to make his final address the next day. The thing would soon be decided, one way or the other.

The next morning, a box of flowers was brought to her; the white roses which he had always sent her. For a moment she hesitated, touched them lovingly, and then at last she took one of them and fastened it in her belt. "It may bring luck," she murmured, as if to excuse her action, and then she bent her head, and pressed her lips to its fragrant petals.

A little later, when she entered the court-room, the eyes of all were fixed on the flower. It was the first touch of color that had ever relieved her black gown.

"You see," one woman whispered, "it's the sign of innocence."

Her companion, less easily moved, replied cautiously: "Perhaps."

Chapter XXXVIII

THE tide of popular sentiment was turning in Elizabeth's favor. It had not been with her at first, in spite of her youth and the pathetic circumstances of her position; nay, against her all the more on that very account with many people, who feared a display of mawkish sentiment, and to whom the cold-blooded character of the crime stood out the more harshly, by contrast with her soft and girlish looks. But now one thing and another—an intangible something in her manner on the witness-stand; Gerard's return and his evidence on her behalf; his apparently unchanged devotion—all this had created a strong revulsion of feeling, which was increased rather than diminished by the District Attorney's charge.

The District Attorney was in a brutal mood. He did not spare Elizabeth, he left it, he said, to the jury to determine the weight of Gerard's evidence. For himself, he would not for the world suggest that a gentleman of Mr. Gerard's high character would testify falsely; yet he might be—mistaken; he might easily make some slight error in dates, misled by his—his interest in the defendant. While he talked Gerard bit his lip, inwardly cursing that dictate of civilization which had abolished duelling, and made even horsewhipping a doubtful expedient. Mrs. Bobby was considering ways by which one could be avenged on "a horrible man, not in society, whom one couldn't snub by not asking him to dinner, or anything of that kind." Elizabeth felt, with a new thrill of pain, that she was involving Gerard in her own disgrace. But Mr. Fenton surveyed the District Attorney unmoved through half-closed eyes, and said to himself coolly that he was going too far.

His own charge was a skillful defense of Gerard's evidence, a criticism, not too violent, of the District Attorney's brutality, and an appeal, not too open, to the sympathies of the jury. Elizabeth flushed as she realized that this was the point, after all; she was to be saved on issues that would not have been effectual with a man. And then the Judge's charge began, and she forgot all sense of humiliation, forgot everything but the thought that her fate hung in the balance, to be decided one way or the other by those carefully-balanced, judicial phrases. Did she imagine it, or was there, through all the calm analysis of evidence, the impartial weighing of this or that detail, a conviction of her innocence so decided that it made itself felt almost unconsciously?

"Strong on our side!" Bobby Van Antwerp's voice, unusually animated and exultant, sounded in his wife's ear at the end. "The prosecution are furious—they say it's horribly unfair. But of course, we won't quarrel with that."

Eleanor was deathly white; her hands were tightly locked together. At Bobby's words she gave a little sob of hysterical relief. "Oh, Bobby," she murmured, under her breath, "thank God that judges are human, after all! Now, if the jury are anything short of brutes, they'll acquit her at once and make an end of this."

But the jury fell short of this test of humanity, and retired to deliberate. Mrs. Bobby scanned their faces anxiously, as she had done at the beginning of the trial. They were care-worn and gloomy—naturally, with a woman's life in their hands; but surely—surely they should look happier, since it was in their power to save her?

"I wish, Bobby," she murmured, with that sob again in her throat, but this time not one of relief, "I wish we had tried if they wouldn't take money!"

"Don't, Eleanor," said Bobby. "They're all honest men—and besides, one can't do such things!" To himself he was thinking that women really seemed on such occasions as this to be entirely without principle, and yet that somehow one liked them all the better for it.

This was at two o'clock. Three, four, five o'clock came, and still they made no sign. The long deliberation seemed ominous to the anxious group who waited in a small, dark room on the ground floor of the court-house, starting at every sound and counting the moments as they dragged wearily along. Mr. Fenton and the other counsel came restlessly in and out, with a cheerful air that covered but indifferently their intense anxiety; Bobby and Julian Gerard stood by the window, talking occasionally in low tones, more often silent and gazing at the prison walls that rose up grimly before their eyes. Elizabeth sat at a small table in the middle of the room, and her aunts and Mrs. Van Antwerp sat around her in a forlorn circle. It was a long while since any one had spoken; all consoling suggestions were exhausted.

Elizabeth's hands were clasped tightly in her lap, her eyes, wide-open yet unseeing, stared steadily before her. Vaguely she was conscious that there were people in the room, that by the window stood the man whose presence might have mattered more to her at some other time than anything else on earth; that her aunts and Eleanor Van Antwerp were beside her, and would bend forward now and then, one or other of them, to press her hand. In a dull, mechanical way, she was thankful to know that they were there; yet nothing they said or did could help her, a great gulf seemed to yawn between her and the outside world.... It is thus, perhaps, that the dying feel when they see, with their failing sight, the faces of friends, and know that even love is powerless to reach them. Elizabeth suffered, during those hours of suspense, the agony of death a hundred times over. But as the afternoon wore on, hope faded and the numbness of despair crept over her tortured nerves.

"I don't like their staying out so long," Bobby Van Antwerp could not help murmuring to Gerard. "After the charge, I thought they'd let her off at once. They all want to—that's certain. But there were one or two of them who looked—infernally conscientious."

"I don't want any of them"—Gerard began, but stopped. "To go against his convictions," was what he had meant to add, but the words remained unspoken. There are limits to even a Puritan conscience. "Good God! Bobby," he whispered, hoarsely, "a man who could convict her deserves to be shot!"

"I agree with you, old man," said Bobby, tranquilly. And then they once more fell silent, and the shadows lengthened, and some one lit a feeble gas-jet, which brought out, in ghastly relief, the look of strained expectancy on each face.

At six o'clock there was a rustle, an excitement. Mr. Fenton came in and spoke to Bobby, and he spoke to his wife. She touched Elizabeth on the shoulder.

"Dear, we—we go up now," she said. Elizabeth rose and mechanically put up her hand to her hair.

"Do I look all right?" she said, and then smiled vaguely at the commonplace question. A merciful stupor had descended upon her in the last hour; when she looked at her aunts, she saw that they were suffering far more than she. "I am not frightened," she said, "please don't be frightened." She was determined that she would be brave. This was the thought uppermost in her mind.

They went up to the court-room, and on the threshold Mr. Fenton said to her: "Remember, that even if the verdict is—is unfavorable, it is not final. We shall appeal." She bent her head, wondering mechanically that any one should speak of things to happen *after* the verdict. Her whole life seemed bounded by the events of the next few minutes; she could not look beyond.... The thought crossed her mind of how slight a thing would decide her fate—the difference between one word or two, guilty or not guilty. A mere trifle—a word in three letters; yet all the difference between honor and dishonor, life and death. Her mind fastened upon the irrelevant detail and dallied with it; the while she was conscious, with sickening intensity, of each movement in the court-room—the breathless atmosphere of a suspense, in which the mere rustling of a paper jarred upon the nerves; the jury filing in, the formal opening question, "Gentlemen of the jury, have you decided upon your verdict?" Her throat was parched, balls of fire danced before her eyes, there was a sound in her ears like the rushing of many waters. Guilty or not guilty? One word or two? The question beat upon her brain with a dull persistence, and she was conscious, vaguely, that the answer was of vital importance, but somehow she could not bring herself to realize it.

"*Not Guilty.*"

The words rang clear and confident, across that gulf which separated her from the outside world. As through a mist she saw the relief on the faces of those around her, but still she herself was conscious of no feeling. She still sat white and dazed, staring before her, while her lips moved mechanically, repeating the words that seemed so meaningless: "*Not Guilty.*"

There was a pause, and then a stir, a murmur of relief. Some women sobbed aloud. But she herself still sat staring before her, repeating the answer that seemed to have no meaning: "*Not Guilty.*"

Chapter XXXIX

BY the next morning, she had realized all that the verdict meant; she had had time even to grow used to it. The first joy had spent itself, the inevitable reaction was setting in.

"Life isn't everything," she thought, and stared before her with knit brows. The fire—it was a long time since she had sat beside one—gave out a cheerful glow, the little drawing-room wore a festive air and was bright with flowers that had been sent to her. A feeling of physical ease and contentment, of relief in the mere change of scene, stole over her wearied senses. But still it did not suffice; she struggled indeed against it.

She took up and re-read a letter which had been left for her a little while before, and had caused her, in her state of exhaustion, something of a nervous shock.

"They have just told me," it said, "that you are acquitted. As for me, I am very ill. They say I can't live much longer. That's why I ask if you will come and see me at once. There are some things I'd like to tell you, and if you don't come quickly it may be too late."

AMANDA."

The address was that of a hospital.

"I didn't know," Elizabeth said, "that Amanda was so ill."

Her aunts, who were hovering about the room, devouring their recovered treasure with tender eyes, looked surprised at her introduction of an irrelevant subject.

"I heard that she had gone to a hospital," Miss Cornelia said, dryly, "and her mother came down to be near her—but dear me, that girl always has something the matter with her! I don't know why you should trouble yourself about her, my dear. Both she and her mother have behaved in a very unfeeling way all this time, never coming to see you, or sending messages, or anything."

"Well, Amanda has sent me a message now," said Elizabeth. "She wants me to come and see her, and I think"—she hesitated a moment—"I think I shall go at once," she announced with sudden decision. The words sounded strangely to her as she uttered them. It was so long since she had said that she would do this or that. And even now, her wishes met with some faint opposition.

Her aunts looked at each other. "But won't that be painful for you, my dear?" urged Miss Cornelia, after a moment.

"I'm used to painful things, Aunt Cornelia." The girl's smile was bitter; there was a tone of petulant wilfulness in her voice. Her aunts still looked at one another unspoken words trembled on the lips of each.

"My dear," Miss Joanna began at last, "Julian"—she stopped.

"He said he hoped to see you this morning," said Miss Cornelia, taking up the sentence. "He hoped that after you had rested"—she faltered as a look crossed Elizabeth's face, which did not promise consent. And then suddenly she took courage and crossed over to Elizabeth and took her hand. "My dear," she cried, "you—you must see him. He has been so unhappy. He—he loves you, Elizabeth." Again her voice faltered. The girl sat passive for a moment, and then she flushed and dragged away her hand.

"I can't see him," she broke out, hoarsely; "it—it would be more painful than seeing Amanda. And—if he loves me, why, so much the worse!" Then softening, as she met their dismayed looks: "Oh, don't you understand," she cried, "don't you understand that the kindest thing I can do for him is—not to see him?" And then the tears sprang to her eyes and she hurriedly left the room.

When she came back a few minutes later, she was dressed for going out, in the black gown and hat that she had worn at the trial. She had tied a black veil over her face.

"I must go to see Amanda," she said, speaking very quietly and without any trace of emotion. "I should always regret it if—if anything happened before I went." She paused as if in expectation of further protest, and then as none came, she went to them and kissed them both affectionately. "You—you don't mind, do you," she said, with a note of apology in her voice. Her aunts sighed resignedly.

"I wish you would let me go with you, Elizabeth," Miss Cornelia said, feebly.

Elizabeth smiled. "Why should you, dear?" she said, quietly. "I've got to face the world alone some time, I suppose. And it will be nice to see what it's like— I've almost forgotten." She gave a little sigh, but checked it instantly, and went out before they could say any more.

Once in the street the world seemed so strange that it was startling, and for a moment turned her faint and giddy. It was a mild midwinter day—the trial had lasted over Christmas and into the new year—almost there seemed a foretaste of spring in the air. To Elizabeth the sunlight was dazzling; she put up her hand to ward it off. She walked slowly and feebly, as if she were convalescing from a long illness. She had not realized before how weak she was. Fortunately there was but a short walk before her, through the quiet regions of Irving Place, past Gramercy Park, and on to the hospital. She met no one she knew, but several strangers glanced at her curiously, or so she imagined, as if they recognized her, even through her veil. They might know her from the pictures with which the papers had been filled; they had seen one, no doubt, only that morning, with an account of the verdict. They were wondering still, perhaps, if she were guilty or innocent.

She was very tired when she reached the hospital, and the meeting with Amanda loomed up before her like a nightmare. Her hand trembled as she rang the bell. A woman in a sister's dress opened the door—the hospital was under the charge of a Protestant order. There was something conventual about the waiting-room, into which she was shown. There was little furniture, pictures of saints hung on the walls, the wide window was filled with stained glass, through which the light streamed faintly and fell in bars of crimson and purple upon the polished floor. The sister, speaking in the subdued voice which the place seemed to demand, bade Elizabeth seat herself and took up her name.

Elizabeth sank down with a sense of physical relief, which obliterated all other feelings. A moment later she looked up with a start. The door opened and a woman entered. It was Amanda's mother.

"Well Elizabeth, so you've got off!" she said, mechanically touching with dry lips her niece's cheek. "I'm sure I'm glad enough, for the sake of the family. And then I never thought you did it."

Elizabeth flushed painfully. "That was kind of you, Aunt Rebecca," she said.

"Well, a great many people did, you know, and probably do still, for that matter. But lor'—what difference does it make, as long as you've got off? Some people might think all the more of you. There was that girl at——who committed that murder that everybody talked about—she got a hundred offers, they say, right after she was acquitted. And everybody knew that she got off, just because she was a woman."

Elizabeth shuddered. "Please don't talk about it, Aunt Rebecca," she said, faintly. "Tell me about Amanda."

A sort of contraction crossed Aunt Rebecca's face, which might in any one else, have resulted in tears. "Oh, Amanda's pretty poorly," she said, in an odd, dry voice. "I guess all those sanitariums and new-fangled inventions, haven't done her much good. Why the doctor sent her here, I don't know. It's a queer Catholic place, and I don't hold with such notions, but Amanda seems taken with the sisters"—she broke off abruptly as one of their number entered.

She was a woman of middle age, with a grave, fine face and musical voice which harmonized with the place and her own costume. In her presence Amanda's mother, for all her uneasy contempt seemed to sink at once into insignificance. The Sister took possession very gently, but completely, of Elizabeth. Her charge had been very anxious, she said, to see her; it was kind of Miss Van Vorst to come. And then she led the way up the stairs, and down the long white corridors, talking quietly as she went of Amanda's case. The girl was suffering from a complication of maladies, and the Sister thought that there was, besides, some trouble weighing on her mind, under the stress of which she grew daily weaker. No, there was, humanly speaking, little hope, though Amanda's poor mother did not realize it, but the Sister thought it would do her patient good to see Miss Van Vorst, of whom she had talked a great deal. All this time there was not a word, not a curious glance, to show that the Sister knew that she had beside her the subject of so much discussion. And yet Elizabeth felt herself enveloped in an atmosphere of sympathy, a tacit recognition of the fact that she had suffered, which held in it not a trace of blame or suspicion. Elizabeth felt grateful.

The private room which Amanda occupied as one of the few "paying patients," was near the roof of the house, at the head of several flights of stairs. Sunlight poured in through the window, the floor was covered with matting, the walls bare and hung with religious pictures. Opposite the small iron bed, and placed where the light fell full upon it, was an engraving, the copy of a famous picture, of

Christ upon the Cross. It was singularly vivid, and the sorrowful dignity of the face had attracted the eyes and soothed the sufferings of many an occupant of the room.

Amanda's strange, light eyes, as they stood out unnaturally large and dilated in her thin, wasted face, were not fixed upon the picture; but turned with eager expectancy towards the door. She was sitting up in bed, her head propped with pillows. Her skin had faded to a duller, more ghastly tint than ever, but a bright spot of red burned in either cheek. As Elizabeth entered she started, and an odd look flitted across her face—it was hard to tell whether it indicated relief, or fear, or perhaps a mingling of both.

"So you've come," she said, and drew a long sobbing breath. It was all her greeting. Elizabeth, embarrassed, murmured a few words of sympathy, as she sank into the chair nearest the door. The Sister, with a keen glance from one to the other, left the two girls alone.

Amanda immediately assumed control of the situation.

"Sit there," she said, in a quick, sharp voice, and pointing to a chair by the window, "sit there so I can look at you." Elizabeth mechanically obeyed and threw back her veil. Amanda's eyes fastened eagerly upon her face.

"Why, you—you've lost your looks," she announced, abruptly. "Did you know it?" There was a note of involuntary satisfaction in her voice.

Elizabeth tried to smile. "Worse things have happened to me than that, Amanda," she said.

"I didn't think anything could be worse—to you," Amanda said, feebly.

Elizabeth was silent. She was thinking that suffering had not yet produced in Amanda any regenerating effect.

"Well, after all, I guess it don't matter," Amanda said, drearily, after a pause. "You're acquitted just the same, and Mr. Gerard is just as crazy about you as ever, they say. I guess you've got the best of me still." She sank into a gloomy silence.

Elizabeth dared not speak. She was wondering if she could not escape, since her cousin had nothing to say, beyond the old jealous complaint. But suddenly Amanda turned to her.

"I've something I want to tell you," she said, speaking feebly and with difficulty. "Sister made me promise that I—would; she said that if there was any—any way in which I'd injured you, it would ease my mind to—tell you. But first you must promise"—she looked about her suspiciously—"you must swear to me on your oath that you won't repeat—anything I tell you."

She raised herself up on her pillows, her breath came in convulsive gasps, she fixed her eyes intently upon Elizabeth. "Promise," she said, in her weak, hoarse voice, "swear to me on your oath that you won't—repeat what I tell you now."

Elizabeth trembled, her brain felt dazed. Those strained, eager eyes held her with a terrible insistence. "I—I promise," she repeated, hardly knowing what she said, conscious only of a wish to have them withdrawn.

Amanda sank back as if relieved, on the pillows, but still she questioned, with a look of doubt. "You won't break your word. You are sure?"

"Quite sure," said Elizabeth. Her brain still seemed dazed, her lips moved mechanically.

Amanda seemed satisfied. Still, she did not speak, she lay quiet, with half-closed eyes. At last, with a painful effort, she raised herself up, and fixed her eyes again intently upon Elizabeth. "I sent the poison," she said. The words came in a hoarse whisper.

Elizabeth stared at her without moving; only a slight shudder passed through her. The words echoed in her ear, beat upon her brain. The odd part of it was that they did not surprise her. She seemed somehow to have heard, or thought them, before.

"Yes," Amanda repeated, after a moment, "I sent the poison. It was after I had left the sanitarium—no one knew that I had left it. I dressed as like you as I could, I copied your handwriting, I knew they would think it was you. But I didn't"—a slight undertone of contempt made itself felt in her voice—"I didn't know how easy it would be, for I didn't suppose you'd do all those stupid things that made them suspect you."

She was silent. Elizabeth still stared at her motionless, aghast. "But why—why," she faltered, "what object, Amanda, could you have?"

A look of intense bitterness crossed the sick girl's face. She seemed to flare up all at once into a red heat of anger, as dry, withered wood will sometimes give out the fiercest flames. "What object!" she repeated. "You ask what object!—and you know how he scorned me! Didn't you wish him to die? You admitted it in court—because he stood in your way; and do you think that is anything to being humiliated—dragged in the dust, as I was?"

She leaned back panting on the pillows; the fierce flame of anger which passed over her seemed to consume her feeble strength. When she spoke again it was much more feebly. "That time when I—I went to him at the studio," she said, "I thought maybe he'd come back to me again—seeing you didn't seem to want him. I thought—but there, I was a fool. Most women are, I guess, when they care about a man. He laughed at me and said that I'd deceived myself—that it was I who did the love-making. That was a lie, but it was what he said, I guess, about most girls—when he got tired of them. I got wild, it seemed as if my brain was on fire, and I—I threatened him. He only laughed. And then I taunted him—about you; that seemed to hurt him more. I said as how you had so many beaux, you didn't care any longer about him. He said then, I was mistaken, that you were just as fond of him as ever—really, that you would do anything he wanted"—

She paused, her breath seemed to fail her. Elizabeth sat listening, stupefied, incapable of speech or motion. Amanda went on presently, huddling one word upon another: "I didn't believe him, I thought it was only to make me feel worse. And then, when I went out, I met you—the thought came to me that I'd find out the truth. I came back, I'd left the door open, I saw you give him money—but there was a look on your face that made me think you didn't do it—for love."

She paused again and struggled for breath. Elizabeth spoke involuntarily. "But how did you know," she asked, "about the pearls?"

"What, that you'd sold them?" Amanda spoke quietly, with a slight smile, as at the simplicity of the question. "I knew it the moment I saw you—that evening, and you didn't have them on. Then when I spoke of them, I saw I was right—I saw how I'd frightened you. There was a secret—I didn't know what; but it was something you were ashamed of. Then, when you got engaged to that other man, I understood—I knew you were afraid of his finding it out. I used to write to him, warning him. He never answered my letters, or paid any attention—I guess he thought I was crazy; but I had to keep on writing—I couldn't help it, somehow. I had to do everything I did. It seemed as if something urged me on. The only thing that kept me from—from having my revenge was that you might reap the benefit. And then this plan came to me, and I saw how I could—get even—with you both."

The hoarse, feeble voice grew fainter and died away, as if from sheer exhaustion. Elizabeth interposed an indignant protest. "And so," she said, "you wanted me to suffer—for your crime? You would have been glad if they had found me guilty?"

Amanda did not answer for a moment. "No," she said at last, "I didn't want you to die. I knew you'd get off—every one said so—because you were so pretty and so swell. They wouldn't"—the bitter smile again hovered about her white lips— "they wouldn't have said that about me. But—if they had found you guilty"—she paused—"I had quite made up my mind to confess. It was horrible lying here, thinking it over—I don't believe death can be worse. You couldn't have suffered— anything like it; for you were innocent."

She looked at Elizabeth with a strange horror in her eyes. Her face was ghastly, beads of perspiration stood on her forehead, and on the little rings of dark red hair, which clung about her temples. "Oh, you don't know what it is," she said, "you don't know what it is. It's the thought of that that's killing me inch by inch; it's not the disease. And yet I'm afraid—I'm afraid to confess"—her voice broke piteously. "You don't want me to—do you?—now that you've got off. It won't do you any good—any longer, and as for me, though I don't want to live, I'm afraid— to die." The feeble voice again faltered and died away.

Elizabeth sat silent, her brain in a whirl. Before her there rose the thought of the long months of torture, the prison cell, the terrible, unnecessary suspicion that still clouded her life.... If Amanda would confess, it would be something. People would never again believe her guilty. And yet!——

Mechanically, her eyes wandered about the room, the incongruous setting for this strange scene—bright, calm and peaceful; filled with the pictures of martyred saints. Her gaze lingered fascinated on the face of Christ in the engraving. It might have been the effect of the light, or the over-wrought state of her nerves which made it appear so real, instinct with mysterious life and power. Almost it seemed as if the lips moved, the sorrowful eyes rested, with a look of infinite pity, on Amanda ... ... "You won't betray me?" the feeble voice pleaded. "I trusted you— you promised? You won't break your word?"

"No"—Elizabeth spoke slowly and thoughtfully—"I won't break my word. I did break a promise I made you once, and repented it, ever since; but this time I shall keep it. If you confess, it must be for your own sake, not for mine. No one I care about believes me guilty. Let it go."

Amanda drew a sigh of relief. Her head fell back, her attitude of tension relaxed insensibly.

"You are very generous," she said, faintly. "I—I won't be ungrateful." And then a silence fell upon them. Amanda's eyes closed, she seemed exhausted. Elizabeth, seeing this, got up.

"I had better go. You're very tired." No answer came. But as she reached the door Amanda's eyes unclosed, she turned her face towards her.

"Good-bye," she said. "I'm sorry you've—lost your looks. Perhaps you'll—get them back." The words came out with a great effort. And then she turned her face away and said no more.

The Sister was waiting outside in the corridor. She accompanied Elizabeth to the door of the hospital.

As they parted she laid her hand for an instant on the girl's arm, her grave, clear eyes scanned the white, exhausted face.

"My dear," she said, "did your cousin tell you—what she sent for you to say?"

Elizabeth met her gaze firmly, with eyes as clear as her own. "It is a secret," she said, quietly. "I promised—not to repeat it."

A cloud passed over the Sister's face; her hand rested for a moment tenderly on Elizabeth's arm. "Poor child!" was all she said. It would have been hard to tell to whom she referred—Elizabeth or Amanda.

An instant later the great hospital door swung to, and Elizabeth found herself again in the outside world.

Amanda lay absolutely still. She was conscious, for the moment, of nothing but the utter vacuity of exhaustion. It was only little by little that her strength revived, her brain began to work, those thoughts weighed upon her again, which were killing her inch by inch.

It is hard to understand the processes of a mind like Amanda's, diseased perhaps from the first, made more so, as life went on, by illness and adverse circumstances. As to how far she was accountable, who can decide?...

One thing is certain, that some sort of moral struggle now took place within her. Her brow was contracted, her lips moved, now and then she stirred uneasily. Her piteous gaze fastened half unconsciously, as Elizabeth's had done, on the face of the Christ in the engraving. For her as for Elizabeth, the pictured eyes held a curious fascination. But we read into inanimate objects, above all the symbols of our faith, our own thoughts and convictions. It was not pity which Amanda saw in the sorrowful eyes which to her, too, seemed alive with a singular power.

When the Sister came in, a little later, she asked her a question.

"Isn't it enough if we confess our sins?" she asked, feebly. "You said that would be enough to have them forgiven."

The Sister looked down at her gravely. "Repentance is not enough," she said, "unless we do what we can to make amends."

Amanda turned away with a feeble moan.

It was late in the afternoon when she nerved herself, as for a great effort. She called the Sister to her and whispered. What she said did not seem to cause surprise. The Sister's face brightened, she left the room quickly. It was evident that she was prepared for an emergency like this. An hour later the small room was filled—there was a lawyer, witnesses.... Amanda's weak voice spoke steadily, without a pause....

When it was over, she sank back exhausted, and her eyes again sought the face in the engraving. She found there what she expected. With a long sigh of relief she turned her face to the wall and slept. The Sister quietly pulled down the blind.

"She will rest now," she said softly, and it was true. Amanda never awoke.

Chapter XL

"DON'T you think," said Gerard, "that I have waited long enough?"

It was five months later. The mellow afternoon sunlight pierced the foliage, which, interlacing, formed an arch overhead. Wild roses grew in profusion along the roadside. Beyond, the fields were thickly strewn with buttercups and daisies. The air was fragrant with the scent of honeysuckle.

Elizabeth wore a white gown; the hands carelessly clasped before her were filled with June roses. So far, she matched the day and the season. But her head drooped languidly, like a wilting flower, the country air had brought no color to her cheeks. Lines of suffering still lingered about her mouth. The eyes which were cast down, almost hidden by their long lashes, held a latent shadow in their depths.

The man by her side, who had just come up from town, noted all this with a keen anxiety.

"Don't you think," he repeated, with an impatience the greater for what her looks conveyed, "don't you think that I have waited long enough?"

A quiver crossed her face, but she did not look up. "It's not my fault that you have—waited," she murmured.

The man made a rueful gesture. "Oh, you need not tell me that," he said. "If you had had your way, you would have sent me—back to South Africa, I believe." He broke off with a bitter laugh. As if in spite of herself, a smile flickered beneath her drooping lids.

"Not quite so far, perhaps." The words sounded with a demure accent. But in an instant the smile vanished, her lip quivered, she looked up at him with a tremulous earnestness. "Ah, can't you understand," she cried, "why I want you to go? Haven't I brought you trouble enough? Do you think that now"—she paused and caught her breath—"now that all this disgrace has come upon me," she went on with an effort, "do you think I would burden you with it?"

"Disgrace!"—He flushed hotly.—"I don't know why there should be disgrace," he said, "when every one knows now—even those idiots who doubted you—how baseless the whole miserable accusation was."

"People don't reason." She sighed wearily. "There will always be a cloud over me—I feel it even here. People at The Mills stare at me, the Neighborhood"—she smiled painfully—"the Neighborhood feels that I have brought upon it eternal discredit. Ah, you can't blame them"—as Gerard muttered under his breath an ejaculation. "It will be the same in town—everywhere. People will always remember that I was horribly talked about, that I have been in prison. For myself"—her lip trembled—"I'm hardened, but for you"—

"For me"—he put out his hand and took hers determinedly into his strong grasp—"for me it is inevitable that, whatever troubles you have, I must share them."

There was silence for a moment. They stood facing each other, the only actors in the peaceful country scene; the man strong, determined, his eyes aglow with the fire of mastery; the woman pale, drooping, exhausted, yet still with some power in her weakness, that opposed itself to his strength. She put out her hand at last in a gesture of entreaty. "Ah, don't let us go all over this again," she pleaded. "Don't make it so hard for me. It's hard enough"—The words seemed to escape her unawares.

"Ah!" A gleam of triumph crossed his face. "It is hard, then?"

"Most things are hard."—She spoke with recovered firmness.—"Life is hard, but one must—bear it. At least I'll try to bear it—alone. The only amends I can make to you"—she clasped her hands suddenly in a passionate gesture of renunciation—"the only atonement is to efface myself, to sink out of your life as if I had never—been in it." She paused, her breath came in convulsive gasps, but still she faced him resolute, the look in her eyes with which some penitent of the early church might have welcomed lifelong immolation. "To efface myself," she repeated, dwelling upon the words as if they held some painful satisfaction, "to sink out of your life—it is the only atonement I can make."

"You can't make it." Gerard's words rang out clearly. He took her hands again resolutely in his. "You can't efface yourself," he said. "It's beyond your power." A smile flickered across his face, his eyes looked into hers with an imperious tenderness, before which they fell abashed. "Do you know," he said, "why I went off in that idiotic fashion into the wilds, tried to cut myself off from the world? I was bitter, angry—I wanted to forget you; I thought, if there were nothing to remind me of you, I might. And then day and night I thought of you, day and night your face haunted me.... Ah, Elizabeth"—his voice broke—"ask me to do anything except—forget you."

There was again silence. Elizabeth's lips parted, her breath fluttered, a warm, lovely color flooded her face. He thought she had yielded. But almost instantly the color faded, she drew her hands from his grasp and shrank away, as if under the weight of some painful memory. "And,—and that deception," she gasped out. "What has happened to change that? You said—don't you remember?—that you could never"—her voice quivered—"never trust me again." She lifted her head suddenly, she looked him firmly, steadily, in the face, with eyes that seemed the index to her soul. "I did deceive you," she said. "Nothing can change that fact. Why should you trust me now?"

"Ah, it would be hard on most of us"—the words sprung impetuously to his lips—"if there were no forgiveness, if strict justice were always meted out." He put out his hand in a passionate gesture, a rush of feeling thrilled his voice. "Elizabeth," he cried, "don't bring up words which I said that night in anger, which I have repented—God knows!—ever since. You had done an heroic thing in telling me the truth at last, just when it was hardest—I—brute that I was—could only think of my own misery. But let the past go—it shall not ruin our lives any longer." He put his arm around her and drew her towards him. He felt her heart beat, her pulses throb; his voice took on a deeper note of tenderness. "The future is ours, and love is ours—my darling, does anything else matter?"

The argument may not have been a wise one, but it has gained more victories than all the logic in the world. Elizabeth, weary of struggling, resigned herself to her defeat....

Later she looked up, gave a little, fluttering sigh, and her eyes sought his with a wistful sweetness. "Dear, I'm not worth it," she murmured, "but I will try— oh, I will try so hard." ... Gerard, smiling, cut the sentence short.

They walked on homeward through the fragrant lanes, in which they two seemed the only wanderers. The Misses Van Vorst, sitting by the drawing-room windows, saw them come with a little thrill of anxiety. Miss Joanna dropped a stitch in her knitting, and Miss Cornelia's thin, silvery curls fluttered, as if stirred by some intangible wave of sympathy.

Elizabeth crossed the flower-studded lawn and came towards them, her white skirts swaying about her in the gentle summer wind. She held her head erect, her color was brilliant, her eyes lustrous. The setting sun shone on her hair and lit it up into a vivid glory. Elizabeth's aunts stole a glance at her, at the look on Gerard's face. Then their eyes met and they smiled softly at each other through a mist of tears.

Lightning Source UK Ltd.
Milton Keynes UK
UKOW02f0803210515

252012UK00001B/86/P

LOOK

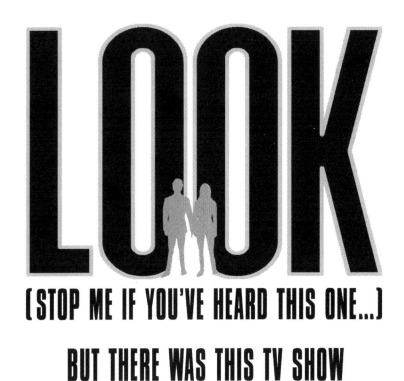

(STOP ME IF YOU'VE HEARD THIS ONE...)

BUT THERE WAS THIS TV SHOW

ROY BETTRIDGE

POTLUCK

LOOK (STOP ME IF YOU'VE HEARD THIS ONE...)
BUT THERE WAS THIS TV SHOW
by Roy Bettridge

ISBN 978-1-326-84306-9

First Published 2016 by Pot Luck

Edited by Roy Bettridge, Alan Hayes and Rebbecca O'Brien.
Cover Design by Jamie Rae
Internal Layout and Design by Alan Hayes

A Pot Luck book

DEDICATION

This book is lovingly dedicated to my father

ROY BETTRIDGE, SR.
(1957 – 2016)

ACKNOWLEDGEMENTS

This book is a tale based on reality with a fictional twist. It would not have been written without the wide-ranging support of everyone involved with the project.

This book is dedicated to my late father, Roy Sr., whom I thank from the heart for his never-ending love, support, guidance, tolerance and patience, and for nurturing my love for *The Avengers*. He was patient through the endless re-runs of the show to which he was subjected – the most amazing man I ever knew. I would also like to record a further, special dedication to my late mother, Iris, for being an amazing mother. Extra special thanks to all of my family for their love and support and extra, extra special thanks to my late grandmother, Rita, for being amazing in all things.

Special thanks to my fiancée Laura for being tolerant and for accepting in one breath everything concerning my adoration of *The Avengers*.

Thanks to Malcolm and Lilian Start for being the exceptional people that they are and for the support they gave me while I was writing this book. My love and respect are always with them.

Thanks must also go to Lucy Wright, Kayleigh Wright, Gemma Wright, Charmian Wright, Neil Griffin, Naomi Keable, Trudi Cope, Sharon Wilkinson, Karen Lenton, Tanya Perrin, Lisa Hunt, Linda Hunt, Karen Needle, Helen Kennewell, Guiseppe Massimo, Darren Howe, Richard Miles, Scott Edwards, Darren Willis (and his family), Aaron Marr, Rod Wildman, Danny Hill, Pawel Kwasnik, Ivetka Kosova and her staff at Tapri, Jack Norn, Andrea Ford, Hannah Brook, Jacqui Gallehawk and all my other friends and colleagues (past and present) at Newlands for their support and tolerance of my eccentricities. And to Mr Neal Dyche for always reminding me to keep smiling!

Thanks also to Craig Chapman, Ann Haines, the Wallis family and all associated, Sharon McDonald and her family, Mark Tebbutt, Jamie Rae, Barry Musgrave, Stefy Cenea, Laura Martin and her family, David Amos (along with his wife Sam and their family), Michael and Sandy Dawson, Dale Knighton and his partner and their family, Trevor Gillman, Katy

MacLean, Linda Kilpatrick, Kelly Bamford, Kim Chilton, Nathan Grooby and all in the Grooby clan, Darren Taylor, Rebbecca O'Brien, Kayleigh Heath, Justine and Jason Mitchell-Bunce, Chris and Mary Kemp, Steve and Priscilla Dodman, Paul and Angela Robertson, Julie Shipton and her family (a massive shout out to her son and my good friend, Mat), the Fleming family (special dedication to Sue Fleming (1947-2011)) and Nick Holmes and his family. A special shout out to my Havelock school chums, the Henry Gotch / Ise Community College survivors, my Tresham College and University friends – you're all diamonds – and to Sam Richards, her partner Pip and their family for their support in everything.

Many thanks must go to Alan Hayes for being my original editor on this project, for always being honest and supportive, for being my mentor throughout the process, and for being my friend.

Extra special thanks to David Hamilton for his research into the repeat dates of both *The Avengers* and *The New Avengers* during the 1990s. His research was the backbone of this project and I thank him for being thorough and diligent.

To all my friends at the time *The Avengers* entered my life, thank you for being patient with me. To those who initially considered me strange but have opened their minds to see that I'm not that bad, my thanks to you. Thank you to all my friends for being the fantastic people they are.

Special thanks must go to the late Patrick Macnee for being such a positive influence on me through my television viewing, for being the first actor I worshipped, and for his quintessential portrayal of John Steed. Many thanks to all of those who were involved in making *The Avengers* and *The New Avengers*; because of those talented men and women I am a fan for life. I must also thank Dave Rogers for his many books on the show which helped deepen my love and adoration for *The Avengers*. Similarly, I am grateful to Andrew Pixley and Michael Richardson, whose own books on the series made me happy to be a fan of this iconic show.

Finally, thanks to the companies who continue to keep the series I love in the public eye: to StudioCanal for giving *The Avengers* another lease of life and for looking after this fantastic show, and to Big Finish Productions for their excellent work with *The Avengers* audio series and bringing the lost episodes of the Ian Hendry series to life. Long may their audio adventures continue.

Chapter 1
FROM THE ASHES OF ROSES

Tape is rolling.
Entry begins.

My name is Chris.

This is my journal. I've been writing journals and making tape recordings of them for many years but as I hit the grand old age of 30 I do wonder why I'm still keeping a journal. But these will be the last of them. The plan is to encapsulate everything into one source and start directly from the beginning. I was nine when I initially wrote them in the back of my exercise book for Geography, each day written down painstakingly in the pages of a lined and stapled yellow book.

Now it's time to finish everything. It's time to stop recording my life and live it. I'm married with two children and this feeling of wanting to stop writing my endless journals occurred recently. The house that was the family home is finally being sold by my father. I spent many happy years stuck in the bedroom listening to my stereo and finally committing my thoughts to both paper and later tape recordings.

I stumbled across the exercise books as I was going through a box of things from the attic. They were all in a box that used to contain my old stereo. It was quite grand for its time with its two cassette decks, radio and vinyl player on the top. I had many hours of fun playing that. The amount of books I found tells me that my dad didn't mind purchasing the endless supply that just kept growing and growing.

I'm considering reading them all just to show me how I thought back then. I'm wondering where I would start and then I see the big black number 1 in the top corner of the book. The handwriting and grammar is appalling. We're off to a good start with the page set up; the same day and date template in each one made in bold black Berol handwriting pen.

I seem to have started off very matter of fact. For the benefit of the tape, I'll read them out loud...

Friday 21st April 1995

"I'm now ten. It was my birthday yesterday and I really enjoyed it. All my aunts came to visit me and give me presents and my mum and dad gave me the biggest birthday cake ever. I couldn't eat it all though so mum put the rest into the fridge."

It's nice to read that aloud and correct my grammar as I did so. I was really thinking about important things at that age! And for the sake of the tape recording I'm making at this moment it gives it all an air of my growing intelligence.

"My friends also came round for my party. My best friend Craig also came. He's great. We sometimes go round each other's houses for tea after school. He looks after me. It's like having a brother. School is a problem if anyone picks on you. I get that a lot. I have a lot of friends there though…"

The power of the written word is something that was impressed on me at school. The teachers would always try and get you to write everything down neatly as well as concisely.

I'm finding this entry a bit boring. Let's find out what the next one is like…

Saturday 22nd April 1995

"I love weekends. Two days of no school. I get to be outside all day and I get to see as many friends as I like. And it's sunny. Weekends are always sunny…"

If I ever met the younger me I think that I would have to sit him down and inform him that as you get older you realise that you live in a world where summer lasts for only a week and is quickly replaced by rain and strong winds. Next page…

Monday 24th April 1995

"It's Monday and I have to go back to school. Mum always gets me up and makes sure I have what I want for breakfast. Dad is

*always in the living room wearing his work uniform as he watches
the TV. When I finish my cereal I have to put my uniform on for
school. Dad and me play a game of who has the better uniform. I
do. It's a purple jumper with a polar bear reading a book with the
name of the school under it…"*

Oh how the routine of school fits in with a routine for life. I now
follow the pattern with my job. I seem to have enjoyed this particular day.

*"Mrs Harris took the assembly today. I always enjoy it when she
does. Every day it's always the headmaster, Mr Hayles, and he
talks to us about how the world around us is changing and
reminds us all about where to get pens from the reception office.
Mrs Harris has been the best teacher that I've had so far. I then
was in Miss Peters class. She always let me and Craig sit next to
each other. Now I'm with Miss Collins. We're her first class. We
had good fun today. We made paper Mache masks before we went
home."*

Arts and crafts were not the best choice for me. I can only imagine
the state I was in. Mum used to complain at how much they had spent on
my uniform for me to go and get it mucky and dirty. The pleasures of
growing up…

Wednesday 26th April 1995
*"It's Wednesday. Mum always takes me to my Auntie Nikki's for
tea. I always get what I ask for. Dad always gets himself
something to eat on his way back from work."*

I'm finding things a little bit ritualistic reading these pages. School
was the mixture of register, lessons, break, lessons, lunchtime, lessons then
home time. At home it seemed to split itself up in the week. Wednesday
was always the day we saw Auntie Nikki and my cousin Rebecca. It was
always a laugh but I don't seem to have written that down in this entry.

11

"Auntie Nikki couldn't get a signal from the TV. She did put on the video player for Mum. The show we watched was good. It was something called Class Act, or so Mum told me. It's a show with Joanna Lumley. The theme song is great. But Mum giggled when I said I like the person who played someone called Gloria because she has such a beautiful face..."

Oh dear. I think I am reading the beginnings of my first TV crush. The Australian actress Nadine Garner does have a very beautiful face and *Class Act* was a good show. Even if you were not interested in the programme, just one look at Miss Lumley was enough to make you change your mind and when she spoke to you in whatever character she was playing you listened.

"Mum is a little angry with me tonight because I won't shut up about Class Act. She cuddled me and apologised for shouting. She doesn't like shouting. Dad is normally the one that shouts when their angry. His face always gets the same look that scares me. I did have a good time at Auntie Nikki's. It was just me and Auntie Nikki most of the time. Mum left for a bit and then came back to take me home..."

This was a little too observant of me. If I could go back in time and talk to Mum about it all and ask why she was doing this I would probably still be confused. I remember that it escalated some time after this entry. I wonder if I can find it. Ah, here we are.

Friday 12th May 1995
"There have been a lot of arguments. Mum didn't want to come home today. It happened again after we had tea. Dad came in and told me to go upstairs to my bedroom. They had a fight. This was the worst one. I heard a lot of swearing. Then it went quiet. I could hear Mum crying from along the hall. Dad then told me go and say goodbye to Mum..."

I still can picture the taxi driving Mum away like she was a prisoner going to jail. It was her fault, of course. Dad later told me that Mum had been seeing another man from over the road. Mike Dowling, the local repair man that seemed to be ideal at breaking things as he much as he fixed them. I think I started hating him from this point on having just read where it all started.

It's been years but it still resonates within me. Looking on it rationally, Mum must've had her reasons for having an affair. I just remained in my little bubble and continued my entries.

Wednesday 17th May 1995
"Tea at Auntie Nikki's again. Dad dropped me off before he went back to work to do some overtime.

Mum is always there to see me. Her cuddles are lovely. I keep asking her if she will ever come back home but she never gives me an answer. I do miss her. I think that Dad does too. He does get grumpy but Mum would always say that Dad works too hard. Mum had to leave quickly tonight. When she sees Dad they both end up arguing.

Mum came back home on Saturday to fetch a suitcase that she had left behind. I watched her leave from my bedroom window. She blew me a kiss and got into another taxi. I really wish that Mum would come home. I know that Dad wants it, too…"

Only seeing Mum when she was around either of my aunts houses was a very strange experience for me. It was either Aunt Nikki or Aunt Cheryl. They were fun but they never quite filled in the gap that had been left by spending a weekend at home. The magic of the routine faded when Mum left the house but, from what I can see in the entries, the whole pretence was kept up.

Friday 19th May 1995
"Dad picked me up from school and we both went to the chippy for tea. Friday is always chippy day. Mum and Dad would

*always have fish and chips. I preferred sausage and chips. We use
biscuit tin lids to put our dinners on because Mum said that it
would save her washing up. Just eat it off the paper and chuck it
away is the rule. It's weird not having Mum eat with us. I think
Dad forgot that she wasn't here. He placed her tin lid out at the
table tonight by accident."*

It did seem like an eternity that Mum was away from us. Dad was
very stubborn and wouldn't take her back. I wish that he had. We both
wanted Mum to be back at home. And from what I can read, we had a
change of pace for a Saturday.

Saturday 20th May 1995
*"I do not like Saturday now. It doesn't feel right. I normally get
up, go downstairs and Mum is there in her dressing gown. It's all
changed. Watching Scratchy and Co, The Chart Show and then
Movies, Games and Videos without Mum there with me feels so
weird."*

Each Saturday was so ritualistic and not having the foundation of
Mum there as Dad slept in was a little disturbing. From what I can read
further in the other pages, this was the most in depth that I went with this
matter. I had nearly forgot that I had placed so many thoughts down on the
page...

Monday 12th June 1995
*"I had a surprise when I got home from school today. It was
Mum. She's come back home! It feels so nice to hear her call out
the way that she always did. She sounds so much better than Dad.
When he wakes me in the morning he puts the bedroom light on
and pulls off the duvet. Mum is so much better because even
though she puts the light on, she gently strokes my cheek and tells
me that it's time to get up..."*

Mum was amazing. Every morning before school it was always a
gentle wake up before breakfast was served. I still remember the first one

14

she cooked when she came back; it was a full English breakfast for all three of us. This was the beginning of the good stuff returning. The mornings were brighter and the school run was a lot more chipper as Dad seemed to have such a spring in his step that I ended up running behind him. The next couple of entries seem to be quite upbeat. No surprise considering that for a while it did seem as though we were never going to be a complete household again. And then it happened.

Friday 16th June 1995
"Mum's gone. Dr Scriven came out from home in his Jaguar. He ran over to her. I didn't see anything else. One of the neighbours came over. Dad told them to look after me. There were sirens every five seconds. I was told to drink my orange juice and given loads of cuddles. Auntie Nikki came round and wouldn't let me go. She held me really tightly like Mum used to. Aunt Cheryl then came. Dad started crying the moment she walked in. I'd never seen Dad cry before…"

The whole day was horrible. Mum went out to get some more milk and it was then followed by screeching tyres and a thud. Dad instantly ran out and was screaming all along the street. It was horrible.

The driver was discovered to have been under the influence. I made it my mission not to find out anything more about him. It was bad enough that he had taken my mother from me.

Aunt Nikki and Aunt Cheryl were around near constantly from this point on. They both knew how much that Dad loved Mum and they wanted to keep the family connection as solid as possible, if anything for my sake as well as Dad's.

I remember that the first few days were like a complete blur. We had gone back to when Mum had left the house but this time there was no chance of her ever returning. How can anybody get their head round that?

Mum was no longer going to be a part of family pictures. She was no longer going to be involved in important events that only Dad and I shared with her. Christmas would never be the same without her waking me to say that Santa had visited and had kissed her on the cheek before he left to visit next door's house. My birthdays felt a little lonelier.

15

School was the worst adjustment from what I can read…

Monday 19th June 1995

"Dad told me that I'm not going to school today. I've stayed in my bedroom all day, staring out of the window looking at the street below. The neighbours were the only ones to give me a wave. We got cards come through the letter box this morning. One of them had been signed by Miss Collins and the class. Everybody's name was written on the card in large black Berol pen. Mrs Harris wrote a card to me and Dad offering her help and support."

Mrs Harris was a good friend to the family as well as being a fantastic teacher. There was nothing that she would not offer to help us with after she had learned of Mum's death. She took me for a few shopping trips and we bonded as a result. She was a wonderful woman who retired to enjoy the fruits of her labour with her husband.

As I read on, I can safely assume that I did not know how to put my exact feelings into words. I would always write the entries at night. Recording them came later and I would tell the pages that I had an interesting day. This had been the case up to this point.

Being off school did annoy me. I liked school. Let's see if there's anything in here on it. If I remember feeling annoyed I must have written something about it. Ah, here…

Thursday 22nd June 1995

"I'm so bored at home. It's fun to be with Auntie Cheryl or Marie from next door but I'm stuck indoors. Dad doesn't want me going out for some reason. Why? What will I do? I'm off school. At least Marie and Auntie Cheryl make things fun, playing the Nintendo for hours until Dad gets back. But even when Dad gets home he won't let me go out. I haven't seen any of my friends for ages. It's not fair…"

I think Dad just wanted to keep me out of sight in case anybody brought in the authorities to complain that a child was not in school. This was the beginning of his descent into a slight depression after Mum's death.

He was working more and hardly wanted to be at home. Both Dad and I seemed to be in a rut at this point. Mum had gone and left a huge void in our lives. As Dad went into overdrive in his work I think I entered a bubble. I created a small world for me to retreat into. I think me doing that allowed Dad to get through things in his own way. It was clear that he was feeling the loss but the minute that he went to work, he became a machine. I suppose I saw this and thought to myself that it was a good idea to do the same thing. I didn't really know what I was doing but I remember that it hit me a good deal of time later.

This black cloud around me and Dad continued to grow. He distanced himself from me a little bit. Weekends became shorter as he insisted on working six to seven days a week and not really dealing with life. He did snap out of it eventually, during the summer holidays according to this…

Thursday 24th August 1995
"Auntie Nikki has been at the house all day. She says that she's waiting for Dad to come home from work. She made dinner for us and told me to go to bed and not wait for Dad to get in. I haven't gone to sleep yet. All I can hear is Auntie Nikki screaming at Dad."

That night was when the bubble burst for Dad. I remember Aunt Nikki not letting up on him and kept throwing Mum's death at him. It sounds harsh but I can see why she did it and she did it to break him. He had built up so big a wall that the only way to get him out of it was by pushing him to the edge. It worked because after that night Dad started staying home at weekends. He always made sure that we went out together to either play a small game of football or going round to Aunt Nikki's to play against each other on video games.

I was being called a tower of strength at this point. Every time that Dad would see a friend and they would ask after him, he would turn to me and say that I was his "…tower of strength". Maybe I was being strong for him. Why would I not be?

The fact of the matter is we needed to be strong for each other. We both wanted to do that for Mum. It's what she would have wanted.

17

But Dad and I were still not opening up to each other. We didn't know how to. It's only occurred to me after seeing these books and reading out the entries just how dark a period it was for us as a family. I can see that I didn't write anything for the day of the funeral.

I also didn't keep much of a journal for a while after that August entry. It did pick up again though in September.

Tuesday 5th September 1995
"Auntie Nikki came round today. She seemed very excited and brought a television magazine with her. There on the second page was my lovely lady with the beautiful face, opposite Joanna Lumley. Auntie Nikki said that Class Act was coming back to ITV. I'm really excited and Dad has said that we can watch it."

Here was where the shell seemed to break for Dad and me.

Thursday 7th September 1995
"The only thing I've thought about today is seeing Class Act again. I stayed in most of the day and have stared at the picture in the television magazine. I think I've got my first crush. That's what Auntie Nikki calls it. The person playing Gloria is called Nadine Garner and she is amazingly beautiful. The way that she's wearing that denim jacket and has her hair so nicely put up is really nice. Joanna Lumley looks lovely all the time.

When the episode came on my stomach went bubbly. The Anglia symbol appeared on screen. I recognised the voice of the announcer. It was the man that does the Birthday Club with B.C Bear before the start of CITV. The theme made me smile. I love it. Dad was laughing at some points of the episode. He found it quite a good show. He's promised that we can watch it again next week."

Did Dad live up to his promise? Of course he did.

Thursday 28th September 1995

"Class Act was on tonight. Joanna Lumley had problems with an old lady and John Bowe who plays Jack got himself a fancy woman in the process of his investigations. Nadine Garner was wonderful as always. Dad was happier tonight. He asked me if I would be interested in seeing Joanna Lumley in something else. It's a programme that he is sure that I will like and that is on BBC 2 tomorrow. I told him I would be. I am wondering what this show is that Dad wants me to watch. He seems happy about it but it's that he thinks that I will enjoy it. I'm not sure. It's got a weird title too, The New Avengers."

The entries from here on reveal to me that I was getting a small fix of Joanna Lumley every week. Dad obviously wanted me to see the whole series. My first crush was Nadine Garner but nobody could deny the presence of Miss Lumley. It looked like he was on team Lumley and I was on team Garner. We both had someone in the show that we wanted to watch. I'm now going through the stereo box and I've pulled out book number three. I'm intrigued because reading the first entry the new show that Dad wanted me to watch had an immediate effect on me.

Friday 29th September 1995

"Oh my god! The New Avengers was great. It came on after The Munsters on BBC2. Dad kept telling me that I would enjoy it. He then told me that this was the show that made Joanna Lumley a star. There are two guys with Miss Lumley. One of the guys is slightly older, carries an umbrella and wears a bowler hat. He also has the coolest name I've ever heard, Steed. The next guy looks really tough and physical. His name is another cool one, Gambit. But Miss Lumley only has the one name and that is Purdey. She also had this weird hairstyle in the credits. It looked like someone had given her a sort of step-style hair cut that's the rage in school."

Here's where a sort of commentary kicks in. From the looks of the page I must have revisited this book at one point. I don't remember having done so. There is red biro over my blue biro telling me what series and episode number was shown.

THE NEW AVENGERS
Series 2, Episode 13
EMILY
Written by Dennis Spooner
Directed by Don Thompson

"They're all after someone that's called The Fox. A meeting has been set up to catch him. There was a car chase. Steed has got a great car. It's a yellow Jaguar XJS, Dad said. Steed and Gambit were in pursuit of this traitor. The chase ended in a garage and Steed got stuck in a mud hole. Purdey had to rescue them both. Then Steed remembered that there's a hand print on the top of a brown car that could identify who The Fox is. Steed put his bowler on top of the print to stop it from being ruined by the weather. Police officers were calling on the radio that a car is wearing a hat. Then it headed for a car wash! Purdey was right on top of it, washing her hair in the process. But her clothes shrunk through the whole thing but the print is safe. The car is then blown up. But the print survived. They caught The Fox! Dad was right; I think this was absolutely brilliant."

Reading that passage out loud reveals to me that I had a good memory. I think that I must have written it directly after seeing the show. *Class Act* was still showing after this episode.

Thursday 5th October 1995
"Class Act was good tonight. Kate found out that her old nanny had joined a church. She wasn't happy about it. Nadine Garner was looking fabulous as always, she even got a little hot under the collar in this one. Dad had a talk with me tonight. He said to me

that if I liked The New Avengers from last week then I would like
a show that's coming up on Channel 4. He told me that it's the
show that started the whole thing. It is called The Avengers. He
even showed me an interview in the television magazine. The
picture looked quite good; it was Steed standing back to back with
a lady tilting his bowler hat against a pink circled background.
Dad has said that he will make sure that we watch it."

I think that this became Dad's way of getting us to find a connection again. I only knew of Channel 4 because of their repeats of the *Batman* TV show starring Adam West and Burt Ward. This time was to be different as the entry reads…

Tuesday 10th October 1995

"The Avengers was unbelievable. The minute that it started I
couldn't stop looking at the telly. There was Steed in all his glory
and he was handing a flower to an absolutely stunning woman
dressed in black. She has an amazing smile. But I couldn't see
Gambit? Dad then told me that he wasn't in the original run.
And why was it in black and white? Was the world all in black
and white until we suddenly got colour?"

Another commentary has been provided for this one, with the red biro informing me of the series and episode number once again.

THE AVENGERS
Series Four, Episode 13
THE TOWN OF NO RETURN
Written by Brian Clemens
Directed by Roy Baker

"A man walked out of the sea in a black bag. Then Steed plays
swords with the lady in black, I think she said her name was

Emma Peel. She's a very beautiful woman. The train ride looked fun, particularly when Steed brought a whistling kettle out of the bag of treats for the journey. The town they've entered seems to be very strange. There's hardly anyone around and everyone seems to be treating Steed and Mrs Peel as though they are not supposed to be there. Seems the whole town is full of bad guys. They've taken care of one man on the beach and another one has stumbled into the school where Mrs Peel is searching.

Oh no, the vicar is a baddie too. The whole town seems to be full of enemies. Steed is now on Emma's trail. How much fun would it be to do what Steed is doing right now? To go around a completely empty place and do what you like to do. It seems that they've found their enemies underground. And all of them are armed. Another fight is on, Steed against an army of soldiers and Emma against the fake teacher and vicar. The Avengers have won! I've asked Dad if we can watch the next one."

My god, is that the time? The wife will wonder where I am.

In finishing this entry, I should really get this box out of here and down to the car. But I really want to leave them here for the time being. There are a lot of memories in this old stereo box and I think that I've only just begun to re-visit them.

End of entry.

Chapter 2
STAY TUNED

Entry begins.

BROOOM-DA-NA-NA-NA!!! BROOOM-DA-NA-NA-NA!!!

What a theme tune even if my voice sounds off key in my attempts to sing it. Mum always told me that if you love the theme tune then you will love the show.

Finding that entry yesterday really brought it all back for me. I'm at the house now sorting through things and I've gone back to that old stereo box. It's hard to believe that I'm still writing things down. The amount of books that I found here yesterday proves that I'm doing the right thing in wrapping things up.

I've been sat here with the box for about an hour, skimming through these pages of my very own history. It's such a thrill to read and listen to everything. Especially this.

Sunday 15th October 1995

"The Avengers, what is one of those? What does it mean? I would get a dictionary and look it up but we don't have one in the house. Not that it matters. My mind is still playing the theme from one ear to the other. All the stuff that happened in that show was unreal. I've never seen anything like it before. Right now I cannot stop thinking about this show. And Dad had already told me that this was the one before The New Avengers came out. That would explain why there was only two people in the show rather than the three people I was expecting. And as for Mrs Emma Peel, to say that she was beautiful would be doing her down, especially since dad then told me that she was the fantasy of many people when he was growing up. Hardly fantasy, especially the way that she handled the false vicar and tossed him into the drain so effortlessly. I think she would be everyone's fantasy. I could learn that move and practice it on most of the school bullies.

But what was with Steed? How the hell did he manage to deal with all those soldiers coming to get him as the metallic door closed? The next thing we saw after Emma had dealt with the vicar was Steed just standing there with the guards unconscious around him – and he managed to defeat them with his hat? This show is amazing!"

I still believe this. *The Avengers* definitely had a power that made you want to watch the screen and disappear for the next hour into whatever situation your heroes were faced with. My adoration carried on to the next week.

Tuesday 17th October 1995
"The week went far too slowly. I was hoping that Tuesday was just around the corner but no such luck. Thankfully though it's that time again; the Channel 4 logo came together and the introduction was given: BROOOM-DA-NA-NA-NA!!! BROOOM-DA-NA-NA-NA!!!

Just the start of it is enough to make my heart race with excitement. I haven't looked at the TV guide to see what's going to happen this week. I am really getting into this show. There is nothing that you cannot like about it. It seems to have its own world that is policed by two people that are the only ones that can understand and deal with it. I love the routine of every Tuesday at six in front of the television. Dad loves it to. I know he does because I see his foot tapping along to the theme tune."

THE AVENGERS
Series 4, Episode 7
THE GRAVEDIGGERS
Written by Malcolm Hulke
Directed by Quentin Lawrence

"This one seemed a little bit dark as it started with a funeral. It hasn't been that long since we all went to Mum's. Memories of everyone wearing black, their eyes full of tears and me stood there wondering why life had been so unfair.

This episode definitely follows that same vein, but the music is ten times better. It doesn't seem gloomy and allows me to keep my interest focused on what's going on. Ten cool points for the TV show.

They then just buried a coffin that had an aerial coming out of it. This show just gets better and better…"

It's fascinating to read all of this now. I remember that I wrote about it but I had forgotten that it was to this extent. The small snippet leads on to an essay about the episode. Plus, as I read on, it seems that I was becoming spoiled by an incoming and new television treat.

Wednesday 18th October 1995

"Dad put the TV guide in front of me tonight. He told me to look at BBC 2 listings. Yes! The New Avengers are on Fridays at 6.25pm. He's told me that we'll be watching it."

But things apparently didn't go according to plan…

Friday 20th October 1995

"I'm not happy. We couldn't get to watch The New Avengers tonight because the telly was on the blink. The TV guide said that it was a good one too. It said that Steed Purdey and Gambit were up against the house of cards. I can dream of what it would've been like."

At that point I had no choice. Not having a VHS player was a bind back then. I was also ridiculed for being one of the only kids in school whose parents didn't have Sky television. We got it eventually but it would have been amazing back then to put each episode into the recording planner. The episode essays soon returned as I turn the page to find...

Tuesday 24th October 1995

THE AVENGERS
Series 4, Episode 6
THE CYBERNAUTS
Written by Philip Levene
Directed by Sidney Hayers

"This one looked spooky. Seemed like a normal office, but what was that noise coming from outside? Sounded like a whip cracking. This man seemed very worried. Even a gun won't stop who's after him. There's that sound again and the poor chap has not only got a broken gun but he's also dead.

I'm seeing faces that I recognise here; Burt Kwouk from The Pink Panther films playing a technology tycoon. Nice one. Oh my god, it can't be. Batman's butler is the bad guy in this one!! This is amazing. I expected him to come out and greet Steed as though he were Bruce Wayne."

I think the fact that the episode was in black and white enhanced the enjoyment. I really did love every second of it. To say that I was getting deeply involved with *The Avengers* is an understatement. I'm reading read on and as I do I'm pleasantly remembering the grip that the show had on me first time round.

Friday 27th October 1995
"Another week gone and I have missed The New Avengers again. Dad forgot to remind me that it was on. He only remembered as we turned on Top of the Pops but it didn't really make up for it. According to the TV guide it was a Cybernaut episode so I'm not

26

happy that I missed it. I wish that we had a video recorder. It would be so much easier than just watching a show and then having to remember it. I have asked Dad for one but he avoided the question."

He continued to avoid the question for a while. He worked a lot of hours to just pay every bill that went into the house. I was very young at the time so I think that I can be forgiven for being a little self centred. Actually, having skimmed a little ahead I can see that another couple of episodes of *The New Avengers* were missed. But it was all down to the fact that Dad was working overtime and I had to go and stay with my grandma. By the time I would get there the show would have been over. At least I could enjoy some time with my grandma.

The essays, as I think I will affectionately call them, continues to fill the pages of these notebooks with *Death At Bargain Prices* and *Castle De'ath* receiving extensive reviews. I'm also still reading that I was, at this point, begging for a VHS player to be bought for the house. But Dad soon proved to me that there was a better idea to capture my favourite show…

Tuesday 14th November 1995

"Dad has surprised me tonight as he happily announced it was nearly time for the next instalment on Channel Four. He produced a small tape recorder. It looked like quite an old machine, possibly from the 1980s. All it needed was batteries and it was good to go. But why was he showing me this? Off air recordings he said to me with a glint in his eye.

The trick was to take the recording from the TV and place it onto the tape to listen to whenever I wanted. He then perched a chair in front of the TV and gently placed the tape recorder near enough to the speakers to pick up most of what was going on. The tape inside must have been a blank one. Dad was very prepared for this and I am grateful.

We were all set. The time was approaching 6pm and the Channel 4 logo was making its way onto the screen. Dad set the tape recorder going and sat down with me to watch what was to appear."

The tape recorder looked like a shoe box but it was quite a novel way of capturing what Dad knew I wanted. It was such a unique idea. And yet I was to be surprised further as the entry continued…

THE AVENGERS
Series 5, Episode 4
FROM VENUS WITH LOVE
Written by Philip Levene
Directed by Robert Day

Steed is shot full of holes
Emma sees stars
I end up having convulsions over colour

"It's in colour! I screamed that out as soon as the rose and gun logo appeared on the screen. I don't believe it. They did episodes in colour. This is amazing! Dad announced to me the next part which was Emma Peel shooting the champagne cork out of the bottle that Steed was opening. Wow. That is so cool. Now they've clinked glasses does the episode start?

BROOOM-DA-NA-NA-NA!!! BROOOM-DA-NA-NA-NA!!!

This is so fantastic."

This was the beginning of it all. The immersion into the show was a slow descent from this point. It also became the same for *The New Avengers* as the recordings on Friday nights were scheduled in promptly at 6.25pm on BBC 2. *Target!* became the first episode placed onto cassette. This one became a favourite of mine. I replayed it over and over. I found the music

28

cues to be quite catchy. *The Fear Merchants* followed on the Tuesday. Scary is not the word. Even the music in this one was chilling. Every time a person's fear was shown a loud and screechy music was played. I didn't replay this one too much as the sound of people screaming sort of put me off.

I find reading these particular entries amazing. I was definitely enjoying the fact that I had something on *The Avengers* that I could listen to. It really did build up my excitement for the episodes that followed as I entered a weekly routine of taping that had me using a lot of C90 cassettes.

Faces from *The New Avengers* continued my now growing collection of cassette recordings. But there was trouble brewing in paradise as the next entry reveals…

Tuesday 28th November 1995
"Tonight the tape recorder has given up the ghost. It refused to play the tape, let alone record anything…"

I became just a viewer again for a short time. I still enjoyed it because I could still watch it. I still continued to write the essays as best I could. Some episodes really stuck in my mind. *The Winged Avenger* was one of them and from what I can read off the page it chilled me seeing someone dressed as a giant bird and clawing his victims to death. But the *Batman* angle was the light touch in that one and made me happily remember watching the *Batman* TV show repeats on Channel 4 a few years earlier. I watched *The Winged Avenger* again quite recently and it still amazes me at how technical it was in making the villain appear menacing and terrifying. The next instalment of *The New Avengers* was to be *Gnaws*. But the entry for it appears to be pretty bare as it appears my Uncle arrived to take us out for the evening. In retrospect it's a good job that he did. The giant rat of this episode at that particular point in my fandom could have scarred me for life. Viewing it again as an adult gave me a more balanced appreciation of the episode with a small chill factor mixed in.

But at the time of writing it appears that the night out was not welcome…

Friday 22nd December 1995

"I never get a say in anything. I have to go everywhere that I'm told to go. I'm not asking for much. All I want to do is watch both The Avengers and The New Avengers on a Tuesday and Friday. Is that too much to ask?"

Thank god I've grown up. A couple of pages along now and we arrive in the New Year's first instalment of *The Avengers*. Dad had got a new tape recorder for me and the recordings came thick and fast.

I still have that tape recorder. I developed a system with the entries where I would record the episode and listen to it immediately afterwards and then again before I went to bed.

The first episode of *The Avengers* that I recorded on this new tape recorder was *The Correct Way To Kill*. But I learned quickly here of a problem and quickly solved it. There were three ad breaks in the show and the trick was to tape the first two parts on side A and then fast forward the tape to quickly turn over to side B. This method gave me the whole episode on one cassette. There was also an extra addition on the end credits that was recorded too.

The announcer for Channel 4 told me of a book that was now available in the shops, "*The Ultimate Avengers* by Dave Rogers in all good book shops at £16.99". I had that on most of the tapes. Dad knew that I wanted it but patience had to be a virtue. The first episode of *The New Avengers* on my new tape recorder was *Dirtier by the Dozen*. It involved an army of renegades, one of them being Boycie from *Only Fools and Horses*.

And there was yet another problem. *The New Avengers* was on BBC 2 and there were no ad breaks. So the whole episode took up all of side A while a small part of side B was devoted to the closing few minutes and the end theme tune. It was a problem that I had no control over but I was clearly relishing the chance that I had to record these episodes.

My dedication to the adventures of Steed continued. I was glued to the TV every Tuesday and Friday. The pages I'm looking at are endless. As *Never, Never Say Die* and Hostage were added to my ever growing collection, *The Avengers* next instalment was called *Epic*. It was a solo one for Emma Peel as she was cast in a film that would end with her literal death. But the next instalment of *The New Avengers* seemed to have really thrilled me. It goes on for roughly four pages and even had a small summation at the end of it. The episode in question was...

Friday 19th January 1996

THE NEW AVENGERS
Series 2, Episode 2
TRAP
Written by Brian Clemens
Directed by Ray Austin

"This was a fantastic episode. An intercept for drugs leading to the villain, a large Chinese man called Soo Toy? Or something like that. In all honesty, he did not look or sound Chinese. Whispering gently and looking like an Englishman does not make you Chinese in any way!

The drop was stopped by Steed, Purdey and Gambit. Soo Toy was not a happy English (trying to be Chinese) man. Revenge was then to be had. Purdey was woken up from her bed; Gambit and a date were interrupted while Steed was torn away from a beautiful woman to meet up at an airport to be flown to a rendezvous. They soon find out that they've fallen into a trap and their plane crashes into Soo Toy's estate. The three are then chased by an army out to capture them. Gambit is caught but Steed had a plan to get the estate. The showdown was brilliant. Both Steed and Purdey take out the group while Gambit deals with Soo Toy. I've listened to this one over three times. I can't get enough of it."

I've still got the cassette in the desk drawer at home. My wife cannot understand why I cherish it so much but it holds great memories. I think it may have been due to the fact of the episode setting being in East Anglia. The sheer factor that I could go to a large playing field and dive among the trees imagining that I was Steed being pursued the army was a dream that was so appealing to my young mind.

The Superlative Seven was the next one recorded. The next episode of *The New Avengers*, from my journal entry, was to instantly become a solid favourite.

Friday 26th January 1996

THE NEW AVENGERS
Series 2, Episode 3
DEAD MEN ARE DANGEROUS
Written by Brian Clemens
Directed by Sidney Hayers

"This was an amazing episode. Poor Steed, he was hunted down by a friend that became a traitor and he had believed shot through the heart. But he came back from the grave and was out for revenge. But Steed, you are amazing. The man hunted you down, shot you, destroyed your valuables, wrecked your home and taunted you by harming those closest to you. But all that matters to you is that he was your friend. You understood his bitterness towards you yet you showed him nothing but compassion, even in death. That is remarkable. I have played this one four times now. I cannot get enough of this episode. Listening to Steed's past and finding out just how much he had accomplished before he became a secret agent is amazing. I wish I could do that well in school. But this episode has also taught me one thing and that is never ever become a Mark Crayford and don't be jealous of anybody better than you."

That's a very good point. I'm onto book five in the pile from the stereo box and just by skimming the pages tells me of the variety in the episodes I was recording. *A Funny Thing Happened on the Way to the Station* was a plot about trying to blow up the Prime Minister. *Medium Rare* involved Steed being framed by an embezzler in the department. *Something Nasty in the Nursery* had officials being put back in the nursery to reveal their secrets to the enemy. *Angels of Death* had *The New Avengers* investigating a health farm that increased mental stress levels to kill members of the department. *The Joker* was an episode that had Emma Peel being lured into a trap from a killer in her past.

From what I can see *The New Avengers* stopped after a few more weeks with the two part episode, *K Is For Kill*. The Emma Peel colour series continued in earnest. I think for a time I was consumed by the Steed and Emma partnership. Dad then surprised me once again.

Wednesday 14th February 1996
"The Ultimate Avengers is absolutely amazing. I was really excited by it before I even opened the first page. I never knew that Honor Blackman from The Upper Hand was in it. That was a shock when I saw the page that began for Season Two. The biggest one was seeing the page for Season One. I never knew that Patrick Macnee was not the original star of the show. It was a man named Ian Hendry and he played a doctor called David Keel. The pictures in the pages look good but the fun is reading the episode synopsis. I also read that nearly every series had 26 episodes in them. That is a lot of episodes..."

The Upper Hand was on the telly at this point in time. I couldn't get over the fact that Honor Blackman had been in *The Avengers*. All I had been exposed to was Diana Rigg and *The New Avengers*. I also still remember how I felt when I discovered about the first series. I never knew that it started off with two male leads. The book became quite an education.

I read *The Ultimate Avengers* in short bits from what I can see in the entries I made about it. I was taking in all of the information like a sponge being fed its intake of water. Plus, it does explain why the red biro appeared at the top of every episode entry.

The Forget-Me-Knot and the end of the Emma Peel era of *The Avengers* arrived on Channel 4. I remember exactly how I felt when Diana Rigg left the show. I was so upset that I cried for a full evening. The new era of *The Avengers* had been put in front of me in the form of Tara King. But from what I'm reading it's clear that I had my doubts.

Friday 10th May 1996
"I'm very worried about Steed's new partner. I've been reading
The Ultimate Avengers and seeing her picture. Every time that I
do I get butterflies in my stomach. I'm a little excited and
nervous. What if I don't like her? She has a beautiful name, Tara
King, and she looked stunning in last week's episode. But what if
I don't see her as Steed's partner and see her instead as an
annoyance that has no right to take the place of Emma Peel? I
don't know what to think…"

Game was the first Tara King episode I saw and taped. It became a favourite from the moment it started it didn't take long for me to warm to Linda Thorson. I've now read through the contents of three exercise books. It's taken up most of the day. I've just checked my phone and I've had at least four missed calls from my wife! I think that I'm going to have to come clean about finding my own personal treasure trove in this stereo box. I seem to be just scratching the surface. Another visit is definitely called for.

End of entry.

Chapter 3
TAKE OVER

Tape rolling.
Entry begins.

I've had to tell my wife about what I have discovered at the old house. The fun I was having was making me late for dinner. The surreal aspect for me is how much TV has moved on since I made the recordings. The Channel 4 logo no longer comes together in coloured pieces. The BBC 2 logo is still the number 2 in a mixture of very well thought introductions; a big cactus closing in on a fly, a flexible slinky style moving backwards and forwards or a squeaking toy that performs like a toy dog performing jumps as it goes along the table. I even taped the introductions on the *New Avengers* tapes. There used to be a still image at least 25 minutes before the episode began. It was a photograph of Steed, Purdey and Gambit surrounded by trees and Steed was doffing his bowler.

I feel sympathy for my poor wife, Anna. She is being very tolerant of all this treasure hunting that I seem to be doing. I set aside the notebooks that I have already read and am now seeing that my yellow geography book has changed into my dark green religious studies book. I did this intentionally marking the change in Steed's partner. The first page confirms that this was now the Tara King era of the show and just by reading out the first sentence I can tell that *The Avengers* was definitely becoming much ingrained in my consciousness.

Sunday 19th May 1996
"I really want all of the things that are in The Ultimate Avengers. Page 330 has nine books and I want all of them. I think four were in the UK and the rest were in the USA. Dad told me that they're all out of print and would be difficult to get hold of. On page 344 I found out The New Avengers have six books. I love the look of The New Avengers annual on page 345. The three of

*them are all on the front in their poses from the start titles. The
Avengers annual on page 333 has Steed's face on it with Tara
holding a gun next to it. There's music as well. I want the theme
single on page 334. And Kinky Boots next to it. I'm trying to ask
Dad for some of the videos on the back page of the book."*

It seems that I was eager to get my hands on something that would
allow me to properly own the show in some format. Looking back I can
now see Dad's point of view. The price of the tapes was a little expensive
with standalone videos priced at £12.99. But I didn't care about price. I just
wanted them.

The episodes also continued on Channel 4. *Super Secret Cypher
Snatch* was the episode that followed the first Tara King show I watched.
The villains were window cleaners and it was this episode that featured the
return of Mother. The next entry was *You'll Catch Your Death* which had
Mr Mackay from *Porridge* (thanks Dad for the classical education in
television) as the villain causing several ENT (Ear, Nose and Throat)
doctors to die from sneezing to death. I was fully loved up and high on my
Avengers fixes but the whole thing started to heat up a little according to
this next entry…

Monday 20th May 1996
*"School was interesting today. The bullies came back. My arm
hurts from them holding me down on the grass at lunchtime. I
dare not tell anybody about it. The last thing I want is a letter to
Dad saying that I'm being got at again. I went through enough
last time…"*

I have never understood why a child picks on another child simply
because they are different to others. But as I read on, I discover the birth of
my stupid solution to this problem…

*"I'm glad that I've listened to the tapes I've made of The Avengers.
I know them word for word. All I had to do today was to be in
the playground and start saying the episodes out loud."*

36

Why did I start doing that? I've read on and found the answer.

"It got rid of the bullies. All I did was say a few lines from the episodes From Venus With Love, The Fear Merchants and The New Avengers episode Trap. They gave me horrible looks but they stopped talking to me. They stopped threatening me. If this is what I have to do to make them leave me alone I will. The Avengers and The New Avengers are saving my life."

Can a TV show be anyone's saviour? I hardly think so. But the bullying was a harsh time. When you grow up you remember being bullied but you forget what you did to either appease them or fight them.

The next repeated episode on Channel 4 was *Split!* It seemed to have made an impression on me at the time according to the entry.

Tuesday 4th June 1996

"The episode tonight was weird. There was a different start to it. It was a light going along outlines and a target followed it. It shot a heart which brought up The Avengers. It then showed outlines wearing bowlers for Steed and lipstick for Tara. Then Tara is chased by the target which ends up shooting Steed's bowler. I wonder if that will be on another episode?"

I later read in *The Ultimate Avengers* that this particular sequence was for the USA broadcasts of the show. The episodes carried on; *All Done With Mirrors* and *Legacy of Death* were both recorded with fervour, such was my dedication for the programme. But the entry from the week of *Noon Doomsday* is quite illuminating.

Tuesday 25th June 1996

"The tape is ruined. I played the episode back and the whole thing sounds like a load of chipmunks. It seemed fine before I put the tape into the tape recorder, so what the hell has gone wrong? And there won't be another episode for three weeks. The Tour De France is going to be on. Three weeks to watch people on bicycles…"

The batteries had run out on the tape recorder so it was recording at a slower speed. All it needed was new batteries. As for the cycling aspect of the entry there is nothing to say. Reading this little entry shows me at how precious I was. It had to be a perfect recording that had no noise in the background and nothing that could cause disturbance.

The first green book is now done and read. Reading the first few entries in the second green notebook tells to me that in the three week break I kept listening back to all of the episodes recorded previously. It must have driven Dad round the twist. All he could hear was the Laurie Johnson theme to *The Avengers* bellowing out through the open door way of my bedroom. It was a consuming passion.

In those three weeks, the tapes were being listened to with an alarming frequency. My weekends were dominated completely. The routine was as I read and listen to it.

Saturday 6th July 1996

"Wake up and have a shower. Play either The Avengers or The New Avengers. Go down for breakfast with Dad before he goes to work. I normally use the time that Dad is at work to listen to a variety of Emma Peel mixed with both Tara King and The New Avengers. Today was From Venus With Love, Target, Noon Doomsday, The Correct Way To Kill, Trap and Mission... Highly Improbable. Dad then gets home and we have dinner. Then it's bed time. For tomorrow I've changed the episodes. The tapes are on my bedroom table: The Joker, Game, The Lion and The Unicorn, Murdersville, Split! and Never, Never Say Die."

Looking at the next few pages, I do nothing but repeat myself. But there was soon to be trouble in paradise, as this next entry proves...

Monday 8th July 1996

"The bullies are really starting to get to me. No matter what happens they seek me out. I was only with Darren and they went for the two of us. It was just shoving and pushing today but they got him the other day with a couple of punches to the face. They got me in the stomach last week just before home time. I think

38

*Dad knew there was a problem. He's threatening to sort the
matter out."*

Dad was true to his word.

Tuesday 9th July 1996
*"I am so embarrassed. Dad came in to see the headmaster today.
Then I was given dirty looks from Gavin Cox, Martin Mayhew
and Michael Ward as they came out from the headmaster's office.
I know things will get worse."*

I was right…

Thursday 11th July 1996
*"The bullies were back today. I'm still using The Avengers to help
me through it all. They do actually leave me alone. Today was
really fun because I actually got to hang out with my friends after
I had given the bullies a burst of The Lion and The Unicorn. I
would love it if they kept doing that. It makes my life a lot easier."*

Looking back on it now, the painful truth is that strange behaviour
alienates you from possible friendships. You are viewed through a
judgmental vision that makes people think you're someone who cannot
even be looked at, let alone spoken to. I read the last entry with an
understanding and yet an anger at myself. Through it all was my love for
The Avengers.

As the schedule for the Tour De France continued to take up the slot
for my beloved show, the entries cover the summer break. I loved the
summer holidays. The six weeks seemed to go on forever. The repeats of
The Avengers returned and the episodes came thick and fast…

Tuesday 23rd July 1996
*"It was really good tonight. It was all about clowns. The end fight
was great. Tara took on a clown that spoke with horns and who
kept disappearing and then re-appearing. Steed took on the clown
that was a quick change artist. One moment he was fighting the*

clown and then he was fighting a boxer, a western cowboy, a washer woman, a swordsman, and a pirate. I've already listened to this one too much. Dad shouted at me to stop playing it."

Look – (Stop Me If You've Heard This One) But There Were These Two Fellers... became a treasured favourite that nearly stretched in the stereo and was the beginning of another fight building between me and Dad. The overplaying of recorded episodes day after day was starting to wear thin with him.

Have Guns, Will Haggle, They Keep Killing Steed and *Killer* were next to be taped. It was followed by *Invasion of the Earthmen*. But a shock occurred according to the next entry that I've just come across.

Wednesday 20th August 1996

"I watched The Big Breakfast with Dad. I can finally watch a full edition of it rather than have to leave as the newspaper review starts after the Phil Gayle 8am news slot. After that I watched The Bigger Breakfast which is presented by Josie D'Arby. They were showing a load of programmes that are on Channel 4 in the week. One of them was The Avengers. The clip they showed was from All Done With Mirrors with Tara talking to Mother about Steed being under house arrest. I played the recording of All Done With Mirrors so I could hear the whole thing from start to finish. The Avengers is so cool. If The Bigger Breakfast is showing it among Sister Sister and Saved By The Bell: The New Class then it proves that The Avengers is one of the coolest things around."

Another couple of favourites were added to the overplayed cassette list – *Wish You Were Here* involved Tara's uncle being kept prisoner in a hotel and *The Interrogators* saw Mr Christopher Lee back as a villain rather than as Dracula, as my Dad always referred to him. This entry appears to have been the beginning of the last term of year 6. The entries are now covering exams that have to be taken. English followed by Maths the following week, just for teachers to determine where you are at in preparation for what happens when you reach the dreaded year 9 exam hall, sat at a desk in front of two clocks perched on pedestals reminding you that you have one hour to complete a paper filled with over thirty questions on one subject. If the exams had anything to do with *The Avengers* I would have sailed through them with flying colours.

False Witness became another firm recorded favourite from Tara's episodes. *The Rotters* was a weird story involving villains that could make wood disappear.

But I still had to contend with what school had to throw at me, or rather what was thrown at me from what I can read.

Wednesday 25th September 1996

"Bullied again. Why can't they leave me alone? I've done nothing to them. I don't care if they keep calling me a weirdo. Being a weirdo keeps them away from me. It's happening in the class room now. I dropped my pencil and Martin Mayhew picked it up, snapped it and handed it back to me.

Dad forced me to tell him about it. I've begged him not to go back to the headmaster. I hate this."

I didn't want to tell Dad anything that happened. He would get angry at the situation and immediately want to rectify it. Looking back, he had the right way of thinking about it. I just wanted him to leave it alone. I did not want the situation to escalate, especially as I was trying my best to protect myself. But I did not help matters by giving daily recitals of the episodes. The teachers must have thought I was barmy. But they never took me to one side and said anything. The headmaster was probably my biggest supporter. He remembered *The Avengers* from his own childhood and was quite happy to allow me to indulge in my game of 'Keep the bullies at bay'.

But as I continue to read on about what occurred during this particular time in my life, it's clear that my love for the show grew deeper.

Thursday 3rd October 1996

"I've done my own poster for The Avengers in art. It's an orange coloured background with the title of the show in bold black in the centre of the page. Everyone in the class thinks that I have an obsession. I don't really care. They still talk to me either way.

41

Robert Gantman told me that he and his dad enjoyed it. I've talked a lot with Robert about the series. he doesn't think that I'm an idiot for being into it.

The tapes are played every night. This week's episode was called Love All. Dad thinks that things are going a little bit overboard. We had another argument that all I was playing was The Avengers. I have put a piece of paper with the title 'John Steed' on my bedroom door that he doesn't like. I stole the idea from a previous episode that showed it was Steed's apartment."

From the next entry, it appears that *The Avengers* was not a group sport…

Monday 7th October 1996
"Robert is a target for the bullies now. I think it's my fault. We've been going round the playground and the field at lunchtimes making up our own episodes of The Avengers.

We imagined that Mother had sent us a secret message in a pencil and we shaved off the side to read a message from Tara to say that she had been taken hostage by Murder International. We had to save her. The bell went and we shot out into the playground to search for her. We found her before Dad arrived took me home. We did it again today. We got word that Emma Peel was arriving in London to meet with her brother, scientist Jamie Peel. He was taken at the airport and he left scientific clues to his location. We found him tied to a tree by the playground railings just before a massive fight with the villain in his underground headquarters underneath the playground."

I think that the teachers were considering telling both our parents that they had issues that they wanted to discuss. Reading on, I see that my indulgence continued.

Tuesday 8th October 1996
"The episode tonight was called The Morning After. Steed and Tara were after someone called Merlin who had stolen a sleeping gas from a secret building. I really enjoyed it."

This escalation was unstoppable.

Wednesday 9th October 1996
"I told Robert about the episode that was on yesterday. We found the window to the staff room and decided that we had found where they had hidden the bomb. We both got there just in time to stop the villain from escaping..."

Breaking point was reached a few weeks later, as this next entry reveals...

Tuesday 29th October 1996
"Dad and I watched the episode tonight called Take Me To Your Leader and was about Steed and Tara following a talking case around London. But me and Dad had a fall out after the show. He told me that he got a letter from the school about my behaviour. He came up to my room and tore the 'John Steed' sticker off the door. He screamed at me. Everything with The Avengers has to stop. He told me how he was getting annoyed at coming home from work and hearing nothing but my tapes at loud volume. I said that I was not coming home in bruises because of the show. But Dad was having none of it. He picked up The Ultimate Avengers and threw it at the kitchen door. It's now broke into two halves straight down the middle. There's also a print mark on the kitchen door where the book hit it. I've been in my bedroom ever since. I don't want to talk to Dad after what he did to my book..."

The letter was the straw the broke the camel's back for Dad. He was working very heavy hours and I wasn't really giving him much of a break at home. I was living, breathing, sleeping and eating *The Avengers*. It was a life blood that was making me feel good. My dearest wish was to walk down the street wearing a suit like Steed, followed by the same style of umbrella and bowler. I wanted to emulate this well dressed, urbane fictional character so much.

I remember the book against the door incident to. Dad spent the evening getting the mark on the kitchen door off with a bottle of Jif cream and a scouring pad. We didn't speak the next morning. But as I read on my attitude in the playground did die down. Everybody knew that I had a love for the show and the whole thing had successfully got the bullies to stay away. I continued to appreciate the show in my fashion…

Monday 4th November 1996
"In English we had to write a story that means something to us before we move up to the senior school. I chose The Avengers. I put down that all the stories I had watched had let me escape from what school had been like for me. I put down at how bad I could be bullied and by believing in The Avengers I could deal with it all. I could let the bullies carry on because the option to fight back was always there with tips in my head coming from Steed himself."

Believing in *The Avengers*? I read that just now and I laughed so hard that tears cascaded down my cheeks. It's clear that my devotion to the show back then that has led my love and appreciation for it today. The peace at home seemed to have been reached also as I read on.

Tuesday 5th November 1996
"Dad gave me a surprise before the next episode of The Avengers. It was a brand new edition of The Ultimate Avengers. He apologised for being so angry. We then watched an episode called Fog. It had Steed and Tara looking around London for someone called the Gaslight Ghoul but I wish that people would stop letting fireworks off. I nearly had the loud whistles and bangs on the tape…"

The next episode that followed, *Who Was That Man I Saw You With?*, went down well with me but I did not like the plotline of people trying to turn Tara into a traitor. But of course, all good things had to come to an end...

Tuesday 19th November 1996

"Tonight's episode is the last one. It was about Mother visiting his two aunts' for his birthday. It had Tara wearing a blonde wig for all of it. Dad said not to worry and keep playing the episodes that I had recorded. He also told me to keep a look out because it might return..."

The next entries made after this last one were just before Christmas 1996. They all feature the same sentence before ending the entry: "still no sign of *The Avengers* returning to Channel 4." It was not too long a wait before my father's prediction of the show's return became a fact. I wonder if I can find that notebook.

Bear with me...

End of entry.

Chapter 4
ONE FOR THE MORTUARY

Tape running.
Next entry.

I brought the box home eventually. My wife has been flicking through the journals. She is quite surprised. She knew about my love for *The Avengers* and has tolerated my passion for it but she never knew the extent of exactly how much it was ingrained into my system. She's finding herself glued to the pages as much as I am.

The books are now blue and the buying of my new tape recorder gave me the idea to put my thoughts onto tape as well as paper. Writing the entry and then recording it was my method back then. Transferring entries from one tape to the current ones I am recording on is proving helpful at this stage of my reminiscence. Finding the necessary date of the tape, I'm now age eleven and the important factor that I was carrying into senior school was…

Friday 12th September 1997
"My first week is over. It's a bit of a scary place at times and the new people in the class are still something that I'm getting used to. I'm playing The Avengers every morning as I get ready. I'm focused on the Emma Peel episodes rather than the Tara King ones. I'm only listening to one a morning. I'm still watching The Big Breakfast before going out to school. Dad said that it's always important to keep a routine…"

I was very nervous about going to my new school. It was bigger and full of more people. The whole environment was so intimidating. I remember that we were given all new things that were alien to us. I had never had a homework diary before and I was now placed into a form year and with a form tutor whose initials made us into their class. We had lessons divided into an A week and a B week and the lessons were in rooms that were at different places in the building. It was like I was in an episode of *Saved By The Bell* but without all of the fun. It took a little while to get used to…

Monday 15th September 1997
"We all had our first PE lesson. We ended up outside and playing football. I didn't want to do. I pretended that I didn't have any kit. The teacher did not look impressed. I walked around after lunch today and it felt like I was in The Joker episode of Emma Peel's colour series…"

Things definitely got worse mid week…

Wednesday 17th September 1997
"I was nearly late for a lesson because I couldn't remember where the room was. I started feeling like Steed running after the villain in The New Avengers episode, Trap. I even had the music from the scene where both Steed and Gambit went after him in my head. I think it made me go faster. I told Dad about the problem I'm having with trying to fit into everything. All he said to me was that it will work out okay. I wish that I could do what Steed did in All Done With Mirrors and stay at home where I feel happy and safe…"

The end of the week then arrived and a past menace returned to haunt me…

Friday 19th September 1997
"The bullies are back. There are more of them this time. It's not just one picking on me its two to three now. Ryan Wilmot is the main one that hits me and shoves me in corridors. He goes around with a friend, Nick Anderson. PE is the worst lesson. I got a basketball in the face yesterday. It hurt…"

I often did wonder what it was that set me out from a very large crowd. Year 7 did not get off to a swimmingly good start.

Aside from the bullying from my new tormentors, I'm reading that I liked some of the lessons and my form tutor at the time, Miss Foreman. She saw that I was in suffering from the bullies. A letter was sent to the parents of said bully and the matter was out in their hands with a very stern warning: either sort out your child or have them face expulsion. These were teachers that seemed to care about the well being of their fresh breed of students.

From that point on, from the notes that I subsequently wrote, things did smoothly work out…

Wednesday 15th October 1997

"Dad placed the TV magazine in front of me. He told me to look at the channel 4 listings. The Avengers is coming back, but it's on at 2.30am. Dad has concerns about me doing what I was doing before with the show. We had another argument about it. I want to record it. It's on next Tuesday. I've looked on teletext and all it says is that Steed and Mrs Peel deal with a gang of masterminds. I'm really looking forward to it now. Dad has brought me a spare set of batteries and a new set of five C90 cassette tapes…"

This appears to be Dad appeasing me because he did not want to argue anymore. The first episode of the re-run was *The Master Minds*. It was quite interesting for me…

Friday 24th October 1997

"I am now watching and recording the black and white Emma Peel's that I have never known. I've read loads about them from The Ultimate Avengers. The episode came on. Straight into the theme, BROOM-DA-NA-NA-NA!!! It was a great episode. On the tape you can hear small pieces of silence that are covered by the music in-between. The fight was really great. Steed went up against one of the thugs and knocked out one of the villains swinging on a gym rope. Emma took out a villain behind a

screen. I thought she was facing a man until it turned out to be a woman..."

The episodes came pretty thick and fast. *The Murder Market* was the next one on the ladder of repeats and was swiftly followed by *Dial A Deadly Number* and *Too Many Christmas Trees*. The Christmas one had an interesting effect from what I can read. I found the tape entry…

Wednesday 5th November 1997
"Santa being a villain was weird. I know that he doesn't exist but if I thought that he still did and saw this again then I would not want any presents from him. And that laugh. I listened back to it and when I hear this horrible Santa I go cold. I did like this one. It even had a mention for Cathy Gale which made me smile. I still want to see her episodes..."

I kept on at Dad to try and find the Cathy Gale episodes in the hope that he could find them. The collection of tapes that I made had formed at least two towers in my bedroom. Dad and I continued to argue that I was staying up late. Back then I did not really consider school or the fact that Dad had work the next day. I just loved the fact that *The Avengers* was back and being relevant in my life. But things then became more interesting from this next entry…

Friday 7th November 1997
"Dad has told me that The Avengers is now being shown two times a week. We had another fight. He does not want me to stay up for two nights of the week. But I want to..."

Anything and everything on *The Avengers* was in the crosshairs and I was not taking no for an answer. The twice a week fixture was something that was gradually phased out. Dad became resigned to the fact that no amount of arguing was going to help the situation. Taping the subsequent episodes on a twice weekly rota had the collection grow rapidly with *A Surfeit of H²O, Silent Dust, Man-Eater of Surrey Green, The Hour That*

Never Was and *What The Butler Saw* being added to the collection. The most important one of the bunch was the episode *A Touch Of Brimstone...*

Thursday 27th November 1997
"Last night's episode was good. Emma Peel being the Queen of Sin with a snake wrapped around her wrist was something to see. Dad woke up during the sword fight between Steed and a villain with one real hand. And then there was Emma being whipped in a dungeon by the head villain, played by Mr Peter Wyngarde. He is a really great villain. It was fantastic..."

These repeats soon came to an end with the showing *How To Succeed... At Murder* and *Honey For The Prince*. From what I've read on the latter episode I liked the way that Steed and Emma interacted at the start as they came home from a night out plus the factor that whole episode revolved around a jar of honey. Only in the world of *The Avengers* could that make sense.

The Avengers was all I was concerned about at this point. I was still continuing to read *The Ultimate Avengers* and I was focusing a little more on the Season Two and Season Three entries as I desperately wanted to see the Honor Blackman episodes. I would look at the videos that were on the back page of the book and stare at the Cathy Gale volumes wanting to own them. The box sets were also something to marvel at. They had one that looked like a briefcase called *The Complete Avengers*, melded in with *The Best of Emma Peel* set and all the individual volumes. Television then returned to its normal and predictable self. Returning to school and facing the bullies was again to be remedied by *The Avengers*. I must have been out of my mind to do repeat this trick but as I read on it's clear that I genuinely thought that the trick would work again.

Friday 12th December 1997
"I did bits from Murdersville and Love All during lunchtime. But I do feel a little bit more exposed. I find myself going down corridors as I'm pursued by the bullies as they wait to hit me. I have to keep going at the act a little longer for the bullies to leave me alone..."

Why did I do this? There were more of them than before and the punches were harder than usual. It's frightening when you are surrounded by bullies making that same punched fist into their hand. My friends knew what was going on but they never spoke up about it. It was a typical situation of a teacher knowing and doing nothing to prevent something happening. I'm now reading through the pages that led up to the Christmas holiday. It's conclusive that my behaviour was freaking people out but was not sufficiently good enough to make the bullies stop. The New Year entered and the reciting out loud trick continued. But it seems to have had a bad whiplash effect…

Thursday 15th January 1998
"I'm getting weird requests from people. They want me to keep reciting The Avengers for them. They think that it's funny…"

School life was going to get tougher without me adding to the whimsical enjoyment of everyone else. In the months that followed I stupidly rose to the bait that was dangled in front of me. I'm cringing at this next entry…

Wednesday 18th March 1998
"I've started a re-run from the black and white Emma Peel's that I recorded, continuing through the colour ones and then onto the Tara King set and finishing up with The New Avengers.

I listen to one episode before I get ready for school and then I listen to more after school. I listen to another episode as Dad make tea for us then I listen to at least two or three before bed. I'm not getting bullied so much but I am being asked to recite everything again. I'm being pointed at and stared at constantly. I hear whispers that I'm the kid that goes around the school and talks to himself but it does not stop them putting a request in for me to do so…"

I can sense from this passage that the act that I started was beginning to wear thin. But it did not seem to ease up and there was a feeling that I was digging bigger holes for myself. The actual reason behind everything was to get the bullies off my back. In that vein, I succeeded. Rather than punch me they seemed to be laughing at me. But I was suffering in other ways. Reading on I've discovered that I was not being involved in many things within my social circle. Not a surprise considering my behaviour at the time. I alienated a lot of possible friendships through this stupid behaviour of mine, but at the time I considered it to be a means to an end. The madness sadly continued as I read on through half closed eyes…

Friday 27th March 1998
"Dad screamed at me tonight as he looked at my homework for Geography. He looked at it and plainly told me that I repeated myself at least four times in one paragraph. He then added that if I spent more time on the work rather than the world of John Steed I would be doing better at it…"

I had a fair amount of detentions handed to me in a variety of subjects but I used the time to complete the work set for me and live my fantasies on *The Avengers*. I just wanted to keep being in my bubble. It allowed me to disappear. But Dad must have been doing his nut. He was constantly thinking on making sure that the ends of each month were met and that every bill was paid on time and food was stocked up. He never made it seem to be a struggle but he was defiant that I do well in my studies. He did allow me to listen to *The Avengers* as I did my homework. The months passed on and my work improved. Detention was replaced with awards for progress and bullying was replaced with teasing about me being a teacher's pet. Is it my fault that I just got on with the work I was given rather than play up for the poor teacher that was trying to educate us?

The Ultimate Avengers was being read every night without fail and like the rat from the *New Avengers* episode *Gnaws*, my love and adoration of Mr Patrick Macnee and his brethren of partners was enormous. I was still continuing the 'performances' and the reputation of me being an oddball that was being widely circulated. If hating yourself at the end of the school day was a subject I would have been top of the class. I've touched upon it in this next entry…

Friday 24th April 1998

"I do not like everything right now. I feel like I'm in a hole and I cannot get out of it. I've kept the bullies at bay but nobody wants to know me. I know that it's my own fault but I cannot exactly go running after them and scream that I'm normal would make a good friend. I wish things could be that simple. I'm also starting to swear. Not when I'm around Dad because he'll kill me. It does feel a bit like a relief for me with all that is going on. I hate feeling like this. I have a great small circle of friends that are tolerating me being a complete fool but I'm keeping other friends away from me. Why the hell am I doing this for...?"

The answer was already in the paragraph. I was desperately unhappy with myself. I just continued to keep my head down and get on with the work that was given to me. It kept home life peaceful and allowed me to escape every night with Steed and his partners. But it seems that with any change there is a backlash...

Thursday 21st May 1998

"I can't win! All I have done is stop being sent to detention, done all my homework and have been given a few certificates. Every lesson now if I get something good said to me about a piece of work that I have done, they all say that I'm the boffin of the class. What the hell have I got to do for them to treat me normally? It's getting impossible. I got my own back on one of them last week in Science. We got a question about eyes and what part of the eye is similar to a camera? I put down the answer as the flash and everyone on the table put down the answer. Mrs Stubberfield was not exactly happy when she shouted at the class and asked us how many people in the world go around with flashing eyes. I found it funny along with everybody else..."

With everything in that paragraph considered I do think that I was being a little hard on myself. I was trying desperately to be accepted when all I had to do was be me. I was trying to change the way that I was viewed but I was being judged on my love for *The Avengers* and the understanding to come on the whole thing would arrive many years later.

As I read on I find that I immersed myself in *The Avengers*. It seems that I wanted nothing more than the world of the show to be real so that I could escape and join in. I wanted to jump into the back of Steed's Bentley with Mrs Peel and join a car chase that would see us being chased by the helicopter from the episode Murdersville as we went after the villains that are causing the department problems with the same trick from *The Bird Who Knew Too Much*. We would then finish the case and head to the buttercup field from *All Done With Mirrors* for a champagne dinner. I seemed to crave for an escapist fantasy life. Not long after I was then placed with something that brought me a lot of joy…

Monday 15th June 1998

"Dad showed me something in the TV magazine. It's an episode of The Lily Savage Show and it's going to have a part with The Avengers in it. The picture on the side is of Lily Savage as Emma Peel and an actor called Simon Williams as Steed. I've already asked Dad if I can tape it…"

At this point in time, it seemed that everything around me was awakening to this wonderful TV show. It got better two days later…

Wednesday 17th June 1998

"Dad has told me that a film is being made of The Avengers. It will have Steed and Emma Peel in it and there is a rumour that Sean Connery will be in it as well with Eddie Izzard and Jim Broadbent who Dad says was in Only Fools and Horses. Now everyone will see just how cool and fantastic this show really is. Everybody will see why it's my passion. Everyone will see why Steed is the coolest secret agent ever…"

I think that my devoted tendencies went into overdrive. Can anybody blame me? Here I was being immersed in my favourite television show and had just received the news that it was being put onto the big screen for millions to enjoy. This was not a thing for ridicule. It was something to cherish and hold close to your heart. It was the past being made relevant.

Lily Savage honoured my expectations from what I can gather in the next entry…

Friday 19th June 1998
"The Lily Savage Show was so funny. The short piece on The Avengers was brilliant from start to finish. It had the start credits made up in the style of the Emma Peel black and white series and it was filmed in black and white to. Simon Williams was brilliant as Steed. He had some really funny moments in the piece especially when Lily Savage as Mrs Peel told him he was well into his first bottle of champagne and the programme had only just started. And then the bit where Mrs Peel says that she's too pissed to fight because she always has a drink in her hands when she and Steed have a scene together. Then there was the mention of the leather outfit that Lily Savage was wearing and her complaints that she can't go to the toilet and felt like a three piece suite from Courts. The diary of the dead man they have found was funny bit to. An army colonel friend of Steed's joined the scene and gave a description of someone tall with a swimmers build with good hair and muscles. Steed asked him if that is the man they're all looking for but the Colonel said it was what he himself was searching for. And to finish Mrs Peel had a fight with what I thought was an enemy agent but was actually a Jehovah's Witness wasn't the funniest part for me. I'm amazed that I was able to not completely laugh through the recording of it. Dad thought that it was hilarious. It's in two parts so the next side of the tape should get that one…"

Indeed it did…

Friday 26th June 1998
"The second part of The Lily Savage Show feature on The Avengers was shown tonight. I didn't think it was as funny as the first one. The theme tune did not sound like the original Laurie

Johnson piece like last week and there were some bits I didn't understand. Steed was trying to rescue Mrs Peel from being tied up and threatened only to find out that it was all part of an annual meeting that she goes to every week. The next bit was funny though. It was Steed finding Mrs Peel tied to a railway line and refusing to untie her from the track because he thought that it was another group thing that she was doing. Of course the train went right over her and then Lily Savage turned up on the train as Tara King. The ending was good to with Steed and Tara comparing their likes and dislikes and finally asking each other if they fancied a shag. Quite a good set of two shorts but I would have liked to have put them onto VHS tape..."

The next few excerpts were devoted to the upcoming movie of *The Avengers*. It was not released for another couple of months but that was not going to stop me going on about it. The next surprise was to come...

Saturday 14th August 1998
"Oh my god! Dad is taking me to see The Avengers movie in the cinema. I've never been there before. From people tell me it's huge. But I cannot wait to go..."

The great day finally arrived, but my reactions were unexpected...

Saturday 21st August 1998
"What a load of crap! The Avengers theme tune was not used on the opening credits but it was put to good use when introducing Steed to the audience. But the training town that Steed fought everyone in was clearly from the New Avengers episode Target. And why didn't Steed doff his bowler to anybody? And what the hell does Steed look like? The umbrella handle is wrong for a start and where are his Chelsea boots? We them met Emma Peel and she's apparently known by Dr Peel. Emma Peel was the daughter of an industrialist and yet nothing was said about her being with Knight Industries. Steed and Emma then met in Boodles. What a

name for a club and I did smirk that Steed was naked and
reading a paper in the steam room that Emma burst into…"

Things got worse for my viewing 'pleasure'…

"Steed's driving a black Bentley. Black! Steed's Bentley was always
British racing green. We then see Mother. He's too relaxed and
not as moody as he was in the TV show. And he has an assistant
called Brenda? His assistant was always Rhonda. And we then see
Father. Both Mother and Father were in the same room? That
never happened in the TV show. If Mother was there he was in
charge and Father was in charge if he was ever away like the TV
episode Stay Tuned proved. And what the hell are Mother and
Father doing getting involved with Emma Peel? It's true that
Emma knew of Mother in the TV episode The Forget-Me-Knot
but never to the extent here. And what is all this with The
Ministry. The Ministry of what? Steed always said which
department he was acting for, plus he was always attached to
security. And what the hell is going on with Steed's Bentley? He
never had a tea pot built into the dash board…"

Things can only get… more terrible…

"The villain, Sir August De Wynter. Great name but Winter
occurs from December to February. And why didn't they give him
an original plot rather than steal the idea of the TV episode A
Surfeit of H²O? Dad told me that it was Sean Connery playing
the villain and that he was also the first James Bond. James who?
And the bit at Wonderland Weather was really weird. A
boardroom full of people dressed as teddy bears. Teddy bears are
not The Avengers! If this was The Avengers the board meeting
would have it raining indoors with everyone under an umbrella.
Or they would have a blizzard going on around them with all the
board members wearing sunglasses and tee shirts. Steed's fight was
brilliant. All with the umbrella just like the TV show. But where
is his metal bowler? He's using a normal bowler hat and Steed

never had a normal bowler hat. And why is there an Emma Peel clone? And now we see the double decker bus headquarters for Mother that we saw in the TV episode False Witness. And Father is a traitor? The more I saw of this the more I felt insulted…"

Feeling insulted was quickly becoming the order of the day…

"What the hell is Emma driving? It does not look like her Lotus. And why send robot controlled giant insects to kill Steed and Emma. Why not use the weather device that he just tested a few moments ago? Sir August was in a full white suit one minute and then was wearing a lounge jacket when he goes and drugs Emma in the next scene. That was a quick bloomin' change of clothes. Then Emma ran through the house in a scene clearly from the TV episode The House That Jack Built, right down to the smashing of a bust to prove she was returning to the same room each time. And then Emma is arrested? What the hell is going on in this film? And Steed needs clearance to gain entry to the archives. Since when did he need that? His security credentials would get him in anywhere…"

Then came a surprise…

"The invisible archive Colonel is from the TV episode The See Through Man but it sounded like Patrick Macnee. It was the man himself. I'm glad he was only a voice because this movie seems to be mocking what The Avengers stood for. We then had Emma in a padded cell wearing a straight jacket. We then had Sir August giving his demands in a full Scottish outfit, Alice re-appearing at Mother's headquarters when we last saw her knocked to the floor by the villain and no explanation as to how she got away and Steed's pocket watch has a tracking device in it to find a now escaping Emma. What is going on? Steed's trackers were never ever in his pocket watch. His bowler hat would be where anybody would find that…"

Was I ever to be happy with this movie?

"Steed and Emma kissing! That should never happen. They should keep it flirtatious like the TV show. From there I just couldn't believe what I saw. They arrived at Sir August's base in two inflated balls that could walk on sea. The "Mrs Peel, you're needed" line was used nicely but how when they got into the phone box how did Emma know to pick up the receiver to gain entry to the base from Sir August when he told her she would remember nothing of being there? The fight with Emma and Eddie Izzard was ridiculous. Steed's fight with Sir August was great with Steed's swordstick making an appearance from the TV show colour series. But I didn't know how he managed to pick up the rest of the umbrella during the fight when Sir August was wildly attacking him…"

The end was nigh…

"Okay, they escaped the exploding building in the escape pod which came back to the Thames with The Avengers theme bringing them back. Steed suggesting the champagne was good but why did he not share it with Emma alone? Did Mother have to be there? The theme tune ending was good but why could it not end like a TV episode?"

I had a habit of reading all of the film credits when Dad and I watched films on television. But looking on this final part of the entry, I was not happy with what I read.

"So the film was 'Inspired by the Thorn EMI TV series The Avengers', was it? Dad tells me that EMI is a record label that has David Bowie on their books. Dad said even Ziggy Stardust couldn't save this movie. And inspired by? There was no real inspiration for this film at all. There was barely anything that truthfully acknowledged the TV show in there…"

Considering at how much I went on about the injustice that I was suffering as a viewer, the point I made in the last entry was probably moot. Watching the film again recently, I was surprised at how nobody from the TV show had any kind of input into the movie. Apart from Patrick Macnee's vocal cameo, I think that an overhaul of the whole story should have been performed. This knocked the return of the series in any sort of way, probably forever. And on that depressing note…

Entry ends.

Chapter 5
THE CORRECT WAY TO APPRECIATE

Tape recording.
New entry begins.

From what I read yesterday, I don't think that the movie went down too well with me. I think that I was on the same page as any movie critic that was watching it. We wanted to see something that was faithful to the television show. Instead we all had the opposite of everything. We all got an episode idea taken onto the big screen with only minor alterations.

Watching it again I end up coming to the conclusion that the actors involved got the beating for it, and quite unfairly. With movies there is nothing that can save it if you have a crap script. And the *Avengers* movie was definitely a casualty that fell into the crap script box.

It's easy for to be judgemental but nobody was going to see these notes so I saw no harm in writing my honest opinion.

I was now entering the realm of the Year 8 student at Harrison Webber senior school. The timetable routines of week A and week B were becoming annoying but I had the perfect escape from the horrid boredom of routine. *The Avengers* was the ideal tool to either relax or prepare me for what lay ahead. But things at home were strained.

Dad was beginning to work round the clock and the kibosh was placed onto my going out to see friends. The only retreat that I had every evening was *The Avengers*. Every night that Dad entered the house from work he would be greeted by the Laurie Johnson theme tune either to his happiness or disgust. This entry sums it up...

Monday 28th September 1998
"Dad has not been talking recently. He has been coming in from work and every time that he reaches my room I can hear him sighing to himself. Every time I ask what is wrong he never tells me. He comes in from work, makes dinner, calls me down for it, we eat, I wash up with him and then return up to my room..."

With a quick flick ahead I see that this was the house routine for weeks. School itself was entering its own dire routine. I was doing the spouting rounds of episodes from *The New Avengers* and *The Avengers* to appease my bullies and keep the people that wanted to laugh at me entertained. It did hurt my self esteem but the goal of keeping the daily beatings away was still working so I stupidly continued playing the fool for anybody that wanted to see it. The school reports were making their way to Dad and he seemed very impressed with what he was reading. But there was still a problem. He was hardly in the house anymore and the stay indoors for me was extended to the weekends. But as I read on, I didn't seem to be complaining…

Saturday 24th October 1998

"This is the third weekend that I've had to stay in. The overtime must be good for Dad. My days are completely filled. I'm spending the days with Steed and friends. Today has been a Tara King day. The episodes played were Love All, Take Me To Your Leader and Split! Another one I had not heard in a while was All Done With Mirrors and hearing Mother talk with an echo reminded me of his location that week being a swimming pool. I did like the fact that he had an office wherever he went. But why did Father only appear in one episode? It would have been nice to see her reappear for at least one more Tara adventure. I threw The New Avengers in today. I played Trap plus Dead Men Are Dangerous because I love the part where Crayford is remembering things and you hear Steed's name being chanted loudly by the crowd…"

The void that had developed between me and Dad led to a very heated debate, according to this next entry…

Friday 30th October 1998

"Dad came home tonight and had a massive go at me. He screamed at me. I was playing The Living Dead and he stormed in, turned off the tape and threw it down the stairs. We didn't hit each other but he did grab my arm a little hard as I went to fetch it back. We then both screamed at each other. I'm angry because

of the way he treated my stuff and how I've been stuck indoors not able to go out and see friends. Dad is angry because he always comes in from work to hear The Avengers playing in the house. He hardly spends anytime here anyway and when he does he never speaks to me. I might as well be invisible to him. I replayed The Living Dead to check that it worked okay. I turned the volume up full blast to annoy Dad but by that time he had asked my Aunt Nikki to come round and watch me while he went out for a bit. What the hell have I done wrong?"

Dad was an easygoing man, but there was only so much that he could take. Since Mum's death he had thrown himself into his work and did not want to stop. So when the time came that he actually wanted to put the brakes on, his work would not allow it. It was a lucrative but a very destructive cycle and Dad was part of it.

I remember that argument. The force that he threw the tape down the stairs was something to behold. I was worried that the tape would never play again.

After this current fall out between us I continued to get my head down with work at school but in doing so I was continuously chided and swore at just for getting on with my education. *The Avengers* may have got me through a lot but I could not take the tapes into the classroom. I wished that I could so that I could block out the whole pantomime and plethora of insults and jibes that were aimed at me.

Soon after, it seems that some surprises took place…

Friday 19th November 1998
"Dad surprised me today. He got me up this morning and said that he had phoned the school to say that I would not be in. He then rushed me to get dressed and we got in the car. We went to this really big shopping centre. It had fountains outside in a walk way that led to the other part of the building. Dad and I had lunch then after we visited a pretzel stand. Dad told me that there was a reason behind him bringing me there. We both apologised for how things had been lately and Dad said that he would not

work as much as he had been. But he then took me into a music shop. It was massive inside and there was everything in it…"

Hold your breath… Here it comes…

"They had videos on The Avengers there. The whole shelf was like a mass of colours. There was a purple one, an orange one, a green one all of them with Emma Peel's face on it. And next to them was a huge box of blue videos with pictures of Cathy Gale, Emma Peel and Tara King on the sides. Dad asked me what I wanted. I wanted all of them but Dad said that he could only afford the one. He got me the purple one; The M Appeal Collection, Mission One of six. The episodes are introduced by Patrick Macnee. The legendary John Steed will be introducing everything. This is AMAZING!!! And then when we got home, Dad showed me that he had gone and brought a VHS player. I put my tape on straight away. It was brilliant to see Patrick Macnee introduce the entire thing and then to see the episodes Death's Door, Honey For The Prince and Never, Never Say Die on the actual screen rather than just listen to them on tape…"

From here my collection took on another level. The releases that followed and bought were happily put onto a shelf in my bedroom. They were all out of sync purchase-wise but the factor was that I now had a collection to boast about. The towers of tape recordings were placed into one side of the room while the VHS tapes took up another. It looked as though Dad was happily indulging in making sure the collection continued as the next entry reveals…

Friday 25th December 1998
"Dad brought me another video of The Avengers for this Christmas. It's the M Appeal Collection, Mission Three of Six. It's brilliant. Once again, Mr Patrick Macnee hosts the whole thing. This volume was a special one as it had the banned episode from the black and white Emma Peel series, A Touch Of Brimstone. It also features the episodes Dead Man's Treasure and The House

That Jack Built which I'm glad to discover is one of Mr Macnee's favourites. I can see now why I enjoyed listening to the tape recordings I made. It wasn't just the music but it was nice to see Steed and Emma go around the whole part of the world that only they knew about. I still laugh that in Dead Man's Treasure amongst all of the modern cars of the time Steed remained faithful to his vintage Bentley. A classic agent has to have a classic car..."

But that was clearly not the only thing that I was surprised with...

"Dad also got me another video with The Avengers one. It was of a show I didn't know anything about but it had been advertised on the video of The Avengers that I had in my collection. It was volume 8 of a show called The Professionals and there were two episodes on it. Dad insisted that I watch the unknown title. I did so because it was clear that Dad wanted to watch and introduce me to this show..."

And introduce me he did...

"The music to this new show sounds familiar. I've heard it used on an advert. The first episode was a little boring but it got interesting at the end. The second episode had to be my favourite of the two. It had a lot of chasing around and gun play..."

But what caught my attention next was the important thing...

"I'm glad Dad wanted me to watch this now. The people behind The Avengers worked on this show called The Professionals. And with a theme from Mr Laurie Johnson that is so catchy. I remember what my Mum said about a show and it's catchy theme tunes..."

And there was an ulterior motive to my father's actions...

"Dad took me to one side tonight. He appreciates that I love The Avengers totally but he said to me that there was a wealth of shows out there that follow the same vein that I could possibly like too. The Professionals was a taste of what was out there and Dad said to me that he wanted to show me the benefits of other shows. He is sure that I would like them..."

I gave the whole thing a very earnest try. The shows that my Dad exposed to me were all either a mix of home videos that he brought home or just happened to be having a repeat session on the television at the time...

Sunday 27th December 1998

"Another video of The Professionals was given to me today. Volume 5 and the episodes on it were really good. Hunter/Hunted had the character of Doyle being hounded by a former policeman that he put behind bars. The next one, Stakeout involved a bowling alley and an atomic bomb. And then I got the fact file on it from Dad..."

THE PROFESSIONALS
Created by Brian Clemens
Televised between 1977 and 1983 on ITV
Starring Gordon Jackson as George Cowley, Martin Shaw as Ray Doyle, Lewis Collins as William Bodie

---

"This show was made by the company that not only were behind The Avengers but were also making The New Avengers at the time that this was in production. It followed the organisation CI5 as they dealt with terrorist threats that were approaching England. I like this show. From the theme tune it hooks you and takes you on an adventure that you don't really want to end..."

My Dad had succeeded a little in opening my eyes to the classics that were out there and we were off to a good start. The follow up to the first show was ultimately successful…

Saturday 16th January 1999

"Dad has decided to choose weekends to educate me in my classic show experiences. I did like the choice this time around and Dad now owes Aunt Nikki a favour for borrowing the tape he played for me today…"

THE CHAMPIONS
Created by Dennis Spooner and Monty Berman
Televised between 1968 and 1969 on ITV
Starring Stuart Damon as Craig Stirling,
Alexandra Bastedo as Sharron Macready, William Gaunt
as Richard Barrett, Anthony Nicholls as Tremayne

"I fell in love with this one the moment that I heard the theme tune. The story is about three agents from an organisation called Nemesis that are made into superhuman beings after a plane crash in the snowy hills of Tibet. The way they use their abilities to help each other in the show was also something I quite liked too and on the tape Dad played me there was an episode that showed Sharron bringing Richard back from the dead. In another episode Sharron was trapped in a massive freezer causing Richard to feel the cold getting worse and allowing him to telepathically contact Craig to say that she was in trouble…"

The Champions is another show that went through a BBC 2 repeat phase. I think it was directly after *The New Avengers* run had finished but Dad was only showing me this very interesting series now. Dad and I were definitely bonding again and my education into his world continued on…

Saturday 23rd January 1999
"Dad seems determined a little bit with this weekend. He wants to keep this up until he's made a certain number of shows for what he calls 'my education'."

MAN IN A SUITCASE
Created by Dennis Spooner and Richard Harris
Televised between 1967 and 1968 on ITV
Starring Richard Bradford as McGill

"The theme tune was something I immediately knew. It has been the theme tune to TFI Friday. This was obviously where Chris Evans stole it from. But the show in general was one that I found hard to follow as Dad described it. It's about a secret agent who is only known by one name and his reputation is that he is a disgrace. He was set up and made to look as though he was a traitor and he is now set out to be used by people who want a scapegoat. I couldn't fathom it all and in all honestly all I could follow was the theme tune. But the actor playing this man called McGill I felt sympathy for. When he got hit and hurt you could see in his face that he really felt the pain…"

My slight confusion was eased with Dad's next choice…

RANDALL AND HOPKIRK (DECEASED)
Created by Dennis Spooner
Televised between 1969 and 1970 on ITV
Starring Mike Pratt as Jeff Randall, Kenneth Cope as
Marty Hopkirk, Annette Andre as Jeannie Hopkirk

"The theme tune gives an eerie vibe and leads into a series about a duo of private detectives. One of them is murdered and comes back as a ghost that can only be seen by his partner. I loved the whole thing that Mr Randall could have been made to look like a lunatic as he was talking to somebody that only he could see. This is definitely a show I would watch again…"

The remake of this classic was yet to be thought of at this particular time but I remember beaming as I found out that Kenneth Cope had turned up as a character in *Brookside*. I wondered if he was going to walk through the wall and if his white suit was still at the cleaners. Onto the next entry…

Saturday 6th February 1999
"Dad told me that this weekend was a lesson involving a certain actor with two classic shows that defined him in his career. I was a little intrigued and then happy as Dad told me that the actor I was set to watch was a friend of Patrick Macnee…"

THE SAINT
Created by Leslie Charteris
Televised between 1962 and 1969 on ITV
Starring Roger Moore as Simon Templar

"Dad told that this show was one of the ones to define the sixties. One of the best actors of screen, Roger Moore plays a troubleshooter that turns up wherever trouble seems to occur. When his name is mentioned at the start of events, a halo appears over his head and one of the greatest themes ever is played. Dad told me that this show began as black and white but these episodes are in full colour. Each episode did get better and better but the one with the giant ant made me a little nervous. After showing me the episodes on the tape, Dad then disappeared for a bit and

returned with a small car that he had since his childhood. It was
a toy jaguar like the one that was driven in the show. He's given
it to me as a gift..."

That toy car sits proudly on top of my desk at home next to a picture of my children. I have yet to give them a classic television education. The second show then followed...

THE PERSUADERS!
Created by Robert S Baker
Televised between 1971 and 1972 on ITV
Starring Tony Curtis as Danny Wilde, Roger Moore as
Lord Brett Sinclair, Laurence Naismith as Judge Fulton

"The two episodes I watched on this were really good. The first
one involved Sinclair being brainwashed into killing a good
friend of his that was too well protected and it was up to Wilde to
stop him doing so. The second one had Wilde being stuck to a
briefcase that was handcuffed to his wrist and contained an
exploding bomb whilst he was being chased by enemy agents that
were trying to kill him and get a hold of the case as it contained
secret information. The theme tune and the beginning of this
show are amazing. The way that shows the two lead characters
coming from different backgrounds and becoming famous
millionaires was great. And the theme tune was definitely catchy
from the beginning..."

I am always amazed at how Roger Moore and Tony Curtis seemed to gel so well together. But I was then given a surprise by Dad's next selection. From what I can gather from the journal entry, this particular classic TV lesson went on into the evening when Dad showed me two tapes of the same show...

"Dad wanted to continue with his 'lesson' in classic television, and so he showed me two very different episodes of the same show…"

MISSION: IMPOSSIBLE
Created by Bruce Geller
Televised in the USA between 1966 and 1973,
repeated in 1996 on Channel 4
Starring Steven Hill as Dan Briggs, Peter Graves as
Jim Phelps, Martin Landau as Rollin Hand, Barbara Bain
as Cinnamon Carter, Greg Morris as Barney Collier,
Peter Lupus as Willy Armitage

"The theme tune I immediately knew. It was nice to see where it was from but it was difficult not to think that I was going to see a squirrel have a daring run on a washing line. The first episode had a man with dark hair leading the team in trying to rescue and old man from a large prison. The second episode had a man with white hair leading the team and they were trying to get scientists out of a bunker underground. I found this show really interesting to watch because it was all technical. The team had a specific part to play and I loved the electrician of the team. I think he was the coolest of the team. But I have to say that I preferred the white haired man as the leader and Dad seemed happy with my choice…"

The first big screen movie of this show was about four years old from this entry, but Dad was more interested in showing the films roots. I stand firm that I did prefer Peter Graves as the leader of the team. I'm surprised that the series did not begin with him but I know that the series would have been nothing without him. Having *Mission: Impossible* without Peter Graves would be like having *The Avengers* without Patrick Macnee. It would never be the same. Watching all of these shows again and being a little older has made me appreciate the time at which *The Avengers* came out. I can see from the next entries Dad had saved some personal favourites for last…

Saturday 13th February 1999
"Dad prepared me for these shows. It was not like him. The routine was he would put the tape into the player and he would inform me of the show as we watched the episodes unfold. But this time round he sat me down and said that the first show was the lead in to the second show…"

DANGER MAN
Created by Ralph Smart
Televised between 1962 and 1968 on ITV
Starred Patrick McGoohan as John Drake

"The opening theme to this was quite catchy and it had an introduction about how every government has its secret service branch. This agent works for NATO and finds himself given a messy job but he can do it. I was happy to see that the one I watched had been written by Brian Clemens. Nice fun all surrounding a girl that mysteriously appears out of nowhere in her pyjamas and tells all around her about a secret government assassination plot…"

But what happened next was to surprise me totally.

"Dad brought out a special case for this next show that he wanted to educate me on. It was a specially made cardboard case that opened up and featured five cassettes and as you closed and sealed it shut it had a very nicely designed penny farthing bicycle upon the side of it…"

THE PRISONER
Created by Patrick McGoohan and George Markstein
Televised between 1967 and 1968 on ITV
Starring Patrick McGoohan as Number Six

"What the hell did I watch? I couldn't make head or tail of it despite Dad's explanation. A secret agent resigns from the service and is then kidnapped. He wakes up in a place called The Village which is full of people that are known only by a number and he cannot leave until he gives a satisfactory explanation as to why he resigned. There is a man there known only as Number Two and his job is break Number Six and find out the reason why he resigned. Any attempt by anybody to escape from The Village then results in the weirdest and chilling thing that I've ever seen. Someone calls out an orange alert and a large white bubble appears out of water from a fountain or from the sea that covers the area. There is then a loud roar as the bubble goes over to the person attempting to escape, suffocates them to unconsciousness and prevents their escape. That's frightening. Maybe that's why people watched it. Did they think that the bubble would pay them a visit if they did not watch the show?"

If you were not confused by this show then you were not watching it properly. Dad was right in this one being a classic because of how well recognised it still is.

The whole saga of shows that Dad showed me were something that I later asked him about. Why did he show me these particular shows? His reply to me was that these particular shows matched my feelings on *The Avengers* from a fan's perspective and the selection he made was part of the cream of Sixties television. Both Simon Templar and John Steed came out of a time when revolution was all around the world, in music and in television. But the moment Dad began to question why I was into *The Avengers* rather than the other shows, I would back away from the subject. I did not want to bore Dad with how fantastic I thought, and still think, that *The Avengers* is. Dad then introduced another character that was in the public consciousness…

Saturday 27th March 1999
"Dad is being a little cryptic today. He tells me that the education of classics that he wants me to be aware of needs the icing on the cake. There is a character that he needs to introduce me to…"

JAMES BOND
Created by Ian Fleming, circa 1952
Film series produced from 1962 to present
Film series produced by Harry Saltzman, Albert R. Broccoli, Michael G Wilson and Barbara Broccoli
Starring Sean Connery, George Lazenby, Roger Moore, Timothy Dalton, Pierce Brosnan, Daniel Craig
as James Bond 007

"Dad knows how I feel about movies. I'm really fussy about some movies. But Dad is insistent that I watch these particular movies that he has had a friend record for him. They've been on ITV. Sponsored by Martini and appearing in a season called 00 Heaven. The man is James Bond. The name I've heard. But I've never really connected with it at all. The first few films that I saw were really tough to get into but Dad insisted that I stick it out. So I did as I was asked and now we're up to the Roger Moore films. This man got around a lot. First it was The Saint, then The Persuaders! and now this. Dad is right about each film getting better and better. They're still making them now, at least that's what Dad has told me…"

I look at the Bond films and wonder why the same thing could not be done for the *Avengers* movie. Each Bond film was grounded in a reality

74

surrounding a central character. Why could that not have been done with the *Avengers* movie? Steed and Emma Peel have their own world and all you have to do is use that world, use what has been given to you, and use the relationship between the leads to drive some of the action. The whole world of *The Avengers* is easy to understand, no matter how compartmentalised it was depending on Steed's partner at the time. But the movie makers got it all wrong. For that, *The Avengers* suffered. The Bond people should work on *The Avengers*, I think.

My love and adoration for *The Avengers* at this precise time in the notebooks seems to be taking on another form, one that I later exploited. I was starting to write short stories that were sending Steed on solo missions for Mother along with him meeting up with Tara King and Emma Peel to fight vicious tailors trying to kill him with a deadly choke hold shirt collar or dealing with a scientist that wants to wipe out the whole of humanity by simply giving them a high fever. All of this was possible in the world of *The Avengers* and I was keeping it alive in my consciousness. I have now entered the Year 9 phase of school and from what I'm reading in the books, me reciting the episodes to keep people at bay was starting to rub a few people up the wrong way…

Wednesday 15th September 1999
"Dad had to take me to hospital tonight. But I had to tell him the reason why I was beaten up today. It was all for The Avengers. A friend decided to teach me a lesson for being so old fashioned and liking a show that was not even successful as a movie. My ribs are killing me and my right hand has been bandaged up. Dad was not angry with me. If anything he thinks that the bullies have gone a step too far in doing this to me. My face looks like it has been cut to ribbons and there is a gash over my forehead where it was brushed hard against the pavement…"

I remember this well. I was walking home from school and it was a day where I had not drawn attention to myself by reciting anything. I knew I was being followed and picked up the pace a little. But they were a full team of five and they pinned me to the ground before I knew where I was. There was nobody about. My hand was bandaged for several weeks with X rays taking place each week. My ribs were kicked and punched to the point of painkillers being needed almost all of the day. Surprisingly the bullies did not come near me again for some time. I never pursued the issue through fear of being hit again.

But it did give me the chance to stop the charade of being a lunatic. I was now given the opportunity to just be me and be accepted by people that were willing to take that second chance on me. With Dad telling me that there were more ways to appreciate things, it seems that I decided to use this as the spring board for a complete reboot of my passion for *The Avengers*.

More on this in the next entry.

Recording ends.

Chapter 6
THE GRANDEUR THAT WAS STEED

New tape is recording.
Entry begins.

The notebooks are now beginning to reveal a change of outlook on *The Avengers*.

I had used this show as a crutch to help me through the hard times of school and the fists that would meet me. It had worked to some extent but as my bruises healed from the last beating up that I received, I was now looking at the show in many different perspectives. But the main focus was the character and portrayal of John Steed.

The eternal gentleman secret agent with an umbrella in his hand and a bowler hat on his head, Steed could face anything with grace, wit and charm. He seemed to float on air in the show and my devotion to him unending.

Each episode that I viewed I was entrenched in what Steed was doing; how he got himself out of situations, how he dealt with the villains that he faced, how he handled relationships with both his superiors and the partners of his trade. It was a deep love and devotion to this character created by Mr Patrick Macnee and I was so happy when I discovered that he was the main person that brought this character to life. He made Steed so real.

The 21st century was in the headlights and all the world was approaching the year 2000 quickly. I remember that I was up all night with Dad watching *The Biggest Breakfast Ever* on Channel 4 with Johnny Vaughan and Liza Tarbuck. I was awake for the whole thing but paid the price the next day. Most of the world was getting drunk and waiting for something to happen.

But what of *The Avengers*? The show that I held close to my heart was undergoing a major change with me…

Tuesday 4th January 2000

"I've been looking at the collection that I've built up so far. I'm impressed. But Dad looked at me the other day and asked me why have I kept the tape recordings? The tapes are not being played as much…"

But with an ever-growing VHS collection of my favourite show mounting, the tide was soon to turn…

Monday 10th January 2000

"I've nearly got the whole M Appeal Collection and Dad treated me to the Movie Commemoration Box Set. I started playing that one today and I'm really happy to finally watch the Cathy Gale episodes. Introduced by the master of ceremonies, Mr Patrick Macnee, I was then blessed to see my first Honor Blackman episode, Immortal Clay. I was quite surprised. Firstly the theme music was different to the Laurie Johnson theme that I have grown up with and become used to. This was really different; repetitive but catchy and very much a jazz styled piece. The titles were also different. Steed and Cathy Gale slowly approached the screen with the different styled logo above their heads to this new theme tune. We then went into the episode…"

I think I experienced a small hit of culture shock at this point…

"It did not seem like an episode The Avengers and yet it was one. I found myself gripped by Honor Blackman and my first sight of Steed's first female partner. But the episode at points did seem a little slow. It was all about an unbreakable cup. I also saw my first sight of One Ten, Steed's boss in the early seasons of the show. This was a Season 2 episode. The next episode was School For Traitors and had Venus Smith in it. I had only read about Venus in The Ultimate Avengers, Steed had three partners in the second series. Three! I thought that did not happen until The New Avengers…"

This introduction to the second series helped in my education of the programme. What I was being spoiled with now was the roots of the show and it was something that I had been craving for. As I read on from this I noted a conversation that Dad and I had about the show. It was a Friday evening and I was deeply engaged with *The Ultimate Avengers* Season Two section. I continued staring at a certain picture that was on page 44 and the picture depicted Steed and Cathy in a stance whilst holding guns. Dad thought that I was getting a little fixated on the Honor Blackman era of the show. The pages that I read about series two made me want to watch the whole thing from the beginning...

Friday 14th January 2000
"Why did Steed have three partners for the second season? I don't get it. Why did Cathy Gale have to share the limelight? She was Steed's only partner for season three..."

I was now in the latter stages of Year 9 and the exams were pretty tough going. I would gladly have swapped a week in front of my videos on *The Avengers* for going through this torture. One of the days had two fights with four different students as we were waiting to go into the hall. I had an exam ritual that was interesting, a case of mind over matter...

Wednesday 9th February 2000
"I wasn't in the exam hall of the school today. I was in the episode of The Master Minds. I am Steed being tested on the inner workings of the human mind and trying to gain full entry into the Ransack organisation being run by the sinister Desmond Leaming and the quirky Professor Spencer. The only trouble is that I cannot place the answers onto my cuffs and finish the tests quicker than anybody else..."

Reading on through the passages, the four letter word that enters every teenager's life finally arrived with me. I had love in my life before in the form of *The Avengers*. But this type of love was the type that was to fully encompass the reality of life. The love of the screen and my passion for *The*

Avengers was now going to have to make way for true romance to enter the equation. But it was to *The Avengers* that I took some inspiration...

Friday 11th February 2000

"There is someone that I like in the year, but she knows me as a babbling idiot. I knew that I would pay for all those recited episodes. She's quite a nice person to talk to and she always says hello, either out of pity or genuine friendship. I do notice that she looks at me across the room at lunch and when we have lessons together we're not that far from each other. Her name is Charlotte Summers. She's in the form 9DY. Very nice to talk to but how the hell do you approach the subject of liking her?"

Help was at hand...

Saturday 12th February 2000

"I watched The Murder Market on The M Appeal Collection – Mission Two and thought about how to next approach Charlotte. With a certain day around the corner, I'm thinking about how Steed was set up on his date with Barbara Wakefield. To start with there could be a small identifiable thing to set them up like a red carnation and then follow it with a small list of things that we could do on the first date. But what could I do along the same lines with Charlotte? Steed handled his date with utter cool and calm. I think I would be a nervous wreck. But I have watched the episode back a few times, to Dad's annoyance. And I've listened to the recording that I made from the late night repeat. Can you pick up tips from an episode of your favourite show?"

I took the gamble with it. I wrote a list of what Steed treated his date to and made comparisons to what I could do myself. I went around the town purposely picking out places that I could afford to take my intended for a date and consequently felt that above anything that I did not want to appear cheap. The card that I bought for her provided a very comical ice breaker according to the next entry...

Monday 14th February 2000

*"I now have a girlfriend. Charlotte liked my card that I gave to
her but it was leaving the price sticker on the back that really got
us talking. Dad wants to meet her immediately but I don't want
to overload her with meeting everyone I know, especially since
we've only just got together. She hasn't been introduced to The
Avengers yet and that is something that I'm going to have to clear
up when I get the chance to. We seem to get on well, that's a good
start. She did tell me that she had admired me for a little while
but still thought of me as the fool that walks around making an
idiot of himself. I think now that I've got the chance to finally lay
that ghost to rest…"*

The ghost was put to rest very quickly…

Wednesday 16th February 2000

*"My image as an idiot has been changed. We did try and organise
a date together for the weekend. We couldn't make our minds up
what to do but I said to her that I would think of something. I
don't know why I said this. How the hell can we go anywhere
when I have no idea where to take her? I've been re-reading the
list that I made on The Avengers episode I took inspiration from
but I've been looking back at most of them. I thought about the
New Avengers episode Hostage, where Steed was having dinner at
his home with a date. Maybe I could cook for the two of us? Dad
still likes the casserole dish that Mum taught me to make…"*

It was a good idea in theory but it was quickly forgotten. But another
was in my mind…

*"I have no choice. I'm going to have to bite the bullet and allow
Steed to be my saviour in this whole matter…"*

It proved to be an interesting decision…

Saturday 19th February 2000

"What a date I've had. Following Steed in The Murder Market; I took Charlotte for lunch at McDonald's followed by a very competitive couple of bowling games at the bowling alley. I finished the date by suggesting the cinema and we went to see a romantic comedy. I must have spent over a hundred quid but it was a day that was not wasted.

Steed has been a good friend to me today. Following his unofficial guide to wining and dining a beautiful date I have successfully had a good date with my girlfriend..."

The magic must have worked...

Sunday 20th February 2000
"Charlotte messaged me earlier. We have another date set but this time she wants to treat me as well as I did her yesterday..."

The bridge I had yet to cross was the passion that I felt for *The Avengers*. It was a television show but it was a major part of me. The important lesson I was learning at this stage was that it was just a television show but it contained a lot of power. I had reached a crossroads with my favourite show and the crunch time was approaching fast, according to the next entry...

Wednesday 23rd February 2000
"I spoke to Dad tonight. I'm worried that my being a fan of The Avengers will cause a problem for me and Charlotte. I am the only person that appreciates or acknowledges it. Being the only one in the crowd to speak up on it was something I have been beaten up for after all. But I want to have the best of both worlds so I can appreciate and love my programme while still having the respect of my girlfriend..."

Thankfully, John Steed was on hand yet again...

Friday 25th February 2000

"The Avengers has been calming me down and helping me think a way through this.

I've been observing the pattern with the relationships Steed had with the partners he used. With Cathy, Emma and Tara he treated them all with respect and as an equal. I think that might be the nest way in which to approach my problem.

Tell Charlotte about my love and passion for the show but do it the way Steed would treat his female partners; no pretentions whatsoever. Tell it how it is and get the proper reaction..."

I then chose the day for the big reveal...

Tuesday 29th February 2000

"This wasn't a bad day. I told Charlotte directly as I intended; The Avengers is my passion. It's deep in my heart and I love the show completely and totally. I was unprepared for her reaction. She quite understood. I made a promise to her not to overwhelm her with the show or any of its episodes..."

The fact that we now had a VHS player in the house gave me carte blanche to look at all that was in my collection. But there was a new format hitting the shelves called DVD. I was not ready to start an argument with Dad about getting a DVD player. They cost more than the video player and he was already working hard enough.

The *New Avengers* videos had also built up a bit for me but I was focusing on The Avengers more. I remember that I ran out of shelf room for the mounted mass of collections that had built up; *The M Appeal Collection, The Movie Commemoration Box, The Sci-fi and Fantasy Box, The Parallel Lines Collection, The Celebrity Guest Collection, The Monochrome Collection Box* adding *The New Avengers* releases kept me busy and entertained for the next couple of months. But there was to be a small backlash...

Thursday 13th April 2000

"It seems as though I have been taking too much time with my collections. Dad seems to feel that I'm losing touch with the outside world due to the religious viewing of Steed and his numerous adventures…"

This was a feeling that was shared by some of my friends at the time. From the entries that follow this one, my promise to Charlotte began to fall through…

Monday 17th April 2000

"Charlotte and I had a massive bust up. She thinks that I've been going on and on about my stupid Avengers obsession. I said to her that it is not an obsession it is a healthy respect and love for a programme that deserves more attention than it gets. But she was having none of it. She was angry that we had not gone out for a couple of weekends. She also said that I seem to want to stay in and focus on The Avengers rather than her. She said that the only proper time we can see each other is at a weekend and all I'm doing is avoiding her. That's not very fair. She wanted me to call her but I'm not going to. She did try ringing but I turned my phone off…"

This was the first chink in the armour with my very first proper girlfriend. The argument was resolved but there was an apparent undercurrent of animosity between Charlotte and my favourite show. The point of acceptance had yet to be reached for her and I wasn't exactly helpful. A couple more months went by and the point of acceptance was finally reached…

Thursday 27th July 2000

"Charlotte surprised me with a gift today as an apology for the last fight we had. She got me the latest video on The Avengers. It's the new one that I've been eyeing up online. The Evolution Collection Volume 1 and it features the only known existing Ian Hendry

episode. The video even came with its own illustrated card inside. To say that Charlotte is amazing would understate the reality…"

Not only did we have acceptance taken care of, it was now time for the tolerance to kick in once again…

Friday 28th July 2000
"Have done nothing but watch the first volume of The Evolution Collection. It's great.

I finally got to see what The Avengers was like during the first series. In all honesty I am a little disappointed because there are points where you can barely hear what people are saying to each other. But the manic Sir Thomas Weller was a treat and the working partnership of Steed and Dr Keel is really a good one…"

The tolerance level stepped up…

"So that's who played Dr Martin King for three episodes. After watching this one, Dead On Course, I'm amazed that he was not given more time in the spotlight as Steed's partner…"

More surprises were to come…

"And we have another Venus Smith episode. I did like this one, Man In The Mirror. But I think that was because I saw another one of Steed's early bosses in the form of One-Six. He's a bit like One-Ten in some respects but not in others. The plot of this one was really good. A man who died a week ago turns up alive at a funfair because he's turned traitor…"

And lastly…

"It's the first Cathy Gale episode. But she is different in this episode with Steed. She seems more chilled and at ease with him rather than having a little bit of spice to throw into his direction.

Charlotte has watched the video with me. I don't think she liked it much but she has not said anything..."

To be as tolerant of my obsession as Dad was and to also sit through four full episodes, I think that she deserved a medal the size of a dustbin lid. But I was to be further surprised by my current girlfriend of the time as the next entry reveals...

Tuesday 15th August 2000

"I got a surprise from Charlotte's mum tonight. She brought out a book from a box that she had been given from her mother. It was a book on The Avengers. It was a novel and it had a picture of Steed and Cathy on the front. Charlotte's mum said that I can have it. I've read it. I remember seeing a picture of this from The Ultimate Avengers. This was the first of a series of books when the show was being broadcast..."

A plan was forming. It was not long before it was put into operation...

Friday 18th August 2000

"I've been searching online all week for the books that were written at the time of The Avengers being on air. After all this time, they can still be found. Even the New Avengers books are out there..."

Stage one was finding them. Stage two commenced a few months later...

Tuesday 14th November 2000

"I've been saving. I really want to own all of these books. I've even found a few of Dave Rogers early books. I never knew that The Ultimate Avengers was a companion to his other volume, The Complete Avengers. It's the main novels that I'm after right now. There were four all written by John Garforth. There were some

86

*American novels that were written but I think I may have
difficulty in getting those ones. But I fully intend to try..."*

The promise I made to myself was to own them all or as near as I
could get to it. Slowly, the books became plops on the mat at home, all
nicely wrapped up and ready for their new owner. Dad seemed happy about
this part of my love for the show but when I asked him about it he stated
that it was because he did not have to come home and find it directly on
the television after he had come home from work. This new collection was
gathered over the Christmas period and into the New Year. Very soon, I
was the proud owner of the nine books written at the time of *The Avengers*
being on the air. I also had all six of the *New Avengers* novels to. Stage three
of the process was a challenge though...

Thursday 11th January 2001
*"I'll give myself a month to read the whole lot starting from
Monday..."*

Challenge accepted. Whether it be *The Floating Game*, *The Passing of
Gloria Munday*, *The Laugh Was On Lazarus* or *Heil Harris!*, something
doesn't seem right. I read the books but I'm detecting an undercurrent of
disenchantment in my recorded journal. I then moved on to the American
books and I'm hearing the same disappointed emotion in my voice. I seem
to have enjoyed reading *The Afrit Affair* and *The Gold Bomb*, both by Keith
Laumer. But I seem to have no mention of *Moon Express* by Norman
Daniels. As my challenge drew to a close, I can now read and listen to the
reason why...

Thursday 15th February 2001
*"All I can say is that I'm not happy. The Steed of these books is
not the Steed that we all know. He has not got any of the
chemistry with Emma in print that he has on screen. There is
nothing that Patrick Macnee has brought to the role been put into
the words on the pages that I read. The American ones had mild
stirrings of it and in The Magnetic Man; Tara King was
behaving as though she was a spoiled heiress. And what was going*

on in *The Gold Bomb?* Since when did Steed and Tara operate from an office? Steed would loathe being an office bound operative. I think that the Steed of the books is nothing compared to the character that Patrick Macnee has created and the character that I have grown to love and appreciate..."

There was a salvation at the end of the tunnel...

Saturday 17th February 2001

"Dad surprised me today. He had gone and ordered two novels of The Avengers. He told me that he knew that I was disappointed with the ones that I had read but the two that he had ordered for me were written at the time the show was on and were a guaranteed good read..."

Then I had the ultimate surprise.

"It's a novel written by Patrick Macnee! It's called Deadline. It's all about the British newspapers and there being bad headlines sent out to neutral territories. Everything that was not in the books I had read previously was in this one. I even looked on the front pages of this particular book and it's a 1994 re-print. So is the second one apparently..."

The second book was then read as quickly as the first one.

Sunday 18th February 2001

"This second book by Patrick Macnee was as good, if not better than his first. Dead Duck, about the poisoning of people using migrating ducks, sounds like a very Avengers type plot from the Emma Peel era of the show. But why couldn't the other books have been like these two? The only problem that I have with them is Steed taking orders from someone called His Nibs. Ideal code name for a boss of his but in the show they both normally operated independently. It had everything that you would expect from The Avengers – even down to the fight between Steed's umbrella and a

bird sent in to a room to take care of him. That is what it's all about. Why did these authors not work with what the actors had given them?"

Mr Macnee's two books had provided me with a tonic to soothe my troubled waters.

But from here it gets hazy. The box I took from Dad's old house is still half full of notebooks but the entries seem a little thin on the ground and there are not many tape logs to provide a background either. I seemed to be distancing myself from the routine of everything. I was enjoying what life had given to me. I had a girlfriend and the relationship appeared to be going quite steadily. Each entry was now plain and reference to *The Avengers* was hardly there. But it was still causing a few arguments between Charlotte and me…

Thursday 17th May 2001

"We had another fight today. This time it was over the fact that I did not meet up with her like I said I would.

I've had enough of being bullied by her. We meet up and we spend time together but somehow that is not enough for her. She keeps telling me that I go on at people about The Avengers but I don't care. I only answer to people's questions in what TV I like to watch but this puts her back up. I have barely watched the show in months. My collections are starting to gather dust.

But it's been good to me tonight after this recent row. I've been watching a few episodes tonight and it's calmed me down.

Charlotte has tried to talk to me and apologise but I keep coming back to the same thing with her…"

There was an underlying feeling that the importance of the show was always going to be there and I had not come around to the fact that I had to keep my head in the real world. But I continued embracing my passion.

Thursday 5th July 2001

*"Dad brought home a new item. It's a DVD player. He told me
that it was because he had got chatting to his friends at work and
they told him that it was a good idea to get one because VHS is on
the way out. But the next surprise came with the next box that he
gave to me. It's a box set of The Avengers. The 1967 set with files
one and two. It's from the Emma Peel colour series and I started
playing it immediately tonight. I told Charlotte about it and did
not expect her to be nice about it. She was and now we're making
DVD nights together."*

But the DVD sets were the start of another collection and Charlotte
suspected that it was going to be another choice of spend time with her or
stay indoors with my favourite show. The next argument was fun from
what this next entry tells me…

Friday 13th July 2001

*"More fights over the time that we're not spending together. I've
offered to not bother watch any television at all if it will make her
happy. But Charlotte then told me it's nothing to do with my
television watching. She tells me that it's down to me talking and
going on about The Avengers. It's apparently driving her mad
and she thinks that I should do something about it."*

I've edited out that the fight had the word 'doctor' screamed at me.
She thought that my love of *The Avengers* needed professionally looking at
but I later found out that she was being sarcastic. With all the love for the
show that I was feeling and Charlotte's shouted criticisms, it seems as
though things should indeed change course.

Thursday 26th July 2001

*"Dad and I got talking tonight. He was looking through an
exercise book that I had from infant school and he as
complementing me on the stories that I had written inside. I did
tell him that I was smaller when I wrote them and as I read them
again they don't even make sense to me. But Dad's point was*

using my imagination to get me somewhere in life and he
suggested that I try a journalistic career…"

At the time I thought that Dad was being sarcastic. But his words soon sunk in and led me to the change of direction that I needed to make.

End of entry.

Chapter 7
MY WILDEST DREAM

Tape is recording.
New entry begins.

I have a lot to thank Dad for. If he had not boxed up everything after I had moved out I may have lost some of these old journals and recordings that I used to keep.

I find myself feeling very nostalgic as I continue reading these journals and listening to the tapes and hearing the changes in my voice as adolescence took hold. It's making me happy that I'm wrapping things up on a high note.

As I read the next book, the school exams had finished. I managed to do pretty well. Dad was very happy with my results but he was insistent that I should stay in education. He had a dream that I could carve a career for myself by using my imagination. He always told me that it was a mixture of hyperactivity and knowledge. The first entry that's here brings back a happy memory…

Tuesday 20th November 2001
"Dad set me a task. He seems to feel that I need to put my brain into gear and wants me to construct a small story for him to read. It can involve anything I like but it has to be a structured piece. I don't know why he has suddenly got this idea into his head. I don't see the point in forcing me to write something just because I have a good imagination. But Dad is certain that a hidden talent could lie somewhere…"

It was certainly a challenge that allowed my imagination to kick into high gear. I re-read the stories that I had written when I was younger but I decided that I should re-write them so that I could understand them now I had grown. The result had a profound effect according to the next entry…

Monday 26th November 2001

"I've been having great fun this last week. I've re-written The Hand That Holds Mine and it's turned out to be a story involving a first girlfriend. I'm in the process of re-writing It's All In The Mind. It's about a day out to a funfair and a child's obsession with what could happen if there was a visit to the funfair hypnotist."

The stories were short but entertaining. The re-write exercise that I began continued as I discovered an old school book...

Thursday 29th November 2001

"It's my old English book with my old red group sticker on it. This is the third story that I've found in there under the heading of 'Be Creative'. The first story, The Lord of The Manor, was a mystery where a policeman was trying his best to arrest a Lord. The second, Summer Rain, was about two kids that watch an old man they think is funny because he seems to be waiting for rain. But the third story, The Happy Time, was about a school kid who kept looking at the clock wanting the day to finish. Each one looked concise in terms of plot but when you're a child you tend to just write and not think about structure. Going back over them and adding to the foundations I had begun has been really fun."

Things changed in the next few months. Christmas came and went. Charlotte and I split and agreed to remain friends. My last year of senior school had me spending a lot of time in the library making my name on internet fan clubs for classic shows. I was busy looking out for sites dedicated to *The Avengers*. But my time was also given over to my new found hobby.

Dad's suggestion of me writing had a bad side effect. I became focused more on being indoors rather than socialise with anybody. It was another one of those occurrences where Dad just intervened where it as necessary. In this case I was glad that he did. With my last year of senior school in full swing, the months seemed to go by at a lightning pace. But I needed the starting point that would give to me the idea that I could follow through from beginning to end. It seems that I was looking anywhere to write about something...

Monday 3rd June 2002
"I've been watching the Golden Jubilee concert and am really amazed at what I saw to give the Queen a good old party at Buckingham Palace. Perhaps it would be best if I looked around for people or things that could possibly help me start somewhere. But where do you start?"

I did not have long to wait. Dad's advice about the world of work and how cruel it can be to the people that were searching for it first time around made me think that college could be the option. I picked up one of their guides from the school library and started reading through what the local establishment, Thornton Academy College, had to offer to me. I did not seem to be too impressed by the prospectus. But all was not lost as the back page offered to the prospective new students the chance to a chance to come to the college at an open day. Dad took a look at the prospectus and thought that there was only one option for me to take...

Thursday 8th August 2002
"Dad reckons that the English course at Thornton is what I should be studying. But I'm not sure. I have no idea what I would do if I did do anything on a writing level. Plus my grades from school in regards to English are as good as they can be so all that college could do for them is boost them up a notch or two. But Dad is insistent. I could be going out into the world of work with the firm knowledge that I have perfect grades and education where English is concerned. The only work that I could possibly is to be a secretary to someone who needs their letters typed quickly and be grammatically correct. I see what Dad wants me to do but I'm really not sure. I looked at the jobs page at the back of the newspaper and all I could find for my first job would be a cleaner of a local chemist. Maybe on a break I could write about the wonders of the carpet in a chemists and how good it can be to clean it up as thoroughly as possible..."

The college open day was quite a revelation for me. I give no mention to it in the pages or tape logs that followed this entry but I was quite happy to see college as my next port of call for the next two years. I was a very dedicated student. I did not do any socialising outside of college time and I kept the day to day routine of Monday to Friday. The weekends allowed me the time to read the endless study book that we were given as a bible and reference guide for the year. We got a different one for the second year but for the first year (2002-2003) we had a lump of a book that covered every angle for the English language. I must have been bored by the whole process of it but from the next entry it appears to be the exact opposite…

Thursday 9th January 2003

"Looking at all of the articles that are featured under the heading of 'Illuminating English' has been great. It looks at playwrights, novelists and writers of the 20th century and how they have used the English language in the profession of making it accessible to the public. What stages that it has to go through and how we as beings take language and process it as thought. It does make you wonder at how true that whole thing is. We all read and we all have understanding of what a piece of text tells us. We all have the ability to form images from the words that we read and it's all down to the minds that have placed the words in front of us. I'm really glad that Dad insisted that I go down this road…"

In the first year we were all given an opportunity to write a small review of something that was important to us. It was to be featured within the next prospectus as a taste for what the English course could offer to its students. I jumped at the chance to do it. My choice of subject was obvious…

Wednesday 12th March 2003

"I've chosen to review my latest acquisition on The Avengers – files five and six of the 1968 set that's been out for a while but I've only just managed to buy it. The selection of episodes on this set is really good. It's got Game, False Witness, The Morning After

and Take Me To Your Leader. I'm leaving nothing to chance with this review…"

The end product was drafted in the subsequent entries and tape logs…

Saturday 15th March 2003

My Review – The Avengers, 1968 DVD set, files five and six

"For the viewers of the 1960s, there were several staples of television. Each week they would be hooked on the adventures of their heroes and how they would outwit their nemesis. One such programme was The Avengers; a staple of the 1960s that covered the television landscape from 1961 to 1969.

The show began its life starring Ian Hendry as Dr David Keel and its origins surrounded the doctor finding the killers of his fiancée. He was aided in this task buy a shadowy secret agent called John Steed, who was played by Patrick Macnee.

The show went through several fresh changes that kept it in people's consciousness. It was at the forefront of women being placed firmly into the spotlight socially and demonstrated this by having Honor Blackman as Cathy Gale, the very first woman on television to be seen not only as a tough and capable woman but was also seen as a man's equal.

It then paved the way for Diana Rigg as Emma Peel who showed that having beauty and brains were a fantastic combination in tackling the masterminds they encountered on a weekly basis. It was then made a complete package by the introduction of Linda Thorson as Tara King and here is where we turn our attention now…"

This was a strong beginning that took six drafts in order to get it right. I was a perfectionist and it was nice to hear on the tape that I was rustling my papers like a newsreader. This strong start then led into...

Sunday 16th March 2003

"In this collection we have some of the defining episodes of a series that left the television screens on a high. It had come from its humble beginnings and successfully taken on the world.

In this set we see our hero, John Steed and his gorgeous partner, Tara King take on all manner of villains inside a world where anything can indeed happen. On volume five we have episode 2, Game, in which a mastermind is torturing his victims in giant replicas of their favourite board games and even places Steed into one himself as he tries to rescue Tara from suffocation in a giant hourglass.

This is followed by False Witness where a glass of milk is drugged and gives anybody the potential to lie. Not a good thing as Steed and his department want to nail a villain for corruption and blackmail and are taking milk with their morning coffee.

These episodes make the way for file six which starts with The Morning After, a tale of London being evacuated so a bomb could be placed in the heart of it to make a ransom demand from a disgraced army General. Sadly, the villains did not take the factor of Steed hanging around to foil their plans.

This is then followed by Take Me To Your Leader where Steed and Tara follow a talking suitcase to several destinations to find a traitor in the department..."

A condensed and capsulated middle that I remember Dad helped me edit. But the ending was all down to me in selling this review to my tutor, I didn't hand in the tape log for marking but I did hand over this...

Monday 17th March 2003

"This set demonstrates the show at the tail end of its life. This was a show that was rich in colour, style and it defined an era of television for many decades. There are many that still talk about the adventures of Steed and his high kicking, sassy and beautiful assistants.

The Avengers captured Britishness completely and had this in its heart from the beginning. It created a world where anything could happen and always had the power to surprise the viewer, keeping them hooked from the start of the episode and whetting their appetite for the following week's instalment.

The Avengers is a statement of classic, it is an example of style and it was also the definition of the 1960s…"

I put a lot of my heart and soul into the writing of the review. It was here that my love for the writing was fully sparked up. I enjoyed handing over the finished assignment. I did not really care if it got anywhere in the prospectus at the time. But in the months that followed…

Tuesday 10th June 2003

"I got called aside by Rachel (my tutor) today. The review that I had written on The Avengers was looked at by all of the tutors on the English course. She told me that it was set to one side along with a few others as the possible start of a creative writing module that they want to kick into next year's syllabus. They want to put my review into the summer prospectus and they also want me to consider joining onto the course. I've spoken to Dad about it and he thinks that I should go ahead with it. I have until Thursday to give a decision to Rachel…"

We got the prospectus delivered to the house and Dad wanted to laminate and frame the piece that I had written. It was like a breath of fresh air.

I chose that summer to look into *The Avengers* online fan groups. The fans were fantastic people to chat to and listening to their stories was fascinating hear about. I wanted to keep the flame alive and I think that writing element of it was something that I wanted to fully consider at this point.

Not soon after I had started my second year of my English course I began on the creative writing sessions. Across the table from me was the woman who I was set to marry, Anna Lucas, not that I guessed anything of the sort to begin with. She was someone who enjoyed the written word and had read endless amounts of books that would leave us talking together for ages in the college courtyard. We soon began dating and my entries slowed up a little as we got closer. I think that I remembered how the entries were during my time with Charlotte. Either way, my romance did blossom considering we're now married.

The creative writing course opened my eyes. We were all allowed the time to go into research mode on the computers and I hit the fan pages once again. I came across one called *The Avengers Hub.* As you typed the website into the address bar you were greeted by John Steed doffing his bowler to you and welcoming you to the site. As I went through the site I found full episode guides, cast details, crew information. This site was one of the few that I could sit in front of for hours and hours on end. Anna had a hell of a time tearing me away from the college computers. But as the lessons continued, I was struck with an idea...

Friday 14th November 2003
"I've been considering taking my review and giving it over to The Avengers Hub. I haven't seen anything on the current DVD sets that are available apart from a notice to everyone that they're available to buy from all good retailers..."

In-between writing for the course and keeping a steady relationship going with Anna, who had yet to find out about my love for *The Avengers*, I put a second draft of the review into the mix. This time it contained the final Contender/Kult TV release on *The Avengers* DVD. It was not much but it added dimension to the original. I added to the information on what the episodes and explained at how the lack of possible features on the discs could put people off buying them. DVDs were well known for the wealth of material that could supplement the original programme. But with these releases, only the Emma Peel colour series had features clubbed together from the repeats on the Granada Plus channel.

I asked Anna to read it. It was here that she finally discovered my passion for the show and she could see the sincerity of my passion. Our friendship deepened rather than create a wall between the two of us. She gave me the idea that I contact the site creator with the idea of a new section on the site specifically for the DVD releases on the show. According to the next entry I was hesitant…

Tuesday 16th December 2003

"I submitted the review to Mike Hannigan of The Avengers Hub. I don't think that he would go along with the idea of having a section on the releases. It's his site after all and the last thing I want to do is be dictatorial. But Anna has been telling me that even if he turns down the review, the important factor is that I've tried and got it out there. She has a way of making me feel on top of the world. She also appears to be very tolerant regarding my passion for The Avengers…"

Over the years her tolerance has become acceptance. She has been captivated by the finding of all of my notebooks and tape logs. She has even been reading the books as we go to bed. Back to the review, it was coming up to Christmas and I was to get a present that was totally unexpected.

Monday 22nd December 2003

"Mike Hannigan got back in touch. He told me that he loved my review and intended to place a section on the releases onto the site. He had all the information on the Contender releases and wanted permission to use my review as a stepping stone to encourage other fans and visitors to the site to submit their own reviews of the releases. I told him that it would be a pleasure to have my work used for this measure and he seemed happy that I had responded happily to his request…"

In June the following year I passed the English course and had two certificates to my name. It had been a hard two years work but out of it. I had succeeded in accomplishing a creative writing course that would allow me to either continue in education or help me finding my way in the world of work. I was in a state of complete bliss.

Things with Anna moved quite quickly after the review was submitted. Living together came up. I was still living at home at this point and college was starting to slowly fade away from my regular routine. Anna and I would discuss at length what I wanted to do and I knew that I wanted it to be involved with *The Avengers*. It was a wild dream but it was something that I wanted to take full grasp of as the entries concurred...

Friday 20th August 2004
"There has to be something that I can do. There has to be something that I can place my imagination to and allow the pen to hit the page running..."

The fact that I wanted to do something concerning *The Avengers* was not present in this entry but it did occur after another chance meeting...

Thursday 16th September 2004
"I met an old school friend today, Luke Palmer. He's done well for himself. I had not seen him for so long and it would have been rude to refuse the invite for a drink. He told me that he was now running his own independent company and writing magazines for corporate companies. It does sound interesting. He asked me what I had been up to and I did feel embarrassed as I explained my current situation. You would like to tell people you're doing well but it's difficult to do so when things are not going well. Luke gave me his number and said that if a job opportunity came up he would be in touch..."

The call came a few weeks later. I started working in Luke's company in the printing room as part of a small team that formatted the papers and printed them before they were distributed. I did pretty well and the work was very much needed. But I still felt a little stifled. I had no idea of what I really wanted. From the next entry, Anna became my salvation…

Tuesday 12th October 2004
"Anna gave me a nice gift today, it was a book called The Avengers Files. It looks like an in depth character analysis of all the characters featured in the show."

I was soon enamoured of this book.

Thursday 14th October 2004
"This book is absolutely amazing. I have read almost half of it and the chapters on Steed are fantastic. They treat him as though the character is a real person and that we as a reader are discovering all that has gone on in this agent's brilliant career.

And it seems to follow on to capture all of Steed's partners from Dr Keel, Dr King, Venus Smith, Cathy Gale, Emma Peel, Tara King, Mike Gambit and Purdey.

This is fantastic and the writer, Mr Andrew Pixley would be thanked wholly and shook firmly by the hand if I ever met him. This is exactly what the show needs. It needs to be kept alive. The characters need to continue going on and reaching out to the world that does not know of them, to reach out to the fan base that already exists and celebrate in this fantastic show…"

The fuse was lit.

Monday 25th October 2004
"I had a meeting with Luke today about an idea that I've had. I love the job he has given me and it's paying the rent on the flat for myself and Anna.

But I told him today that I wondered if it was possible for me to use the facilities to make my own fan magazine for The Avengers.

He went silent for what appeared to be a lifetime but he's asked
me if he can think it over..."

The wait was unbearable. I remember the meeting. He looked at me stone faced as I told him that I want to write a magazine about a forgotten show from the 1960s. He just looked at me with a steel glare. I didn't write or record another entry after this one. He seemed to be avoiding me at work. I thought that I had better leave him alone seeing as now we were reduced to a simple nod to each other. Then it happened.

Thursday 4th November 2004
"Luke called me into the office at lunch today. He had given my
request consideration and he said the only way it could be done
would be outside of the company time due to the demands put
upon the company by outside clients."

I was unprepared for what followed.

"He then said that we would have to consider the people the
magazine would reach, how much we could charge per copy,
where we could sell.

We? He's openly offered to help set up and distribute the magazine
that I have in my head and has given me total control over
content. But I insisted that he take some portion of the editing
duties. He looked at me and said that when the finished copy is
ready he'll look at it gladly.

Anna and I have celebrated my triumph at securing what she calls
my first freelance job, even though I have another job that is going
towards half of the bills..."

But the work had only just begun.

End of entry.

Chapter 8
THE BIG THINKER

Tape is recording.
New entry begins.

The last of the stuff from Dad's attic has come out. The contents were full box folders clearly marked with "The Avengers" in bold blue permanent marker.

Both Anna and I were shocked when I opened the first file. It contained the very first magazine that I managed to create while working at Luke's. The cover was still in good shape if only for a few bends of the pages in the corner. I was amazed that Dad kept hold of anything, but this was a man that hoarded everything for over thirty years. I remember that Mum would tell him that there was clutter that she wanted him to finally sort out. The magazine was a labour of love for some time. I had help from all corners. Luke helped nearly every day with the editing and formatting after he had finished a very long day. Anna helped me find pictures that could be used for inclusion and even suggested what features to place into the first issue. The next entry reveals how Dad then placed his hand into this creative pocket...

Thursday 9th December 2004
"Dad has been going around some of the shops in town and has been calling in a few favours from his friends. He has asked them to place some copies of the magazine in their place of business, but he also asked them to only charge at a small rate. The charges were a subject that I had not considered as this is really a pure labour of love for me. But Dad said that you have to make some small profit from the endeavour.

I would prefer it to be a non-profit idea because this was something for fans of the show. For people that are interested in keeping the show and the characters alive and continuing to be glorious in our support and love for The Avengers. He thought that I was mad. He gave me one of those speeches that begin with the term 'these days…' I know that he means well but his vision for me includes a large leaning towards money. I can understand that but it will not be the case with this project."

I became bloody-minded about the whole thing after this entry. For the next few weeks I was hardly ever home. Luke and I were flat out exhausted by the end of the year. We had already decided against trying to push for a Christmas printing because at that time of year the whole factory was going into overdrive due to the needs of the clients on Luke's lists. As December made way to January, I was exhausted. Reading the notebook entries reveals I had never worked so hard in my entire life. But the next entry reveals that my overall energy level was taken from me a little bit.

Friday 7th January 2005
"I've just got in the door. I'm still a bit jazzed but I know that it's temporary. I know that by the time I eat the sandwich that Anna has left out for me, I'll be finding it hard to keep my eyes open. I really think that's it's been worth it. Luke and I are now in the process of making certain edits to the features that I have put into the issue."

I was soon surprised when the issue was printed in a run of over 500 copies. Luke decided to make it that number at first with a possible more to come. Dad had already found locations for me to place them; the chemist, the chip shop, the two corner shops that took up two sections of where Dad lived. The final place was a suggestion made by both Luke and Dad and it was to put some in the factory just in case anybody at work wanted to look at our efforts and pass the word around. With 100 copies at each location, we prepared for the big day. Luke and I went around to each place and handed over the first issue, bound in tight ribbon.

Looking at this first issue again, the front cover speaks out to me. It made an impression at the time as the entry reveals…

Monday 17th January 2005

"Well, there we go. The first issue of my new magazine about The Avengers has been given to the unsuspecting public. I love the title I came up with for it – Cult Champagne. It has a very Avengers ring to it and the logo that Luke came up with of a champagne bottle with the label reading 'Vintage Avengers' was quite fun with a small silhouetted picture of Steed in the champagne glass."

The first issue will now be broken down by its very proud creator.

"The front picture was Steed and Emma standing back to back as they did on the Lumiere video releases. Surrounding them were teasers of the upcoming features inside the magazine placed inside of bowler hats. The first page had the full table of contents inside next to a credits table. It then had a small letter from me welcoming the reader to a celebration of all things Avengers. The first feature then met the reader - a full on review of the only existing Ian Hendry episode, The Frighteners, with a descriptive plot synopsis, character outlines and production dates. In the bottom of the page I added a teaser. I knew from the various sources on The Avengers Hub that a second Ian Hendry episode had been discovered in America so I placed a 'Watch this space…' box with a small hint that we may be able to review this fantastic find."

From the first feature we now go to the middle section.

"The middle reveals a 'Villain of the month' section. Mr Teddy Bear was chosen for this issue. There was also a small table of Steed's favourite quotes, the top one being "Mrs Peel, we're needed." There was another table that I titled 'Driving Me Crazy' and was devoted to the cars driven by our favourite agents. The last part was done just for laughs: 'Mother Knows Best', a small instruction guide for anybody that wanted to work for the department in any capacity."

We then head to the final part of the issue…

"The section before the end of the issue was given to the DVD
review. I then put in another review, this time for Mr Andrew
Pixley's book, The Avengers Files. Luke then placed a few puzzles
onto the page - guess the agent through a mixed up picture
followed by a detailed crossword puzzle featuring all clues and
answers Avengers related. The back page was a small laugh put in
by Anna and is was to have Emma Peel holding a card telling the
reader that they're needed to keep more issues coming."

Anna was quite inventive in adding that to the back of the issue. In a short space of time I had convinced my partner and my boss to help me in creating a small, not very important magazine to help me get me enthusiasm for my favourite show out there into the world. After all the hype making the first issue of *Cult Champagne*, I returned to work. Luke had this great quality of reminding me that it was important to keep the money rolling in for the business. The dull routine came back to haunt me. But then, after a few weeks had passed.

Tuesday 8th February 2005
"I went into the chemist today to get Dad some cold and flu
tablets. I was taken aback by what happened. The chemist, Andy,
looked directly at me and asked me where the other copies of the
magazine are. Apparently, he has been endlessly harassed by some
customers who want a second issue."

Only a few weeks had passed since the first issue had been delivered and one place of delivery had already run out of 100 copies. The instinct to not charge anyone had been right and it had reached out to a certain target audience. I had some thinking to do.

Wednesday 16th February 2005
"I spoke to Anna about the so called demand for Cult Champagne
to return. She seems to want to go ahead with it and suggested

*numerous articles that I could place into the second issue. I'm a
little worried about a second issue…"*

I was filled with a blind panic but I went straight to Luke.

Friday 18th February 2005
*"I went into Luke's office to tell him about people wanting a
second issue of Cult Champagne only to find that he already had
a template for the second front cover up. I guess that he was aware
of how many we had 'sold' to the public."*

Easter was fast approaching and the second issue of *Cult Champagne*
was made to order. The work that we had done on the first issue had
prepared us for how tough it could be but strangely enough it became a
little bit easier. The hard task was finding different features as there was
only so much that you could cover. But it got underway, as the entry
reveals…

Thursday 24th February 2005
*"Work on this one has been thick and fast. We're all set to make
sure that the second issue gets to people for Good Friday. The focus
of this one has been on the personnel side of the show. The stars
will have the spotlight soon but both Luke and myself felt that
some people behind the scenes needed to be given some time in
Cult Champagne. I've been having great fun writing about Mr
Brian Clemens. This was a man that had written not only movies
but also for nearly every television series in the UK. That is what
you call an impressive CV. We've also touched on both composers
for the series – Mr John Dankworth and Mr Laurie Johnson.
Both of them appeared in pivotal moments of the shows history.
One composer was at the beginning where we saw the
introduction of a much emancipated woman. And the other
composer that saw the show become and international hit. We've
also looked at stunts from the show for a small section in this issue,
in particular the fight scene from the episode Mandrake where*

Honor Blackman famously knocked out a professional wrestler. The finishing touches are now being decided…"

An executive decision was then soon made.

Tuesday 8th March 2005

"Luke asked me into his office today. With all of the time that was being devoted to my little magazine it had been taking time away from the orders that he needed to send out and process. He has solved the problem. He has brought in some temps and gave some of my work load to them. Luke then told me that both he and I will work on the magazine so it can reach its target date. He also instructed me to go home and think up more ideas for more issues. He senses that the people interested in the magazine will want it to continue."

How many other bosses would do that? I think that I was extremely lucky. The second issue hit the places we had designated as our place of 'sale' on Good Friday as we had planned. But there was no time for me to rest as the next entry reveals…

Monday 28th March 2005

"Luke asked me about further issues. I told him that I had done nothing but think about further issues. He leapt upon the whole thing and told me to give over the ideas that I had. It was a weird ten minutes where he took the notes I had placed on a page in biro from my hand and with a large grin looked at me and said that we will do them…"

The ink had hardly got dry on the second issue before the third and fourth issues were being planned and put into motion. The third issue was devoted to the Cybernauts from the Emma Peel era. They appeared in two episodes and had their own episode in *The New Avengers* and Luke saw this as the series having a recurring villain. The features placed in the issue were quite fantastic. We gave a very sufficient piece of the limelight to the *New Avengers* episode *The Last of the Cybernauts…??* and gave attention to the reaction of Professor Mason when he sees traitor Felix Kane without his face mask. Issue 3 of *Cult Champagne* was very well received…

Wednesday 27th April 2005
"The chemist friend who is giving out my magazine has run out of copies we gave him on Monday and wants more. I told Luke and we delivered another 150 copies round to him. It seems that the features in this issue have struck a chord with some people."

It seemed like *Avengers* fans had united in support of my magazine. Issue 4 focused on the Emma Peel era mainly and I gave it the title of 'Diabolical Masterminds'. It was the second issue that we had produced in a four week timetable. We placed number four in the points of 'sale' on 23rd May 2005 and we made sure that we gave extra to everyone just in case we got another unexpected rush of people wanting the issue. Looking at the next entry, it's a good job that we had foresight…

Friday 27th May 2005
"Anna and I did some calculations today. Issue 3 of Cult Champagne made 450 copies and Issue 4 was at 400. So far, the magazine has accounted for 1650 copies 'sold' across its first four issues."

I took a little break from it after this entry. I needed a breather. I returned to the natural run of things whilst thinking on further issues. In the six weeks that followed I entered a level of creativity that I had never known before. I was thinking about *The Avengers* from the moment that I woke up and the ideas of what could go into the next edition were fun. But Luke was always trying to think further ahead than I was. Typical of a good businessman, he had made a plan in his head for us to follow as closely as we could. It was then time to resume *Cult Champagne* duties.

Tuesday 14th June 2005
"I was honest and told Luke that I had enough in my head to make more than one issue. His eyes lit up. But then he told me to give him all the information that I had."

I soon found out his reasons...

Thursday 16th June 2005

"Luke placed a large sheet in front of me with a plan of how all the information that I gave him could be put to good use. He told me that if the plan can be followed then we could keep to a monthly release date which would be good to keep the magazine alive..."

Over three months Anna, Luke and I went into overdrive on my little magazine. We made nine issues in three months, all of them devoted to Steed's female partners. In October 2005, we printed an up-to-date release guide for all of the books and videos on the show in Issue 15. But from reading the next entry, I needed to step back...

Saturday 12th November 2005

"I'm exhausted. I feel like I'm the servant of two masters. None of them are placing an unfair demand upon me but I'm struggling to get a little rest time."

Anna and I had hardly seen each other due to each other's work commitments at that time but she tells me that she insisted that I put the brakes on for a bit. It was not an easy task but I followed orders, to a small extent.

Friday 18th November 2005

"I've been doing hardly anything for nearly over a week. Work has been light at Luke's insistence and home life has been interesting as Anna wants me to strictly obey her orders. I've been re-reading the book by Mr Andrew Pixley, The Avengers Files. I've been devouring the sections concerning Steed. I find them fantastic as well as fascinating."

The light bulb above my head went on...

Saturday 19th November 2005

"I phoned Luke today for an idea about a special edition of Cult Champagne all about Patrick Macnee. Luke liked the idea but I told him that I wanted to stretch it over three issues so that it covers his career both pre- and post-Avengers."

The hard part was the research of Mr Macnee's career. But we eventually got there and on 12th December 2005 we presented the three issues. We definitely ended the year on a high but the strain of it showed...

Monday 19th December 2005

"I've told Luke that I need to consider the future of Cult Champagne. I think we went at it with passion but we also went at it like it was something that was feeding a business. The satisfaction at having produced 18 editions of a fan magazine that is being welcomed by the fans is brilliant. But the rate of it was something that I was not expecting..."

My small exhaustion was then replaced with creativity.

Thursday 22nd December 2005

"I think that Cult Champagne is worthy of a few more issues. But I'm thinking of spreading them out through the year. Maybe two or three editions as a collector's bundle?"

The idea went down a treat and the first issue produced for January 2006 was an interesting double feature.

Wednesday 4th January 2006

"Okay, we have printed the Patrick Macnee editions. They were fantastic. But now I've had an idea do an edition devoted solely to John Steed and cover the whole period of the series. Best episodes, favoured cars, favoured flowers for his buttonhole. I'm planning the works for it..."

I then added an unusual point.

"I also think that some consideration could be given to the amount of champagne used in the series. Especially when a fictional brand was used, Meudon and Heim. I think that's worthy of a contribution."

I listed exactly how many episodes the champagne appeared in. They were mainly the Tara King episodes but nevertheless we included the Meudon and Heim champagne guide as separate Issue 20. For the summer, I chose to focus on the various criminal groups that bugged *The Avengers*. Issue 21 focused on Intercrime, Issue 22 focused on the Golden Fleece Fund and Issue 23 focused on Bibliotek. It was a raging success when we got them out in July 2006. As an extra addition, we made Issue 24 to coincide with the villain group series. It was an in depth feature on the Ian Hendry episode *Hot Snow*. We titled it 'Hot Beginnings'.

The autumn releases would cover Issues 25 to 28 and I decided to make each one about the variety of bosses that Steed had reported to. We called it 'The Boss Bonanza' and the selection that was sourced for the issues were One-Ten, Disco, Charles, Quilpie and Mother. I remember that the winter ones were a rush because Luke wanted to get anything printed and out of the place before the Christmas holidays and that included *Cult Champagne*. So to finish the year off we printed Issues 29 and 30 as 'Unsung Partners' and devoted the issues to Dr Martin King and Venus Smith.

The year had gone by quickly but as I look at the issues of *Cult Champagne* in the box folders it was quite a fruitful year. But things did need to change according to the next entry…

Tuesday 9th January 2007
"All of the features that I've written have taken a bit out of me but I feel that unless I take a step back I'll hit a block on a subject that I know pretty well…"

I panicked about writer's block. There was a substantial breather between the next editions that were put out due to my fears and concerns.

For April 2007, we made the second to last bundle of *Cult Champagne*. It was called 'The Undercover Series' and covered the undercover roles performed by Cathy in *The Gilded Cage*, Emma in *Room Without A View* and Tara in *Whoever Shot Poor George Oblique Stroke XR40?* I think after this effort I was truly exhausted. The bundles did split the year up but they also required twice the effort to make them reach the deadlines.

I requested a holiday from work. I took Anna to our favourite cottage in the country. I also proposed and we decided to marry quickly. On 19th May 2007, I became a happily married man. From this next entry, it appears that I returned from my honeymoon to a proposition.

Friday 8th June 2007

"Luke rang and left me a message to ring him immediately. He told me that he understood that I did not want to feel pressured with work but he suggested that we ease the burden by allowing the fans to bring in some fan fiction. Whole issues of Cult Champagne could be devoted to their stories. I immediately agreed we've arranged to make the factory a place for all the fiction to be sent to. I've said that I will do another special edition so they could know where to send the fiction to."

Cult Champagne Issue 34, released July 2007, was called 'Let's Find Doctor Keel' – a small plea to anybody if they knew where all of his missing episodes were. As Luke's idea took hold, the magazine went back to a monthly format from August to November 2007. It was a much needed breather where the only work being done on it was reading and placing all the letters and stories that we got sent. But as 2008 approached, the entries reveal that I was feeling contemplative.

Thursday 20th December 2007

"I haven't really adjusted to everything I've gone through recently. I'm a husband now but I've hardly spent time with my wife. And to top it off I'm still writing a journal like a silly school boy. I suppose I'm just griping for the hell of it. I'm quite happy thinking about Cult Champagne, but I think I need to return to work. I need to be a wage slave for a while."

My words proved themselves a little prophetic come the New Year…

Friday 11th January 2008
"Luke brought me into his office today for the first time in ages.
He told me that we would soon have to call it a day on the
printing of Cult Champagne. The books need to be balanced at
the factory and work needs to resume quickly. In one way I'm
relieved but in another I'm sad to let it go."

It was a very good run and we ended it by making another bundle package. *Cult Champagne* finished with Issues 39 to 41 devoted to 'Medical Criminals' and spotlighted the episodes *Second Sight, From Venus With Love* and *You'll Catch Your Death* respectively. I added a thank you letter to everyone that picked up and read a copy of my little magazine, telling everyone that it had been a pleasure to give them something that they enjoyed. I remember feeling very saddened. I suppose when you devote a lot of your time to something it becomes a part of you and a lot of hard work went into the 41 editions of *Cult Champagne*.

But from what I'm reading, the work done on the magazine had ignited a spark in me.

Wednesday 23rd January 2008
"I can't switch off. I've done so much writing that I cannot seem
to get it all out of my system. Maybe it's because my writing on
The Avengers has fulfilled and awakened a desire in me…?"

My awakened desire was to be fully explored over the coming months.

End of entry.

Chapter 9
REQUIEM

New tape is recording.
New entry has begun.

I had roughly three productive years with the making and success of *Cult Champagne*. It was unbelievable. The features that I produced for the Issues were time consuming and it would give me whole days to come up with the text required as I ended up writing five to seven features at a time. I remember being happy that I was allowed a breather because I had painted myself into a corner with the production of the whole thing. I was extremely lucky to have two people that were supporting me in the whole venture. Without that, I don't think that it would have got passed one issue let alone forty.

My love for *The Avengers* was still there. The tide had not turned. If I had to choose a favourite issue to write and work on it had to be the 'Boss Bonanza' series. I think One Ten was the strait laced one, Disco was the keeper of secrets, Quilpie was the man for the official records, and Charles handed out the assignments and loved to bend or break the rules. And then we had Mother who ran the whole roost with a rod of iron, a temperament that was sometimes more down than up but a trust in his top agent John Steed that was unfaltering. It was not much but for me it was a definite labour of love. But as things died down, this next entry reveals that there was a whiplash effect.

Monday 12th May 2008
"I've been so bored recently. All of that work on Cult Champagne is now to become a memory. I have had the thought of asking Luke of we could restart the whole series but I know what the answer would be. I was staring out the window so hard that my eyes kept relaxing every five minutes. I would love to still be doing Cult Champagne. It was a chore at times but I thought it had a

*few more issues to give. I've re-read the last Cult Champagne issue
over a million times through this week. We were doing so well
with it. We had features that were being rated as fantastic by our
readers. We had fan fiction coming in that was absolutely
fantastic. Why is it that in life we want something so much that
when we get there something has to happen for it to be taken from
us?"*

With *Cult Champagne* I can only look back on it more with pride
than regret. I achieved something with my fandom of *The Avengers*. It may
have been small but I got there. I knew that I was not going to give up on
the dream. It was almost as though I was a preacher selling the importance
of *The Avengers* to his congregation. I had a religion in *The Avengers* and I
was happy to shout it out loud. I would religiously watch it, after all. But I
refused to give up on the dream.

Thursday 15th May 2008
*"I wonder what would happen if I approached the rights holders
of The Avengers with the idea of making Cult Champagne into a
fully fledged fan magazine. I spoke about it with Luke in the
canteen today. He thinks that it would be a challenge in itself. My
response was simple; I don't care."*

The idea soon fizzled…

Friday 16th May 2008
*"Anna sat me down tonight. She caught a glimpse of a letter I've
written to The Avengers rights holders and thinks that it would be
a wasted exercise.*

*She supports the thought but she does not want the mood to be
broken when they tell me that they would prefer any projects to be
done by their in-house team. But my argument was that there is
nothing new being done on The Avengers."*

I went a little bit mad…

"Why wouldn't anyone welcome an idea that could celebrate one of the greatest TV shows to come out of the 1960s? This is where I blame the movie for everything. It's made everybody think that The Avengers should stay in the past to gather dust without ever being allowed to move forward into a new territory. Why would they be so closed minded? It would keep the characters in people's minds and it could finally shake away the bitter aftertaste left behind by that stupid movie."

Ouch!

"Here we have a show that lasted the entire length of the Sixties, was a television staple, launched the career of some of its major stars, set several trends including the fashions that were worn in the programme, showed that a woman could be the equal of a man, had a style of its own which makes it endurable… and yet everyone refuses to allow a breath of fresh air to be blown onto this absolutely brilliant show."

I was planning to take this argument to the rights holders of the show. I would have begged for them to consider what I was telling them and to allow me the chance to try and re-awaken the visions of the show. But as the next entry reveals, the dream was soon over after some thought…

Saturday 24th May 2008
"I've been thinking on what Anna said to me and I hate to say that she has a point. Why would the rights holders of The Avengers consider that I have anything to offer in keeping this classic series alive in the minds and hearts of any viewer and fan…?"

The main problem here was that the creative tap still wanted to run but everyone wanted me to turn it off. I just did not want to give up on the dream of somehow knowing that I had contributed to someone learning how great a TV show that *The Avengers* was and still is. I spoke about it to Anna and she got onto it straight away.

Thursday 28th May 2008

*"Anna contacted a friend of hers today that runs his own
publishing company. She told him that I was responsible for Cult
Champagne and he was a fan who owned all of the issues that we
printed. He phoned me this afternoon and said that although
there is hardly enough money in it to make me a fortune it would
at least give me the opportunity to keep the creative muscle flexed.
It was probably the most productive and quickest phone call I've
ever had in my life. We talked over some possible ideas that I
could work on and then he told me to keep thinking and call him
if I have anything to hand over to him."*

I was scribbling away like a maniac trying to forge together a story
that could make sense. I had no idea of what I could write but I believed
that I could do it.

Anna then had the master stroke of telling me to make a list of all the
trials that my character would go through. I looked to my muse and once
again, *The Avengers* had come to my rescue. The next step happened
instantly according to this next entry…

Friday 29th May 2008

*"I've got my central character and I'm currently building the story
around him. This guy will not have it easy. His father left him
and his mother when he was a child and he was very nearly put
into care because his mother who was working so hard to try and
keep the roof over their heads. He then finishes school and goes
straight into working for a local supermarket chain. He then puts
himself through college and immediately decides that he wants to
follow in the footsteps of his favourite film icons. The big screen is
his big adventure and he wants to get there at whatever cost. He
leaves his mother and sets himself on the path to riches by scoring
an audition playing his own agent. But he gets laughed out of the
audition due to the fact that he is not well educated. He goes to
college and studies hard to get his qualification and in that time
he studies the classics of theatre. He then gets an agent and puts*

119

him to work. He then scores several auditions while working various jobs to try and pay the rent."

And breathe…

"I showed this rough outline to Anna. She was quite critical of it and has showed me where points in the plot can be brushed up and pulled back on. She then insisted that I send this to her publisher friend. I called him and told him that I had been figuring out a story to write and present to him. He was all over it and gave me his email so I could send it immediately."

Soon after that email was sent…

Sunday 31st May 2008
"Anna's friend, Mark got back in touch about my storyline possibility. He loves it and insists that I begin writing it immediately."

In June 2008 I was once again the servant to two masters. Only this time, the pace of everything was being decided by me. Within the first month I had written two chapters and placed my character at the beginning of his struggles to get to his goal of stardom. I told Luke about what I was doing and he instantly asked whether he could edit it for me. I said yes instantly. But I was not prepared for how brutal his edit was going to be as the next entry reveals.

Tuesday 24th June 2008
"I've only just managed to finish the polishing of both chapters one and two. It's as though Luke went through every word of every sentence to assess its meaning in relation to the story. I almost don't want to hand it back to him in case he takes the edit and rips it to pieces."

Luke and I knocked the whole thing into shape. Mark had an input also. He was publishing it after all. Within five months we had a completed story. My character, John Jason came from nothing. He admired all of the movies he watched and adored the stars in them He then thought that he could take a gamble and enter the world of the spotlight. He struggled through the ridicule, the scorn and the rejection. He pursued his dream and became an understudy to one of his favourite actors in a West End stage play. Although he had rehearsed the part backwards, a bout of the flu met his favoured actor and thrust John into the spotlight on the centre of the stage. From that one performance he was hailed as a success. He was a man that had come from rags to riches. The story ended with his return home to his mother to give back all that she had given to him. But there was a problem…

Thursday 9th October 2008

"I still cannot think of a title for this book. My first attempt at something and I've written the whole thing without giving it a title…"

Anna then gave me a title and also gave her publisher friend an idea for the front cover. The title was 'Food for the Soul' and the picture was to be a boy looking at a giant cinema screen, smiling at his favourite scene. It was quite a fun piece of work to write and it was my first venture away from the world of John Steed.

But the world of *The Avengers* was never going to be far behind me. I started thinking about how I could immerse myself in another goal. This time I could try putting a stamp on my favoured classic TV show. But I was also looking for someone who shared my vision, somebody who also thought that the show was wonderful. Then by chance I discovered something online.

Saturday 11th October 2008

"I was trawling through some things online and I just thought I would type in The Avengers to the address bar. The page hits that came up pointed to something. It was a site called The Avengers Forever (TAF for short). I clicked on the site. Anna said that today was the most she has seen me stare at the computer screen. This site is quite comprehensive. It even has screen shots of the Ian

Hendry episodes that they found in America. Plus the episode
guides are quite detailed with fun facts and trivia, including the
stars that graced the Bond series after being associated with The
Avengers. Even the pages on The New Avengers have been given
the same due care and attention which is something I applaud..."

This new find was to be the mainstay of my enjoyment for the next few months. I went through the whole thing section by section. All the pages garnered my interest and I was a fan that was hooked on what the site had to offer. But no updates were occurring. I did check regularly but nothing.

I carried on looking at TAF. The connection with it was not as strong as I wanted because I felt that this site had somehow given up the ghost. It seemed to have been a labour of love that was now a museum piece for anybody wanting to visit it.

That Christmas saw the pressing and printing of my book and although I was happy with this, I returned to Luke's factory to pick up the pace on my day job. He had offered me a pay rise of £3 due to the demand that I had kept up with over that period, but I later discovered that he had sold an issue of *Cult Champagne* to a friend of his in the publishing world for the hand to hand price of £3. The book reached 77 copies before the heat on it went cold.

The New Year was then entered with gusto but I was asking Luke to give me as much overtime that he could offer. The reason for this is in this next entry…

Thursday 15th January 2009
"I've never felt so low. It has nothing to do with the book neither.
I knew that there would not be much interest in my story and
there is only so much door beating that you can do and hear the
word no. I sent an email to Mark and thanked him for putting
the book into print. He did help me out of a creative jam. We
have a massive amount of back log at the factory. I offered to stay
on with the night staff to get everything done. The last thing that
I want to do is to be sat at home and pondering all that has not
happened. All that I want to happen could never happen…."

The work became more over the next couple of months and it caused many arguments between Anna and me. I had a routine of get up, go to work, come home, eat dinner, watch an episode of *The Avengers* to de-stress from work, go to bed. I followed that routine for over three months and it was coming up to April before a massive head to head clash occurred...

Tuesday 31st March 2009
"I just had one of the worst fights with Anna since we married.
She keeps telling me to snap out of the depressive state that I've
put myself in. Her words were that it was degrading to know that
she was married to somebody that was being so pathetic."

My wife has a plain way of speaking. I had hardly been out of the house for months and I had not engaged with anyone on a social level, including her. I must have been a nightmare. I seemed to be angry at the world. Anna decided to add her own remedy and dragged me out of the house to dinner away from home. By the end of the night I was telling her how disappointed I had been with myself. All my effort and hard work had come to nothing and nobody seemed to be paying attention to the ideas I had. I still thought that I could contact the rights holders to *The Avengers*. Anna then surprised me.

Wednesday 9th April 2009
"My wife is someone very special. After all of this time telling me
not to follow any direct avenue in my appreciation of The
Avengers she is now championing me to come up with something
to send off to the powers that be..."

I began jotting down an idea for a possible book. I was not sure how I would present it to anybody but the next task was to get the correct name for the rights holders to the show. I went back to *The Avengers Forever* website and found out that most of the pictures on the site had the name StudioCanal upon them.

Tuesday 21st April 2009

"I sent off an email to StudioCanal. I simply asked them if they would consider giving me the permission to write a book with the characters from the show. A story surrounding John Steed and his association with Dr David Keel seeing as it's the first partner Steed worked with and it's the first series that is still thin on the ground in terms of episodes. I just thought that it would be a way to slowly open the opportunity of more than one book and open a new generation's eye to this fantastic show."

I kept checking my emails for over a month and I even telephoned the company to check that the email had arrived. The patience level was tested right up until I received the reply...

Monday 25th May 2009

"StudioCanal replied to me. They're not interested in my ideas. They prefer to handle something in-house and thank me for my interest in this great series."

Anna was right but at least I gave it a shot. The depressive cycle returned quickly. The main reason was because the fights with Anna became more but my week was set to get worse.

Wednesday 27th May 2009

"Luke called a meeting today. He announced that he was planning to sell over the company. He thanked us all for our service and told us that our contracts would last until next year as per everyone's individual agreements. He then offered us the hope that the company that took over would keep us on."

Trouble came in threes, it would appear...

Friday 29th May 2009

"Anna left me a message on my mobile today telling me to ring her urgently. She told me that Dad had collapsed at work. I rushed to the hospital and they told me the worst; he has a blocked

artery and they needed to perform emergency surgery. He was in recovery when I got to the hospital but it was still touch and go. I kept telling him to retire. There was no need for him to keep being stressed out by a job. He had put in enough hours over the years. Give it up, Dad. You've done your duty and along the way you've proved yourself to be an amazing father that taught me everything I hold dear..."

That was not a good week at all as I contended with a possible dream turned down and in ruins, a redundancy coming up and my father critically ill. I took leave from work so that I could visit Dad frequently. He was home a couple of weeks later but Anna had made sure that a bed had been set up for him downstairs. It was at this point that he allowed us to look into a bungalow for him. I was feeling so low. The only things that were able to console me were my wife and *The Avengers*. But even that was wearing a little. Being knocked back by the rights holders was trying to leave a taste of ash in my mouth. Instead I was trying to give my own style of counselling. I would tell myself that *The Avengers* is great. It is fantastic and it will be given the due that it rightly deserves. I then went back to my online searches and found the perfect tonic as the next entry reveals...

Wednesday 24th June 2009
"I went online to look out for my fellow enthusiasts on The Avengers. I did not expect to find anything new in the lists that I normally trawl through. I then came across a new site. It's called The Avengers Declassified and from the moment that I saw the home page I've become hooked. This site is completely amazing. It's full of images and from the looks of it and it seems to want to go in depth with everything that the show is..."

I had found a kindred spirit in a website and it had allowed the fire in my heart for the show to be relit. The surprises from this wonderful find continued to keep coming.

Thursday 23rd July 2009

"Oh my god! The Avengers Declassified is lifting the lid on the first series. This is amazing. The articles about the whole creation of the show from its beginnings lying in the Ian Hendry show Police Surgeon and from that programme's ashes came The Avengers with a whole creative team behind it. The pictures are also great. Some of them I recognise from the books that I own. I cannot get enough of this site."

My enjoyment was to continue...

Wednesday 19th August 2009

"I am having the greatest day as an Avengers fan. Today, I have read the entire set up of the missing first episode of The Avengers. Hot Snow has finally been given the once over and now we know what happens during the second and third acts which are still missing. This is brilliant! We get to see the first meeting between Steed and Keel and we also find out the whole story of what was behind Peggy's murder and why Steed sought Keel out in the first place. It's brilliant. The Avengers Declassified is the greatest site in the world."

It was not long before my soul was fed once again.

Friday 21st August 2009

"At last! The first and second series of The Avengers is to be released on DVD by Optimum Releasing, a division of their owners StudioCanal. I have a little bit of a wait but it promises to be good..."

It lived up to its promise...

Friday 23rd October 2009

"I finally managed to buy and order my set of The Avengers first and second series. It arrived in the post today. My jaw dropped immediately. Finally, the show has been given a home video

126

release that is worthy of its greatness. The features on it are absolutely amazing. It has interviews with cast, audio commentaries on episodes, documentaries featuring the shows very first producer Mr Leonard White, it has a reprint of the brochure to advertise the second series in 1962, it has PDF content for the computer, filmed introductions on some of the episodes. I'm in seventh heaven."

My joy was uncontained…

"Every episode from Series 2 is here. And finally I get the chance to see what is left from the Ian Hendry era. The first act of Hot Snow, the shot live and recently found Girl on the Trapeze and the stalwart episode that was thought to be the only one left from the first series, The Frighteners. But the fantastic edition to this set has to be the scrapbook from Leonard White. It's fantastic; it gives us a glimpse of what the missing episodes looked like thanks to John Cura's Telesnap photographs. It's a pity that they start from episode thirteen, One for the Mortuary, rather than the start but at the end of the day, who cares? This is amazing and shows us all what we are missing. This shows us what the Ian Hendry era gave to this brilliant show and it makes me firmly believe that the other missing episodes could still be out there. If they found Girl on the Trapeze, which was shot live and should not exist at all, then anything is possible…"

I was drowning in my love for *The Avengers*. I went through all eight discs in the series two set with joyous abandon. I then would re-watch them. I was making the scrapbook in the set look weathered with my constant reading and looking at the images of the missing episodes.

I then felt a little bit reflective. My *Cult Champagne* magazine was an attempt to show people just how brilliant this show was and it appeared that StudioCanal were firmly in the process of doing that. I felt a little let down that I could not be a part of it in some way. Further sets were to come on the show. The next one was the third series which was the last series to feature Honor Blackman as Cathy Gale. As I waited patiently for my next addition to my collection, Luke finally admitted that he had a new job in the offering which was why he was selling the business. I understood his wanting to progress in his career but he would not tell me what his new prospective job was. He apologised for my redundancy which I chose to take on the chin. Series 3 then arrived in my possession.

Friday 19th February 2010

"I may already possess this third series but this collection and its bundle of features puts the Kult TV set into the shade. This set contains the Avenging the Avengers documentary that was only available on VHS, filmed introductions from the early 1990s repeats of third season episodes on Channel 4, another brochure reprint from 1963/1964, more audio commentaries with episode writers and directors and more PDF material."

I was then to be firmly elated with the next find on this particular set.

"Oh my god! They've produced a full reconstruction of two episodes from Series 1. This is brilliant! Double Danger is on disc four and, having watched the reconstruction twice, I wish that this episode could be found. On disc five was A Change of Bait and from the look of it appears to be a weird tale involving fraud over a cargo of bananas. That part of the story I found quite funny."

As the year went on the Diana Rigg series were released and I was hooked on the reconstructions that were done for each set. They were an absolute thrill with even the smaller reconstructions being given an equal taste of the limelight. But I was happier about the fact that *The Avengers* was being dusted off and being taken out of the world of complete reference. The show was now being given back to both its old and its new audience. I was now feeling liberated to shout out on the roof tops that *The Avengers* was the best series in the whole world. I would have succeeded if Anna had not threatened to divorce me if I even attempted the stunt. Christmas that year was a little bittersweet as the entry reveals.

Thursday 23rd December 2010

"Luke surprised me with a visit today but it was not with his usual cheerful outlook. The company had kept me on in spite of wanting to replace staff. Now it was my turn and the new chairman wanted Luke to break the news to me in case I went into a towering rage. I had seen it coming for months so I knew it was only a matter of time before the new broom brought in staff from other territories to take over the old guard. I telephoned the chairman, Michael. I thanked him for keeping me employed passed the year grace period that I had on my contract. It was civil and I was proud of myself for not being spiteful. Both Luke and Anna made me smile again with their early presents – The Avengers Series 6 Optimum set alongside The New Avengers Optimum release set that features commentaries from Mr Brian Clemens and the late Mr Gareth Hunt. A wonderful Christmas thanks to wonderful people."

The tide was not about to turn any time soon on the job front for me. I was searching for a new source of income at the start of the New Year…

Tuesday 11th January 2011

"The factory shifts that are being offered are mainly for cleaners. Sadly the people that want a job can't get one due to the fact that there is nothing out there. Of all times to be placed jobless in a recession it had to happen to me."

My melancholy, my spirit and my dreams were soon to be soothed, uplifted and re-awoken as *The Avengers* rescued me once again with the announcement of its 50th birthday celebrations.

End of entry.

Chapter 10
A SENSE OF HISTORY

Tape is recording.
Here goes my final entry.

Upon the discovery of the *Avengers* 50th anniversary proceedings, I desperately searched for a job with the goal to try and secure tickets to both days celebrating the show. It was an event that I did not want to miss. I went onto *The Avengers Declassified* and saw a large orange poster on the site advertising the event. But the world of work was a tough scenario. We were still in a bad recession and the job market was rising in unemployment. I had used the last of my factory overtime money on paying the bills and there was no way that I was going to allow Anna to carry me with my responsibilities. The whole house was near flooded with job papers scribbled on or highlighted to within an inch of their life. I was desperate for anything. With Anna's support and my determination to fully celebrate *The Avengers*, I spent a month looking for a permanent piece of employment. But as this entry reveals, luck was thin on the ground…

Tuesday 8th February 2011
"I've been searching for months now for a job. People are reading my CV and just tossing it aside. Does my experience of getting up in the morning and working all the hours under the sun really go against me?"

I had a goal that I wanted to achieve and it was attainable if somebody would give me the chance to prove my worth. I eventually did get to the interview stage about a month later. I had to sign onto the dole. But then the tide turned…

Thursday 17th March 2011

"I had an interview today at a supermarket store. I think that it went well. They told me that they're celebrating their fifth year in business and were always on the lookout for new staff members to join their team. They seemed impressed by my CV and the reference from Luke would give them more than adequate ammunition to consider me for one of their backroom workers..."

I was told that I could start that Monday. It was nice to be back at work but this work was a little bit lighter than what I had been used to. We were a very small team and we were all expected to perform a shopping list of things each day. You were given more than your own allotted shift to do. In any day it was always a mixture of sorting the pallets out the back and then there was the endless double checking of the orders that came from the suppliers.

I was now able to try and put some money to one side to attend the 50th anniversary celebration of *The Avengers*. The pay was okay and I only had a small handful of money each month left for me after I had deducted my half of the bills. Anna did offer to help me out. I refused her help. She worked hard for her money and I did not want her to be paying for me when she could treat herself to something.

Working in the back rooms of a supermarket compared to a proper factory is not much of a change but the treatment of the staff is very unique. At the factory there was a sense of comradeship and laughs were to be had all over from the staff to the upper management. Here at the supermarket it was a case of know your place, mind your manners and speak when you are spoken to. There were times when it really did get on my nerves. I piled up the overtime. I was even working a number of night shifts. It would make a considerable sum at the end of the month. What could I do? I needed the money.

I had made the choice of getting the tickets to Chichester for the event at their University in May. Anna had looked around for places to stay and we were all in the process of putting the final touches to everything that I had planned and aimed for. But as this next entry reveals, trouble is never far away...

Monday 2nd May 2011

"We were warned at work today that there was a problem with payroll. They had made mistakes with a few people's hours and the money they were supposed to be given. I've been silently praying that it does not happen to me."

My prayers were not answered...

Monday 9th May 2011

"I went to check my wages and found there was less there than there should be. I then checked my wage slip and the amount of over £2,000 that I've earned in the last month or so has not been paid to me. I've received £300 for the month and a hearty apology from my manager. I wanted to throw myself over the desk and throttle him."

All the work and all the wages that could have gone towards me and Anna having a wonderful time in Chichester celebrating *The Avengers* went immediately out of the window. Anna could not help me at the time either and I was not going to beg friends for financial help to get me out of the rut I had been put in. June came and went. I wanted to cry like a child at having to miss the celebration of the show I loved so much. I was left wondering what the days would have been like. To add insult to my injury, the event was being hosted by Mr Paul O'Grady who is one of the best enthusiasts of *The Avengers*. To have met him would have been amazing as Anna and I love his daytime show. When the wages were corrected the following month, I handed in my notice. The treatment I was receiving at the hands of everybody would make me feel horrible nearly every day. I went straight back to the job searches.

Thursday 14th July 2011

"I've never felt more liberated by leaving the supermarket behind but the job market is still as low on the ground as it was before. My dream of celebrating The Avengers is up in smoke, my writing ideas have joined them and I'm barely scraping by with my half of the bills..."

Bitterness mixed with self pity. It did not remain for long as there was a saviour in the darkness as the entry unfolds.

Tuesday 26th July 2011
"Luke telephoned me today. He leapt for joy when I told him that I was jobless as he wanted to offer me some employment. It's the same position that I had at the previous factory but the location is about fifty miles away from where I'm living. It would mean early starts to get to work each morning but the pay is good and all the other extra's that I had before in my favour would be there also. I accepted instantly. I start on Thursday."

It was not long before I was back on track financially. The environment was a much friendlier atmosphere and I was made to feel like part of the community rather than an outcast.

But I was still sporting wounds from missing the 50th anniversary event in Chichester. I went online and found videos from the event. It looked amazing and the pictures that were taken of all of the various guests were fantastic. But the video that brought most pride, joy and a tear to my eye was Patrick Macnee's video address to everyone. At 89 years of age at the time, he still had a twinkle in his eye and even now I can still picture an *Avengers* world where John Steed has been knighted on his 90th birthday for service to his country. I then had an interesting moment whilst out shopping with Anna…

Thursday 11th August 2011
"I ran into my old headmaster in town today. He recognised me instantly but he remembered that I was a massive fan of The Avengers. He asked if we could swap numbers and we did so."

The reason why came a little later…

Saturday 13th August 2011
"My old headmaster revealed to me why he wanted my number. He has become a chairman of a Culture Society and after seeing me he wondered whether I would be interested in doing a talk to

the society about The Avengers. He revealed that he had a copy of my book, Food for the Soul and thinks that I could impress on the society the cultural impact of Sixties television."

I was flattered but immediately laid down a ground rule.

"I told him that I would not cover all the television of the Sixties and would only focus on The Avengers. For me, that particular show is paramount. He agreed to let me talk about any aspect I wanted. I agreed to do it."

I spoke to Anna about it and she likened me to a church minister about to talk to his congregation. I was happy to be billed as the guest speaker and it would occur one afternoon when I was available. I was never good at making speeches and if I wanted to preach about *The Avengers* I would do it from a car with a good sound system that could blast out the theme tune around every street. I asked Luke if I could have the time off. He allowed it instantly and told me that he would be there in the crowd cheering my cause.

I spent a couple of weeks deliberating what I would cover in my talk. I considered my audience. These are people that take pieces of history and go in depth of how important they are to Britain or people as a whole. I was unsure whether television entered the equation. But it was *The Avengers* and I was full of beans to talk about it. Anna had got me the *50th Anniversary Collection* from Optimum Releasing for my birthday and I started to watch the 39 discs all in order. I was writing away like a mad demon. Within two days I had constructed what I wanted to say. It was a beautiful Saturday afternoon for the speech and I was ushered into a hall that was littered with fine examples from British history. There was a makeshift stage that had a podium placed upon it. I did not focus on anything other than what I wanted to say with the John Dankworth version of *The Avengers* theme playing over and over again in my head.

I was then introduced and took my place at the podium. I committed the finished speech to tape before it was drafted.

Saturday 3rd September 2011

"Ladies and gentleman… Television captures us all. We all have favourite characters that we follow every day or every week. We love to know every aspect of their personality that has been channelled so well by the actor playing the role. We love to view the situations that they're a part of because we know deep in our hearts that they can either escape it, have created it or are a part of a plot that requires them to be a pivotal part of our enjoyment. Television gives us an escape. It gives us a world that we can admire and see as the ideal place to retreat to. It is the bubble where anything could happen. I have existed in this bubble for a good number of years and it is this that has brought me here today."

Subtle introduction.

"In 1960, the world was at the beginning of a new social time. Throughout that decade people went through a variety of points that are still with the world today. It was the time of what is seen now as a Golden Age. Art, culture, music and television were at the forefront of this Golden Age. And one particular television show demonstrated its potential to speak to its audience. It gave them the escape that they were looking for and it invited them into the world where anything could literally happen."

Good build-up.

"The Avengers was created by a team that consisted of Canadian producer Sydney Newman, producer Leonard White and a pool of scriptwriters. It was forged from the ashes of a series called Police Surgeon that starred an upcoming young actor whose talent shined out from the screen like a beacon, Mr Ian Hendry. The vehicle was found for him and the first paving slab for this remarkable series was laid down. The premise was a simple one; a young doctor has his fiancée murdered in front of him with no explanation and it becomes the catalyst for the doctor to meet a

shady secret agent that helps him track the killers. This shady contact is a debonair and suave man and the gods were shining down from the sky with the actor chosen and cast into the role of this contact. The secret agent was John Steed and the man that played him is the fantastic Mr Patrick Macnee."

Upcoming sadness...

"My description of this first year is sadly all that we have in existence of its inception. Most of the Ian Hendry era is lost apart from two and a half episodes of the 26 that were made. There is anger at this on my part, ladies and gentlemen, mainly because nobody likes an incomplete collection."

Pause for laughter...

"But the problem with this is that we are not able to see how things were within the television landscape. The Avengers started off as a male partnership and the world of the male was not to be challenged as forcefully as it would be. The appeal of The Avengers first series is all encompassing. I am one of the many that want the remaining twenty four episodes discovered and put into formats for the fans to enjoy. That first year laid the foundations of a strong show. A show that was to change with the times with each year and it preceded all of the contemporaries that stood side by side with it. But Ian Hendry's year with The Avengers has suffered, ladies and gentlemen. Due to the nature of business and the way history has chronicled its inclusion in the television landscape, Dr David Keel was made to seem like a one hit wonder. A character that was not as pivotal to The Avengers make up as everybody else. This is a stigma that has endured for over thirty years and it has buried the main factor of the series ultimate success. The Avengers was the vehicle for Mr Ian Hendry. Without Mr Hendry and his character of Dr David Keel, The Avengers could easily have not forged ahead and

136

continued. We would not have seen the innovations that came out of it without this first laid paving stone."

End of Act One…

"As we entered the second year of this fantastic show, Mr Hendry had decided to leave. Mr Macnee came to the forefront and the producers chose to make John Steed the central character. We then saw the next paving stone being laid and it was a very important one, ladies and gentlemen. 1962 was to begin a new age in the way that the world saw the female of the species. For too long a woman had been seen as someone who belonged tied to the kitchen sink, someone who should be subservient to a male's needs and someone who should know their place without being told. The Avengers changed the entire perception of women being a wallflower and it was with the creation of a character called Mrs Catherine Gale. A strong woman from the first moment, this was a lady that was a successful anthropologist. A woman that could handle herself in any situation no matter what it was or who she was up against. This character was embodied by Honor Blackman who showed to all of the viewers that were watching that if a woman was hit, that woman could hit back twice as hard. Liberation had begun and The Avengers was the first to demonstrate this by having John Steed partnered with this strong woman. But he was not only partnered with this lady. She was his equal and he knew it. He knew that she could rescue him for a change and he revelled in the fact that the woman was an independent sex that could handle itself. But the stigma from year one followed a little into year two. Around the world we do not hear of Cathy Gale as a pioneer for what a woman was capable of. She was one of a kind and is a little pushed aside by what happened for The Avengers in the intervening years. It was 1964 and the show was unparalleled with its fandom. There was a buzz happening because The Avengers was changing the landscape of television and it was pioneering the social changes that were occurring in the world."

End of Act Two...

"By 1965 the world was in full social change. Everybody was making a statement and everything was opening its eyes to every possibility. In the world of The Avengers, John Steed became partnered with Mrs Emma Peel, who was just as strong as her predecessor. Formerly Miss Emma Knight and the president of her father's company, the emancipation of women were firmly thrust into the open. Emma Peel was embodied by Dame Diana Rigg and became a template for many women as The Avengers ushered itself out of the black and white and firmly into the colour where they once again heralded the changes occurring in the world. The invention of the mini skirt and the answering machine were all pioneered first on The Avengers along with the martial art technique Kung Fu which was first practiced on television by Dame Diana. But as the sixties rolled on, it was time for more change. When Mrs Peel left Steed and rejoined her husband in 1967, the world shed a little tear. I know I did..."

Pause for more laughter....

"But the show then ushered in Miss Tara King, a strong example of how free the Sixties had been and the opportunity to show it by giving John Steed his first single partner of the entire run. Carrying high kicks alongside a lethal brick in her handbag, Tara was seen to grow as an individual under Steed's wing. But it was in this part of the Sixties that we were to say goodbye to the show. But we did so wistfully and we looked back upon it as being one of the staples of Sixties television."

Back on the soap box I go.

"But as I look around here today, ladies and gentlemen, I see your faces asking me one question; why is this particular show important? I can only answer you from my own personal understanding. Viewed with both my eyes and heart, The

Avengers is more than just a television show. A series of fantasy mixed with spy elements, I find the characters appealing and the situations they find themselves in amazing. The show feeds a desire in me to be a part of the world that it created. From its gritty beginnings in 1960 to its established formula for the unexpected in 1969, I would be there for the whole thing. But The Avengers is important because it foresaw and resonates with so much of the change that occurred in British culture and society. Look around today and you will see how strong a woman is in industry and any walk of life she wishes to attempt. Look at the well dressed men on the TV shows and you will see them wearing the exact style of suit that was made and created for John Steed. Look at how British the show is and where its imitators fail because they do not pick upon this element of the show. But it is just a television show. It is just a programme meant to entertain for fifty minutes. Everyone has told me that all The Avengers stands for is a television programme. I disagree. And I invite anybody to disagree with someone that tells you not to believe in your passions. It was a passion that kept the James Bond films in the cinemas. Is Bond just a literary character or is he more because he has endured for so long? It was a passion that kept The Beatles music in the hearts and minds of its fans. Are they just four men that played music instruments or did they change the face of music with their own compositions in a world where that was considered the wrong thing to do?"

In summary…

"Ladies and gentlemen, The Avengers represents part of the face of the 1960s. It depicts the social changes within the world and it glorifies the British stiff upper lip alongside the eccentricities that live with it. The show is important because it welcomed the social changes and placed them on the screen. Without the show doing that, we would not be talking about the strength of women, the equal rights of a woman or any individual, we would not be remembering the 1960s at all. For me, the show is a part of

British history. It may be just a television show in many people's eyes, but for me it is an institution that should be celebrated and allowed to prosper and to continue. Not to be sidelined and never to be forgotten. Thank you."

The moment that I uttered the last line I was met with applause by all. I went home and sat down in my chair completely exhausted. I went back to my own little world. I returned to the factory and became happy in the knowledge that I had at least informed the small gathering of people of how good *The Avengers* was and how important it should be from a fans perspective. Going back to reality was hard but it was something that I knew that I had to do. I had to now let go on the idea that I could contribute to *The Avengers* in any way. Soon after, Luke told me that he was forced to close that particular factory because of the lack of business it appeared to be doing. I seemed to be going back into the familiar ruts that I was climbing out of.

But this dark cloud had a silver lining. Although Luke still had not told me what his new line of work was away from his small line of factories, he did say that he himself had been inspired by what I had spoken about on *The Avengers*. He had been in touch with certain people and they were willing to pay me to go and speak about the same topic on a convention-type circuit. The next entry reveals that it went rather well…

Thursday 17th November 2011
"I gave my talk in Peterborough. It was like every person was looking at me and hanging on every word I said. Anna was sat in the crowd like a proud mother and Luke sat next to her grinning like a Cheshire cat. I've come home on a high…"

The talks continued as I re-entered the world of work in the February of 2012. My new job as a warehouse worker for a stationery company was quite fun. My boss there was a fellow lover of *The Avengers* and we would talk at length about how wonderful we thought the show was and what our favourite episodes were. I revealed to her about my struggles with the show ever since school due to the fact that the show was from another time. My boss then told me that *The Avengers* is an asset as well as a show. For a company to have something like that in their archive makes it a gold earner as there are many territories around the world that loved the show then and still very much do now. She then joked that I could be a campaign master that kept up the image and memory of *The Avengers*. But the talk with my boss had made me look at things a little differently. From this next entry, I was considering her sage words…

Friday 24th August 2011

"Have I been preaching all of this time? Have I taken The
Avengers to another level and tried to impress on everybody what
this show is? And do my feelings on the show match with some
other people that watch it and live it as religiously as I do?"

As I continued the talks up to Christmas 2011, I then made a bittersweet decision.

Thursday 20th December 2011

"I think it may be time to hang up my imaginary bowler hat. It's
time to put all of my love for The Avengers back into my little
world that exists only in the four walls of my home. I have not
failed in my task to bring this wonderful TV show out of the
darkness that I felt it had been placed in. I have not failed to
point out just how important it is to love something wholly
whether it is a TV show or anything else that you want to hold
close to your heart. But I think I have failed in my own attempts
to add something new to it all. I think I've failed to take it to a
level where I'm happy to look back and smile. Maybe everyone in
school was right; I should just shut up as it is only a TV show. I've
failed to say that they were wrong. I have failed to prove that they
were wrong. I've failed…"

This was the last entry that I can find in this notebook. In January 2012 I contacted the rights holders to the show again. I asked them if I could possibly get permission to use *The Avengers* in a book idea. It was met with the same negativity as the first time. I just looked at my copies of *Cult Champagne*, patted myself on the back and went back into the world of work where I belonged. The dream I had pursued for so long was closed. But I still loved *The Avengers* from the living room of my home, pouring through each series and each one of Steed's adventures with a love and raging fire of passion. The next entry that I've found in the last of the notebooks is quite an eye opener.

Friday 24th August 2012
"Anna and I keep fighting. I don't fully understand why but she always brings it back to me falling into a rut of some kind. How? I'm working and earning. I'm doing my job day in and day out so what is the problem? She then gets wound up when I put The Avengers on. She screams at me telling me that it's The Avengers that is the problem. I don't understand how…"

It was because I had given up. I had taken the knock back and I was settling for what cards I had been dealt. I was depressed. I turned down the invite to return in glory to the Culture Society to follow up on the speech that I had made before. I had turned it down without thinking but they kept the door open for me to return. I soon snapped back into my old self after putting down the phone to my old headmaster. Anna watched with pride as I rang him back and told him that I would write another address for people. Once again, it was tape recorded after drafting.

Monday 17th December 2012
"Ladies and gentlemen, this year has been a year of personal discovery for me with my favourite show. My faith with it has been tested and my confidence to keep going on in what I'm doing has been the biggest mountain that I've ever had to climb. The factor of giving out something to the people does not always mean that they will welcome you doing so. It was this that shook my foundations. I was attempting to keep my personal flame for The Avengers alive but somehow the flame was blown out. I was not sure whether I could relight it with the same amount of passion and enthusiasm that I had with it before. But as I sank in the chair at home and watched the series again, the flame ignited. I stand here before you as a reborn and devoted fan of The

Avengers. And I think that the rebirth needs to be as far reaching as humanly possible. This show is absolutely amazing, its characters are enthralling and its look is instantly appealing. Ladies and gentlemen; the revolution has begun."

The show had come to my rescue again. The talk circuit became my life again. I fitted it in between work shifts and took a hefty pay for the people that were gathering just to hear me talk. The resurgence was then confirmed.

Wednesday 23rd June 2013

"I visited The Avengers Declassified today and I am buzzing. It seems as though the audio book company Big Finish have secured the rights to remake some of the lost Ian Hendry episodes. This is amazing!!! A new audience can be reached and this amazing show can live on..."

My happiness was uncontained as I told everybody about this new adventure that *The Avengers* was embarking upon. But it was to hold a lifeline for me…

Monday 28th June 2013

"Luke telephoned me today. He finally snapped and told me what his new job was. Aside from running the factories he has been busy securing a job as an editor for publishers in London. The reason he rang me was to suggest that we resurrect Cult Champagne – only this time we would make it an official publication by securing the rights properly. My love for The Avengers could reach the new generation of fans. Would I be interested in doing it?"

The trials that had gone on before with legal issues were still present back then, so *Cult Champagne* gathered a lot of dust. These are the last recordings I'm intending to make. Every log and notebook will disappear. The end result is now encapsulated within the three new tapes I have made. Where will they go? I wish I knew. Will they be hidden away? No, they will not. They will serve as a template to my children to believe in the dreams they have.

But Luke's idea about the magazine was a good idea. Did I go for it? What do you think...???

Recording ends.

ABOUT THE AUTHOR

Roy Bettridge has been involved in the creative arts from a young age and gained a BTEC in performing arts in 2006. He has also studied at the University of Bedfordshire. He has many passions with television, performing and writing being at their forefront. He has written essays about the 1960s cult television series, *The Avengers*, about which he is passionate. Among these writings is a chapter in the *Avengerworld* anthology. He currently resides in Kettering. This is his first published book.

THE AVENGERS: AGENTS EXTRAORDINARY...
ITS FANS: WRITERS EXTRAORDINARY!

AVENGER WORLD

www.hiddentigerbooks.co.uk

KEEP 'EM PEELED FOR

POLICE
SURGEON

DR BRENT'S CASEBOOK

www.hiddentigerbooks.co.uk